LAST KNOWN PORT

A Southern Mystery

by Sue Anger

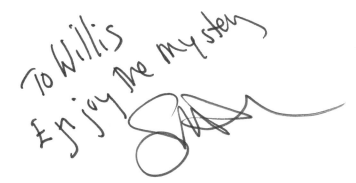

DORRANCE
PUBLISHING CO
EST. 1920
PITTSBURGH, PENNSYLVANIA 15238

Dorrance Publishing Co
585 Alpha Drive
Suite 103
Pittsburgh, PA 15238
Visit our website at *www.dorrancebookstore.com*

Visit Sue Anger's author website at *www.sueanger.com*
Beaufort Harbor illustration by Kyle Dixon
Cover design by Dennis Mathias

ISBN: 978-1-6393-7460-1
eISBN: 978-1-6393-7513-4

DEDICATION

This story is dedicated to the memory of my mama who loved Beaufort and always laughed at my jokes.

And to Keith, Daniel and Kaitlin, with love and gratitude.

And to the working folks living in Carteret County, North Carolina.

NEWPORT RIVER

RUSSELL CREEK

NORTH RIVER

MOREHEAD CITY

BEAUFORT

BOGUE SOUND

LENOXVILLE POINT

CARROT ISLAND

HORSE ISLAND

FORT MACON

SHACKLEFORD BANKS

BEAUFORT HARBOR
NORTH CAROLINA
1923

ATLANTIC OCEAN

LAST KNOWN PORT

A Southern Mystery

ACKNOWLEDGEMENTS

My deepest gratitude goes to the families of Carteret County, North Carolina, who are dedicated to their communities and keeping their heritage alive.

I stand on the shoulders of Charles O. Pitts, Jean B. Kell, Pat Dula Davis, and Mayor Katherine Cloud. In their lifetimes, these historians were dedicated to preserving the history of Carteret County and encouraged me to record invaluable oral histories. Also, thanks to Ann and Bland Simpson, who showed me it could be done.

Particular thanks to the research and written accounts by Nancy Duffy Russell, Sonny Williamson, David S. Cecelski, Debbie and Mike Lester, Mamré Marsh Wilson, Jack Dudley, Mary Faith Warsaw, Neal Willis, Linda Willis Slater, and Ginny Costlow.

I would also like to recognize the Beaufort Historical Association; the Core Sound Waterfowl Museum and Heritage Center; Rodney Kemp, Dee Lewis, and Juanita C. Paull of the History Museum of Carteret County; Paul Foutenou, Michael B. Alford, William Prentice of the North Carolina Maritime Museum; the North Carolina Map Collection; and David M. Bennett of the North Carolina Maritime Museum System.

Many thanks to Norman Gillikin, Roderick Hill, Timmy and Don Morris, who, although no longer with us, were generous with their time and support.

Finally, thanks to Geoffrey Adair for all of his amazing stories, and to my two high school English teachers, Mrs. Sunny Newton and Mrs. Barbara Yeomans. I hope they give me an A.

CHAPTER 1

∾

"Hang on, Pilot! Here comes another!"

Propelled by a fair southeast wind, a gentle swell lifted Jake Parson's thirty-five-foot sailboat as he steered through Beaufort's shipping lane. The waves grew in strength as they approached the shore, causing Jake to tighten his grip on the tiller.

"Woo-hoo!" cried Jake as the sloop momentarily surfed the crest of the wave. Pilot, Jake's Labrador retriever, answered him with a bark and danced on the deck.

On the horizon, Jake spotted a thin ribbon of land, a welcome sight after two weeks at sea. His nautical chart indicated that he was approaching Fort Macon on his port side. For nearly a century, this brick citadel had protected the narrow inlet between Bogue and Shackleford islands, two of North Carolina's Outer Banks. As the swells pushed the *Jamison* into port at a comfortable seven knots, Jake could see turbulent water between the two islands.

Jake wasn't fussed by the messy chop; he'd trusted his sturdy boat through many storms. One final ocean surge heaved his boat into the clashing currents, where it bobbed like a ragtime dancer.

And then, as quickly as it started, the wind pushed the boat past the briny conflict into the calm, shallow sound. In the gold and reddening light of dusk, Jake exhaled in relief. His arrival was a week late due to a storm and a shift in wind, and he longed to see his brother, Wade, who was waiting for him in port. Pilot cast his nose into the air to catch the savory smells of supper accented with fish house debris. The Lab was anxious to be reunited with his best friend, Yawg, the hound who'd sailed with Wade on his boat, the *Amelia.*

The cry of a gull startled Jake, and he turned his head to track it through the brilliant sky. It was the first land animal he'd seen in days. He navigated through the channel, catching the last low rays of sunlight illuminating a white church steeple and the sails of a windmill on the horizon. His mother called this time of day the magic hour: the moment when a day passes into evening, when the earth is suspended before darkness and slumber.

When the waterway narrowed, the current strengthened, and he used the steeple to sight his course towards town. Jake held fast to the tiller as a tiny line of houses and stores came into view, reminding him of a doll-size village. After the *Jamison* rounded the west end of Carrot Island, the Beaufort Harbor opened to him, welcoming him like a safe embrace.

Jake turned his gaze to the row of brick buildings. He could see Beaufort wasn't a swanky port like Charleston, where grand houses and gardens were built right down to its sea wall. At first glance, Beaufort appeared to have the right mixture of working grit balanced with provincial propriety. Workboats were rafted six deep behind the stores, all grimy, salty, and rough from years at sea. Shouts of the crews on these boats drifted across the water.

After he passed the row of stores and fish houses, Jake steered his boat to come about and approach the public town dock. As the *Jamison* glided up to the platform, two small boys emerged from behind the pilings to catch his bowline. The boys secured the *Jamison* while Pilot trembled with anticipation, waiting for Jake's command. Once he heard, "Off ship," the Lab soared off the boat, landed on the dock, and raced to the shore. Jake felt an urge to join his dog, rolling on the sandy beach and running through the tall marsh grass. As much as he loved the sea, it was always exhilarating to return to land.

"Hey, mister, you got a nice dog there," said one of the boys. His voice resonated with the local dialect, a mixture of Southern accent and Scottish brogue that drew out the vowels.

"Thanks. I 'preciate you helping me dock." His voice was thick and slow from lack of use.

2

"That's okay. This is our dock. My name is Michael, but everybody calls me Marbles, and this is my friend, Tobias."

Tobias's face split into an enormous grin, revealing several missing front teeth.

"Nice to meet you. I'm Jake. That's my dog, Pilot."

"You want us to watch your boat while you're in town?"

Jake considered the boy's proposal. "Well, I might. What'll it cost me?"

"Nickel for the evening," said Marbles.

"Nickel each?"

"Nah, we'll share it between us." As if to emphasize his point, Marbles threw his arm around Tobias's shoulder. The little boy nodded his head vigorously.

"It's a deal," Jake said as they shook hands. The boys exchanged jubilant glances.

In a more somber tone, Jake added, "But just so you know, my dog knows his job. He will not want you to board my boat. He'll feel like you're taking his work away from him."

The boys turned to study the Lab, snapping at several small fiddler crabs. "No, sir," answered Marbles. "We won't mess with him."

Jake bent over to pull the door of his cabin closed. "Maybe y'all could help me in another way."

"How's that?"

"I'm looking for a boat called the *Amelia*."

"We know her."

"Know where she might be docked? Last I heard, she could be at a boatyard called Lowell's."

"She hain't there now," replied Tobias. "Everybody's looking for her."

Jake jerked up his head. Inside his chest, his heart pounded wildly while his eyes darted back and forth between the two boys. *Hide.* He'd learned to take cover when he felt like this. Mask his feelings. Hide himself so people wouldn't know.

"She left Beaufort, but she never got to her next port," said Marbles.

Wade is missing. Jake felt the town spin around him. His knees folded and he sat down on the boat's bench. *But he's only missing.* He breathed in and breathed out. *He's only missing. I can find him.* Jake was no stranger to panic; he'd suffered from shell shock since returning from The Great War five years before. Sitting on the bench, paralyzed with fear for his brother, Jake concentrated on hiding his agony from this new town. He recalled returning from France when people he'd known all his life turned their back on him.

Now, the familiar sense of suspicion and distrust began to surge inside him. Bile rose in his throat. He needed to shield himself and keep his head down.

"Mister, you okay?"

Jake swallowed and focused on the boys' faces. "I guess I might be a little hungry." They watched him closely as he pulled out a large handkerchief and mopped his face. He was so accustomed to hiding and secrecy; he wasn't ready to share his kinship with Wade. He cleared his throat. "That's a shame. I needed to do business with the captain." He took another deep breath. "So, how long's the *Amelia* been missin'?"

"I don't rightly know," answered Marbles. "It was in the paper. Want me to run and get you one?"

Jake nodded and handed the boys several coins.

Once they were out of sight, he reached into his pocket for a pack of cigarettes. His hands shook as he struck a match to light one. Leaning over, he rested his elbows on his knees as he recalled all he knew. Wade was expecting Jake and would not have left port unless there was some urgency. He closed his eyes as his mind raced. *Maybe he sent a telegram to Mama and Daddy. Wade would never have left port without letting them know.* He studied the shoreline and noticed a large hotel that might have telegraph services, but his body wouldn't move. He often felt this sense of detachment in the trenches in France.

A few moments later, the boys returned with a newspaper, and Jake read the short article on the *Amelia* printed on the front page of *The Beaufort News*:

> *Beaufort, NC—The schooner* Amelia *set sail from Beaufort Harbor en route for Bristol, Rhode Island, on April 17, 1923. She was captained by Wade Parson of Johns Island, South Carolina. When the* Amelia *never made landfall, the captain's father, Mr. Clarence Parson, reported her disappearance to the Coast Guard. Commander Elijah Midgett of the U.S. Coast Guard is leading the seaboard search from Fort Macon. Anyone with information should contact him.*

The article went on for several more paragraphs about searches and witnesses, but the print swam incomprehensively in front of Jake. The two small boys were looking at him expectedly. Forcing a casual tone into his speech, he said, "Well, boys, since the *Amelia's* not in town, I don't reckon I can do much onshore right now. Think I'll moor for the night and come back when there's more light." The rising panic in his chest told him to stay away from people to process the *Amelia's* disappearance.

Jake noticed their disappointed looks, and Marbles fingered the coins he still held in his hand.

"Keep the change for your trouble."

Their faces brightened, and they untied his bowline.

Jake whistled for Pilot, who bounded down the dock and jumped onto the deck of the boat. After the boys cast him off, the *Jamison* glided across the harbor. The further he got from the town, the more his breathing calmed. After tying up to a mooring, Jake collapsed on the bench while a cry of anguish ripped from his chest. Eventually, he entered his cabin, pulled out the bunk, and retrieved a bottle of whiskey from a hidden compartment. Hope burned in his chest, but he knew he would probably never see his brother again. People who grew up on the water often faced losing loved ones at sea.

The glowing sunlit moment of entry into town had vanished, and the sky settled into a deep velvet twilight. As the evening darkened and the air chilled, Jake worked on the whiskey, his thoughts swirling around and around in his head until he passed out.

The next morning, the harbor was heavy with boat traffic when Jake woke up. Feeling detached and vacant, he mechanically prepared his coffee. In his mind, he walked himself through the day. First, he would go to the inn and telegraph his parents. Then sail to Fort Macon and talk to Commander Elijah Midgett, the officer mentioned in the newspaper. Tomorrow, he would provision his boat, and if the weather favored him, he would set sail for his home in South Carolina.

Climbing out of the cabin with his mug, Jake settled into the cockpit to drink his brew. Pilot lay next to him, and Jake stroked his head. How different Beaufort looked this morning. Yesterday, wrapped in the glow of the sunset, the town was charming and welcoming. Now, it was the place that hid the secrets of his brother's disappearance.

He was turning his head away from the town when his dog began to bark. Trusting Pilot's guarding instincts, Jake looked around to see if another boat was approaching. The Lab rose to his feet, but instead of a defensive stance, he trembled and whined in excitement while staring at the shore. Jake followed his gaze, but his vision was still blurry from his nighttime binge. From the dock, he heard the mournful bay of a hound. Pilot answered with a long howl that split Jake's head. Unable to focus, he reached into the cabin, grabbed his binoculars, and adjusted them to bring the town into view. After several clumsy attempts, he locked the glasses on an animated dog on the dock. Jake's body stiffened as a cold chill enveloped him. "Yawg?" he said in disbelief when he recognized his brother's dog, wagging his tail and dancing with joy.

CHAPTER 2

∽

Dear Mama and Daddy,

I arrived in Beaufort yesterday and heard about Wade. I was all sad about it, but then Yawg showed up! That got me thinking. Wade would never have left port without Yawg, and he knew that I was coming up to meet him, and I don't reckon he would have sailed before I got here. So, something hain't right.

I'm sending you a telegram today. But I'm planning to stay here and find out what's what. Please let me know if Wade wrote another letter to you since I left. I reckon I can learn more if people don't know I'm Wade's brother, so I'm gonna call myself Jake Waterson. So, when you write to me, use that name. And I won't telephone you 'cause I'd have to use your name and people would know I'm Wade's brother.

I know you're worried about me, but I got Pilot and Yawg with me, so I'm alright.

I wish I was with you right now.
Your loving son, Jake

Tucking the letter into an envelope, Jake wondered if this was the right path for him. He longed to sail home and not question Yawg's return. Maybe the hound had run off after a rabbit when Wade cast off, or his brother thought his dog was onboard when leaving port, or Yawg fell overboard and made it to shore somehow. He was weighing all these scenarios when his glance fell on Yawg, sleeping on a pile of soft rags. Ever since he had boarded the *Jamison*, Pilot had not left his side. Although Yawg had several small wounds and his fur was muddy and matted, it was the dog's mangled front paw that concerned Jake.

After Jake had retrieved Yawg from the dock earlier that morning, he'd returned to the mooring, anxious to hide his connection to the dog. After he was a safe distance from town, Jake wept while he cleansed and treated the dog's injuries. Yawg whimpered in pain while simultaneously thumping his tail as if to say, "No hard feelings." Now, Jake shuddered as he thought of the bloody wound beneath the bandaged paw. Yawg had a story to tell him.

Once he sealed the letter to his parents, Jake pulled out a coffee can from under his bunk and extracted Wade's last letters.

We had trouble coming through a storm. The mast on the Amelia *broke, but we made it into Beaufort. I sold the lumber to a ship headed north. I'm sending the crew home on the train, but I'm staying with the* Amelia *til she's ready to sail and you get here to look into growing the business. . . .*

. . . The town has been nice to me. The Amelia *is coming along good at Lowell's on Front Street. There's a man named Isaac that is good with wood. I think I can make the* Amelia *faster. You can never have too much speed.*

Speed. The ever-faster boat. That's all they talked about in the speakeasies, in the boatyards, on the water. Speed to outrun the law. Speed to chase down pirates. Bigger engines. More power. Whispered. Coveted. *Where did all that horsepower take you, brother? What did you get yourself into?*

Their mama always said Wade was a special kind of smart. Over the years, Jake's family built numerous boats in the yard behind their home on Stono Creek. Wade had a special gift of seeing a boat before it was made. Sometimes, he would draw the vessel if someone asked him, but usually he just built right from his head. Once their daddy asked him how he could do that and he replied, "I just take away the part that's not boat."

Jake couldn't imagine how Wade could navigate the dark, shadowy world of bootlegging, because he was simple with people. Once in grade school,

Wade looked panicked when their teacher declared, "You look as happy as a June bug in the springtime!"

Wade had turned anxiously to Jake and whispered, "Am I turning into a bug?"

Jake returned the letters to the coffee can and caught a glimpse of his haggard face in a small tin mirror that hung in the boat's interior. Red, swollen eyes stared back at him. Rubbing the stubble on his chin from two weeks at sea, he began to form a plan to find his brother. First, he pulled up a bucket of seawater and retrieved his safety razor from his shaving kit. As he began to shave, the saltwater brought a sting and a burn to the operation, but he couldn't spare his freshwater. While he worked the razor up his neck, he tried not to think of a rogue wave jostling the boat. But he didn't want to enter town with an unshaven face looking like a hobo. Or worse, a shad-boat fisherman. He shaved off the beard but left a mustache in the hope that it would hide his physical likeness to Wade. When he finished shaving, he set a cap low on his forehead to further hide his face.

It was nearly noon when he sailed the *Jamison* back to the town dock. Before he went ashore, he shut Yawg and Pilot in the cabin. Accustomed to long stretches on a boat, the two guard dogs barely stirred. He surveyed the busy hotel with a small wading beach where several families splashed in the chilly spring water.

A familiar clammy panic swept over Jake. His shell-shock disorder had grown incrementally when he served in France. After he was wounded and hospitalized for the third time, Jake had fallen into a near-catatonic state and could not return to the Western Front. Believing that his cowardice was contagious and would spread to other soldiers, his commanders deemed him mentally and morally deficient. Before he was shipped stateside, he was not allowed to say goodbye to his regiment.

Returning to South Carolina felt more foreign to him than stepping off the ship in France. Since he had enlisted with childhood friends who remained with him throughout the conflict, several of whom had been killed, he was shunned by his neighbors. Privately, Jake and his family struggled with the torture of his night terrors. Everything that had been home to him was now alien. If a stranger glanced at him on the street, he was filled with fear and distrust. During his fits of distress, his sensory awareness was often heightened.

The clip-clop of horses on cobblestones sounded like a stampede that would trample him. The backfiring of a car would send him into a full-body sweat. And, on occasion, his sense of smell was impaired. Once, he was sitting in his mother's kitchen when she pulled a loaf of bread from the oven, but all he could smell was the choking stench of cordite smoke mixed with the fetid mud of the trenches.

It was his brother who pulled Jake through his recovery. When Jake's hands were shaking, Wade simply handed him a wood planer and said, "Could you help me shape this bow, brother?" Once he held the tool, his hands seemed to remember their purpose.

Over the following years, Jake learned to approach life as if every task was a mission. Before he entered town, talked to people, or negotiated a sale, he would break down the steps of each of his actions and mentally tick off his list as he accomplished them. *Greet person (tick), touch hat (tick), ask if their family is well (tick).*

Standing on the deck of the *Jamison*, Jake pictured his brother's face as he willed himself to step off his boat onto Beaufort's town dock (*tick*). He secured the boat lines against the pilings (*tick*). He breathed deeply to steady himself, and waited for the pounding of his heart to slow (*tick*). Trembling, he walked down the dock to cross the street to the hotel (*tick*). When he reached the street, he turned and focused on the sign that read "Inlet Inn" on the elegant hotel across the street (*tick*). Blocking out peripheral sights and sounds, he crossed the street and entered the building (*tick*). At the registry desk, he posted his letter and placed a telegram to his parents in care of the General Store on Johns Island. *Arrived in Beaufort (stop). Letter follows. (stop) Jake (stop).*

Once he completed these tasks, his body unclenched, which allowed him to become aware of the hotel lobby's sights and sounds for the first time. A family with a passel of laughing, sandy children scurried across the entrance hall. His stomach growled when he smelled fried chicken and a buttery cream sauce. *An army marches on its stomach.* He was anxious to put his plan into action, but his appetite overtook him, and he floated toward the savory scents emanating from the dining room.

When a young, blushing waitress served him a second piece of pie, Jake asked her where he could find Lowell's Boatyard. The question sent her into a fit of giggles before she managed to sputter, "Walk through the town, and you'll see it on the harbor side just before the end of the block of stores." After he nodded his head in thanks, she nearly ran from the table.

Revived and strengthened from his first hot meal in weeks, Jake paid his bill, left the inn, and began to walk along the seawall into town. Jake planned to build a small boat to ferry him back and forth between the *Jamison's* mooring and the shore. Working in the yard would allow him to observe the people who might have been the last to see Wade. Initially, Jake planned to make a standard dinghy, but as he strode along the harbor, he noticed it was filled with small working boats that drew shallow drafts. Finishing a flat-bottomed working skiff might be a good introduction to the local fishermen.

As Jake entered the town, his anxiety increased, and he began to scan the street for dangers. He noted a Model T car on rickety, unsteady wheels that moved quickly past several drays. To avoid eye contact, he kept his head down as he passed storefronts with large plate glass windows displaying dry goods, groceries, china, medicines, and hardware. Nearing the end of the shops, he heard the faint drone of a motorized bandsaw and steady hammering so typical of a boatyard. This noise increased as the waterfront opened to a boat launch running from the shore into the water. A partially constructed schooner sat on the rail line where a lanky boy nailed planks.

Jake removed his hat before he opened the door to the boathouse. Inside, the hum of the bandsaw pitched into a high whine as a workman ran planks into the blade. The back entryway to the building was open and a sea breeze blew in off the water. The smells of cedar, dust, and motor oil transported Jake to his father's yard on Johns Island, while a thousand memories of Wade ran through his mind: building boats, hunting for squirrels as kids, fishing in their creek. Once his eyes adjusted to the dim light, he turned to the right and saw the flimsy interior walls that created an office. He knocked on the door and heard a scuffle inside, but no one answered. After a minute, he tentatively opened the door and peered into the dingy room. Behind a desk littered with papers, a weathered man was lifting his head from a grimy blotter. His sallow complexion and drab hair blended with the gray office.

"Are you Charlie Lowell?"

The wizened man looked up and snarled, "I might be."

"I'd like to rent a space in your boathouse for a week."

Lowell's eye roved over Jake's scruffy, sun-bleached hair, rumpled pants, and work shirt. It wasn't like Jake had a washtub and iron on the *Jamison* to smart himself up.

"What boat are you off 'un?" the man asked. His scratchy voice sounded like an untuned fiddle.

"The *Jamison*. Got in last night."

The man continued to stare at him, but Jake returned it with equal measure. Strangers often mistook Jake's wiry body for scrawny weakness. His war service may have aged Jake beyond his twenty-four years, but a life on the water and building boats had made him agile and strong.

Lowell made several clumsy movements to light a cigarette. "What you want space for?"

Jake could not imagine anyone being so suspicious of new business. "I want to build a skiff to ferry me to my boat. I don't reckon I'll want to swim out to my mooring every day."

Lowell exhaled a long trail of smoke. "Most folks just tie up to the dock."

"Not all of them," said Jake, looking out at the harbor through the back door of the building. "I can see half a dozen anchored from here."

It looked like heavy gears were grinding through Lowell's head.

When he didn't answer, Jake insisted, "You don't want my money?"

"I like to know who I'm doing business with."

"Waterson. Jake Waterson from Charleston way." There was no hint of shaking hands.

"I can't say that I know the family."

"Do you know any families in Charleston?"

"Maybe I do."

Lowell stood up but kept one hand on the desk as he made his way around it. Jake was downwind from him and winced as he was overpowered by the odor of tired booze, cigarette smoke, and sweat. Lowell approached Jake and squinted up at the taller man. "I'll charge you one and a quarter," he spat. "A day."

Jake laughed. "I won't give you more than three a week." Still an outrageous sum, but the boatyard was Jake's only link to Wade, and he wasn't going to let it slip away. He turned to leave.

"Not so fast," said Lowell, taking a long pull from his cigarette. "I'll have to make room for yer." He thought for a minute. "Three and a quarter."

Jake stared into the rheumy eyes.

Finally, the man added, "A week. But you have to bring your tools. And I don't want you underfoot. I'll have Isaac get you some wood."

"I select my own wood."

Lowell ignored him as he shuffled to the door. Dithering over the price exhausted him. When he opened the door, a man dressed in rugged work clothes was waiting outside the office. Since Wade had mentioned a man named Isaac in his letter, Jake studied this enormous man whose bulk filled the door frame. He recognized the strong intelligence in his dark eyes set against a deep russet skin tone. Around his neck, he wore a small leather pouch on a chain. "Isaac, this is—ah," Lowell fumbled for Jake's name like he was searching for change in his pocket. "This is—"

"Jake. Jake Waterson."

Isaac nodded at him.

"He wants to pick out his own wood for a skiff," said Lowell. "Why don't you show him what we have?"

Isaac turned away from the office, and Jake fell in behind the man's easy, deliberate lope. The confrontation with Lowell left him feeling tense and flighty. He inhaled deeply as he walked away from the office and felt relieved when Lowell closed the door behind him. They stopped on the other side of the warehouse in front of a stack of boards.

"We use juniper," said Isaac. Jake nodded in approval; the local evergreen wood was a popular choice for boats since its high pitch content made it resistant to saltwater. Isaac's low and even voice was a welcome contrast to Lowell's raspy interrogation.

Over the next half hour, Jake examined each board in a large stack of lumber. As he scrutinized the boards for warping knots, and damage, he pictured the boat he wanted to build. Eventually, he chose two planks and asked, "Is this all you have?"

"Yes, sir," answered Isaac. "How much do you need?"

"I'm thinking a thirteen-foot, flat-bottom skiff, with maybe a four-foot beam."

"Two hundred feet of board?"

Jake thought for a minute. "That sounds about right."

Another builder might downplay the importance of wood in a small boat, but Isaac didn't question Jake's choices. There was a calmness about Isaac as

13

he looked over Jake's selections. "I knows you want good wood, and you knows what you want. I taking the dray and mule out to the lumber yard first thing in the morning."

Jake considered him for a minute. "Should I get here by six or seven o'clock?"

"Seven be fine," Isaac answered with a nod.

"I'd appreciate that."

The two men carried the wood to the far end of the workspace. When they finished, Jake left Lowell's Boatyard and made his way back down Front Street to Guthrie's Hardware. As he walked into the cool shade of the store filled with tools and building supplies, he felt the same gentle breeze flowing from the back entrance, but now it was mixed with a delicate rose scent. In the center of the store, a young woman stood behind a counter, leaning over a large ledger. When he entered, she looked up from the thick book, and Jake glimpsed a delicate face surrounded by fair wispy hair. As she stowed the ledger under the counter, he saw a long, heavy plait down her back. He knew it was fashionable for girls to cut their hair into crisp bobs these days, but he thought her hair looked swell.

"I imagine you're off the *Jamison*." It was a statement, not a question.

"Yes, ma'am, I'm Jake Waterson."

"I'm Nell Guthrie. This is my daddy's store."

She extended her hand. Jake was startled to feel a thick layer of callous on the palm and fingers of such a delicate hand.

When he didn't release her hand, Nell said, "I'm gonna need that back."

His ears warmed with embarrassment as he released her. "Oh, yes, ma'am."

Grabbing a small slip of paper from the counter, Nell asked, "So, do ya know what ya need?"

"I'm thinking I need two oar sockets and locks, a fifty count of copper rivets and burrs, a bow eye, and about ten feet of manila line."

Without looking up from the list she was writing, Nell nodded. "Sounds like you're building a small boat," she said, stepping out from behind the counter.

"Yes, ma'am." He'd never thought about talking to a girl about building a boat and watched her in awe as she moved unapologetically through the store.

"Please tell me you're not building it at Lowell's."

"Ah . . ."

"Oh, my Lord, honey," she sighed and shook her head. "Guess you'll keep Lowell in whiskey for the month for what he charges."

"I thought that was illegal." His mouth twisted as he tried to keep a straight face.

"I could only wish for Charlie Lowell."

Jake chuckled. "He didn't seem like a trusting man."

"You reckon? He doesn't like 'foreigners' in his warehouse," she said as she stepped toward the bins of rivets and screws lining the wall.

"I'm from South Carolina, not South America."

"A different continent for him." She stopped in front of the wall and searched it for Jake's rivets. "My daddy says he puts the 'cur' in 'curmudgeon.'"

"I figured, but I'm not planning to dock the *Jamison*."

"Well, then you'll need a dinghy."

"I was thinking more of a skiff."

Nell nodded. "Are you gonna add a sail to that?"

Her ease in the store was impressive but distracting. As Jake watched her move around the merchandise, he barely heard himself speak. "The sailmaker is my next stop. I figure I'll rig her to sail in a week's time."

"You'll need more line after your sails are finished." She deftly counted out his rivets before adding, "Sounds like you work fast." She looked up and smiled. "Or optimistically."

It was a casual glance, but its warmth transported Jake. Nell's genuine smile reminded him of a steady wind pushing the *Jamison* into port on a rising tide. He smiled back.

Turning to the wall of hardware, she asked, "How 'bout the *Jamison*? Need any grease for your winches after being offshore?"

He nodded, thinking he would buy a zebra if she offered it. "What do you like?" he asked, pulling himself back to reality.

"I'm liking this heavier grade." She pulled a small canister from the wall and handed it to him. "It sticks better and lasts longer, so you don't have to buy it as often."

"Sounds good." He pretended to examine the label.

"What width did you want the line?"

"About a half-inch."

Arriving at the spools of rope, Nell began to deftly measure out the line. Turning away from her, Jake wandered around the store to see if he needed anything else, but he kept imagining Nell sailing on a broad reach with him. When she looked up and caught him staring at her, she stopped measuring and asked, "Is this the line you wanted?"

"Oh, yes, ma'am," said Jake, a little startled. "But if you don't mind me saying," he hesitated and looked around at all the hardware lining the walls.

Nell finished the question for him. "You're wondering why a girl would be working in a hardware store."

Jake felt relieved. "Yes, ma'am."

She glanced over at the counter and, for a brief moment, her eyebrows knitted together. "That's sort of a long story." She turned around to measure his rope.

Jake felt like he was intruding and moved away from her. While pretending to examine bins of nails, tables filled with tools, and a barrel of piping, his heart began to pound in his chest. When he came to the far wall, he saw a job board with multiple requests for work. He chuckled at one notice reading, "Sober Man: Good for Oystering."

"Sounds like somebody wants to take the fun out of oystering."

Nell finished coiling the rope and strode over to him, bringing her soft rose scent with her. "I always liked this one," she said, pointing to a small notice. "'You tried the best, now try the rest!' I think a little boy posted that for raking leaves."

They both chuckled, and when Jake glanced at her, their eyes met. Nell hesitated before she put her hand up to her hair and then returned to the counter. Lifting his gaze, he watched her walk away and wanted to follow her. Exerting a great effort, he turned back to the job board and noticed several framed watercolors of boats surrounding it. Studying the art closely, he saw it was detailed and accurate without being mechanical. "These are good paintings."

Nell looked up from writing the receipt. "My friend Emma Grace makes them. You may have met her little brother at the dock. They call him Marbles. Boat owners love her pictures. They bring in good money."

"She could have been a boat builder with that eye," he said.

"You might be interested in her latest work." Nell returned to the wall and pointed to a crate filled with watercolors. "I haven't had time to frame these. Maybe she can paint the *Jamison* before you sail away."

Jake stepped over to the crate and began to flip through the paintings. But he stopped abruptly when he saw a picture of Wade's boat with Yawg on the deck. Blinding anguish gripped him, followed by the familiar tightness in his chest. He stared at the image for several moments before he strained to steady his voice. "This looks like an unusual boat."

Nell crossed the room and glanced over his shoulder. "Oh, that's the *Amelia.*"

He closed his eyes. It made Wade's disappearance more real to see this image of his brother's boat, its name spoken by someone else. His heart began to race, and sweat broke out over his body. He strained for control as he asked, "Is that right?"

Nell nodded. "Kinda sad," she said, looking down at the picture. "His family just reported that she went missing." She walked back to the counter. "He was some kinda funny—the captain, that is."

"In what way?"

Nell wrapped his items in paper and tied the package with a string. "Well, when Emma Grace was painting the boat, he came up next to her, and she about jumped outta her skin 'cause he came out of nowhere. He was right interested in her picture, but then told her all the things she was getting wrong. And he could not smile to save his life."

Nell described his quirky brother perfectly. Jake's hand shook as he reached out to touch the watercolor. He wanted to buy it, but feared it would draw attention to himself.

"Was there anything else, Jake?" she asked him from the counter.

"No, ma'am. That's everything." He inhaled deeply and turned away from the crate, feeling like he was leaving part of himself in the painting. He walked back to the counter. "I'll come back another time to place a work posting."

"We don't charge for that," she said with a grin. "But your hardware and grease come to $1.35."

He reached deep inside his pocket and placed a dollar and two quarters on the counter.

When Nell turned her back on him to open the cash register, Jake felt his anxiety build. Before she could turn around, he picked up the items and left the store without waiting for his change.

CHAPTER 3

Later that evening, a rain cloud moved in from the ocean and drenched Beaufort, leaving a languid humidity in its passing. After supper with her parents, Nell Guthrie stepped out on her front porch to wait for her beau. She settled into a rocking chair and studied the quiet waterfront. Since land and sea were in a constant tussle for wind in Nell's coastal town, it unsettled her when it died. As the western sky became streaked with shades of orange and fuchsia, she spotted her fiancé striding toward her home with a powerful gait. She felt a warm pulse surge through her body.

Although Asa Davis had only proposed to Nell the previous week, she had loved him all her life. With affection and amusement, she studied his walk and wondered why Asa never looked like he belonged in his clothes. She knew he liked to smart himself up before he went to work as a druggist, but his starched shirt under his jacket strained against his massive chest and looked wilted in the moist air. A straw boater hat was clamped down on his head to rein in his unruly hair. Smothering a slight chuckle, she rose from the chair and cooed, "Hey there, Asa."

"What's so funny?"

"I was just thinking that you always look like you're wearing your cousin's clothes."

"Maybe my wife will dress me better." He glanced toward her house before caressing her face and giving her a swift kiss. She took his arm, and they stepped off her porch. As they fell into step together, he squeezed her hand. Easy contentment settled over Nell as they moved away from her home.

Asa laid his arm around her shoulder and asked, "Where you been hidin' out, lover? I didn't see you at the store this morning."

"Daddy let me have the morning off when the tide was low so that I could dig some clams for supper."

"I thought I saw you leave the store. Then I stopped by your house to deliver some laudanum for your mother, but I couldn't find you there either."

She looked down at her shoes, secretly tickled that he was watching and thinking of her throughout the day. "You know you have boys to make deliveries for you."

"I wanted to see my girl."

She cuddled against him and inhaled his familiar musky scent mingled with spicy bay rum. The walkway glistened with moisture, so the couple dodged puddles as they strolled toward town. Nell's eyes drifted to the harbor. "She looks slick ca'am," she said, using a local expression for calm water.

Asa followed her gaze. "That's a fact."

A haunting penny whistle melody drifted across the harbor from one of the anchored boats. The still water magnified the notes, making them unusually clear and distinctive. "Have you ever heard that tune?"

"What tune?" Asa paused to listen. "No. Guess not."

She concentrated on the song. "Unusual for a penny whistle."

"You would know. You're the musician."

"I can't remember such a quiet night."

"That's one thing you notice when you're inland. There's not near as much wind as down here."

Nell thought for a moment before she turned to look up at him. "You loved college, didn't you?"

"You know I did."

When Nell looked wistful, he added, "Shame your mama got so sick."

Nell had finished high school the year before, and planned to attend a conservatory of music, but her mother required constant care.

"College was the best damn party on earth," said Asa.

"Wouldn't have been my reason for going."

"The boys just wanted to put the war behind them. And live the good life."

"Nothing wrong with that."

"Don't worry about college and all that, Nellie. There'll be plenty of music when we move to Richmond."

She looked down at the engagement ring on her finger. "I guess I'll know soon enough." After their wedding, Asa and Nell were planning to move to Virginia's capital, where Asa wanted to open a chain of drug stores. Walking together past the houses that lined Front Street, now dimmed and quiet, Nell realized she knew the families in each household. A twinge of uneasiness gripped her as she realized she wouldn't know any people in the houses in Richmond. "It just sounds so big."

"Nah, it's only Beaufort with row houses."

A new thought occurred to her, and she turned to him with excitement. "I'd like to study at the Richmond Music Conservatory."

He tucked his chin into his neck. "That's a good idea. You missed out on school, and you deserve to go."

Nell squeezed his arm, and her step became lighter as they approached the town. "So, how's your mama taking all this? I can't imagine that she wants you to marry someone from Beaufort."

"Well, that was the darndest thing," Asa replied in surprise. "Daddy brought her around."

Nell lifted her head to stare at him with skepticism.

"I talked to him first, and he was the one who told her. I don't know what he said, and maybe I don't want to know, but she came around."

Raised in a prestigious Richmond family, Mrs. Davis would undoubtedly want her only son to marry a wealthy social debutante. When Nell attended Mrs. Davis's cotillion classes as a child, the elegant lady always referred to Beaufort as a backwater fish town. "We'll see about that when I have supper at your house tomorrow."

The couple entered the commercial part of town, and Asa said, "May I interest you in a hot fudge sundae?"

"I'd love one, but I believe the drug store is closed."

"I happen to have a set of keys."

"In that case, I would love a sundae," she giggled.

The couple stopped in front of Mason's Fine China and Jewelry Store, lingering to study the dinnerware selected by engaged couples. Small white cards with names and wedding dates adorned each pattern in the window. Nell winced at the frumpy willow design chosen by Mary Jane Fulcher.

"I don't see our pattern displayed yet," said Nell as her brow furrowed.

"Give the man time; it hain't been but a week." Asa drew her closer to him and nuzzled her ear. It tickled Nell, and she scrunched up her shoulder.

As they turned toward the drug store, Nell realized that Asa was opening a door to a dazzling new world. On the other side of the street, Nell glanced over at her father's hardware store and wondered what it would be like in a year after she was gone. It would be hard for her daddy to replace her, but she wouldn't miss his interminable disappointment.

When they approached the Davis Drug Store, Asa unlocked the door and they slipped inside. After the salty sea air, the familiar dusty hints of menthol, licorice, and sulfur greeted them. Asa flicked on the lights and flung his boater across the room, where it landed on the ice cream counter. Nell watched him swell with pride as his eyes swept over his domain. Wooden shelves covered the walls from floor to ceiling, filled with packaged remedies such as Lydia Pinkham's Vegetable Compound used for lady troubles and Dr. Miles Restorative Blood Purifier. At the back of the shop was the dispensary with rows of glass and ceramic jars that stored compound ingredients. During store hours, Nell loved to watch Asa mix and roll these components into remedy pills by following the formula cards stored in his card catalog. On one side of the shop was his state-of-the-art soda fountain, where a large mirror filled the wall behind the white marble counter.

"Nell, could I show you something in the back?"

She smiled up at him. "Why yes, I believe I could, sir." Leading her into his darkened office, he pulled her to him for a lingering kiss. His lips traveled down her neck, and she could feel his desire as he gently pressed her into the wall. As his kisses became more urgent, she imagined waking up next to him in a luxurious bed in Richmond.

A soft rap on the back door made Nell jump.

"Jesus Christ," Asa swore in aggravation. "Let me run back and get that. It might be a late delivery."

"Asa, maybe they'll just go away if we don't answer." She tried to pull him back to her.

He cupped her cheek with his hand. "Let me take care of this or they could start pounding and wake up the whole town." Smiling, he turned away from her. Pointing a finger at her in jest, he said, "Stay right there. I'll be right back. Don't move."

After he left, Nell made her way to the doorway. Asa dropped his voice and spoke to the visitor in a muffled tone. She couldn't make out the words until Asa exclaimed, "No, I'll meet up with you later."

Nell clamped her hand over her mouth in surprise. Asa closed the door, and she heard his footsteps coming toward her, but she didn't move from the office doorway. After he rounded the corner, he pulled her toward him. "Now, where were we?"

Stepping out of his reach, she replied, "That didn't sound like a drug store delivery."

Asa started to say something but checked himself after glancing at her face. "It was just Chadwick; he wanted to know when I was coming over to the inn."

Nell crossed her arms over her chest. Betrayal and anger rose inside her. "It didn't sound like that."

"Nell, look, he just needs a little help." He placed his arm around her shoulders, but Nell shook him off.

"You promised me you would stop running liquor. It's been fun for boys down here, but things are starting to change. They say gangsters are entering the game now. I can't live like that."

A cloud passed over Asa's face. "I told you this is just to help Chadwick take over."

She raised an eyebrow and pointed toward the back door. "That didn't sound like you're stepping away. You're still supervising."

A sullen pause settled between them. Nell saw their new life slipping away from her.

"So, if I give up whiskey, does this mean Emma Grace will stop making wine?"

Nell trembled with rage. Asa's comment referred to Nell's best friend who made a variety of homemade wines. "She's not breaking the law, but you are. You're allowed to make wine, just not sell it. I don't reckon the local police would be bothered with Emma Grace, seeing as they love her elderberry brew." She poked her finger into Asa's chest. "The revenue men will chase you down when you pick it up offshore and carry it into port." Nell was referring to the strong-arm men of the Federal Treasury Department who enforced Prohibition laws. "That's importing it into the country. You could go to jail."

"If I get caught."

Nell threw her hands up in exasperation. "I can't wait at home for my husband, wondering if he's out getting shot on the water."

He barked out an explosive laugh. "Nell, you've been watching too many newsreels."

She took a deep breath and gritted her teeth. Her eyes were hot with unshed tears. "I can't have my children raised by a bootlegger."

"You won't."

"I'll hold you to that."

"Of course, sweetheart, I want to build a life with you."

The vision of her new life and elegant home marched across her thoughts as she pulled a hankie from her pocket and dabbed her nose. The stiffness in her shoulders eased.

"Come on," he moved in closer and wrapped his arms around her. "Let me make you a sundae."

When they reached the soda fountain, he wrapped his hands around her waist, lifted her, and set her on a stool. Despite her anger, she felt swept away by his strength. Once he was behind the counter, Asa began to build the sundae with hot fudge, nuts, and a cherry.

"Did I ever tell you about the music halls in Richmond?" Asa painted a picture of the city with his words: going dancing at night clubs, promenading by the James River, and being recognized in the Fan, the city's elite neighborhood. His enthusiasm infected her, and she eventually pushed his rum-running antics out of her mind.

Finishing their sundaes, they left the store and strolled back to her modest white clapboard home. The windows were dark when they arrived, so Nell knew her parents were in bed. As they stood on the veranda, Asa gently stroked her hair. "Running booze was just something fun to do while I was stuck in Beaufort." He leaned in to nibble her ear lobe and whispered, "It doesn't mean anything to me." She pulled back to study his sunburned face just as he dipped his head.

Nell wrapped her arms around Asa as she stood on her tiptoes to look him in the eye. "I believe you." And she did. Asa pulled her into him, and they shared a last kiss on the veranda.

After Nell watched Asa walk away, a restlessness overtook her. She realized she wasn't ready to go inside. When her brother, Harrison, had been killed in the Great War, her father built a bench in honor of him. It called to her now, and she walked around the house to sit with his memory in their back yard.

Mr. Guthrie had designed the circular bench to wrap around the pecan tree in the center of the garden, now filled with sprouting vegetables and herbs. When she passed her henhouse, Nell's flock of chickens rustled and clucked softly. Cigarette smoke greeted her when she entered the spring garden. The dim light revealed her dear friend, Emma Grace Willis, wrapped in a dusty rose dressing gown embroidered with black trim. Her presence didn't surprise Nell since Emma Grace lived on the other side of the yard with her aunt and uncle. Twenty years earlier, the two families planted one large garden that blurred the property line.

"Hey, Emma Grace."

"Hey. Were you out with Asa?" Despite the light tone, Nell could hear the thick sadness in her friend's voice. Emma Grace had been engaged to Harrison when he died. Without answering her, Nell sat down on the bench and wrapped an arm around her friend. They sat in silence as Nell traced the remembrance her father had carved into the bench: "Harrison Guthrie 1899–1917, Sheltered and safe from sorrow." After Emma Grace squeezed her hand, Nell answered, "We had a sundae at the drug store."

Emma Grace followed her friend's finger as it traced the name so dear to both of them. "I went to bed early after a long shift at the clinic, but the dream returned."

Nell could feel Emma Grace's body tense while she paused to inhale her cigarette. "I get those nearly every night. So does Mama."

"He's calling to me. But when I pour medicine into a spoon, it turns into vapor and floats away." She pressed a handkerchief to her eyes. After Harrison landed in France to fight on the Western Front, he contracted influenza and died within weeks. To assuage her grief, Emma Grace began to assist the nurses at the Davis Emergency Clinic. Asa's father, Dr. Giles Davis, the owner of the small infirmary, recognized Emma Grace's talent and encouraged her to enter nursing training. Nell knew Emma Grace was trying to save Harrison's life with each patient.

After a time, Emma Grace blew her nose in a loud, indelicate fashion. "How's Asa?"

Nell could hear the edge in her friend's voice. "Please don't sound so bitter," Nell answered, more concerned than irritated.

"I remember how he broke your heart last summer. You see something in him that I don't."

Nell twisted her mouth into a smile. "Well, his house, of course. His daddy's big, dreamy house."

Emma Grace looked up at her in the dim light before laughing a throaty chuckle. "So, you're marrying the house, not the man?"

"Don't be silly, Emma Grace. Men go to sea and never come back, but a good house will always keep you warm."

Emma Grace snickered along with Nell. "You're a mess." She used the local endearment mothers said to their children when they tucked them in at night.

Nell leaned back against the pecan tree and inhaled the rich earthy loam of the garden. "I get mad at Asa, but I can't think of a time when I didn't love him." And as she said it, her current spat with him dissipated. "Remember in high school how your brothers didn't want us to play in their baseball games, but Harrison got us in?"

"Yeah, I do. We beat the pants off them."

"I think I fell in love with Asa then. When he's not around, it's like a part of me is missing." Neither of them spoke while the steady hum of garden crickets grew louder. The still, muggy night pressed down on them.

Emma Grace took a drag from her cigarette. "I hope you're right. But you were always a pushover."

They stood up and locked arms while they meandered down the garden path. They were passing a bed of snap bean seedlings when Emma Grace said, "I stopped by earlier this evening when I got off from the clinic. Your mama said you were down at the store."

"I worked there all afternoon. A captain came in who looked like someone you might want to modernize. He's trying to grow a mustache but doesn't know how. He came in on that sharpie, the *Jamison*."

Emma Grace nodded as they made their way through the garden labyrinth.

"Oh, and he really liked your paintings."

"He has excellent taste."

"Said he was from South Carolina. Had a nice accent, definitely Lowcountry. Said he was building a skiff down at Lowell's."

"Bless his heart." This local expression expressed contemptible pity for a helpless soul.

"I think we should add him to the harbor log."

"Yes, indeed, he should be logged."

Nell kept a register of the boats in the harbor for her father's hardware store. Boat design trends reflected the conversion from sail to engine power, which was invaluable to her father's business. Between Nell's interest in her customers and Emma Grace's medical experience, they noticed shifting patterns in their entries. Emma Grace found a connection to yellow fever from boats arriving from New Orleans, which helped prevent the disease from spreading throughout Beaufort. "Daddy needs me at the store tomorrow," said Nell. "Why don't we walk into town together?"

"That sounds swell," said Emma Grace. They reached the edge of the garden, and Emma Grace turned to embrace her friend.

"Please be happy for me," Nell pleaded.

"Don't be silly."

As they held onto each other, Nell cherished her friend who loved her brother so passionately. She heard one deep, slow blast of a tugboat's horn signaling its departure from the harbor. Their hug ended, and she watched Emma Grace make her way across the garden to her home, her safe port.

CHAPTER 4

Later that night, Jake stowed his penny whistle in the cabin of his boat. Playing music often soothed him after a raging panic. As he lamented Wade's disappearance, a slow, melancholy lullaby emerged from the instrument. Following his visit to the hardware store that afternoon, Jake's distress and wariness had dimmed but he wouldn't be able to sleep inside his cabin. These episodes often brought on claustrophobic reactions, and the walls of the small interior closed in on him. Jake invited his two dogs to settle down on the bench on his deck for the night. When a tugboat sounded one final blast, he glanced across the harbor and watched it glide out to sea with gentle ripples fanning out behind it.

Jake knew it paid to be cautious the first nights in a new port. Prohibition had brought out a pirate element on the water, so it would not be unusual for someone to visit him after dark. Killing the light from his lantern, he scanned the waterfront with his binoculars. Wade's letters alluded to a rum-running operation at Lowell's, so he turned his attention to the waterfront entrances of the stores that lined Front Street, now dimly lit from the few streetlights in town.

The calm night magnified the muffled laughter and voices from the large fishing boats. When a dampening chill began to settle on the deck, Pilot and Yawg sought warmth by wedging themselves between their master and the side of the sloop. Absently stroking his dogs, Jake studied small disturbances along the shoreline. Based on Wade's correspondence and Charlie Lowell's curious demeanor that morning, he suspected that he might be in for a show.

An hour passed before Jake saw three people walk down to Lowell's dock while another man rowed a small skiff against the tide to meet them. The low lighting from the street silhouetted the men and the approaching boat. One of the men on land was significantly broader and taller than the other two. Jake adjusted the binoculars and saw the smaller man was carrying an outboard motor. Although he couldn't make out their words in the heavy air, Jake recognized Charlie Lowell's distinctive squawking tones. Another voice answered with the low, rumbling rhythm of a steam engine.

After the three men walked down the finger dock and attached the outboard motor to the boat, the smaller figure stepped into it. From the man's light step and agile movements, Jake sensed he was younger than the others. Soon, the oarsman was pulling away from the dock with steady rowing strokes. The two men on the shore watched the boat as it moved out of the harbor. Once it rounded Carrot Island, Jake heard the motor jump to life and listened until it was out of hearing range. Lowell and his broad-shouldered companion returned to the warehouse, continuing their muted conversation as they walked.

After an hour, Jake went below and drew heavy canvas curtains across the cabin windows before lighting a candle. He poured three fingers of bourbon and reached into a crevice behind a lower storage bin to pull out a small bound notebook.

He spent the next twenty minutes writing down everything he'd witnessed that evening: the time, the boat, and the people. He made a note of the large man's voice and sketched the skiff. From its silhouette, he estimated it was a fifteen-foot sloop. The men didn't use their running lights on the boat and delayed the start of their motor. If they were catching the tide for fishing or setting nets, they would have used their lights so other boats would know their position in the dark. Jake assumed they held off starting the motor so it wouldn't be detected as it left the harbor. In all likelihood, this small boat would be a runner from the larger ships outside the three-mile boundary along the coastal waters. After picking up booze, she would elude the federal revenue agents and either run her booty back into the harbor, or temporarily hide it on one of Beaufort's isolated islands. Another possibility was the small boat was picking up hooch hidden in the area. Jake stowed the notebook and began a letter to his parents.

Dear Mama and Daddy,

I'm glad I stayed in Beaufort because there's a lot of action here. I think it's more than likely that Wade may have tried to make a ship-to-shore hooch run. When I was home, you would know when certain boats passed by Charleston from Nassau, because their loads of booze would circulate in batches through town. If I can find out which liquor surfaced around the time Wade was in Beaufort, I might be able to figure out who he was working with.

I think Wade might have made alterations to the Amelia *to make her go faster—maybe even installed an engine. Or he could have made a hidden cargo bay with a false floor. I don't think he would have done this work at Lowell's because it's so open on Front Street and all. I'm going to try to find out other places where boats could be outfitted.*

Yawg was pretty boogered up, but he's coming along right well. His paw looks like it might've got caught in a trap.

Your loving son,
Jake

His cup now drained, Jake refilled it and gathered a couple of blankets. He put the letter in an envelope and leaned over to blow out the candle. He paused when his gaze fell on the nautical chart that lay on his bunk. Picking up the coastal map and studying the sounds, rivers, and waterways, his eyes followed numerous secluded coves and secretive landings in this low marshy land. Weariness enveloped him, and he sighed deeply. *Where did you go, brother?*

Setting the chart aside, he blew out the candle and climbed out on the deck. He wrapped the blankets around him and leaned against the cabin to finish his drink. He planned to sit sentinel to see if the boat returned, though he deemed it unlikely. Jake felt the comfort of Pilot and Yawg nestled against his legs and focused on the gentle sound of waves lapping against the boat. His mind wandered back to the small sloop slipping out of the harbor. He didn't like to think Wade would be involved with Charlie Lowell and his friends, but he could understand the temptation. Wade had been traveling to apprentice at the Herreshoff Manufacturing Company, a prestigious ship designer and manufacturer in Rhode Island. Although this was a coveted position, Wade was impatient to start his own boatbuilding business on Johns Island. If someone in Beaufort had spoken to Wade in the right way, Jake could see how he might have been swayed by the possibility of making quick money.

The whiskey slowly warmed him, and his thoughts drifted to the cheerful faces of Tobias and Marbles on the dock. Kids like that could help him keep a pulse on the town. He remembered how the French military forces often paid local children to notice shifts in supply lines or find hidden paths through forests. His eyelids grew heavy. Smiling, he remembered how Marbles bartered with him at the dock. As he drifted into sleep, Jake was walking down Front Street and entering the hardware store, where he could smell a delicate rosewater scent.

✧

When Jake awoke the next morning, he checked to see if the skiff had returned, but nothing was docked behind Lowell's. He checked his pocket watch and saw he had an hour before he was to meet Isaac. When he arrived at the town dock, Marbles and Tobias were nowhere in sight, but there was a small, lumpy parcel on the bench with "Jak" scrawled on the outside. He unfolded the paper and read:

> *Deer Mr Jak and Polot*
> *We at skool. See you latr.*
> *Tobias and Marbles*

Jake chuckled. *Stay in school. Learn to spell.* The note was wrapped around three crackers. "Looks like you'll be on your own most of the day," he said to the two dogs as they gobbled up the treat. When they wagged their tails and looked at him for more, Jake ordered the dogs back onto the *Jamison*. Pilot's tail dropped, but he obeyed. Once inside the cabin, he gave an exaggerated yawn and settled down with a deep sigh.

Carrying his carpenter's bag through town, Jake could see Isaac waiting for him in the dray in front of Lowell's. After Jake sat down in the cart,

Isaac snapped the reins, and the mule began a steady clop down one of the side streets.

Outside of town, the road grew rutted and muddy. The dray was the better choice over the company truck that would have become stuck on the unpaved road. More than once, Jake hopped out to work the cart out of the soft earth and to coax the mule to continue.

The second time this happened, Isaac said, "This road get better when the summer dry it out."

Jake watched the mule's hooves sink into several inches of muck. "I hope so."

Isaac chuckled softly. "We mighta done better if'n we'd taken the boat instead. This New Bern Road follow the Newport River. The mill's on Russell Creek."

Jake nodded, recalling the nautical chart he'd studied the night before. Coastal folks often used the waterways as a highway system when the roads were particularly treacherous.

By the time Isaac pulled the wagon off the road several miles later, Jake's boots and trousers were covered with mud. Isaac directed the mule down a path until the woods opened to a field with several warehouses, sheds, and piles of wood curing in the open air. Behind the storage buildings, Jake could see a small cove with several boats tied to a dock. No saws were working this early in the morning, but several dogs barked out their arrival when they drove up. A thin man with graying temples walked toward them. His rumpled clothes and hair suggested he had slept in one of the sheds.

"Mornin', Mr. George," said Isaac, touching the brim of his straw hat.

"Hey, Isaac, Mr. Buddy'll be back at dinnertime."

"I'm picking up Mr. Lowell's bill of sale. And we need some planking for a new boat," he said, nodding at Jake. "He want to build a skiff."

"Need about 150 square feet of premium juniper. Nothing knotted," said Jake.

Within twenty minutes, the three men had loaded the wood, and Isaac and Jake began the slow journey back to the boatyard.

When they were still outside town, Isaac began to talk. "My boy, Tobias, mentioned that he met you when you first sailed up to the dock."

Jake chuckled. "That he did."

"I hope he didn't get in your way none."

"No sir, he and Marbles were right helpful. Helped me dock and got me some papers. I 'appreciate their help."

"He talked a heap about your dog."

Jake nodded and a long spell passed before he asked, "Have you built a lot of boats at Lowell's?"

Isaac nodded.

Although Isaac leaned forward and rested his elbows on his knees in a relaxed manner, Jake noticed how his eyes darted cautiously. The rutted road made the planks bounce and slide in the flatbed behind them.

"I reckon y'all see a lot of action on the water nowadays."

"Some, I suppose."

"I've been thinking about getting in on some of that new trade off the coast."

Jake noticed Isaac stiffen slightly, and his jaw hardened. "I wouldn't know anything about that."

As they neared the town, Isaac pulled out a pocket watch on a chain from his trousers. Jake's eyes widened as he saw that the timepiece was identical to his own. Jake's grandfather gave the male children a silver pocket watch with their engraved initials on their seventeenth birthdays. Resisting the impulse to reach out and grab the heirloom from Isaac's hand, Jake leaned forward to adjust his boot while turning his head to study Isaac's watch more closely. By squinting, he could make out an engraving similar to the initials on Wade's timepiece.

"That's a nice pocket watch," said Jake.

Isaac turned to him, smiling in a simple, easy way, and chuckled several long, lazy laughs. "Yes, sir. A sailor paid me with it when I helped him with a boat. He ran out of money." Jake could see Isaac's demeanor change into a façade of ignorance as wariness crept into his eyes. "Why, you think I stole it?"

"Oh, no," answered Jake quickly. "I've just never seen one like that." He turned his head away as his heart raced. Wade had mentioned Isaac in his letters, and Jake could see why his brother would trust the man. When they were selecting wood for his boat, Jake recognized Isaac's raw intelligence for boat building, which would have appealed to Wade. An uncomfortable tightness gripped Jake's chest. Isaac might know where Wade had gone for alterations to the *Amelia* after he left Lowell's boatyard, but Jake wasn't ready to tip his hand and reveal his identity. Jake glanced at Isaac, who was staring straight ahead at the road in front of them. It was as if he was wearing the mask of a dulled smile that gave him a blank look. It reminded Jake of men right before a barroom fight; they appeared serene, but their tense bodies were ready to uncoil into a fight.

Jake knew Isaac had little reason to trust a white man. The Klan was on the rise in North Carolina, and lynchings were increasing throughout the South. Two decades ago, white vigilantes swept through Wilmington's Negro community, killing residents and burning buildings. While it was reported as a race riot, many considered it a coup d'état when the aldermen and mayor were forced to resign at gunpoint. These elected officials were replaced with members of the white mob.

Jake fidgeted and strained to control his growing panic. Each time the dray stalled in the mud, he was grateful to hop down from his seat and dig out the cart since the physical activity calmed his nerves. After a mile or so, Isaac began to talk quietly to his mule and then hummed a tune.

Eventually, the wagon re-entered Beaufort. While the two of them had mucked their way out to Russell Creek and back, the town had started its business day. Like all Southern towns, Beaufort abided by Jim Crow laws that forced the races to live separately. As Isaac's mule cart passed through his neighborhood filled with stores, churches, a school, and a movie theatre, several folks nodded or waved.

A small woman stooped with age approached the street and Isaac stopped the dray in front of her. The frozen mask melted away from Isaac's face as he looked at the ancient woman with genuine affection. "Mr. Waterson, this is my grandmother, Tulla Jaspers."

Jake jumped down from the seat to help the woman into the wagon. "Hello, Miss Jaspers."

She chuckled softly. "People call me Tulla."

Once she was settled, Isaac snapped the reins, and they advanced toward Front Street. "Where you off to this morning, Grannie?"

"I need to check on Miss Evelyn Jane's new baby."

"Grannie's a midwife and a root doctor."

"We had a midwife stay with my mama after my brother was born," said Jake. "She more than likely kept both of them alive."

"Is that right?" commented Tulla. "I reckon I delivered 'bout half the county."

Jake continued to talk to Tulla until Isaac stopped the mule on Front Street in front of a small house, and his grandmother disembarked.

"Bye, Grannie, see you tonight," Isaac said as he turned the dray in the opposite direction toward the boatyard.

When the two men rolled up to Lowell's, Jake slipped Isaac a quarter. "Let me pay for your help."

Isaac nodded and accepted the money. The two men unloaded the lumber and carried it into the boathouse. As Isaac walked away to work in a far corner of the building, Jake balled his fists in frustration. He felt Isaac could hold a valuable key to Wade's disappearance. Steadying his breath, he pondered how he could gain the man's trust.

With a great effort, Jake turned away to give his full attention to building his boat. First, he secured a sawhorse and his stem stock by nailing them to the wooden floor. He planned to build the open vessel upside down on these supports. Once the hull was complete, he would flip it over to finish the interior. Humming an easy ragtime tune, he anchored the chine plank to the stem. While a gentle breeze stirred from the back door, he molded the flexible juniper to create the skin of the boat.

As he worked, Jake listened for the baritone voice of the silhouetted figure from the previous night. But it didn't surface in any of the men working in the warehouse or any of the customers who passed through the yard. When the sun began to heat up the boathouse, Lowell emerged from his office and walked out to the trawler that was dry-docked in the boatyard. The workers climbed down from the boat's frame to listen to their boss as he gesticulated angrily and roundly criticized their progress. Jake studied the build of a tall, slim youth working on the deck and thought he could be the right height and build of the person who stepped into the sloop the previous night.

When Lowell walked back to his office, the young man shook his head, pulled out a packet of Lucky Strikes, and sauntered to the back of the yard while his companions returned to work. Jake followed the younger worker and said, "Reckon you need a cigarette after that earful."

" 'At's a fact," said the young man as he took a long drag. The boy had a thicker brogue than the other people Jake had met in town. It had a Scottish lilt that stretched his vowels into long, rounded cadences.

Jake extended his hand. "Jake Waterson."

"Frankie Chadwick," the boy replied as they shook hands. "Hain't nary a person that calls me that. Everybody calls me Chadwick. You been building boats long?"

Jake nodded. "My daddy taught me."

"Same here. Charlie always wants new labor."

Jake glanced over at the office. "That would be a hard way to make money."

Chadwick shook his head wearily. "I hear that shit, buddy." After a moment, he added, "Ol' Charlie's his own man, I reckon. My daddy sent me in from the Island to work with him."

"The Island?"

"Harkers Island. 'Bout fifteen miles east from here by boat. My uncle's a Rose, so we built just 'bout every boat on the Island. Daddy knew I wanted to come to town, so he set me up so that I could work with Lowell."

Nodding, Jake patted his pockets, making a show of searching for matches. "Sounds like a high price to pay to live in town."

"You got that right," answered Chadwick, throwing a rueful look in the direction of Lowell's office.

Jake pulled out a variety of items that included a pocketknife, several nuts and bolts, and a large wad of folded bills. While he continued to search through his clothing, he peeked at Chadwick, who wasn't taking his eyes off the cash in Jake's hand. It reminded Jake of Yawg at dinnertime when he wouldn't break eye contact with the food bowl. In reality, the stack was several bills wrapped around a number of pieces of paper. "What do people do for fun around here?" he asked once he found his matches.

Chadwick pulled his eyes away from the money. "Er's a time going on to the inn." Jake remembered the stately Inlet Inn where he'd sent the telegram to his parents.

"Them rich folk come down from Raleigh on the weekends."

The sandy beach and the hotel's dock full of skiffs waiting to taxi people to Shackleford Banks would be attractive to people from the inland, who visited to escape the heat.

Jake nodded, "Good to know. Do you only work on new boats?"

"Nah, lots of people want to change up their boat."

"I've been thinking about putting an engine in the *Jamison*." He cupped his hand around his cigarette as he struck the match to light it. "I need a fast boat."

"There'd be some power in that," the youth said with a smile full of crooked teeth.

"I'd need to haul her out of the water on a marine rail, and I don't reckon I want to do it here," Jake said, indicating the rail next to the boatyard. "Kinda out in the open."

" 'magine so."

"Know anyplace that could do that?"

"I'll ask around."

"I'd 'preciate that."

The two men talked amicably until their cigarettes burned down to their fingers. Then they returned to work.

Working on the boat brought a sense of normalcy to Jake. Although Wade and Jake had learned the boatbuilding craft from their father, Wade taught Jake the art of design. At the end of the afternoon, relief and satisfaction flooded Jake when he stood back and admired the nearly finished watercraft.

As dusk brought long shadows to Front Street, Jake strolled back to the *Jamison* at the town dock where he found Tobias and Marbles waiting next to his boat.

"Hey, Mr. Jake, is your skiff done?"

"Almost. You gonna row her for me before my sails are made?"

"Will you pay me a nickel?"

❧

The next morning broke clear with a strong northeast wind pushing clouds out to sea. From the cockpit of the *Jamison*, Jake treated Yawg's wounded paw while his boat bobbed and fought her mooring. While he worked, he remembered Yawg and Wade had been inseparable in South Carolina. Jake's brother, who was naturally laconic with people, would have long conversations with Yawg.

After pulling up his anchor, Jake fought the headwind during the short sail across the channel. He planned to post a request for carpentry jobs on the work board at Guthrie's Hardware. The night before, he'd recalled a military strategy used during his service. Enlisted men were encouraged to fraternize with civilians to build loyalty and glean local information. Working inside people's homes in Beaufort might help Jake learn more about the town's rum runners.

After docking the *Jamison*, he studied his two dogs in his cabin. Although he knew how devoted they were to each other, Jake felt he needed Pilot to steady his nerves while visiting Nell. "Sorry old boy," he said to Yawg as he closed up the hound in the cabin. Then he and his Lab walked off the dock toward town. He ignored his quickening pulse as he approached the shop and repeated his mission focus: to find Wade at all costs.

When he walked into the store, Nell was standing with another young woman behind the counter. Leaning over a thick ledger opened in front of them, Nell furiously wrote as they giggled and elbowed each other. Today, she wore a periwinkle-blue dress, and his gaze lingered on the simple cross around her neck. Then his smile faded when she swept her hand across the page of the book, making the small diamond ring glint on her left hand. Surprised by his disappointment, he reminded himself that he'd just met the girl. Still, he scratched Pilot's head to settle himself.

"Hey there, Jake," said Nell. "This is my friend, Emma Grace Willis."

With some reluctance, he turned from Nell's dancing eyes to face Emma Grace. Even in the drab nurse's uniform, Nell's friend was striking. Her black hair was bobbed and styled in a Marcel wave, and she scrutinized him with thoughtful brown eyes.

"Miss Willis," he nodded.

"So, did Charlie Lowell give you a proper Beaufort welcome?" asked Emma Grace.

Jake forced a small laugh. "You might say that. I try to stay upwind from him." Both girls giggled.

"Good luck with that," Emma Grace replied. Turning to her friend, she added, "I best be going." She came around the counter and headed for the door.

"Bye, Emma Grace. I'll pick you up after work," said Nell.

"As long as they don't need me at the clinic tonight," Emma Grace called over her shoulder.

Looking down at Pilot, Nell asked, "And who might this charming gentleman be?" She slipped a dog biscuit out of a jar on the counter and presented it to the Labrador retriever.

"This is Pilot, who will always behave like an orphaned child within ten feet of a biscuit."

While Nell scratched the dog behind his ears, Jake reached into his bag to retrieve the posting written on the back of an envelope. "We should all have such good friends," Nell said softly to Pilot. She stood up, noticing the envelope in Jake's hand. "So, are you ready to post for work?"

"Yes, ma'am," he replied. "And I need a gallon of white paint."

"I'll need to get that from storage." She moved out from behind the counter to walk to the back of the store. Jake exhaled as he watched her walk away. *Lordy, that's one good-looking girl.* Shaking his head, he reaffirmed his mission: to find Wade at all costs.

When Nell was out of sight, he glanced down at the ledger open on the counter. Quietly turning the large book around to read the entries, he read detailed accounts of boats entering the harbor. In different handwriting, there were references to illness and transactions of the crew. Scanning the page, he quickly found:

> *May 7, 1923 "Boat Name:* Jamison, *Owner: Jake Waterson*
> *Homeport: Charleston, S. Carolina*
> *Business of Craft: Fisherman? Skiff builder? Candlestick maker?*
> *Bootlegger? Traveler?*

He let his fingers linger on the entry, imagining her curiosity as she wrote it. Then his mind snapped out of his ruminations and began to race with all the possibilities that this harbor record could offer him. Hearing bumps and scrapes emanating from the backroom, he furiously flipped through the pages looking for entries of the *Amelia.* Blood pounded in his ears and he felt a surge of optimism as he searched. She may have tracked the *Amelia* through town, and he could learn what happened to the boat after it left Lowell's. He longed to slip the ledger into his bag and walk out of the store but knew that could draw attention to himself.

The sound of footsteps moving out of the backroom forced him to hastily return the book to its original spot before he stepped over to the work board to post his request and scan for jobs.

Nell returned, set the can of paint on the counter, and began to write up his receipt. "That comes to $1.15."

Jake casually walked back to the counter as he said, "So, you were going to tell me how you came to work in a hardware store."

"Well, I reckon it is a little strange to see a girl working here." Without looking up from the receipt, she cleared her throat and forced a brittle laugh. "It just became necessary after my brother . . . passed." The last word caught in her throat, and she turned to the pillar behind her. For the first time, Jake noticed the framed photograph draped with a black ribbon. The picture showed a doughboy infantryman. "This was my brother, Harrison," Nell swallowed. "When he didn't come back, my daddy needed someone to help him in the store."

A wave of anguish surged in Jake. "It never really leaves you," he said.

Turning back to him, Nell held his look. After Jake came home from Europe, most people didn't want to talk about the war. They wanted to put it behind them and drown their memories in booze and dancing. But Jake could see that Nell wasn't like that. She was one of the people who carried the war with her. After several years, others would often chide them for being overly somber and serious.

She was studying him now and asked, "Did you lose someone?"

He cleared his throat. "Yes, ma'am. I was a sergeant in the 118th Infantry. The battle at Montbrehain was particularly hard—I lost more than half my troop. Most of them I'd grown up with."

The hardware store melted away, and all Jake could see were the gray, lifeless faces from his last battle. While recuperating in the military hospital, he lapsed into a vacant, thousand-yard stare and he stopped feeding and caring for himself. The disgrace of a cowardly discharge still clung to him. Drawing a long, shaking breath, he repeated, "And it never really leaves you." Pilot sensed the distress in Jake's voice and pressed himself against his master's leg. Jake closed his eyes in silent gratitude to his dog.

Nell's composure crumpled as a bleak, stunned look swept over her face. "It doesn't feel like five years ago. He enlisted and got sick. And . . . I never saw him again." She closed her eyes and drew a deep breath. "He never treated me like a little sister. He was always looking out for me. And then he was gone." Her hand went up to the small cross on her necklace, but she couldn't stop two tears from rolling down her cheeks.

A strong impulse to protect her and lift her sorrow overtook Jake. He ached to jump over the counter to stroke her hair and comfort her in his arms. He moved forward, but her engagement ring glittered on her hand as she held the necklace. He stopped abruptly and remembered her hands' calloused strength and roughness, but now they looked small and vulnerable.

She pulled a small handkerchief from her pocket and dabbed her eyes and nose. "It nearly killed my mama. She'd been poorly before, and the shock put her in a wheelchair. So, when I'm not caring for her, I help Daddy in the store. He needed me after Harrison . . . well . . . Harrison loved working here. I feel him in here, and I want to do him proud."

A look of longing and loss passed between them. Then she stiffened when her eyes shifted to look behind Jake. He turned to see a stout, middle-aged man enter the shop.

"Well, hey there, Daddy." Nell chimed with forced bravado. "This is Jake Waterson off the *Jamison*."

Mr. Guthrie grunted while hardly glancing at his daughter. There was a tightness around his mouth and eyes. "Nell, did you finish those entries?"

"Yes, sir." Nell closed the ledger in front of her and handed it to her father.

Without another word, Mr. Guthrie took the ledger and walked toward the back of the store.

Remembering the gallon of paint, Nell turned to the counter but didn't look at Jake. "That'll be $1.15." Her hands trembled as she pulled the receipt off her pad.

Jake paid while trying to catch Nell's eye, but she pointedly looked away from him. He picked up the gallon of paint and moved toward the door. "Come, Pilot." The dog fell in line behind him as they walked away.

CHAPTER 5

∽

The next morning, Nell and Emma Grace took advantage of a favorable tide and set sail to Harkers Island to deliver engine parts for the hardware store. The two young women boarded Nell's skiff and sailed an easterly course. Beaufort was located on the south side of a peninsula that extended into the Atlantic Ocean. Cape Lookout marked the land's end and the beginning of the East Coast's most shallow and volatile waters. Since the low country from Beaufort to Cape Lookout was more water than land, the roads were often impassable; people tended to travel via their sounds, ditches, and creeks.

On the return trip, Nell's *Harmony* dodged the sailboats and engine-powered watercraft that filled the sound. The light wind shifted to the southeast, and she detected a delicate southerly balminess. As they approached the inlet and Beaufort came into view, Nell became restless. She turned to her friend and said, "I believe I am having sinful desires."

Emma Grace, who was relaxing against a boat gunnel, straightened up to give her full attention. "Gracious; do tell."

"Jake Waterson—remember how he came into the store yesterday?"

"What happened?" Emma Grace asked with concern.

Nell glanced at the church steeple and gripped the tiller. "Well, nothing really, but I just felt—I must have still been really upset about Harrison. Remember how we talked about him the other night?"

Emma Grace nodded.

"I didn't mean to—" Nell stumbled over her words. She looked away for a moment when a rush of confusion engulfed her. "We were standing by the cash register, and I was fixin' to check him out. And then he asked me why I worked in the store, and we started to talk about the war. Probably half a dozen people mention Harrison's picture every week, and I don't think a lick about it."

"Okay."

"And then, I don't know, I just started to tell him everything—everything I ever felt for Harrison and how I missed him, and he talked about when he was in the war." Nell wiped her eyes with the back of her hand. "There is just something about him. He could feel what I was feeling. Oh, Emma Grace, I wanted to kiss him." She paused and put her fingers to her lips. "I shouldn't be feeling this way when I'm engaged."

"You scarlet woman," Emma Grace teased.

"Oh, please don't make fun."

"Honey, these are human feelings. All you've ever known is Asa," said Emma Grace.

"The Bible says that when you look at someone with lust, you've already committed adultery in your heart."

"Yes, well, I think you're safe from condemnation. I'm not so sure the men who wrote the Bible always had women's welfare in mind. Like when it says, 'Wives, submit yourself to your husband as you do to the Lord.'" Emma Grace sniffed. "I don't think so."

Nell jerked her head away from the water to stare at her friend, aghast that she could be so casual about eternal damnation. "Emma Grace— you're being sacrilegious." Although Emma Grace attended church with her family every Sunday, Nell knew she had lost her faith after Harrison died.

Emma Grace sighed. "And you're being silly about Jake. There are bigger things to worry about."

Nell's insides twisted in agony. Her throat felt dry as she scrunched up her face to fight her tears.

"Oh, Nell, I'm sorry," Emma Grace said. She reached over and squeezed her friend's hand. "Look," she said softly, "once you've nursed a child with a fever through the night, you get an idea about what's important in this life.

So, you poured your heart out to him, and he comforted you. Now you know you can't do it again."

Emma Grace had a straightforward way of simplifying things. "I suppose you're right," said Nell, returning Emma Grace's squeeze. "It's always hard to know what to do with men."

"Don't I know it," sighed Emma Grace.

Emma Grace took over the helm so her friend could dab her nose and eyes with her handkerchief. The wind rose, but only a gentle chop greeted them in the estuary protected by barrier islands. As they sailed along, Nell could hear the rollers crashing on the ocean side of the Outer Banks, but they sounded distant and remote.

Later that day, Nell smoothed the back of her hair, which was swept up in a loose twist and secured with horn combs. She stepped back from the small mirror on top of her vanity. Since she couldn't see her full reflection in the mirror, she turned several times to check all the angles of her dress. Feeling like the cat's meow in Emma Grace's elegant chiffon frock trimmed with a lacy Peter Pan collar, she lifted one shoulder seductively before smiling at herself in the reflection. She could hear Asa and her daddy talking in the next room, and a nervous flutter rippled through her belly. Taking a deep breath, she walked out of her room to step into the parlor of the small home.

Since her parents owned few luxuries, their front room was simply decorated with handmade quilts and crocheted doilies. Although the family owned a telephone, a large wireless radio, and a phonograph that connected Nell's mother to the world, they had parted with many valuables in recent years to pay for doctors' bills. Dressed in his ill-fitting suit, Asa was sitting across from Nell's father. The two men were locked in animated conversation and filled the room with their cigar smoke. Nell's mother sat in a wheelchair next to her husband and turned her head when her daughter entered. "Oh, Nell, you look like you just stepped out of *Ladies' Home Journal*."

Thomas Guthrie and Asa turned to look up at Nell. "Well, don't you look swell," said Asa taking her in from head to toe. He beamed at her as if she were a jewel in a display case.

Nell smiled at him before glancing at her father. "You're pretty as a picture," Thomas said gruffly. Clearing his throat, he stood up and walked behind his wife's wheelchair.

"Thank you, Daddy," Nell replied in a soft voice. She crossed the room to a small table that held her cloche and clutch bag. While she settled the hat on her hair, Asa and her father took up their previous conversation.

"Well, I think Harding can pull this around," her daddy said to Asa.

Asa nodded enthusiastically. "I know he can. He's a good ol' boy from Ohio. There's not a doubt in my mind that he can create a whole lot of jobs."

From the corner of her eye, Nell watched her father. It was nice to see her daddy talk and argue with Asa. When Harrison was alive, Thomas had often cut up with his son's friends when they stopped by. He'd been more outgoing and at ease with the world in those days. Now, he kept to himself. Nell shifted her gaze and saw that her mother was watching her. "Oh, Mama, I forgot to tell you. The Inlet Inn hired Emma Grace's cousin, Winston, to play with the ragtime group tomorrow."

Thomas shifted uncomfortably.

"We can only hope Beaufort is ready for it," replied Alice stiffly as she patted her husband's hand resting on the handle of her wheelchair.

Nell looked up at her father. "The manager asked them if I could open for the family crowd. Will that be okay, Daddy?"

"What sort of music will you play?"

"Waltzes, tangoes. Pieces with an easy tempo so fathers can dance with their daughters and the little ones can ride on their daddies' feet."

Thomas nodded but added, "As long as that's all it is. I'll not have you playing that hellacious monkey music in public. Lord knows what people would think."

"Yes, sir," Nell replied. She glanced at her mother, whose eyes were burning with excitement. Playing at the inn would be Nell's first public performance outside of their church. Before Alice Guthrie was crippled with rheumatoid arthritis, she had taught music to Nell, Harrison, and most of Emma Grace's family.

Alice turned to speak to Asa. "As far as music is concerned, I'm afraid Nell's father isn't ready to enter the twentieth century."

45

"Yes, ma'am," Asa replied politely. He walked over to Nell and gave her his arm. Nell slipped her arm into his and looked at her parents in their modest living room. She thought of the days ahead when she would plan her wedding, move out of her parents' home, and away from their town. A dull ache rested at the back of her throat, and she swallowed with difficulty. Her mother pressed her lips together and turned her face away, now softened with emotion.

∽

To escape the direct pummel of wind and salt from the harbor, the couple walked up Ann Street, one block inland. As she strolled along with her beau, Nell's mind drifted to her future mother-in-law, Sylvia Whitestone Davis. Asa told Nell that his parents met while his father, Giles Davis, studied medicine at Johns Hopkins University in Baltimore and shared rooms with Sylvia's brother. When they married, Sylvia assumed her husband would accept a position in a metropolitan area. But when Giles's father became ill with cancer; they returned to Beaufort to continue the family practice. Having accompanied his father as a child on many house calls, Giles felt a devotion to his father's patients and hometown. He eventually opened the small Davis Emergency Clinic on Front Street. The practice had four patient rooms, an operation room, and a kitchen. It served Beaufort, as well as the coastal communities east of town.

"Your mama seems to miss Richmond a whole lot," Nell said to her beau.

Asa snorted and said, "Oh, little girl, you don't know the half of it."

As she walked arm in arm with Asa, Nell remembered the cotillion lessons Mrs. Davis taught when Nell was growing up. The local girls learned to walk with graceful poise, sip quietly from their soup spoons, and maintain creamy complexions. Now that Nell was engaged to Asa, she concentrated on recalling these etiquette lessons.

Climbing the steps to the lower veranda of Asa's refined childhood home, Nell felt like she was leaving small-town Beaufort behind. Once inside, she likened the vestibule to the halls of English castles, where ancestral portraits strengthened the family's sense of lineage and purpose. When they entered the parlor, Nell's eyes traveled over the walls of the room, taking in rich velour curtains that framed the windows, and oil paintings of Confederate generals and Civil War scenes interspersed among bric-a-brac shelving holding exquisite eggshell porcelain. It felt like a magical world to Nell, and she longed to be a part of it.

Nell searched the room for Asa's parents but only saw a stranger on the settee. He wore an impeccable three-piece suit that was the color of a mourning dove, garnished with a ruby-colored tie. His pale skin contrasted sharply against his jet-black hair. A small smile twisted out of the corner of his mouth.

"Ramsey! You old dog," Asa boomed to the stranger. "When did you get in?"

"I swept in on the iron horse around three this afternoon." His voice emanated from his chest with deep, steady resonance.

"Nell, this is our cousin, Mr. Edgar Ramsey from Richmond."

"How do you do, Mr. Ramsey," said Nell.

When she proffered her hand, he enveloped it in a warm clasp. Pulling his words into a long, sensual drawl, he answered, "May I congratulate you on your upcoming nuptials, my dear. I hope you have a remarkable wedding, followed by an amicable marriage."

Nell returned the smile and glanced down at his hand to see a silver ring set with a bloodstone. She couldn't remember a man in Beaufort wearing any ring other than a wedding band.

"Dr. Davis is delayed with his house calls, but I'm so glad you have arrived," Mr. Ramsey continued.

Asa looked over Mr. Ramsey's shoulder and searched the room. "Where's Mama?"

"Oh, here and there. I believe she is finding fault with the roast at the moment."

The conversation paused, and Nell remembered it was a young lady's duty to sustain a cordial exchange at a social gathering. She addressed Mr. Ramsey. "I hope you are enjoying Beaufort."

Mr. Edgar Ramsey grinned as he answered, "I always enjoy Beaufort. The people here are so . . . Beaufort. The town could have been Morehead, but it's Beaufort."

Nell's tension eased, and she smiled despite her frayed nerves. This newcomer understood the rivalry between Beaufort and Morehead City, the modern town built on the Newport River's west bank. Asa walked over to the buffet while Mr. Ramsey returned to the settee. Nell made an effort to sit erectly in the plush chair while keeping her back straight and her ankles crossed as Mrs. Davis had shown her.

Straining to maintain the formal diction she'd learned in cotillion lessons, Nell asked, "May I inquire as to your profession in Richmond?"

"I dabble in antiquities," drawled Mr. Ramsey. When Nell looked a little confused, Mr. Ramsey elaborated. "Mostly old artifacts from the Civil War and maritime relics."

Nell could imagine how his demeanor and appearance would remind people of a Confederate general. "Then you must know Buddy Taylor at the lumber yard."

Mr. Ramsey brushed the knee of his pants. "Oh, yes. Buddy and I are old friends."

Asa was picking up various wine bottles on the buffet and reading labels. "So, what did you bring us from Richmond, Ramsey?"

His cousin rose from the small couch and walked toward Asa. "I brought a bottle of Cabernet. May I offer you some?" asked Mr. Ramsey.

"Is that a fancy French name for red wine?" asked Nell.

"It is."

"From grapes?"

Mr. Ramsey chuckled. "It is."

Nell hesitated. "I'll have a small taste," said Nell. The Methodist in her felt conflicted about drinking so openly, but she knew this was the social norm in Asa's home.

"Sounds like you have been enjoying the homespun version of wine," said Mr. Ramsey.

"Yes, sir. My friend, Emma Grace, brews raspberry, strawberry, apple, and dandelion. And the occasional brick."

Mr. Ramsey paused and looked at her in confusion. "Brick?"

Nell nodded. "Bricks are mailed from a farm. They're supposed to be compressed, dried grapes, but we're never real sure what kinda plants are in them. They come with explicit instructions about how to avoid fermentation. So, everyone ferments them into wine."

Mr. Ramsey roared with laughter. "Our Noble Experiment has made you very creative indeed."

Nell smiled as she thought of Emma Grace's concoctions stored in the shed in their shared garden. Her hand trembled when she accepted the small wine glass from Mr. Ramsey.

"I'd love to try the dandelion sometime." He raised his glass and toasted, "Santé!"

The smooth, even taste of the wine lingered on Nell's tongue, reminding her of a lulled melody. "No," she said, once she'd swallowed the delicate wine. "I don't think you'd care for dandelion wine in the least."

Mr. Ramsey chuckled, brought the bottle over to the small table in front of the settee, and raised his glass a second time. "Here's to the French vineyards; may they always make an excellent Cabernet, and may we always be able to sample it. Somehow."

They raised their glasses and took appreciative sips. Nell picked up the bottle on the table and admired the illustration of a black horse with a windswept mane. "Wow, they really have swell labels." She tried to read the French words. "What do they call this?"

"*Le Cheval Noir*," the name rolled off Mr. Ramsey's tongue. "It means 'the black horse.' I brought it with me from Richmond."

Asa choked on his wine and set his glass down.

Nell set the bottle down and began to rise in concern but stopped when she saw Asa's face darken. Mr. Ramsey was studying Nell and remained unaware of the shift in Asa's temper. Her fiancé crossed the room in two strides, took the bottle from Nell, and examined the label. "So, you brought this from Richmond?" he asked Mr. Ramsey. "That's right interesting."

"Asa, what in the world—" Nell began, but she was interrupted by a woman's shrill voice emanating from the dining room.

"Oh, blast."

Nell recognized Mrs. Davis's scolding timbre that was answered by her maid's low and soothing voice. The door opened, and Asa's mother entered the room. "Well, it would appear that supper will not be served at six o'clock," she stated crossly. Dressed in a subdued, ecru shift, the small lady set off the ensemble with a long string of red garnets. She knitted her brows in angry consternation.

"Never mind that," said Mr. Ramsey, pouring a glass of the French wine and handing it to her. "Dr. Davis is delayed and I know you wouldn't want to start without him."

Mrs. Sylvia Davis sniffed. "Oh, Ramsey, we'll not wait on him. Lord knows when he'll wander home." She took a large swallow from the glass and looked around the room, seeing Asa and Nell for the first time. Her face broke into a wide smile. "The two of you are betrothed!"

"Yes, ma'am," said Nell, holding up her left hand and wiggling her fingers.

Mrs. Davis crossed the room and held Nell's finger to examine the diamond in its setting. "Oh, I do love a wedding! And Richmond will not see the likes of yours for quite some time. I was able to reserve Centenary Methodist on Grace Street."

"Ma'am?" said Nell, looking confused.

"The Methodist church in Richmond. It will be a wonderful way for you to enter Richmond's Fan," Mrs. Davis said, referring to the city's affluent neighborhood. She took a dainty sip of the Cabernet.

Nell shot a distressed look at Asa. Her father could never afford such a lavish wedding. "I'm sorry if there has been some sort of misunderstanding, Mrs. Davis," she stammered, "but I was planning for a small family wedding at our church here in Beaufort."

Scowling, Mrs. Davis replied, "Nell, dear, you must make a statement in Richmond. If you're presented there, it will only help Asa's business." She took a generous sip from her wine class.

"Mama," interjected Asa, "This is Nell's wedding—"

"Fiddlesticks," interrupted Mrs. Davis as the color rose in her cheeks, "This will launch you into a successful marriage." She turned to Nell. "A lady must support her husband in his endeavors. You need to make a statement when you enter his world."

The room began to spin as Nell's parched mouth couldn't form words. Closing her eyes, she thought of the modest items in her hope chest that she and her mother had assembled since she was a child. In it, she had stored her father's hand-carved figurines, along with the bedspreads and tea towels sewn with friends at quilting bees. All treasures laced with memories but pitifully thin additions to a marriage.

While Nell stood frozen in the middle of the drawing room holding her wine glass, Mr. Ramsey drifted over, picked up Mrs. Davis's hand and stroked it reassuringly. "Sylvia, let's think this through for a moment. They could have the small wedding that Nell has always dreamed of with her family here in

Beaufort. Then you could send them off with a big ol' ball in the Capital of the Confederacy. That would be all your doing."

The deep red splotches faded on Mrs. Davis's face.

"We could take it a step further," the elegant man continued. "And have a grand reception in Morehead City at the Atlantic Hotel. You know how the governor likes to come down to that watering hole."

"Mama," started Asa, "I don't think—" But Mr. Ramsey silenced him with a conspiratorial look.

"In Morehead?" Nell squeaked; the thought of crossing the river to her rival town was unthinkable. "At the Atlantic?" She knew everyone in Beaufort believed Morehead stole the Atlantic Hotel after the original hotel on Front Street had been destroyed by a hurricane in 1899.

But Mrs. Davis's face brightened, and a distant look settled on her features. Turning away in thought, she walked over to the buffet table, where she refilled her glass. "Now, Gov. Morrison does visit there from time to time."

"The governor at my reception?" Now it felt like the air was leaving the room, and she gasped in panic. "Goodness, what would I say to him?"

Asa and Mr. Ramsey looked at her in sympathy.

"You could start with 'How do you do?'" offered Mr. Ramsey.

"Mrs. Davis?" said a hushed voice. They all turned to the dining room door. Nell saw that Annie Jasper, who worked as a maid in the household, had silently entered the room. "Supper is served, ma'am."

Asa walked over to Nell and put his arm around her waist. "Don't even think about it, sugar. We'll sort it all out later." He brushed her forehead with his lips in a light kiss.

She looked at him for a moment and wanted to say something, but her mouth felt like it was glued shut. Taking a fortifying sip from her wine, Nell leaned into her fiancé and walked toward the dining room.

To her relief, Mrs. Davis started a new conversation while Asa carved the roast. "Cynthia Noe was telling me about some sort of brawl on Front Street this afternoon," said Mrs. Davis. "Did you see what happened, Asa?"

Nell was studying her silverware, wondering which fork she should select.

"That I did," said Asa quickly. "As a matter of fact, I was in the middle of it. I was behind the counter when two little deviants tried to pinch one of the ivory handle brush sets. I ran out from behind the counter and pulled them outside and started hollering for Jimmy."

"Oh, Asa, how awful for you," said his mother.

"They call Jimmy the sheriff," Asa replied, "but he's worthless. Before I knew it, that useless drifter had jumped on top of me and flattened me to the ground, yelling at those boys to run for it. Then he told his black dog to attack me."

Nell jerked her head up in surprise. Her hand flew to her mouth when she realized that Asa must be talking about Jake Waterson with Tobias and Marbles in the drugstore.

"There is just something that's not right about that man," said Asa.

"Why would you say that?" asked Nell, pressing her knuckle against her lips. She thought of the sincerity in Jake's eyes when he expressed sorrow over her loss of Harrison.

"He's over there at Lowell's asking all sorts of questions, poking around where he shouldn't be. Charlie don't trust him, and that's a fact." Asa gulped a large swallow of wine. Nell noticed the heat in his face.

Mr. Ramsey laughed as he passed a tureen of mashed potatoes. "Charlie Lowell doesn't trust his mother."

Nell's eyes darted to Mr. Ramsey. There was obviously another side to this Jake Waterson. Had he tricked her with all his sympathetic talk? Who would do that? Who would use her brother's death for his own gain?

Asa's agitation increased. "Why would somebody come into town, ask for workspace in Lowell's warehouse, and then take off to the lumber yard with his nigger?"

Nell glanced at Annie, setting more serving dishes on the table. Nell knew she was married to Isaac, who worked at Lowell's. For the briefest moment, Annie's eyes flashed, but her face remained impassive while she offered the serving bowl of sweet potatoes to the guests. With some hesitancy, Nell answered, "Maybe he wanted to choose his wood."

"Maybe. But it seems like he's doing it behind a white man's back. I wouldn't be surprised if he turned out to be a revenue man," bellowed Asa.

With trembling hands, Nell picked up the serving spoon and put sweet potatoes on her plate.

"Jimmy let that bum just walk away," continued Asa. "I tell you, they should have locked up that maniac right then and there." He stabbed the roast in anger and sat down. Then he reached for the bowl of sweet potatoes and began to load his plate.

"Amen to that." Mrs. Davis raised her glass.

Nell's heart raced. What would have happened if she'd been left alone with that stranger in the store a minute longer? "It does sound strange that the law didn't do more."

"Oh, Jimmy sat there and went on to that moron about civility in town and we don't want any bad influences in Beaufort. He may as well have blessed him and sent him on his way."

Mr. Ramsey studied her for a moment. "Did you see what happened, Nell?"

"No, sir, I was at Harkers Island most of the day." She looked down at the table and pushed her food around on her plate, wondering how a perfect stranger could have so completely fooled her.

"Sylvia, you simply must see the latest antiquities that I'll be transporting," Mr. Ramsey said. Nell felt enormous relief that Mr. Ramsey had changed the subject. She looked down and smoothed Emma Grace's bold dress, remembering how strong and infallible she'd felt when she left her home. Now, she felt like an imposter. First, Mrs. Davis was taking over her wedding, and now she was beginning to think Jake was behaving like the deceptive seducers she'd seen in the movies. They start off acting like a swell guy, then they deflower and abandon the heroine.

Mr. Ramsey was droning on about antebellum chandeliers. Nell took a sip from her wine glass and caught her reflection in a mirror hung over the sideboard. She looked so pale and queasy; she didn't recognize herself. Bobbing around from one conversation to another, she felt untethered, drifting out on the tide.

CHAPTER 6

Earlier that afternoon, after the pharmacist pummeled him, Jake ushered the two boys away from the sheriff and a group of angry citizens of Beaufort. A rather odd, tiny woman with a strong local brogue helped comfort Marbles and Tobias. "Don't you think nary a time on them," she said as she wiped their tears. Jake thanked the small woman who called herself Tisdale, and then returned to his boat to doctor a swelling eye and cheekbone. After supper and three fingers of whiskey, he settled on the deck to enjoy the soothing comfort of the *Jamison's* gentle rocking.

The water surrounding the boat made Jake feel protected, like a moat that he could cross at his discretion. Falling into an uneasy sleep, the veteran drifted back to the Western Front where the earth erupted with artillery fire and threw him into the air. When he awoke, he thought a mortar shell was tossing him before realizing the *Jamison* was frantically bobbing in a fierce, rising wind. Although the air was filled with ocean salt, all he could smell was the stench of sewage, spilled blood, and the broken earth of open trenches. In the darkness, Yawg and Pilot whined inside the cabin. Lightning filled the sky, followed swiftly by a loud clap. As the wind gained strength, Jake stowed loose objects flying around the boat's interior.

When loud raindrops began to pound on the boat, he closed the cabin door, which had become unlatched during the heavy weather. After Jake and the two dogs hunkered down, the *Jamison* tossed and twisted as she fought her mooring. Lighting a lantern while the boat moved so violently could easily cause a fire. So, the three of them remained in the dark as the storm raged wild and angry. As panic engulfed him, Jake focused on slowing his shallow breathing while the two dogs pressed themselves against him. Occasionally, Jake cried out as the distorted faces of his platoon swam around him in the sea of darkness. When Yawg climbed into Jake's lap, he buried his face in the dog's back, still unable to smell the dank fur.

The squall raged for several hours and then abruptly eased; the wind began to die and the rain became lighter. Only then did Jake unfurl himself to stretch out on the bunk, drenched in cold, clammy sweat. Eventually, he fell into a broken sleep and when the sun woke him a few hours later, he staggered across the cabin to open the hatch. Although the harbor was filled with sparkling light, he could only smell the rancid trenches. Still locked in his nocturnal trauma, he focused on his breathing until he could smell the briny essence of the sea.

It was some time before he could move to the deck to eat cold biscuits and canned meat, but he marveled that the food did not taste like gunpowder and bloody dirt. After Jake fed his dogs and treated Yawg's wounds, he and Pilot boarded the *Miss Mary*, the dinghy he completed the day before. He was still shaking from his ordeal, but the outgoing tide was strong, and he welcomed the fight against the current.

Rowing across the harbor, he thought about the day ahead of him. Nell's father hired Jake to build a ramp off his back porch, which would allow his crippled wife to take her wheelchair down to the garden. Once the *Miss Mary* was docked, Jake strolled down Front Street with Pilot at his side. There was a lightness in his step despite the rough night and the throbbing in his head because he would soon see the fair Nell Guthrie.

Glancing at the water, he noticed a ketch with an overhanging stern similar to the *Amelia*, his brother's boat. His light mood dimmed as he remembered his sobering mission: *I must find Wade*. His steps became more measured as he recounted what he knew so far. First, Chadwick and the pharmacist were likely running booze with Lowell from his boatyard. Chadwick had the size and build of the man who rowed the skiff on the first night Jake was in port. When the pharmacist scuffled with Jake the day before, he recognized the man's deep baritone voice. He was the man who stayed onshore and talked to Lowell. Second, Jake figured Lowell would sell his mother for a bottle of rye but couldn't be the brains behind an orchestrated smuggling operation. The pharmacist was a likely candidate for the escapades, but it was still too soon to tell. Third, Isaac knew something and feared something. Jake shook his head. *I reckon I suspect 'bout half the town.*

The man and his dog arrived at the Guthrie family address and began to walk up the driveway. Voices greeted them as they approached the back porch. Through the screen door, Jake could see Nell and her father seated at their kitchen table. When Jake rapped on the door, Nell gave a small jump, while Thomas Guthrie looked up from the table and announced, "Nell, this is Jake Waterson. He'll be building the ramp for your mama."

Jake removed his hat before opening the screen door. Nell's eyes widened and stared in disbelief, first at her father and then at Jake. Disappointment flooded the young man. *She must have gotten the wrong end of the story.* Silently cursing the belligerent pharmacist, Jake said, "Sorry to startle you, Miss Nell."

"Have y'all met?" asked Mr. Guthrie.

Nell was too flustered to answer, so Jake replied, "Yes, sir. We've talked at the store." Pilot, sensing distress, began to pace in agitation on the porch. Nell pushed back a lock of hair from her forehead and twisted her hands in dismay before saying, "If y'all will excuse me, I need to check on Mama."

Thomas Guthrie watched his daughter push back her chair and leave the room. "Jake, take a load off, and help yourself to a biscuit," he said, pointing to the breakfast table.

Jake politely sat down.

"I'll be right back," said Mr. Guthrie, leaving the room.

Jake's mouth watered when the scent of fresh biscuits reached him, but his stomach was too upset to take any food. A pot of soup on the back burner simmered on the large, cast iron stove in the corner, and drying herbs hung from the rafters. The small house was built with thin walls and hardwood floors so he could easily overhear the conversation in the other room.

"I know your mama and I raised you better than that," boomed Thomas Guthrie. "That is not how we treat guests in our home."

"No, sir, but I think it best that you know what people in town are saying about Jake Waterson."

Jake closed his eyes in dismay. *Damn that pharmacist. Why couldn't he have left the kids alone?*

"He whupped up on Asa yesterday, and Jimmy pulled him off," Nell cried. "There's not a lot to trust in a man like that."

There was a pause before Mr. Guthrie replied in a lower voice, "Well, I know he's one good carpenter. I watched him build a skiff in less than a week."

"But, Daddy—"

"And I expect you to treat him as a guest in this house."

"Yes, sir."

"I also don't want you to trouble your mother with this talk."

"Yes, sir."

Jake's eyes darted around the kitchen as his chest tightened and his breathing became ragged.

"Just let me know if he puts a toe out of line." Her father's voice was sharp and severe. "Now, I need you to ride out to Buddy's with Jake and help him get the best price on lumber."

"But, Daddy," his daughter's voice became high and strident. "I can't ride around in a truck with a man like that—"

"Nell, you know Buddy Taylor from high school, and I'd feel better if you would bargain for the best price. And if this Jake character is so wily, you can keep an eye on him for me."

"Daddy," said Nell, dropping her voice. "I wouldn't feel right with him in the Ford."

"You want me to hand over the keys to him and let him go by hisself?"

"No, sir."

When Jake heard the stomp of heavy footsteps nearing the kitchen, he slipped quietly out the back door and lit a cigarette as his heart raced. A few moments later, Mr. Guthrie stepped out on the small porch and spent several minutes showing Jake the layout of the ramp before leaving for the hardware store. As Jake was marking the placement of posts with stakes and string in the yard, someone cleared her throat behind him. He looked up to see Nell standing on the bottom step. She was eye level with him and trembled like a skittish colt. Gripping the hammer in his hand, he fought an urge to pull her to his chest, stroke her hair, and soothe her.

"Mr. Waterson." She swallowed. "Mr. Waterson," she repeated, "some very ugly stories are circulating in this town regarding you."

"Nell, I—" He leaned toward her, but stopped when her eyes widened, and she jumped up a step.

"I think it's best if you call me Miss Guthrie." Her tone was sharp, but it wavered slightly. "I think you're an untrustworthy man, and I'm not taking any phony-baloney from you."

When he stepped back from her, she looked relieved. "If you're referring to my visit to the drug store yesterday, I'd like you to hear my side of the story."

Pilot nuzzled Nell's hand. Without looking at the dog, she moved her hand up to the cross on her neck. "I don't think that will be necessary," she replied, looking away. "I've heard and seen all I need to know. My father would like me to take you to the lumber yard. Please let me know when you'll be ready to leave."

He grimaced. "Yes, ma'am."

Jake was turning back to his work when Nell added, "Just so you know, the man you attacked at the drugstore is my fiancé." Jake closed his eyes and swore under his breath as she walked back up the steps. It sickened him to think of Nell coupled with the arrogant druggist. He reminded Jake of the old-money gentry who dominated Charleston. When Wade and Jake sailed into town, it was not unusual to see well-to-do men visiting the bars and brothels on Saturday night, and then rise the next morning and sit in the front pews of churches, seats reserved for honored patrons. Watching Nell enter the house, Jake's mind drifted back to the moment he shared with Nell at the hardware store when he considered her a kindred spirit.

Trying to put the specter of Nell and the angry pharmacist out of his mind, Jake pounded stakes into the ground with his hammer. The earth was wet from the rainfall the previous night, so the work went quickly. As he toiled in the yard, he absent-mindedly whistled "Melancholy Baby." Ironically, the song always cheered him up. He thought of his patient daddy, who'd taught him that it didn't pay to get angry or agitated while tracking deer. Exhaling, Jake imagined himself on a hunt now as he searched for his brother. All he wanted was to find him and get out of this town.

Once he'd marked off the placement of the ramp, he calculated how much lumber he would need and knocked gently on the back door.

"Be there in a minute," came the girl's voice from within the house.

He moved to the edge of the porch and lit a cigarette while he surveyed the site plot. When the screen door slammed, he turned to see Nell setting a large bowl of water on the porch. Pilot fell on the bowl as though he hadn't seen water for days. Keeping her eyes on the dog, Nell stated, "I think it's best we keep Pilot here while we go to the lumber yard. We might not have room for him in the truck bed once the wood is loaded."

Pilot looked up from the water when Jake commanded him to stay. The dog answered by licking his lips and looking as if he'd swallowed paint. Nell stooped to collect a small spade and garden fork from a toolbox on the porch and put them in her purse. Tossing her hair as she walked past Jake, he caught the scent of her delicate rosewater. As she walked toward the truck, Jake noticed her flushed face and her hands clenched into fists. Jake put out his cigarette. "Nell—Miss Guthrie."

She turned to look at him.

"Would it make you feel better if I rode in the back of the truck?" Jake asked.

She glanced at the flatbed while the sun beat down on them. Jake watched her and thought about his daddy and brother, who could wait out any game.

Finally, her shoulders slumped slightly. "No. That won't be necessary."

Positioning herself in the driver's seat, Jake went to the front of the vehicle and muscled the crank to start the engine.

He climbed into the cab before she could change her mind and closed the door. Without looking at him, she shifted into first gear, and they inched down the driveway.

CHAPTER 7

∽

Gripping the steering wheel and grinding the gears on the Ford, Nell focused on the road. She downshifted when turning onto Live Oak Street and drove the truck out of town. They were soon on the rough, unpaved New Bern Road that had stalled Jake and Isaac in the dray. The midnight storm made the road rough and rutted, so she urged her truck to power through the muck. She tried to ignore the thick, chilly silence in the truck's cab.

She'd been a fool to trust Jake when he first came into the hardware store. People in Beaufort were often wary of strangers. And for good reason. Emma Grace's mother had trusted a sailor, and it was disastrous; she was abandoned and died in childbirth.

The truck strained against the increasingly treacherous road, and after an eternity, Nell pulled off and heard the whining saws beyond a grove of pine trees. They bounced along before the sandy road opened to a field stacked with lumber.

Buddy Taylor came out of a small building and made his way over to their truck. Although he was a grown man with curly chestnut hair, Nell always thought of him as the freckly carrottop she'd known since kindergarten. Short and wiry, Buddy's humor and mercurial antics lit up any room. When the liquor flowed freely in impromptu speakeasies at the Inlet Inn, he always made the room buzz. But being a rascal often vexed Buddy's staid family that included three older brothers and a formidable mother.

"Well, hey there, Nell Guthrie," Buddy exclaimed. "What brings you down here?"

"Stopped by to keep you out of trouble."

"Good luck with that." Buddy noticed Jake climbing out of the Ford. "Who's riding shotgun for you today?"

Her back stiffened. "This is Jake Waterson. He's helping my father this morning. He'll be giving you an order, but I'd like to look over the wood before I pay. We need heart pine for house construction."

"Any friend of Nell's is a friend of mine," said Buddy. Nell looked away as the two men shook hands.

Buddy turned to his assistant. "George, could you work with Mr. Waterson here? I need to talk with Miss Guthrie for a moment."

Nell turned to Jake and said, "Don't load that truck 'til I see the wood."

"Yes, ma'am," replied Jake with a strained smile.

Nell followed Buddy through a maze of stacked lumber in the yard. Her friend started working in the family's construction business while still in school. Now, he was the lumber yard's chief operator, while his brothers led the construction side of the business. As Beaufort prospered in the early 1900s, Taylor's Lumber Company grew along with it.

They approached a large shed near his office. "So, who's your new bodyguard?"

"Daddy hired him to build a ramp for Mama to get around the garden." She dropped her voice. "Asa thinks he's a revenue man sent down to spy and get the lay of the land. He's been asking a lot of questions—real nosy-like."

Buddy glanced back over Nell's shoulder. "Is that right?" He stopped in front of a small building. Before he opened the door, he searched the landscape as if he were expecting his mother to jump out from the corner of the building. Putting the key in the door lock, he whispered, "I wanted to show you my Sugar Shack and all the treasure I procured in Norfolk. It will intoxicate your senses."

"Does that mean you ply your customers with bourbon? Then after they're all corked, you pounce on them like a praying mantis?"

"Noooooooo," Buddy chuckled. "It means you'll never feel the same after you leave."

Nell knew about Buddy's magpie-like tendency to seek out and salvage building detail. As a summer watering hole, Beaufort attracted wealthy people who wanted to build vacation homes. Buddy was always on the lookout for finishing touches that could dazzle these people. But she wasn't prepared for what greeted her in the Sugar Shack. Instead of stepping into a dusty warehouse with haphazardly stacked salvaged items, the shed was decorated as a genteel parlor with an upholstered settee, matching chairs, and a shaded lamp. An elaborate Oriental rug graced the floor, while the walls displayed rows of delicate crownwork and exquisite exterior gingerbread trim. Small shelves of porcelain figurines, painted drawer pulls, and translucent eggshell china mingled among the moldings. On the small writing table sat a bowl filled with cuff links and several rings with large stones set in them. A panel of stained glass hung from the ceiling, catching the eastern light. Several marble fireplaces leaned side by side against the wall, adding a stately charm to the staged room.

"I'm speechless," Nell said in genuine amazement. Although she could hear the whine of the lumber saws a short distance away in the yard, nothing was dusty or broken.

"These are my treasures," beamed Buddy, his face flush with unabashed affection. "Every single item is special to me. I wanted to surround myself with refined elegance."

"All you need are slippers and a smoking pipe," replied Nell, caught up in the wonder of the room.

"Oh, I've got those," Buddy replied, as he bounced across the room and flung open the doors on a small wooden wardrobe. Stored inside the closet was an assortment of smoking jackets, robes, and slippers. "I knew you could 'preciate all this. My family thinks I'm wasting my time." He leaned toward her to share his delicious secret. "But I think I'm on to *something*."

Leading her to one corner of the room, Buddy stood in front of a dark, draped tapestry hiding a nine-foot-high structure attached to the wall. Gripping a handful of fabric, he turned to Nell and whispered, "And this is who I wanted you to meet." Like a magician, he dramatically swept the cloth off the covered item, crying, "Ta-da! Nell, meet Nadine!"

Nell looked up at a magnificent wooden mermaid figurehead designed to lead the prow a ship into oncoming surf. "Wow, Buddy. You've outdone yourself."

Buddy shrugged his shoulders. "Thought you'd like it."

"What in the world are ya going to do with it?"

"Thought the Beaufort Methodist Church could use it at the gateway into their Sunday school garden."

Nell looked aghast at the bare-breasted woman protruding from the wall. Then she noticed Buddy's sly smile and they both burst out laughing. Taking a step in Nell's direction, he asked, "So when ya gonna leave that ol' fancy pants, Asa, and get to know a real homegrown man?"

"Oh, Buddy, Buddy, Buddy." Nell sighed, looking down at him.

"Not the right type? And what type would that be? Tall and brooding? Given to fits of temper? Popular with ladies? All of the ladies?"

Nell raised one eyebrow. Although Buddy was genuinely fond of her, he was a notorious flirt.

Buddy hesitated. "Well, you've got a point there," he conceded. "But really, Nell, you can do so much better than Asa."

"I'll keep that in mind," replied Nell, turning away with a bemused look.

Gazing affectionately at the wooden sea nymph, Buddy said, "I acquired Nadine near one of the shipyards in Norfolk. All sorts of things are going on the market since the Navy started chasing runners. Those boys need money for faster boats."

"You seem to know a lot about it."

"Shoot, that's all anyone was talking about up there."

Just then, Jake poked his head in through the doorway. "We're all set, Miss Guthrie."

"Thank you, Mr. Waterson."

Jake remained in the doorway, taking in the unique interior.

"Well, we best be going," said Buddy. Nell got the feeling her friend didn't like his lair polluted with other adult males.

The three of them left the shack, and Nell carefully looked over all the wood selected by Jake.

"He about run me all over the mill, pickin' out wood," said George as he mopped his forehead. Buddy named his price and then took two dollars off since it was Nell. After a brief pause, Nell accepted. She paid Buddy, and the men loaded the lumber onto the flatbed.

Driving back in silence, Nell concentrated on making their way through the rutted road. When they arrived back at Nell's back porch, Pilot greeted them like a half-drowned sailor. Jake unloaded the truck while Nell entered the kitchen and retrieved the bowl of bread dough rising on the windowsill. After sprinkling flour on the table, she smeared her knuckles with bacon grease before pulling the damp tea towel off the bowl. The dough had risen to double its size. She drew her arm back to punch it down. As it deflated, Nell pummeled it with both fists. *Why did Daddy make me go out to the lumber yard with Jake? Will I ever be able to have my own life?* She thought of Jake's smug calmness in the Ford. *I'll treat him like a guest in this house when Hades freezes over.* Reaching into the bowl to lift the dough, she recalled how her daddy had so readily dismissed her concerns. She looked up from the table and out the window at the pecan tree in the back yard. *He didn't even listen to me.* It hadn't always been this hard. When Harrison was alive, the three of them had gone sailing and fishing together, spending endless afternoons on the sound. When her gaze drifted back to the floured worktable, she felt as deflated as the bread dough, now reduced to its original size. The strength returned to her arms, and she started to knead it and eventually divided it into four loaves. What she would give to see her daddy laugh with her again.

After washing her hands, Nell walked into the parlor to join her mother, who was adjusting knobs on the wireless. "How are you getting on, Mama?"

"I'm a little stiff today, but Tulla will help when she comes later." Alice Guthrie began life as an active girl with a strong love for music. She and Thomas married after high school, and Alice taught music to Beaufort's children. After Nell's birth, the doctors diagnosed her with chronic infectious arthritis. She continued to teach piano for several years. But when her only son died and was buried on foreign soil, her limbs curled up, and she lost her ability to play the piano.

"I thought I would practice some of the music I'm going to play at the Inlet Inn tonight." Nell was scheduled to play classical music during the supper hour. "Would you listen with a critical ear?"

"Of course, dear."

Nell pushed the wheelchair over to the piano as her mother asked, "So, how was supper last night?"

Nell shifted uneasily. She didn't want to worry her mother about Mrs. Davis's hijacking of her wedding. Instead, she replied, "Oh, Mama, everything was so divine: the china, the food, and their store-bought wine. And there was this dandy from Richmond who dresses better than Emma Grace."

Her mother studied her face. "Did Sylvia mind her manners?"

"Oh, yes, ma'am. She was talking about having a big reception for us in Richmond."

Mrs. Guthrie studied her only living child. "It's strange and wonderful to think of you going to Virginia."

"I know." Nell stared at the floor. "I couldn't be leaving you if I didn't know Miss Tisdale and the Oyster Shuckers will be helping out every day." In their youth, Alice Guthrie and her friends worked in Leonard's Oyster Factory. The long hours, hard labor, and irregular schedule bonded them. Now, in middle age, the friends frequently met for quilting bees and after-church Sunday dinners. They all agreed to help with the care of Alice Guthrie after Nell moved away.

Alice Guthrie's face softened as she turned and looked out their front window. "We all lost so much when Harrison died."

Nell remembered how everything stopped when they received the telegram from the war office. Her daddy disappeared for several days and reeked of liquor when he returned. Nell barely recognized his drawn face strained with grief and anger. Her mother's limbs stiffened, and she took to her bed. Nell and their local healer, Tulla Jaspers, tended to Mrs. Guthrie. Within a few weeks, Nell and her mother realized that her daddy could no longer run the store by himself. Between caring for her mother and the operation of the hardware store, Nell couldn't pursue her dream of studying music in college.

"This is your second chance." There was a slight catch in her mama's voice. "It's time for you to spread your wings."

Nell swallowed hard, feeling hot tears building in her eyes. Through the open window, Nell heard Jake sawing lumber and humming a tune. His music irritated her, and she shook her shoulders, attempting to shrug it off. Turning her attention to the sheet music on the piano, she smiled at her mother. "I reckon that's why God invented the Norfolk Southern. As long as the train stops in Beaufort, we can see each other whenever we want."

As she practiced Strauss and other waltzes, her mother counted off the beat by tapping her hand against the arm of her wheelchair.

"I think the tempo is a bit stronger there," Mrs. Guthrie offered at one point in the song.

After several songs, both of them felt satisfied with the music. Nell lifted the lid on her music bench and pulled out sheet music for a ragtime tune.

Mrs. Guthrie instinctively looked over her shoulder.

"Was Daddy planning to come home for dinner?" Nell asked, referring to the noonday meal.

Her mother shook her head.

Nell pounded out the jaunty tune for several minutes before she stopped and frowned at the sheet music. "That doesn't sound right."

"No, it doesn't," her mother agreed. "I heard this tune on the wireless the other night and I think they put a half note in the third measure." Nell played through the portion of the tune a few more times until both of them agreed it sounded better.

"So many of the musicians of this new music improvise as they play," said Nell's mother.

Nell nodded. "I love it. I think rag is ready to turn a corner."

Mrs. Guthrie laughed softly. "The Rev. Billy Sunday would like it to turn down a long dark alley."

Nell chuckled. "Well, it may not be his cup of tea, but they love it at the inn. It's kinda hard not to dance to it." She sighed deeply. "I wish Daddy would let me play with Winston." While she was growing up, Nell often practiced this syncopated music with her brother and Winston. While Nell rested her hands, she could hear the rhythm of Jake's saw counting out a beat.

"I know your daddy's got your best interests at heart. In his mind, girls don't play in pool halls and speakeasies."

Nell scoffed. "The inn's not a backwater dive."

"I think he's been listening to the preacher. He's worried about how people will perceive his little girl."

Nell turned to look at her mother. "He hardly even looks at me anymore."

"He's changed," Mrs. Guthrie agreed. "I think . . ." she paused. "I think he's afraid to love. He hardened his heart." Nell's mother sighed deeply. "You have to understand, Nell, that your daddy carries a lot of guilt."

"What do you mean?"

Alice Guthrie searched for the right words. "Your daddy feels like he should have fought in the war, not Harrison."

"Mama, he was too old for that. And Harrison enlisted."

"He knows all that—in one way—maybe in his head, but in his heart, he felt he needed to protect us, and he didn't. It's hard for him not to feel bad about it."

Nell nodded as she thought about her daddy with new understanding. They sat without speaking, the sawing rhythm filling their silence.

After several moments, her mother suggested, "Why don't you play me the piece you were putting together after your sail the other day? Do you have a name for it yet?"

Nell inhaled deeply and pushed memories of her daddy out of her mind. "I was thinking of 'Salt and Harmony.'" Her fingers found the keys as she started a classical music piece. As she played, she thought of a wake fanning out behind her boat, sunlight filtering through the small prisms of fractured light from ocean spray, and a sea breeze cooling her in the late afternoon. She stopped playing and the last note hung in the air.

"You need to finish that, Nell. Or at least write it down."

"Yes, ma'am. It's growing on me, too." She folded down the piano's fallboard over the keys and stood. "I best put dinner on the table."

"Be sure to invite Mr. Waterson to eat with us," said Nell's mother.

Nell had nearly forgotten Jake. With polite stiffness, she answered, "Of course, Mama."

Within half an hour, Nell laid the table with cooling bread, sliced meat, store-bought cheese, and sweet pickles. After everyone was seated and Mrs. Guthrie led grace, they began to eat.

Mrs. Guthrie turned to Jake. "So, I hear you come from Charleston way."

"Not the proper, ma'am. Johns Island. My family has a cove on our land. We fish, build boats, and make cargo deliveries."

"Whatever brings you to Beaufort?"

"My daddy wanted me to look into expanding his delivery business up here."

As he talked to her mother, Nell listened closely to Jake's voice. It was a soft cadence that reminded her of singing crickets, but there was something familiar about it.

"You're mighty quiet, Miss Nell," said Mrs. Guthrie.

"I'm right tired, Mama."

"I reckon you are. All the work you've been doing." Mrs. Guthrie looked back at Jake before she said, "I understand you were involved in an altercation at the drug store yesterday."

"Yes, ma'am."

Nell inwardly groaned. *Couldn't people stop talking about this?*

"Miss Tisdale is a close friend of mine. She was in the crowd."

"Yes, ma'am. She helped me with the boys after we walked away."

Nell looked up in surprise, "Miss Tisdale was there?" Asa hadn't mentioned her mother's eccentric Oyster Shucker friend. Although she tended to wear men's trousers and walk her pet goat, Nell loved Miss Tisdale's ability to spin stories without prompting.

Mrs. Guthrie continued. "She thought Asa was being a horse's behind."

"It was a big misunderstanding," Jake replied. "Marbles and Tobias helped me unload my clams down at Leonard's. I gave them both a nickel. They were a little too excited when they ran over to the drug store by themselves. While I was getting hired by your husband in his store, I heard some shouting and looked across the street. That's when I saw the druggist pulling Marbles out by the ear. From what I understand, one of them reached into the candy jar before paying. I believe the pharmacist thought they were trying to steal from him."

Nell looked up and stared at Jake in disbelief. "Do you mean to tell me that whole big to-do in the street was over a few pennies worth of candy?"

"Yes, ma'am."

"That's pretty much what Tisdale said," confirmed her mother. "I hope you won't think badly of Beaufort," Mrs. Guthrie added, looking at Jake.

"No, ma'am," answered Jake.

Nell remembered the outrage and anger Asa expressed at supper the night before and wondered how the two accounts could be so different. Feeling both angst and confusion, she opened her mouth to question Jake but caught her mother's eye. Clearing her throat, she said, "I understand the sheriff arrived?"

"Him and half the town." Jake closed his eyes before biting into a slice of the warm bread spread thickly with butter. "I believe this is the best bread I've ever ate."

Nell felt heat rising in her cheeks. "Thank you."

"Why don't we send you home today with a loaf?" said Mrs. Guthrie.

"I'd 'preciate that," replied Jake.

They ate in silence for a few minutes before Mrs. Guthrie said to Jake, "It sounds like you have a musical ear, Mr. Waterson."

Jake looked at her in surprise. "Yes, ma'am. Everyone in my family plays. How did you know?"

"I heard you and Nell harmonizing this morning."

The two young people stopped eating to stare at Nell's mother.

Mrs. Guthrie chuckled. "You were humming 'Melancholy Baby' first thing this morning," she said to Jake. "And Nell fell in with a soprano key."

When neither of them answered, she continued, "I went out on the front veranda to catch the sea breeze, and I could hear both of you as plain as day."

An awkward silence settled on the table. Nell's face flushed as she tried to remember the moment.

Without looking at Nell, Jake cleared his throat. "I heard you playing earlier. You got a strong talent."

"Thank you," Nell stammered. And then added, "Jake."

"That Joplin can swing a tune."

They locked eyes, and Nell noticed a clear serenity in his gaze that she hadn't noticed before.

∽

When dinner was over, Jake returned to the back yard to work on the ramp while Nell cleaned the kitchen. With her hands deep in sudsy water, she looked up when she heard a gentle knock at the back door. She turned to greet Isaac's grannie standing on the porch holding a large satchel. "Hey there, Miss Tulla. I saw Annie last night at Miss Sylvia's."

"Yes, ma'am," Tulla answered in a delighted voice. "She mentioned you this morning."

"Mama's looking forward to working with you," replied Nell, walking the lady through to the parlor.

"I heard you and Asa are getting married," Tulla replied. "Blessings on you both."

"Thank you. Mama said the liniment you gave her last week helped her sleep through the night. Let me know if y'all need anything."

Later that afternoon, Nell finished all her housework and began to dress for her musical performance at the Inlet Inn. She slipped into a floaty, rose-colored chiffon dress. As a child, she'd watched her mother struggle into rigid corsets, stiff petticoats, and ankle-length, frothy dresses trimmed with yards of lace. But she came of age as Coco Chanel and a new generation of designers brought easy, simple lines to dresses. Nell twirled in front of the mirror, watching the gentle skirt flow around her. As a finishing touch, she added a matching headband and a long string of beads around her neck.

"Oh, Nell, you look stunning," exclaimed her mother when Nell walked into her bedroom to model her ensemble.

Tulla was in the process of packing her medicine bag. "You'll have a string of boys following you."

"Thanks, y'all. I hope they make Asa mad," said Nell. Gathering her sheet music from the piano, she walked to the kitchen, picked up a bowl of food scraps, and two loaves of bread wrapped in paper. Drawing a deep breath, she stepped out on the porch.

Jake was packing away his tools when he looked up to see her stylish dress and hairdo. "Well, don't you look . . . swell."

She set out the bowl of food scraps for Pilot, who gobbled down the food while thanking her with an appreciative tail wagging. Nell paused to watch the dog's happiness for a moment. Dogs were so easy to understand: they ate, they chased your chickens, they slept, they pooped, they loved. She sighed deeply. A dog might dig up your flowers, but he would never lie to your face about it. How could Asa tell one story, and Miss Tisdale and Jake say something so completely different?

The screen door opened a second time, and Tulla joined them on the porch. She set down her bag to adjust a small hat on her head.

"Are you walking all the way home by yourself?" Nell asked the elderly lady.

"No, ma'am. Isaac's meetin' me in town."

"May I give you one of the bread loaves for your family?" asked Nell, as she offered one of the parcels.

"Yes, ma'am. Much 'preciated," Tulla smiled as she accepted the loaf.

Jake hoisted his carpenter's bag onto his shoulder as he spoke to Tulla, "I'd be happy to walk with you since I'll be heading that way."

"Much obliged."

Nell handed Jake the other wrapped loaf of bread. "I believe my mother wanted you to have this."

"Thank you," Jake answered. "And please thank your mama."

Nell nodded and smiled at him.

The three people watched Pilot finish the last of his food. The moment stretched on in comfortable silence.

Looking up from the dog, Nell saw Asa come around the side of the house from the driveway. Taking in the sight of Nell, Jake, and Tulla Jaspers all standing amicably on the back porch, the druggist stopped in midstep. His face darkened. "What the hell are you doing here?" he demanded of Jake. Pilot's head snapped up in alarm.

With a steely look in her eye, Nell approached her fiancé, "Asa, you can't cuss like that here." Asa glared at her. "My daddy has hired Mr. Waterson to build a ramp because my mother's in a wheelchair."

Asa looked around the yard and noticed the posts and ramp boards set in place. Then his eyes moved to Tulla. "Is he hiring voodoo witch doctors to take care of your mama, as well?"

The elderly lady shook her head. Jake shifted uneasily while Pilot remained taut, ready to jump into action at his master's command.

"You don't need to be disrespectful. My family 'preciates Miss Tulla," answered Nell.

Pilot emitted a low growl and the hair on his back rose. Without taking his eyes off Asa, Jake addressed Tulla Jaspers, "I believe we were just leaving, weren't we, Miss Tulla?" Offering the woman his hand, he helped guide her down the steps. Given Tulla's age, the two of them began to walk slowly toward the driveway past a sneering Asa. Pilot followed them with his hackles still raised.

Asa watched until they were down the driveway, then turned to Nell and demanded, "Has that bastard been causing you trouble over here?"

"Of course not, and I'll ask you not to swear where my mama can hear you." They glared at each other. "Jake remembers a very different interpretation of the incident yesterday, and Miss Tisdale backs up his story."

Asa tucked his chin down into his neck. "If you ask me, that woman is a bit off in the head."

Hot rage bubbled up inside Nell. "She's one of my mother's dearest friends."

Watching Jake and Miss Tulla walk away, Asa replied, "That boy hain't right either."

Asa didn't acknowledge Nell's fury, but she knew it was time to get to the inn. Her fiancé fell in step alongside her as they left her back yard and walked toward Front Street.

"Well, it's just not right," said Asa stubbornly.

"Tulla Jaspers has been a godsend to my mother. I don't appreciate your rudeness."

The angry tension brewed between them as they continued in silence. Nell knew ladies shouldn't make a scene, but Asa needed to apologize.

Glancing over at Nell's face, Asa continued in a lowered voice, "I'm just worried about your safety—darlin'." He attempted to pick up her hand, but she drew it away.

"By insulting my daddy? I reckon he can hire whoever he wants to work in his yard."

"I want to be able to take care of you and protect you. How could your daddy have a deviant like that work around you and your mama?"

"Asa, my beau, I live in my father's home, and I don't make the decisions. You don't need to talk about my daddy that way."

"I don't trust that boy. He's asking too many questions at Lowell's."

"I swear," Nell replied, her voice becoming strident, "sometimes you pout worse than a five-year-old."

They walked in silence down Front Street, Asa's resentment clinging to him like the stench of a dog's roll on a fish kill.

CHAPTER 8

As Nell and Asa climbed the steps to the Inlet Inn, Asa pulled out a small vial from his breast pocket and said, "I need to make a prescription delivery to one of my customers upstairs. I'll come down later to the ballroom to hear you play."

The two of them stood on the veranda awkwardly facing each other as the tantalizing scent of hush puppies and clam chowder wafted out of the hotel kitchen. Asa's harsh words to Jake and Miss Tulla were still ringing in Nell's ears. Clenching her fists in frustration, she fought the urge to launch herself at her fiancé's chest and pound him with her fists. "Asa—" But before she could finish, he pulled her into an embrace.

"You know how stupid I can get," Asa whispered, "but I can't see straight when I'm worried about you, Nellie."

Turning her face away from him, her body remained rigid. "It's no excuse—" She fumbled for words. "You're a hard-headed man, Asa Davis."

Pulling back and smiling at her, he replied, "That I am."

Without returning his smile, she walked with him into the hotel. As Nell turned off to go upstairs to the ballroom, Asa said, "Knock 'em dead, sugar. This is your night."

Ascending the stairs, she did not reply or look back. Instead, she focused on calming the butterflies in her stomach.

The late afternoon light slanted into the large hall from the western windows, making the polished wooden floors and brass fixtures gleam. Although the ballroom was not as grandiose and elegant as the Atlantic Hotel

73

across the Newport River in Morehead City, Beaufort considered it their jewel. This weekend marked the hotel's summer opening that transitioned Beaufort from a quiet, smelly fish town that processed menhaden over the winter into a fashionable watering hole for visitors. Fed by the ebb and flow of the rumbling train, the town's population doubled during the warmer months.

Nell's footsteps clattered across the empty dance floor as she made her way to the piano. Her high school friends were serving supper to the family crowd. Although the air was filled with the savory aroma of seafood and creamy sauces, hints of rose and violet scents also floated through the hall. Out-of-town families filled the tables bordering the dance floor. While the women and children stayed at the inn all week, they were now sitting down with their menfolk who had arrived on the afternoon train.

Nell opened with a Strauss waltz and followed it with the popular foxtrot, "Alabama Slide." Amid the married couples, daddies danced with their crinoline-dressed daughters. Nell played on as shadows grew longer in the fading daylight. She moved into favorites, such as "On Moonlight Bay." Nell glanced up during her last set to see Emma Grace's cousin arrive with his trumpet case. Winston smiled at her after he sat down. Soon, he was tapping his foot to the beat while waiting to play with his band.

Parents drifted off the floor carrying sleepy young'uns nestled against their shoulders. At the same time, ingénues with their beaus began to drift into the room, clustering around the dance floor. More young people from town and officers from the Camp Glenn Coast Guard Air Station in Morehead City and the Fort Macon Coast Guard Station on Bogue Island arrived.

The crowd became louder and more animated as it anticipated the band. Winston unpacked his trumpet and polished it, while Asa drifted in with the younger crowd. Relieved that he returned to hear her play, she nodded to him when he waved at her.

When Nell's set ended, Winston and the leader of the band walked onto the small stage. "Good evening, ladies and gentlemen," he said to the audience. "Let's all say thank you to Nell Guthrie on the piano." The audience applauded politely. "Now, please stay where you are for the newest tunes out of New Orleans." Winston shot off a Satchmo riff on his trumpet, and the flappers and their beaus exploded with applause and cheers.

Feeling envious of the excitement, Nell reluctantly packed up her sheet music while the other musicians moved onto the stage. Stepping onto the dance floor, she heard someone calling her name. Turning toward the voice, she saw a bobbing head of chestnut curls make its way through the pressing throng.

"You sounded *stupendous*," said Buddy Taylor.

"Thanks, Buddy. Time for me to take leave of the piano."

Buddy looked puzzled. "But you're the ragtime queen."

"My daddy doesn't think it's such a good idea."

"Lord have mercy," exclaimed Buddy. "'The sins of our fathers shall live on in their children.'"

Nell giggled. "Well, I wouldn't put it that way. But I'm right disappointed." She paused for a moment before she added, "I didn't see you on the dance floor."

"I'm a real heeler in the ballroom. Ladies don't seem to 'preciate dancing when there's a nose in their bosom."

"Picky, picky," said Nell. "You should stick around, though. When you dance these new dances like the Charleston, you don't need to hold the girl like you do in a waltz."

Buddy leaned in toward her and lowered his voice, "I'm really more of a backroom kind of man."

Nell knew that Asa and his friends often visited the impromptu speakeasies that popped up in private rooms around the hotel. Second to that, she thought of the treasures Buddy stored in his Sugar Shack collection that would appeal to potential clients. "That doesn't surprise me at all," she answered. "I've seen some of the rooms you've furnished at this inn. You got talent."

"Well, this Raleigh crowd's got some money. That's a fact." Looking around the room, he gave her the impression of a short Daddy Warbucks scanning each person's wallet and worth. "Yeah," he answered without taking his eyes off the dance floor. "The lumber yard pays the bills, but decorating is what I love. It's a lot more fun to spend the afternoon drinking Boiler Makers and hanging wall art than planking wood. Oops! Is it against the Eighteenth to say that?"

"I 'magine," she answered with a laugh. Buddy could always put her in a good mood.

Nell looked over his shoulder to see Asa walk up with the burliest man on the floor at his side.

"You're hittin' the right notes tonight!" the enormous man boomed.

"Thanks, Midgett! You're a sight for sore eyes." No one was surprised when Elijah Midgett enlisted in the U.S. Lifesaving Service at the onset of the war. Nell knew him as a fearless ballplayer from pick-up games in high school. After years of rowing, Midgett's arms had grown to the size of small tree trunks.

"Fort Macon keeping ya busy?" asked Nell. In 1915, the lifesaving service had merged with the Revenue Cutter Service to become U.S. Coast Guard.

Midgett sighed, "It's a mess. This rum blockade is about to kill me."

"I hear that," answered Asa.

"Prohibition's making everyone thirsty," agreed Buddy.

Midgett took a sip of his drink and let out a long sigh of exasperation. "When somebody gives us faster boats, then I might could enforce it."

"Don't try too hard. The local boys are enjoying the game," said Nell.

At that moment, everyone turned to the stage when The Bees Knees broke into the pounding drive of a Joplin tune. The sparkle of the Raleigh crowd ebbed from the edges of the room to burst onto the dance floor. It was soon a hopping mess of legs, feet, and arms flying to the pulsing rhythm. Nell listened carefully to Winston's distinctive trumpet signature. His notes were crisp and clear, and the bass was keeping a beat, but the piano wasn't pulling them through the melody.

"They're moving it tonight," Asa exclaimed.

As Buddy and Asa fell into a conversation, Midgett leaned into Nell and shifted uncomfortably from one foot to another. "Uh, Nell."

Nell smiled as she watched Midgett shuffle his feet for several moments. She knew this massive hero adored her closest friend since primary school. "I think Emma Grace's planning to be here tonight, but she's been right busy with the fever in town." Relief flooded Midgett's face. Nell wondered how Midgett could fearlessly prowl the treacherous North Carolina coast but felt mortified every time he asked about Emma Grace.

"Actually," she said, looking behind the big man, "here comes Emma Grace now." Midgett turned around, and they both watched her friend saunter across the dance floor filled with youthful dancers swinging to the hard-pounding ragtime sound. She wore a shimmering, lime-green dress accented with sequins and a long string of polished shells and gems around her neck. The bold ensemble made her rich complexion glow like polished nutmeg. As she moved indifferently through the swarm of swirling pink and white dresses, she made the other girls look like they were out for their first ice cream. Nell noticed that the men and boys on the floor stood speechless as she glided by, while their partners cast her vitriolic looks.

Oblivious to her effect on the dancers, Emma Grace rippled through the crowd without concern. Although the *Ladies' Home Journal* would call it "sex appeal," Nell knew Emma Grace's air of nonchalance was exhaustion following a long work shift.

"Hey, y'all," Emma Grace greeted them with her eyelids at half-mast.

"Well, good evening, you sultry vixen," said Buddy.

She smiled at him through her curtain of fatigue.

"You make the other girls look like collard greens," said Buddy.

"Well, now, thanks, dear friend," retorted Nell.

"I didn't mean you, my lovely. I was just watching Emma Grace part the seas through that pastel pit over there." Buddy indicated the girls on the dance floor.

Emma Grace looked behind her and let out a throaty chuckle. Turning her attention to Midgett, she said, "Well, hey there. Long time no see." She reached into her beaded clutch and pulled out a slim case. She plucked out a cigarette and tapped it against the side of the silver box. "Would you have a light?"

"Yeah," Midgett replied, reaching into his pocket. "You look nice."

"You look nice, too." She examined his massive chest and arms as if she was checking for scurvy. "Looks like working with boats has been good to you."

"We row a lot," said Midgett, as he struck the match.

"So I hear." She bowed her head over the match to light her cigarette, and Midgett's clumsy hand passed dangerously close to the spit curl over her right eye. Emma Grace lightly touched Midgett's hand to steady the match. She inhaled deeply as she lifted her head, but her smile faded when she looked over Nell's shoulder. "Oh, hell."

Before Nell could turn around, a cloud of gardenia scent enveloped her as Luanne Fulcher and her friend, Selma Ward, entered their circle. Wealthy and pampered, Luanne was the ringleader in leading offensive snubs against Emma Grace in high school. She was outraged when Nell's striking brother coupled with Emma Grace. She'd retaliated by starting rumors over Emma Grace's frizzy black hair when style dictated young girls control their long hair with neat bows and buns. Luanne and her family began a whisper campaign insinuating Emma Grace didn't belong at the school for white children, and several mothers stopped welcoming Emma Grace into their homes.

Luanne's hair was a brighter blond than Nell remembered. Both girls dressed in similar blue dresses and their necks were weighted with ropes of imitation pearls. Ignoring everyone else, Luanne addressed Midgett and Asa. "Hey, you reckon y'all want to dance later?"

Her voice sounded deeper than Nell remembered, as though Luanne was fighting a head cold. Then Nell realized the girl was attempting to speak in a sultry tone.

"I believe I'm spoken for this evening," Asa replied quickly, clearing his throat. His voice sounded so harsh and emphatic that Nell glanced at his stony expression. Midgett gave Emma Grace a paralyzed look.

The conversation halted until Emma Grace tilted her head toward Nell and quoted, "*Beware the Jabberwock, my son! The jaws that bite, the claws that catch!*"

Nell nodded sagely. "*Beware the Jubjub bird, and shun The frumious Bandersnatch!*"

Buddy erupted in laughter as Luanne and Selma gave them looks that were both confused and dismissive. During high school, Nell and Emma Grace developed a stratagem for countering Luanne's reign of terror by speaking gibberish in her presence. By the time they graduated, they had memorized most of Lewis Carroll's nonsense poem, Jabberwocky, for this purpose.

Emma Grace sighed and turned to Midgett to ask, "Mind if I take a sip of your drink?" Without waiting for an answer, she took Midgett's glass from his hand and tasted it.

"That's disgusting," Luanne said. Selma sneered at Emma Grace.

"No, I don't mind," said Midgett, belatedly.

"Hmm . . . needs something . . . , mused Emma Grace. She handed the glass back to Midgett and pulled out a thin flask from a hidden pocket in her beaded bag, and poured a generous slosh into the tumbler. After slipping the thin container to its hiding place, Midgett handed the glass back to her and she took a long pull. "Mmmm, much better."

"Want me to get you a fresh one?" asked Midgett.

"Maybe in a minute," she said, her gaze lingering on his lips. "I don't mind sharing if you don't."

"Not really," said Midgett.

"I'd like a drink," Selma said to Asa.

"They're right over at that bar," interjected Emma Grace, without taking her eyes off Midgett.

Luanne looked murderous.

"I hear you two are walking down the middle aisle," Buddy said to Nell and Asa.

"You heard right," said Asa as he placed his arm possessively around Nell. Luanne looked like she'd swallowed her tongue.

Buddy turned to the newcomers. "Why don't we head up to Chadwick's suite? I hear they got a *full buffet* up there. If you know what I mean."

"Might as well," scoffed Luanne. "There's nothing going on here now that the Raleigh crowd showed up." She turned away from the group. "See ya, Midgett," she tossed over her shoulder. Her sickly sweet gardenia scent lingered in her wake.

Nell stood on her tippy toes and gave Asa a quick peck on the lips. "I need to powder my nose."

Asa pulled her in for a real kiss, but when their lips touched, she felt none of their usual heat.

Emma Grace wiggled her fingers in a little wave at Nell as she and Midgett migrated toward the dance floor. "Bye, now."

"Those . . . are nice beads," Midgett said to Emma Grace as they walked away.

"Thanks," replied Emma Grace. "Those are nice arms."

Nell's gaze lingered on them for a moment, and for the first time in several days, she felt real happiness. Emma Grace had never been short of suitors after Harrison died, but now she showed genuine affection for Midgett.

Once Nell was in the bathroom, she slipped into one of the stalls. A few moments later, the door to the bathroom opened, and gardenia perfume saturated the air.

"So, Little Nellie's playing her piano here tonight. That'll put a damper on the party," came Luanne's nasal voice.

"Oh, Lulu, she is handcuffed to Asa, after all," replied Selma.

There was a pause before Luanne said, "In public anyway."

Nell froze as the other girl gasped, "Lulu! Do you mean to tell me—"

Luanne giggled and spoke in a sing-song voice, "Nellie, Nellie, Perfect Nellie, why are you so gosh darn smelly?"

The two girls shrieked with laughter.

"It's no wonder her only friend is that freak show out there. Did you see that unnatural color she was wearing? She's always been shameless."

"That Nell doesn't even have the sense to cut off her hair."

"She looks like an old granny."

"Goodness, little girl! It's 1923, not 1843," she snickered.

"She just teases Asa to death. I don't know how he can put up with it."

"He needs a modern woman like me," answered Luanne.

A few moments later, the two young women left, but Nell remained paralyzed in the stall. *Could this really be true?* Her head pounded as it spun with confusion. Luanne was a notorious liar throughout school, but Nell remembered Asa's surge of anger when she asked him for a drink. Feeling dizzy, she grabbed the partition of the stall for support. Luanne's biting ditty rang in her head, and doubt rose inside her. *Why wasn't she enough for him?*

Opening the door of the stall, Nell dragged herself to the sink and hung her head. After a wave of nausea passed, she turned on the faucet and cupped her hands, and drank water. Longing to cry and rage, she was terrified that her ravaged face would broadcast her feelings to the people in the hotel. Last summer, Asa turned to flirtatious girls off the train, but he had returned to her at the end of the season. *Could that be happening again?* But he had proposed to her and promised himself to her. A sob settled in her chest. *Should I listen to Asa's side of the story?* Pulling her handkerchief from her purse, she wet it in the sink and pressed the cool comfort on her face, taking care not to smudge her powder, lipstick, and rouge. The band stopped playing to take their first break. She knew the powder room would be filled within minutes.

Steeling herself, she opened the door as several ladies entered the bathroom. Determined to find Asa and clear this matter up, she marched into the corridor just as Winston rushed up to her. "Nell, I've been looking everywhere for you." His face was stricken with concern.

"What's wrong?"

"We got a problem with the band."

When the break ended, Winston opened up his horn to call the audience back to the floor. He blew a long, sensuous note that pulsated around the hall like an electrical charge. It hung in the air and reverberated in the joyful faces around the room.

CHAPTER 9

Winston's long, clear note drifted out of the inn and down to the water, magnified by the still evening. On the far side of the harbor, Jake caught the sound while nursing a rye on the *Jamison* and watching town folk entering the hotel for the first night of the season.

As the streets emptied, he chewed the inside of his mouth. It was an opportune time to break into Guthrie's Hardware to borrow Nell's harbor log. Fighting with Asa propelled his desire to uncover what happened to his brother and confirmed his suspicions that this town was hiding something. Nell's harbor log might give him information about Wade's movements after leaving Lowell's Boatyard. Still, he struggled with himself. *Breaking and entering and stealing! What would Mama say?*

Glancing down at the well of his boat, he grimaced when Yawg gingerly licked his wounded paw. The hound looked up at Jake and thumped his tail. Since Yawg was alive, maybe his brother was nearby as well. Wade could be suffering and need help. Closing his eyes, he steeled himself with one last gulp of whiskey. *Sorry, Mama, hope you understand.*

After settling his dogs for the night, he climbed into the *Miss Mary* and began to row towards town. His oars created small ripples as they silently dipped into the water. Without a mast, the small boat would be barely visible from shore.

Determined and focused on his mission, every muscle in Jake's body was tensed and coiled. An enhanced sensory perception guided his peaked awareness. As a boy, he used this same steady focus when he hunted game with his father, and again when he fought on the battlefield.

He planned to enter Guthrie's Hardware from the water's edge, unseen from the street. Music from the Inlet Inn was muffled and distant here, but the deep, vibrating bass notes resonated over the water. When the *Miss Mary* aligned with the hardware store, he steered the boat across the harbor. The tide was low enough to slip the skiff under the store's dock and tie up to one of its pilings. After listening for noises, Jake threw his rucksack on the dock and hoisted himself up. Lying flat, he scanned the harbor one last time before slinking up to the back door.

The skeleton-key lock was easy to pick, and within a few moments, Jake was inside the store. Taking several deep breaths, he flattened himself against a wall and scanned the interior. A streetlamp cast a beam of light through the front windows, and Jake took pains to stay in the shadows. Straining to hear any movement, he detected a faint, irregular, rumbling sound. The variability of loud and low bursts of noise indicated the reverberations were not mechanical. Standing still, he determined that it was emanating from the store's office. Reaching into the rucksack, he retrieved his flashlight and aimed the soft beam toward the floor so he could light his way without being detected from the street. Cautiously creeping forward, he peeked through the office window and saw Thomas Guthrie sitting in his chair, slumped over the desk with a bottle of liquor next to his head. His loud, sporadic snores vibrated the windowpanes.

Jake pulled his head back from the window and sank to the floor to think. A logical whisper in his mind told him to scrap the project and come back on another night, but a louder, angry voice screamed at him to push forward. In the trenches, battle taught him to deny his fear and crawl over the top. Now, the strong pull of duty rose in him. Jake sat on the floor, waiting for his racing pulse and breathing to settle.

Cautiously scanning the cluttered store with the weak beam of his small flashlight, he spied a large steel pipe in a bin. Positioning himself to watch the snoring Mr. Guthrie, he dropped the steel pipe. When it landed with a loud crash that clapped through the store, Thomas Guthrie shuddered and raised his head slightly off the desk. Then his head dropped back down with a thud. Within a few minutes, the deep, rhythmic snore resumed.

That settles that. Recalling that Nell stored the ledger on a shelf under her service counter, Jake cautiously made his way to the center of the store. He crouched low to avoid detection from the windows that faced Front Street. After searching all three shelves of the desk and finding nothing, he heard voices approaching the building on the sidewalk. Jake snapped off his light and dropped facedown on the floor. While breathing dust and dirt, he listened to the footsteps approach. The walkers gossiped about people at the inn without breaking stride and moved on down the street. Exhaling, he pushed himself off the floor and sat to collect his thoughts.

The erratic rumbling continued from behind the office door. The ledger could be anywhere in the store, but in all likelihood, it was in the office. Moving stealthily toward the interior room, Jake switched off the light and gently turned the door handle. Once inside the small room, the clamor of Mr. Guthrie's drunken slumber increased tenfold as it reverberated around the office. In the dim light, Jake noted a picture of Nell's brother near Mr. Guthrie's hand. Underneath the framed photo was the harbor log. Dropping to the floor and creeping up to the desk, Jake carefully pulled the ledger toward him. Just as he was ready to snatch the account book off the desk, Mr. Guthrie's snoring broke, and he sat up in the chair. His empty eyes wandered around the room and landed on Jake. The veteran remained motionless and held his breath. Then Mr. Guthrie's unfocused eyes rolled back in his head before he swayed and fell back on the desk with a thud. Jake exhaled, whipped the book off the desk, and reset the photo in its place.

Several minutes later, Jake stood outside behind the store with the ledger tucked in his rucksack, silently closing the door behind him. He took a few minutes to reset the lock before making his way down to the *Miss Mary*. Hearing a small engine purr through the water, he flattened himself on the dock while a boat glided by, reduced speed, and cut power. Once it was out of sight, Jake dropped into the *Miss Mary* and untied her.

He'd planned to sprint back to the far side of the harbor, but now he was curious about the small powerboat tying up behind Lowell's. Using his oar to pole his skiff underneath the line of docks, he strained to hear the muted voices. Peeking out around a corner, Jake could see Chadwick securing the boat to one of the pilings. When two figures walked out of the shadows and passed beneath a streetlight, Jake recognized Asa Davis and Isaac Jaspers.

Chadwick lifted up several wooden crates to them, and they carried them up the dock to nestle them in Asa's open car trunk. After several trips, the sheriff's car pulled up, but the men didn't pause in their work even when the vehicle's headlights swept over them.

After Sheriff Jimmy Styron stepped out of the car, the pharmacist casually walked over to him, carrying a bottle from one of the crates. He reached into his breast pocket and handed the sheriff an envelope and the bottle. Jake maneuvered the *Miss Mary* a few feet closer to the boatyard and caught part of their conversation. "There's some Black Horse on the street," Asa was saying. ". . . name. Let me know if you come across it. . . . our delivery so I want to know the son of a bitch who got to it first."

The sheriff touched his hat and muttered something Jake couldn't hear. They both laughed, and then the lawman walked back to his car and drove away. After the men emptied the boat, Chadwick hopped up on the dock while Asa passed some bills to Isaac. As the large man walked away from the boatyard, Chadwick and Asa climbed into his car and drove off.

After the car pulled away, Jake worked the *Miss Mary* out from under the dock and rowed up to read the name on the transom of the boat that Chadwick had piloted. After turning his boat away from shore, he quickly rowed the *Miss Mary* out of the pool of light toward the *Jamison*.

It didn't surprise Jake that the police were involved in smuggling booze through the offshore blockade since this was true in every port. As he pulled hard on his oars, the altercation with Asa outside the drugstore came to mind. Was the scene staged with the sheriff simply to discredit Jake? Small towns were wary of strangers, but Davis seemed particularly hostile to Jake. Maybe the plan had been to haul him off to jail right there, but Tisdale interrupted them.

Jake reflected on the trip with Isaac Jaspers out to the sawmill. Recalling that Isaac was reluctant to share any of his knowledge, Jake knew if he ever gained the man's trust, he might have a chance at finding Wade.

Once Jake was back on the *Jamison*, he sat down with Nell's log. He quickly confirmed that traffic from the Whiskey Road that ran from Nassau to New York must be connecting with runners along the Carolina coast. There was an entry for Wade's arrival in Beaufort in early April, listed with other boats damaged in the same storm. At that time, Nell noted a deluge of Bacardi, Canadian Mist, and various wines that she traced from the *Three Sisters*, a schooner from Nassau. She'd also made a note of the double seal on the bottles that prevented people from tampering with a high-quality product by watering them down with moonshine or bathtub gin. Many of these loads circled back to Lowell's boatyard—no surprise there. But she also listed other boatyards outfitted with marine rails that could have made alterations on Wade's *Amelia*.

There were several entries for ad hoc speakeasies in rooms at the Inlet Inn. Jake looked up from the book to the hotel across the water. The party was still going strong, and maybe he could learn something about the booze trade from it. Stowing the ledger deep under the bunk of the boat, he smarted himself up for another trip to shore.

The syncopated ragtime rhythm spilled onto the lawn of the Inlet Inn as Jake approached the hotel's side entrance. Fighting his discomfort caused by the noise and crowd, he stole up the stairwell to the second story that held the dance floor.

Inside the ballroom, music blasted while the hopping, writhing crowd on the dance floor bounced in front of him. Jake hugged the room's perimeter with his back to the wall and focused on his mission as the crushing crowd circulated around him. He moved to the front of the building and settled near the terrace that faced the harbor. Here he had a vantage view of the dancers and an escape route to the terrace if he felt hemmed in by the throng of people. By concentrating on his breath and keeping time with the music, his racing heart slowed. A trumpet player with considerable talent led the band, while the bass and a girl on piano synched with his melody. After a double-take, Jake recognized Nell Guthrie on the piano. Mesmerized by Nell's syncopated brashness, he barely heard the voice of a woman standing next to him. "So, fancy seeing you here, Jake Waterson. Man of mystery."

He turned his head and was startled to look into the exquisite face of a woman dressed in a shimmering green dress. Her coal-black eyes expressed a smoldering awareness. She knew his name, and there was something familiar about her, but Jake struggled to place her. Her mouth twitched as she studied his face. "We met in the hardware store the other day. I'm Nell's friend, Emma Grace."

"Of course . . . you look so . . . different . . . out of your nursing uniform."

"Girl's gotta have fun." She continued to stare at him with a bemused but critical look.

"I didn't know Nell would be playing tonight."

A smile parted her ruby lips. "Neither did she. The boys needed a piano player, and she obliged. I think she sounds great."

"More than great." And he meant it.

"She knows there will be hell to pay when her daddy finds out. But I'm so proud of her I could bust."

"Her father doesn't want her to play?"

"Thomas Guthrie considers this jungle music and does not want any daughter of his playing it in public. If he had his way, she wouldn't play it at all. Nell's mama stuck up for her."

Jake looked back at Nell. "It certainly does agree with her." Nell's face glowed with contentment as she pounded out the tune.

They both looked on in admiration.

"Thomas wasn't always such a fuddy-duddy," Emma Grace said. "Harrison's death knocked the moxie out of him. It changed all of us, but Thomas is still struggling with the bottle."

Uneasy, Jake shifted as he thought of the large man slumped over his desk in the back office of his hardware store.

Emma Grace continued. "He would have lost his store if Nell hadn't stepped in. She pretty much runs it. Shame how Thomas can't see how happy music makes her feel." She took a small sip from her drink. "He's scared. Afraid to lose Nell like he lost Harrison." Emma Grace paused for a moment before she said, "So, how do you like Beaufort?"

"It's a beautiful town," Jake said automatically.

"You're a terrible liar," she answered without apology or embarrassment.

The blunt remark felt as refreshing as a wind lifting his boat out of an afternoon of doldrums.

"So, let's try this again," Emma Grace said, with a wisp of a smile. "How do you like Beaufort?"

"There's lots of secrets here. I prefer the honesty of a backwater town, myself."

She let out a throaty laugh. "Now, you can take that to the bank." Still chuckling under her breath, her gaze wandered back to musicians performing on the small stage. "But just in case there's any confusion, Nell Guthrie is the real McCoy."

"I can see that. They've got an authentic sound." Jake turned back to Emma Grace, "If she's the real deal, what are you? You look like you don't want to be here."

"I'm an aberration. Someone who never belonged here. Should never have been born, maybe. People remind me of that every day."

"That sounds like a hard life. Why don't you leave?"

"I'm a girl, you dolt. We have to be chaperoned. Or something."

Jake laughed as he shook his head. Then he turned back to Nell and the band. "The boys she's playing with hain't half bad, either."

Emma Grace smiled, this time with actual warmth. "The guy on the trumpet is my brother. Well, first cousin, if you want to split hairs."

When Jake looked confused, Emma Grace explained, "My mother died when I was born, and I've always lived with my aunt and uncle. They're the only parents I know."

Jake nodded and noticed that Emma Grace made no mention of her father. He tore his eyes away from her face when an enormous man carrying two drinks walked up and stood behind her.

Without turning around, Emma Grace said, "Let me introduce you to Elijah Midgett. Local Hero." She turned her face up to the behemoth, and her hardened expression evaporated as she accepted a fresh drink from the man.

When Jake shook hands with the Coast Guardsman, his adrenaline surged. The article in the paper had mentioned Midgett as the man leading the search for Wade's boat. "Jake Waterson from South Carolina. I'm living on the *Jamison*."

"She's a beaut."

"Thanks. I built her with my daddy."

"You must have a real boatyard down there."

"So we're told." Jake turned his attention back to Emma Grace. "I was right impressed with your watercolors at the hardware store. How long have you been painting?"

"When I was shunned by polite society in high school, I took it up as a hobby."

Midgett nodded as he surveyed the room. "It was either that or horse diving or wing walking on a bi-plane. We all think you made the right choice."

88

She smiled up at him. At that moment, the band moved into a slower song. Emma Grace set her drink down and picked up Midgett's hand. "Bye, Jake," she said as she pulled the big man toward the music.

Jake watched the couple on the dance floor for a moment before walking to the bar to purchase a root beer. He moved out to the hotel veranda with his drink in hand and found a chair in the shadows. The sounds of music, clinking glasses, laughter, and dance steps floated out to him. Once he was a safe distance from the crowd, a great weight lifted off his shoulders.

Before long, a pair of men strolled out on the balcony. Both had a more citified appearance than the local population. The taller man had black hair and wore a tweed suit with a silk handkerchief displayed in his breast pocket. His portly companion could easily have stepped off the train that afternoon. The men didn't notice Jake, and they spoke in low tones, smoking cigarettes. The taller stranger nodded, and a few minutes later, they eased off the balcony and returned to the ballroom. The secretive nature of the conversation prompted Jake to follow them. When they were a safe distance inside, Jake got up from the chair and tailed them, making sure he stayed far from the dance floor.

Ducking into the hallway, Jake caught sight of the tweed coat as he rounded a corner. When he caught up with them, they were knocking on Room 201. Chadwick, from the boatyard, answered the door. Hearing music and laughter from the room, Jake assumed this was a speakeasy. *So, everyone is back from the boatyard after re-stocking down at Lowell's.* Mr. Tweed Coat spoke to Chadwick for a moment before the two men entered the room. Jake slipped back to the ballroom and was crossing over the mezzanine at the grand entrance when he heard a familiar voice float up from the lobby.

"I'm not a Negro," a girl was shouting. "My father is Italian!"

He looked over the banister to see Emma Grace in the grip of a man dressed in uniform with a small, bronzed nametag. The hotel manager was steering Emma Grace toward the front door, when Midgett bounded up and intersected them. "May I ask what you are doing?"

"I'm very sorry," the manager replied. "We have received a number of complaints regarding this woman's . . . er . . . character."

Emma Grace turned a fierce face to Midgett, "He's calling me a whore."

Several ladies in the lobby averted their faces, and the manager looked flustered. "State law prohibits us from serving Colored people. We received complaints from patrons that this loose woman is carrying liquor on her person."

"Miss Willis has accompanied me this evening," said Midgett. "One of her cousins is playing in the band."

The manager hesitated before answering, "Regardless, Mister . . . "

"Midgett. Commander Elijah Midgett, decorated war hero, stationed with the U.S. Coast Guard at Fort Macon. Evidently, you're not from around here."

The manager straightened in an attempt to match Midgett's height. "Nonetheless, several patrons have complained."

"The men from my fort have other dance halls to visit that are more welcoming."

"Forget it," Emma Grace retorted. She roughly broke the man's grip on her arm. "I'm leaving."

"You'll regret this," said Midgett, stubbing a finger into the manager's chest. The strength of the jab caused the man to step back. "You just made a big mistake." He turned and followed Emma Grace out of the hotel.

Jake hastened toward the grand staircase, but slowed when he noticed two girls leaning over the railing watching Midgett and Emma Grace leave. They fell on each other, laughing. Both of the girls wore pastel blue dresses, and one looked like her hair color came from a bottle. "Oh, my, but that was fun!" The blonde exclaimed; her speech was slow and slurred.

They snickered some more. "Did you see her face when she said, 'he called me a whore'?"

"I'm so glad you thought to go to the manager, Luanne," said one of them. This sent them into fresh peals of laughter.

Thinking of Emma Grace's striking face and her piercing jet-black eyes, Jake advanced toward them in anger. Then he reined himself in when he remembered his purpose in this miserable town: to find Wade without bringing attention to himself. He felt the walls were closing in and recognized the claustrophobic feeling that preceded a shell-shock episode. Hastening toward the servants' entrance, Jake rushed down the stairs, threw open the door, and gasped the fresh salty air. For a few moments, he bent over to breathe and calm himself. When he straightened up to walk away from the inn, piercing pain ripped through the back of his head. Then the ground rushed up to meet him.

CHAPTER 10

Every morning, Nell awoke with music playing in her head. When practicing classical pieces with her mother as a child, the melodies would start in a dream and increase in volume as the sun rose through her bedroom windows. In high school, Nell often heard jaunty marching tunes and popular songs she practiced with Harrison and Winston. When her brother died, "Amazing Grace" swam in her head for months.

After her first public performance at the Inlet Inn, the syncopated beat of Scott Joplin's "The Entertainer" danced through her mind all through the night. By the time she was awake, her feet were a-tapping. Knowing how much her father hated these tunes, she squelched the song as she dressed. Once she was out of the house and on her way to the Saturday market, she picked up the beat and nearly cakewalked down the driveway.

Farm folk and fishermen made their way into town by road and water on Saturday to sell their bounty and greet their neighbors. Nell made her way through the throng on Front Street, greeting several friends while buying staples for the week. She was on her way to Mason's Fine China and Jewelry Shop to check on her wedding dinnerware registry when Sophie Ann Joyner from high school stopped her. "Well, Nell Guthrie, I heard you playing at the inn last night. We could've danced all night long."

"Thank you, Sophie Ann," stammered Nell. "It was the best." The euphoria of the evening flooded back to her. The music's syncopated beat, coupled with the crowd's high-steppin' dancing, put her over the moon.

She instinctively looked over her friend's shoulder and lowered her voice, "My daddy would not 'preciate me playing ragtime, so I'm hoping he won't find out."

Sophie Ann giggled. "You'll have a time keeping that from him. Everybody's talking about it."

Nell glanced at the hardware store. "Well, maybe he won't hear about it today."

They both giggled, and Nell waved goodbye to her before she continued up Front Street. She stopped in front of Mason's and searched for her bridal china in the storefront window. Following her engagement, Nell and Emma Grace picked out a geometric design. The strong lines and shapes reminded her of sharp, decisive jazz notes.

She peered through the shop window, searching for the bold pattern. When she didn't see her selection displayed, she read the cards on the china sets. "Mary Jo Williams will marry Grady Lee Epton . . ." she read on the Bending Willow pattern. Her eyes drifted over to the next setting, and she caught her breath when she saw, "Nell Guthrie will marry Asa Davis at the. . . ." But the card was resting on a dinner plate decorated with a delicate rosebud pattern. She laughed. *Old Mr. Mason is not as sharp as he used to be, and he's put my name on the wrong china.* The bell over the door jingled when she walked into the shop.

She waited while the jeweler finished talking to another customer. "Mr. Mason, I saw that you displayed the wrong pattern for my wedding registry in the window. Don't you remember when I selected the modern pattern with my friend, Emma Grace?" Her words came out in a rush.

"Why, yes, ma'am, Miss Guthrie, I remember it well. But Mrs. Sylvia Davis came in later and said you changed your mind. She said you selected the rosebud pattern instead."

Nell stared at the store manager, feeling queasy. She stopped herself when she opened her mouth to correct him. Mrs. Davis's cotillion lessons emphasized that families should never air their disputes in public. Still rattled, Nell stammered, "Thank you, Mr. Mason," and slipped out of the store. Once on the street, she dodged the light-hearted Saturday market crowd and hurried home. Was everything going to be this hard? Did all engaged couples go through this much turmoil?

Back in her house, Nell put the food away in the kitchen before seeking out her mother in the bedroom. Since it was time to change the sheets on her mother's bed, she helped Mrs. Guthrie move to her wheelchair as she recounted her exchange with Mr. Mason. "I don't understand," Nell said as her mother leaned on her, moving from bed to chair. "It's my china and my home; why does she get to choose my dinner plates?"

"You'll do well to pick your fights with Sylvia—she likes to win." Nell heard the weariness in her mother's voice just before the back screen door slammed.

"Nell?" Emma Grace cried out.

"In my mama's room."

Nell was snapping a clean sheet over her mother's bed when Emma Grace entered the room. Glancing at her friend's face, Nell let the sheet fall to the bed. The dreary starched nurse's uniform drained the color from Emma Grace's face, but today her complexion was as gray as oatmeal. "Emma Grace, what's wrong?"

"Good morning, Miss Guthrie," Emma Grace greeted automatically. "I've just come from the jail. They called me down at around five o'clock this morning. It's your carpenter—Jake Waterson. Jimmy found him behind the inn last night and put him in the drunk tank. When he didn't wake up this morning, they saw his head was bleeding."

"Land sakes," cried Mrs. Guthrie, putting her hand to her throat. Nell's jaw dropped as she stared at Emma Grace, open-mouthed.

"I went over right away. Doc was busy with some brawl on a workboat. Jake was awake by the time I got there, but he needed sutures. So, I stitched him up in the jail, but I'd feel better if we could get him over to the clinic. I asked Doc Davis to release him, but can you believe they want a bond for 'Drunk and Disorderly?' He's worried sick about his dog."

Nell sank onto the half-made bed.

"It doesn't make sense," Emma Grace continued. "I talked to him at the end of your second set, Nell. He was as sober as a judge."

When Emma Grace mentioned her music, Nell automatically looked through the bedroom doorway before remembering her daddy was at his store. The three women were lost in thought as they imagined being imprisoned inside the damp city jail. After several minutes, Mrs. Guthrie said, "Something doesn't sound right about all this. First, that whole brouhaha with Asa downtown, and now this. Jake has not seen the better side of this town."

"Asa thinks he may be a revenue man," Nell replied.

"That's nonsense," snapped Mrs. Guthrie. "A revenue man would never travel with such a nice dog."

The clock in the bedroom ticked loudly as the three women sat in silence.

"I'll post bond for him," Mrs. Guthrie stated flatly.

The two girls turned to stare at the woman in the wheelchair. "Mama, you barely know the man."

Mrs. Guthrie's mouth flattened into a strained grimace. "I had a son once." Her voice quivered. "I haven't forgotten how easy it is for a boy to crack his head." Swallowing with difficulty, she smoothed the blanket on her lap.

"Oh, Miss Alice, I didn't mean for you—" started Emma Grace, but Mrs. Guthrie cut her off.

"It would be unseemly for you girls to be involved in all this." Pivoting sharply on the wheels on her chair, she rolled up to her dresser and opened a jewelry box. "Do you know what the bond is?"

"Twenty dollars."

Mrs. Guthrie lifted an inserted compartment of the box, counted out several bills hidden in the bottom, and held the money out to Emma Grace. "Why don't you send Winston over there and get him released to the doc?"

When Emma Grace remained frozen, staring at the cash in the gnarled hand, Mrs. Guthrie raised her voice, "Don't make me go down there and spring him myself. You take this money, now!" she cried, shaking the bills with force.

"Yes, ma'am," said Emma Grace as she darted across the room to accept the cash.

Nell kneeled in front of her mother so she was at eye level with her. "Mama, you don't have to do this."

Mrs. Guthrie's determined face began to crumble. She turned away from Nell and looked out the window. "If Harrison were far from home and needed help, I would hope strangers would give him the benefit of the doubt."

Nell leaned over to embrace her mother while Emma Grace quietly slipped out the bedroom door.

Later that afternoon, Nell was hanging her wet laundry on the clothesline when she heard Emma Grace's voice behind her. "Hey, Nell, look what floated in on the tide."

She turned to see Emma Grace standing next to Jake. "Miss Guthrie." With a weak smile, Jake touched his hat brim in greeting. A glimpse of a bandage peeked out from under the cap.

"Well, you both look worse for wear," Nell said to them, taking in their ashen, haggard faces.

"Can't argue with that. Lord, honey, we've been mommicked," said Emma Grace.

Nell noticed Jake looking at Emma Grace in confusion. "Mommicked is a word we use around here. It means 'torn up.'"

"Well, then, last night I was mommicked," Jake said as he gingerly touched the bandage.

"You reckon we could sit down for a minute?" said Emma Grace.

They walked over to Harrison's bench, where Nell stood to allow the exhausted people to rest. Emma Grace leaned her back against the pecan tree and closed her eyes. Nell shifted uneasily before saying, "I hope you're feeling better, Jake."

"I'm much better now, Nell." His voice sounded tired. "A cuff on the head won't slow me down that much. I understand Miss Alice bailed me out. Do you think I could thank her?"

"I just got her to lay down for a bit. She had a busy morning, as you can imagine. Were you planning on hammering? She needs to rest right now."

"Doc Davis said Jake isn't supposed to do any work today," Emma Grace replied without opening her eyes.

"I don't plan on staying long," said Jake. "I need to wet the concrete around the posts so they'll cure by tomorrow."

"Do you have any idea who might've hit you in the head?" asked Nell.

"Not really," he chuckled. "Somebody probably had a snootful and thought I looked at his girl the wrong way." Although the answer was plausible, it sounded rehearsed.

"You sure you want to stay alone on your boat tonight?" asked Emma Grace.

"Yes, ma'am. Best place for me. But I 'preciate your help."

"Well, I think I'll go see if Mama Beatrice needs anything before I fall over," said Emma Grace, rising from the bench.

"Oh, Emma Grace," Jake called to her. The nurse turned to look back at him. "I'm real sorry about the way they treated you last night."

Scowling, Emma replied, "So am I."

"What's all this?" asked Nell.

Emma Grace briefly explained how the manager of the Inlet Inn had thrown her out.

When she finished, Jake added, "I was coming down the stairs when I overheard two girls having a good laugh over the whole incident. I reckon they set you up."

"What did they look like?"

"They had on blue dresses that looked like they were made for their sisters. One had yellow hair of an unnatural shade. I remember she called the other one Luanne."

Nell and Emma Grace exchanged looks. "High school all over again," said Nell.

"That's a fact," said Emma Grace. She looked both aggravated and weary. "They must've thought they could have some fun with the new manager over there—because everyone in town knows who I am. I have a feeling Winston will take care of this. Thank goodness Daddy Donnie is out on a trawler, 'cause he'd probably take his shotgun over there." Her fatigue caught up with her, and she broke out into an enormous yawn that she quickly covered with her hand.

"Emma Grace, get on home now. You look like you haven't slept in a week."

"The fever at the clinic has 'bout wore me out."

As she turned to make her way through the garden, Jake said, "Thank you for helping me, Emma Grace."

"My pleasure, Jake," answered Emma Grace. "You're good people. I know what it's like when people don't believe you." While Emma Grace meandered toward her home, Nell reached down and picked a wild violet before taking a seat on the bench some distance from Jake.

While Jake sat slumped and ragged, Nell remained upright with her ankles crossed and her hands in her lap. She idly watched one of her laying hens scratch at the gritty soil in front of her. "I . . . ah . . . " Nell cleared her throat. "I'm real sorry Asa was so rude to you yesterday. I hope you didn't get the wrong impression of him."

Jake involuntarily barked out a laugh that morphed into a cough. "I think that ship has sailed. That boy don't like me."

"No, I guess he doesn't," agreed Nell. A long moment stretched between them, but Nell felt like a weight had lifted. "Do you remember anything before you blacked out?"

"Not really. I'd stepped out of the side entrance when you were playing Joplin's 'Cascades,' and I was walking away from the hotel. I got about thirty feet from the door, then it was lights out."

"Sounds like someone followed you."

"That would be my thinking."

"I wonder why." Nell furrowed her brow in concentration.

Jake snorted. "Could be anything. When you come into port, you never know who you might set off. Sometimes, it's somebody's way of saying 'howdy.'"

Nell tried to stop herself from laughing as she replied, "That's just common." She stared down at Jake's weathered hands, so different from Asa's. Thinking of her fiancé, she recalled her humiliation when she overheard Luanne in the bathroom. The violet slipped from Nell's fingers, and she bent down to retrieve it. Jake leaned over at the same time, and they bumped heads. "Oh, Jake, I'm so sorry." Without thinking, she reached out to touch his head. Jake winced in pain and lifted her hand from his recent wound. A warm pulse radiated through Nell when they touched. When Jake didn't release her hand, she shyly pulled it away. They sat on the bench in silence. Feeling engulfed in a flurry of confusion, Nell turned her attention to her hen, who was stalking a grasshopper.

Finally, Jake shifted and cleared his throat. "I heard you and the boys play at the inn last night. You sounded better than most of the bands I've heard in Charleston."

Without replying, Nell turned away, so he couldn't see the blush spreading to her cheeks. "Thank you. The boys will want to know that." The heady feeling began to dissipate, so she added, "Please don't mention it to my daddy. I would get into all kinds of trouble."

"Emma Grace said something about that. It's a shame. I'd be proud of any daughter who could play like you."

"I think he's concerned about my soul. Devil's music and all that."

A soft breeze lifted the leaves on the pecan tree. "I heard you playing your own music with your mama yesterday morning; I would put that in Gershwin's league. He's making jazz respectable."

Her eyes swept over his face and when she saw he was sincere, they exchanged a slight smile. People in Beaufort hadn't heard Gershwin's classical jazz yet, which didn't make good dance music. Sometimes when she was playing his work, she felt like the composer was taking her to a secret island. Now, Jake was saying he'd been to that island. She felt shy and wicked at the same time. Staring down at Jake's fingers, she wanted to reach out and stroke them, hands that played Gershwin. Instead, she squished the violet in her hand and looked away. "Not sure if the folks down here are ready for the piece I was playing yesterday. I don't see the Raleigh crowd finding a beat to 'Cadences of Crashing Ocean,' or 'Seagulls Crying in Anguish.'"

"Something like 'Ghosts of Yesteryear's Shipwreck?'" Jake chuckled. "You might be surprised. I heard Gershwin's jazz opera 'Blue Monday', the last time I was in New York. He's working it—half jazz, half classical."

Nell turned to look at him; her eyes widened. "You were in New York? And you heard Gershwin?"

"Well, he wasn't playing, but I saw his show. My bro– our crew always hits the music halls when we're up there. My whole family is musical. I'd love to go to New Orleans. They say the streets are filled with notes."

Nell pictured a city made of music. She could almost feel the rhythm on her skin. "It was great to play last night. I thought I would be scared, you know, they asked me at the last minute when their piano player couldn't sober up. But it was so much fun to see everyone hopping to my sound." She moved her hands to the side of the bench and gripped it. Jake rested his hand next to hers. She closed her eyes when their skin touched. "It made me think I could give a concert of my music."

"I never really thought about doing that," mused Jake.

"Do you write music?" Nell's eyes opened in surprise.

"It's more of a family thing. We play together."

"You can make people happy or thoughtful or sad with music."

Jake looked away for a moment. "I can't speak for my family, but I write more for myself."

Nell glanced over at the laundry basket, waiting for her. Then a new thought rushed into her head. "Hey! Was that your penny whistle I heard the other night?" She stood up from the bench and began to walk back toward her house.

Jake fell in behind her. "Guilty as charged. That is about the only instrument that's not destroyed by salt spray on a boat."

"I 'magine."

When they reached the back porch, Jake tested the post for the ramp.

Nell bypassed her laundry basket and walked up the porch steps. "Don't leave before you say goodbye. Mama wanted to give you something before you went back to your boat."

"Nell, I really—" protested Jake.

"Hush now; we all want to make Mama happy."

Jake stayed in the yard, drawing water from the pitcher pump and pouring it on the post concrete while Nell worked in the kitchen. Several minutes later, she came out with two small dinner pails. She moved to the edge of the porch and handed one of the buckets down to him. "It's a little Brunswick Stew. And this," she said, handing him the other bucket, "is a chunk of ice for your head. It's important to keep it cold to bring down the swelling."

"Yes, ma'am," said Jake, taking the pail. "It's much 'preciated."

Both of them lingered for a moment. Nell thought of Gershwin's unpredictable riffs that swelled so unexpectedly.

"Well, I best check on my dog and my boat," said Jake.

Nell began to hum "Blue Monday," though it sounded lonely without a full orchestra. Jake joined her by softly whistling the melody as he walked away. Reaching the driveway, he glanced back at her. Nell smiled at him. Then he disappeared around the side of the house and was gone.

CHAPTER 11

On Sunday morning, Nell was sitting in the Davis family pew of the Beaufort Methodist Church. Wearing white gloves and a small bonnet, she sat with this prominent family near the front of the sanctuary. While overpowering organ music reverberated throughout the interior, Nell turned around to glance at Emma Grace and her family several rows behind her. Winston anchored one end of the pew while Mama Beatrice sat near the aisle with her infant. In the middle sat the younger children, including Marbles looking miserable in a starchy collar. It felt odd to Nell to be sitting between Asa and Mrs. Davis, so close to the pulpit. She had hoped her father could join her, but her mother needed extra help that morning.

When the service was about to begin, Nell saw Jake shuffle into the church. His movements were stiff and awkward from his injury. She almost didn't recognize him in a jacket and a white-collared dress shirt. He took his cap off when he entered the church, exposing the clean bandage covering half his head. Her face grew hot as she remembered their conversation about Gershwin. She turned away and stared at the pulpit.

Service began with announcements, local news, and hymns. Then everyone grew silent as their new minister, the Rev. William Sanders, plodded up to the podium. Tall and stately, this man began his sermon with a commanding stature in his holy robes. "We are blessed to live by the sea, where we can reap the fruits of the surf: the mullet, the clam, and the humble oyster."

With each sea creature, he paused and punctuated the name as if he were savoring the sound. "We are blessed with the rhythm of the tides and the changes of the season. The poor souls who live inland will never know the pleasure of catching a high tide at four in the morning."

Nell tittered along with the rest of the congregation, but her gaze shifted to the exquisitely detailed, stained-glass windows, now radiant from sunlight. This church always felt like home to her.

The preacher's brow knitted together. "But a new tide—a dark tide is flooding our small paradise. A tide with a voracious undertow that can pull the strongest sailor into the depths of a watery hell."

Nell, along with most of the congregation, was startled when the preacher's voice rose in timbre. "It drowns our righteousness in the flotsam and jetsam of evil," he boomed. "As we separate the wheat from the chaff, we must learn to separate poison from the bounty of the sea. This evil tide washes up on our shores in the dead of night in wooden crates. This is not the bounty of our generous ocean. These are harbingers of sin! It is an evil reaping. It will leave death and destruction in its path."

Nell sighed. *Another "dry" sermon on the evils of alcohol.* She missed sitting with Emma Grace, who could always put a funny spin on a sermon. Her attention drifted away to the row in front of her, where Buddy Taylor sat with his withered mother, corseted in a dour black silk dress with a full-length skirt indicating that Mrs. Taylor was still mourning her husband, now dead for ten years. As she studied this harsh, forbidding woman, Nell understood why Buddy was careful to hide away in the splendor of his Sugar Shack.

Nell turned her attention back to the pulpit. "This is the harvest of alcohol!" The preacher struck the podium with his fist. "The highest court has cast out this devil and closed our saloons, yet, like the cockroach of inhumanity, this evil returns on its midnight feet. There are those amongst us who do not heed the Lord's message. Good citizens may burn the saloon to the ground, but the speakeasy rises from its ashes. This blight destroys families, corrupts the morality of our youth, and works in tandem with the devil to destroy the fabric of our society."

Nell's gaze wandered around the congregation and accidentally locked eyes with Edgar Ramsey, who winked at her. For a moment she was startled, but then she returned his bemused look. To her surprise, Jake was sitting on Mr. Ramsey's immediate left. This time she didn't look away from him. His attention remained on the minister, so Nell studied his face.

The reverend's voice rose and fell. "What happens when you take a match to moonshine? Every schoolboy knows it burns. It burns with the flame of the devil." The reverend raised his fist and shook it. "Alcohol decreases productivity and makes your mind less agile by weakening the spirit and the soul. We know that forty percent of sin and immorality is prompted by drink. It is the alcohol that degrades our morality. It drops the veil of propriety and opens the door to depravity. Once this veneer has been destroyed, there are no limits. Men will lie with beasts. Men will lie with other men. Drink turns them into perverts who corrupt your children."

A ripple swept through the congregation as some men snickered, and several mothers pulled their children towards them while they searched the congregation for perverts. Behind her, Nell heard a man mutter something about keeping those pansies away from him. She noticed several boys sitting in a corner of the church, who chuckled when one of them batted his eyes and gestured with a limp wrist.

With a stern eye from the preacher, the disruption quieted, and Nell's eyes drifted back to Jake, sitting in front of the stained-glass window. *There's something familiar about his silhouette. Where have I seen it before?* Her eyes drooped. *What was he talking about at dinner with Mama the other day?* The *Jamison* floated through her memory, the special way it purred down the harbor. In her mind's eye, she read the homeport on her stern: *Johns Island, South Carolina.*

"This is the devil's work," Rev. Saunders roared. "Lucifer does not come to you and say, 'I am the devil.' He is more cunning because he comes to you as a false god. Before you know it, you are under his spell. First, you drink the alcohol. Then the alcohol consumes you."

She stared at Jake. *Where have I heard that accent before?* She looked back at the reverend, who was perspiring heavily in his robes. His sermon was nearly over.

"I ask you now to drink from the goblet of righteousness." The minister's voice took on a more calming tone. "To allow the word of God to flood your soul; to cast out the evil brew of deception. Drink deep at the Lord's trough. Or will you be pulled into the undertow of Lucifer?" He paused before adding, "Let us pray."

Well, that wasn't too bad, Nell thought as she bowed her head. When the congregation rose, Nell turned to walk out of the pew with Asa and her future in-laws. Their small cluster joined the rest of the crowd gathering on the sidewalk outside. "Mama will be so disappointed that you can't join us for Sunday dinner," Nell said to Mrs. and Dr. Davis.

"I'm so sorry, I can't stop by," Dr. Davis said sincerely. "But I need to make my rounds."

"I'm afraid your invitation caught me unawares," said Mrs. Davis. "And I have a long-standing engagement this afternoon."

But you still had time to swap out my china. Nell forced a small smile and slipped her arm through Asa's. "How disappointing," Nell answered in a light-hearted lilt. She watched the older woman stiffen before she walked away with her husband toward their home.

"Hey there, Nell and Asa," greeted Buddy, stepping towards them with his fragile mother clinging to his arm. "My mother wanted to say hello." Mrs. Taylor looked like she wanted to do nothing of the sort.

"Hello, Miss Taylor, I think Robert's house renovations are divine," said Nell, who remembered to use Buddy's Christian name.

"I understand that you're quite the musician in town, is that right?" The ancient woman's mouth puckered like she was sucking a lemon.

"Yes, ma'am, I often help with the church organ when they ask."

Asa draped his arm around Nell's shoulders. "This little girl can play just about any tune you put in front of her."

"I heard that some girl was playing down at the inn the other night," said Mrs. Taylor.

Nell stole a glance around the church crowd before remembering her daddy was home with her mama.

Buddy noticed her panicked expression and quickly answered, "I think it was some out-of-town girl, Mama. Came in on the train."

"That's no place for a young girl," retorted Mrs. Taylor fiercely.

Buddy leaned into the small woman and guided her away. "Look, Mama, there's Jefferson Brooks; I know you wanted to talk to him about his pigs." Buddy threw an apologetic look at them as he steered the older woman away.

"Let's get out of here before she comes back," whispered Asa.

Asa and Nell strolled down Ann Street several paces behind Emma Grace's large family. In springtime, Nell thought Ann Street was the most beautiful place in the world. The trunks of the elm trees were whitewashed up to six feet from the ground. Most yards had white picket fences that kept their livestock close to the house but were always filled with flowers.

But today, Nell felt eager to set things right with Asa. With an eye on Emma Grace's family, she slowed her pace so they could not be overheard.

She cleared her throat. "Your mama seemed pretty upset about our wedding plans at supper the other night."

Asa laughed a little too hardily. "That's my mama. She loves to fuss."

"I think it might be a little more than that."

"Really?" he said without interest.

Nell's anguished feelings bubbled out of her. "Your mama changed the china pattern that I picked out at Mason's!"

Asa stopped to look at Nell. "What are you talking about?"

"Every bride in town picks out their tableware pattern for their wedding. Not their mother-in-law. I picked out what I wanted, and she went in behind my back and picked out a different pattern."

"She probably knows what will work best in Richmond."

His logical tone irritated Nell, and she threw her arms up in exasperation. "I want this to be my china in my home. And when I look at my plates and saucers in Richmond, they would remind me of Beaufort."

"I'll tell you what. Once we get up to Richmond, you can see what the other girls are using, and then I'll buy you whatever you want." He spoke as though that was the most obvious solution to the problem.

"I don't want to do that. This is part of my wedding." She was on the verge of tears. "I want to share my china at Mason's so all my friends can see it."

"Nell, what has gotten into you? What are you so mad about?"

Luanne Fulcher's hateful words swirled around and around in her head. *"Nell doesn't even have the sense to cut off her hair. . . . She looks like an old granny. . . . She just teases Asa to death. . . . He needs a modern woman."*

She glanced ahead to see if anyone could overhear them. "Do you think I'm *modern* enough for you?"

Asa looked perplexed. "Huh?"

She thought of all the times they'd fumbled around in Asa's Model T, but Nell had always stopped him from going too far.

"Well, Luanne Fulcher was saying the other—"

"You don't need to be talking to her," he roared at Nell.

Startled by his outburst, Nell stepped back from Asa. Something in his venomous tone didn't ring true.

He turned and started to walk after Emma Grace and her family. Tucking his chin into his neck, he replied, "She's nothing but a liar."

"Asa, slow down. We need to talk about this."

When he stopped to look at her, his face was red with anger. "Luanne Fulcher is nothing but a lying tart. She certainly spread enough rumors about you and Emma Grace in high school. I'm surprised you listen to her at all."

A swarm of confusion engulfed Nell. It was true that Luanne couldn't go a week without spreading a new falsehood.

"Now, you can believe her, or you can believe me," Asa spat at her, then waited for an answer. Nell was opening her mouth to reply when a fast buggy turned on to Ann Street. As it got closer, she could see Chadwick was driving. He stopped it alongside the couple and gave Asa a taunting smirk. "So, Asa, how was church?" Chuckling to himself, he slapped the reins, and the buggy took off toward town.

Asa's demeanor changed. Gnawing his lip for a moment and looking distracted, he said, "I just remembered I need to run over to the drugstore. I need to mix a compound for Jerry's granma."

"Asa!" Nell cried. "What about Sunday dinner with my family?"

"I'll get over to your mama's before they put the ham on the table."

Before she could protest, Asa abruptly set off at a trot after the buggy. Remembering that it was unseemly for ladies to make a scene in public, she automatically glanced up and down the street, but it was empty. She watched her fiancé lope away, round a corner, and disappear.

⌒

By the time Nell arrived at her home, Emma Grace was wearing an apron and laying the table with biscuits, gravy, green beans, and sweet tea. "Hey,

105

buttercup," she said as she handed her friend an apron. "Mama Beatrice and the brood will be here shortly." There were six children in the Willis family, four of them under the age of twelve, so Emma Grace had set the kitchen table for the younger children. Nell went through to the parlor room to set the dining table, now expanded with a leaf. She heard the smaller children arrive, and one of Emma Grace's cousins ran up to her and hugged her around the waist. "Hey, Nellie. Sunday school was fun. They gave me this book."

The coloring book was filled with the evils of drinking. Nell shook her head at the gruesome pictures of drunkards destroying their families, but she smiled down at Emma Grace's little cousin. "Well, now isn't that special." She kneeled to give the girl a hug. "You reckon you could help me set the table?"

"Hey, y'all," Emma Grace said, entering the room and speaking to the children, "Go wash your hands and sit at the kitchen table. It's Sunday, and this hain't no barn."

The food was served, but two seats remained empty at the grown-up's parlor table.

"Asa stopped by the pharmacy," Nell explained to no one in particular.

"Where's Winston?" asked Emma Grace.

"In big trouble," scowled their mother. Beatrice Willis expected all her children to attend Sunday dinner. Mr. Guthrie bowed his head, and everyone at the table followed suit as he said grace.

As they settled into their food, Emma Grace said, "I drank a glass of wine last night, and now I feel my spirit weakening."

Nell giggled but attempted to cover it with a slight cough.

"Y'all can laugh all you want, but the preacher made a lot of sense," said Mama Beatrice. "Look at our family—drink destroyed so many of my cousins. Billy Sunday set my family on the straight and narrow, and now we can hold our heads up in this town."

"I meant no disrespect, Mama Beatrice," said Emma Grace.

"I know you didn't, honey." The older woman's brow furrowed with concern. "But I think the preacher's got a point."

Nell pushed the food around on her plate. When she looked up, she noticed her mother studying her. "Did you want to say something, Nell?"

"It's a mess," replied Nell. "There are people who are ruined by drink, but when they outlawed it, more people started drinking. More women, that's for sure. And in the big cities, and even here on the water, people are starting to shoot each other."

At that moment, they heard the backdoor slam.

"Winston! Is that you?" asked their mother.

"Yes, ma'am," replied Winston over the sound of water splashing in the kitchen sink. "I'm just washing my hands."

The young man appeared in the doorway. Nell looked behind him, thinking that Asa would follow him in, but he was alone. Winston slid into his seat. When he reached for a slice of ham, his mother slapped his hand. "It is the day of the Lord, and you need to give thanks."

"Thank you, oh Lord," began Winston as he closed his eyes with reverence, "for the best mama in the world. And the best food she can fix. Amen."

Mrs. Willis smirked at him, but she allowed Winston to serve himself some ham.

"The preacher makes a good point," continued Emma Grace. "Half the people in this town supported the Eighteenth Amendment. But nary one of us was ready for the Volstead Act."

"Amen to that," replied Winston. "We thought the amendment would just take away the hard stuff, but the Volstead took beer and wine and half my back porch."

Nell glanced at her father's face with some apprehension. She knew he hated political discussions at the table. But he was unfazed by the conversation and focused on his food.

"So, tell me why I can legally make my own wine, but not beer?" Emma Grace said.

"*Ach, Nein!*" cried Winston imitating a German accent, "Zee filthy Germans drinks zee vile beer!"

"Here's what I want to know," Emma Grace stated with a straight face. "The preacher said forty percent of sin starts with a drink. What does the other sixty percent start with?"

Nell pressed a napkin to her mouth to suppress a giggle.

"Sin!" replied Winston, with his index finger pointing to heaven, "begins with the humble oyster. Because it puts lead in your—" Catching his mother's eye, Winston didn't complete the sentence. He lowered his voice to imitate

Rev. Saunders, "So I ask you, brothers and sisters, which tide does the sin of the mollusk ride? The dark tide, or the fruitful tide?"

Emma Grace snickered.

"I think you've said enough." Mr. Guthrie glared at Emma Grace and Winston. The young people froze and a chill settled on the table.

Winston's mother reached over to clock her son, but he ducked out of her reach. "Be glad your daddy hain't here. You wouldn't be using those nasty words on Sunday."

When the meal was over, Nell, Winston, and Emma Grace carried the dirty dishes from the dining table. Before they sat down to eat, Nell had carried water from the outdoor pitcher pump and placed it on the large cast-iron stove. Now, she poured the warmed water into the kitchen sink to wash the dishes.

While Winston shepherded his younger siblings into the garden, the two young women began to wash the pile of dirty dishes. It was usually a time to laugh and gossip together, but today Emma Grace was silent and Nell noticed a look of thoughtful concern on her friend's face.

After she had tucked the remaining sweet potatoes into the icebox, Nell asked, "Emma Grace, what's wrong?"

"Oh, nothing," answered Emma Grace. But when she looked up from the sink and saw Nell's anxious expression, she added, "Well, I was just thinking about what the preacher said."

"He tends to be right ham-fisted."

"He's that, alright. But I was thinking about when he compared 'men lying with men' to having sex with an animal."

Startled, Nell whipped her head around to make sure no one else was in the room. "Emma Grace," she hissed under her breath, "you can't let my daddy hear you talking like that."

Distracted, Emma Grace looked up at Nell and chuckled. "Oh, sorry." Then she turned back to the dishwater in the sink. "Well, it got me thinking about a man who came into the clinic a few weeks ago. He'd come down by train and was having a bad angina attack. We pumped him up with nitroglycerin, but I reckoned there had been some heart damage. Doc wanted him to get some rest, so he didn't discharge him. Part of it was that he didn't know anyone in town, and he'd have to stay in a hotel. Doc Davis wanted to keep an eye on him."

While she wondered what this story had to do with sex, Nell continued to dry the dishes and listened patiently. "I think I remember hearing about that—wasn't his name Howard?"

"Horace," Emma Grace corrected. "He was traveling alone and was in so much pain. So, I asked him if I could contact his next of kin, and he gave me the name of his cousin. I ran right down to the inn and sent out a telegram to him up in Norfolk."

Nell turned away from Emma Grace to put away a stack of the dinner plates.

"So, the cousin came down right away. When he walked into that patient's room, Horace started to get better. Before he arrived, Doc Davis wasn't sure if Horace was gonna live, but we soon saw the color come back to his cheeks and his circulation was getting better. It was like he'd been all clenched up and when his cousin walked in, he just relaxed."

Nell smiled. "Family can do that."

"Well, see, that's the thing. One night, I was coming in on the late shift around midnight and I happened to pass his room. The cousin was in bed with Horace. They were wrapped around each other like they were spooning."

Nell made a short intake of breath. "Did they have their clothes on?" She had heard of this sort of lust.

"Oh, yes," Emma looked up from the soapy dishes and stared out the window. "But there was real . . . love between them."

"They must have been so embarrassed when they saw you."

Emma Grace shook her head. "They never saw me. The thing is, I wasn't embarrassed for them at all. I wasn't disgusted. Horace was doing so much better."

Nell knew that Emma Grace often measured success in life by how well someone healed.

"And about three days later, he was well enough to travel, and he went home with his so-called cousin."

The two friends stood side by side at the sink, washing and drying dishes for a few minutes before Nell answered, "Hain't that sumthin'."

Emma Grace nodded.

At that moment, Winston opened the back door, and several children chased each other through the kitchen. Eager to change the conversation, Nell asked Winston, "Did you see where Asa went to? He was supposed to have dinner with us."

"I hain't seen him, but I was downtown."

Nell gave him a confused look. "He ran an errand at his drugstore."

"I didn't see him when I walked by. Could have been in the back." Lowering his voice and looking over his shoulder to see if the older adults were nearby, Winston said, "It's more than likely he needed to check in with Chadwick."

"What do you mean?" A mantle of dread settled over her.

"Everyone was talking about the delivery of Canadian Mist and Bacardi in Room 201 on Friday night while we were playing at the inn. Lowell was getting a liquor drop in this week."

Nell's hands shook as she carefully set down the cup she was drying. "So, he's still running booze?" She kept her voice low and neutral despite her building panic and rage. Asa was breaking his promise to end his rum-running operation.

Winston studied her face and shifted uneasily. "Well, yeah. You knew that."

Emma Grace looked up from the dirty dishes, "I saw Asa at the speakeasy at the inn the night you were playing."

"I thought Chadwick was running the speakeasy at the inn now."

"Hardly. Chadwick couldn't run himself out of a paper bag."

"When I accepted Asa's ring, he promised to stop smuggling liquor."

Winston looked surprised. "Nell, look, I don't know what he told you, but I can't 'magine Asa giving up so much money. And I 'magine he's doing this to make a big splash in Richmond."

"What do you mean?"

"His trips to Richmond. Everyone up there knows him and they rely on him when they can't get hooch through the blockade at Norfolk—you know, the naval base and all that. So, Asa brings it in by land."

"How did he carry it up there? How would he get it on the train?" She felt the room spin around her. All those trips to Richmond. Asa had never been truthful.

"Well, I hain't sure about how he moves it, but they surely love him up there for it. Sometimes they visit at the doc's house and they talk all about it."

For a few moments, Nell replayed the last year in her mind: Asa's frequent trips to Richmond, always flush with cash and his talk of his new business connections in Virginia. She always assumed he was just a local smuggler, helping his friends make a happier party. Now, she felt like she'd stepped off the end of a dock, and it was a long drop to the water below.

Winston was watching her face. "Look, Nell," he answered gently. "I think this is about more than money. Asa always felt like he couldn't be a doctor like his daddy—or his granddaddy. He wasn't that good in school, but that family wants more out of him. This is giving him respect in Richmond, but it's more than that. Running booze gets him up in the morning. It's the thrill; it's the chase of it all."

Nell nodded and turned back to the dishes in the sink. A few moments later, she heard Winston leave by the back door.

For most of the afternoon, Nell sat with Emma Grace on the harbor shore, watching the younger children wade and splash in the water. On any other day, Nell would have hitched up her skirt and waded with them, but her whole world had shifted since her talk with Winston. When the afternoon light faded into dusk and the Willis family drifted back to their home, Nell went out to Harrison's bench under the pecan tree and traced his name with her finger. She closed her eyes and listened to the slow, steady hum of evening's first crickets and the clucking of her hens.

"Hey, darlin'," she heard a voice call. She opened her eyes to see Asa walking toward her through the garden. Nell felt like she was looking at a stranger. After briefly kissing her on the lips, he sat down next to her.

"Hey, Asa," she said lightly, "Where ya been? You missed Sunday dinner."

Asa's head twisted to one side, and he tucked his chin into his chest. "I just got real busy down at the drugstore, Nellie. My daddy called in with a mess of orders that needed filling right away."

Nell was quietly studying his face. There was something familiar about the way his head almost involuntarily twisted. The night Asa made sundaes at the drugstore, and they talked about their plans in Richmond, he tucked his chin into his chest. She studied him now as he lit a cigarette, while trying to recall what they had talked about that night in the drugstore. Then it came to her. "I wrote to the Richmond Music Conservatory and they want me to come up, and audition for them. Maybe we can take the train up together the next time you go." She noticed his chin dip a second time.

"That would be grand," replied Asa.

He was lying to her. The way he twisted his chin told her it was a lie. When they were walking away from church earlier that day, his head had rotated in the same manner when she mentioned Luanne. This same mannerism surfaced when she asked him to stop running booze. Rage brewed inside her as she realized she couldn't trust anything he said. When she didn't answer, Asa's gaze wandered indifferently over the garden and back yard. When they rested on the ramp, he started to chuckle.

"What's so funny?" asked Nell.

"You know that hobo that's building your ramp?"

Nell nodded.

"He got thrown in jail the other night," Asa said, laughing softly.

"Yes, I heard that," she was watching Asa more closely now. "He came by yesterday afternoon to cure the concrete."

Asa whipped his head around to look at her. "Your daddy hasn't got ridda him yet?"

"I reckon he thinks he's doing a good job building the ramp."

Asa whistled softly, shaking his head.

"At least he's not raising his children to be bootleggers," Nell retorted, feeling her color rising.

Asa sat up straight. "I told you I quit."

"But you didn't, did you, Asa Davis."

His face was rigid as his chin tucked in toward his neck. "I don't know what you've heard, but not everybody knows I've gone out of business yet."

But Nell read the chin, not the man. "You're flat-out lying to me." Her lip trembled as anger coursed through her body. It made her strong.

"That's a fine thing to say to your fiancé," he bellowed at her.

"Asa, I can't marry you." She pulled her engagement ring off her finger and held it out to him.

Asa didn't move. "Nellie, this is good money for our family. A way to build our future."

She stood up and set the ring down on the bench next to him. Asa didn't move and continued to stare at her face. "Nell, honey, you're taking this way out of proportion. It's just a little fun."

"Running booze up to Richmond? That's crossing state lines."

"Who told you that?" he demanded.

She laughed. "You just did." She turned away from him and marched toward her house. Asa followed her. "I wouldn't worry too much on this, Asa," she said over her shoulder. "Summer's coming. There'll be plenty of distractions around to make you happy." He was walking alongside her now, and she looked him in the face. "In fact, I wouldn't be surprised if Luanne isn't waiting for you right now over at the drugstore."

"What are you talking about?" Asa sputtered, but his chin betrayed him.

"I was giving you the benefit of the doubt. She claims to know you pretty well."

"That hussy is a liar."

"Well, you would know." When Nell reached her back porch, Asa grabbed her arm. "You taking other people's word over mine?"

"Yes, sir." She pulled her arm out of his grasp, stomped across her back porch, and entered the house. Once inside, she shut the heavy inner door that no one used in the summer.

⸻

Later that evening, after Nell helped her mother settle into the parlor, she walked down to the small beach in front of their house. She sat on the sand, took off her shoes, and let the waves lap her toes while staring into the endless horizon with its infinite possibilities.

Her anger and hurt were raw. It was hard to turn away from Asa. He had been such a part of her life for so long. She thought of the softball games with Harrison as kids, and how he wooed her back last winter with gifts from Richmond, ending with a Louis Armstrong record and a silver oyster pendant necklace. He said he had needed her then, and he loved her more than he realized. Despite her pain, she felt something rich and vital growing inside her. Nell heard footsteps behind her, and Emma Grace sat down next to her.

"Your mama said you'd be down here."

"I broke up with Asa."

"You okay with that?"

"Yeah, I think I am." But despite these words, Nell sniffled.

They dug their toes in the sand and didn't speak while the last rays of the sun warmed them. With her friend at her side, Nell felt her bruised heart strengthen.

Exhaling, she said, "It was always easier for me to put Asa before myself. Maybe you can't blame him for that."

"Maybe."

"I lost so much of myself when Harrison died, and I couldn't go away for school. It wasn't time to run off when Mama and Daddy needed me so much, but a part of me fell away."

"It was probably easy to let Asa step into that loss," answered Emma Grace.

"You think so?"

"It was simple for me to see, but it's always harder to see in yourself. You loved him, Nell, and that's a risk for anyone."

Nell glanced over at her friend. "I guess I'm kinda wondering why I don't feel sadder than I do."

"I guess I am, too. You tend to take these things more seriously than I do."

"Maybe it's been coming on for a long time."

"Maybe. But I think you're a little smarter now. The way you always talked about Asa, the way you would go on and on about Sylvia Davis' house. You always made it sound like a fairy tale. I didn't think you ever saw the whole man."

The sky darkened while the western horizon became an indigo blue with the first glimmers of stars. Nell closed her eyes and dug her fingers into the sand. The grains of sand felt like every star above her. She felt herself growing larger: her joy reaching out to be a part of the lapping water, the briny air, and the marsh grass that swished in the breeze.

Emma Grace stood up and held out her hand, and the two friends waded in the water as they'd done as children. "Remember when we used to jump off the end of the dock at night?"

"Yeah, the phosy-light lit up in the bubbles around us," replied Nell, referring to the phosphorescence that brightened when seawater was disturbed. It was a mysterious element of the ocean that never ceased to amaze her.

They both looked at the end of the dock. "What are we waiting for?" asked Emma Grace.

They ran to the end of the dock, stripped to their camisoles, and jumped into the harbor. As they plunged into the water's depth, a million glowing bubbles rushed up all around them, tickling them before they burst on the water's surface. Their magical essence reminded Nell of Harrison. For the first time since he had died, she felt joyous at the thought of him.

Later that night, after Nell rinsed the salt out of her hair in the backyard pump, she went inside to help her mother prepare for bed. Alice Guthrie was resting comfortably with several pillows propping up her head. Nell quietly told her mother that she had broken her engagement with Asa.

"Well, thank goodness for that," sighed Mrs. Guthrie.

Nell's jaw dropped in surprise. "I thought you liked Asa!"

"Asa's alright, but I never saw it working out between the two of you. Sometimes I felt he wasn't really housebroken."

Nell stared in disbelief, and then both of them broke into laughter.

"I certainly didn't feel he was making you happy," continued her mama. "You were trying so hard to make it work."

"Why in the world didn't you say something, Mama?"

"Darlin', it is not my place to tell you who to love."

"Maybe not, but I would've listened," said Nell.

"Nell, you never know what's going on between two people. It's always hard for a parent to interfere. "I kept praying you would work through it." Alice Guthrie paused, then added, "How ya feeling, sugar?"

"I think I'll be okay." Her lip trembled despite her words.

"I'm so glad you're not downhearted, my girl." Mrs. Guthrie paused. "But I think your daddy's gonna be right upset about all this."

Nell slowly nodded her head while she looked at nothing. "He does like Asa."

"He does," agreed Mrs. Guthrie. "But I think he was relieved when you got engaged. It showed him that you were moving on. You got stuck here after Harrison died, and you needed to stay here, and he felt bad about that."

Nell thought of her father's stormy moods and icy distance since Harrison's death. This new interpretation of his behavior was insightful.

Her mother continued. "I think first thing tomorrow morning we need to call an emergency meeting of the Oyster Shuckers."

"What in the world?" said Nell.

"Sylvia's not gonna take this lying down."

Nell looked away from her mother for a moment before she replied, "I hadn't thought about that."

"Oh, my little lamb."

CHAPTER 12

Jake's tool bag bumped against his leg while he walked with Pilot up Front Street the next morning. He planned to finish the ramp at the Guthrie household, but he couldn't steer his mind away from the extra weight he was carrying in the satchel. Before leaving the *Jamison* that morning, Jake stowed two additional items. The first was his Smith and Wesson revolver. After he was attacked at the Inlet Inn, he figured Beaufort was the type of port where he might need a pistol. The other item was Nell's harbor log. Although his head still ached from his injury, it was his conscience that was causing pain. While Nell's ledger gave him invaluable information about Wade when he was in Beaufort, the theft weighed heavily on Jake.

Nell's rooster crowed at them when they arrived at the Guthrie family's back yard, so Pilot chased it until he tired. While Jake began to saw planks, he frequently glanced up at the back door, wondering how he could sneak the harbor log into the house.

After the family breakfast, Nell pushed her mother's wheelchair onto the porch. Jake stopped sawing and walked up to the women. Nell smiled shyly before looking away. Touching the brim of his hat, he spoke to Mrs. Guthrie. "Mornin', ma'am. I appreciate you posting bail for me."

"How's your head?" replied Alice Guthrie.

"Still attached."

As he chatted with Mrs. Guthrie, Nell ducked back into the house and returned with a bowl of water for Pilot.

"I'm looking to finish planking and getting a coat of paint on today if the weather holds." All three of them looked reverently at the sky. Weather was paramount to anyone living on the coast, where sudden storms often blew up from light breezes.

"It's clouding up," agreed Nell.

"Be sure to rest if you feel weary," said Alice.

"Yes, ma'am."

"Nell, will you take me back inside, please? I underestimated the heat." As Nell turned the wheelchair around to enter their house, her mother added, "Jake, we'll expect you for dinner."

"I look forward to it, ma'am," replied Jake.

At noon, Jake washed at the outdoor pump and presented himself at the back door. After they all sat down and began their meal, they talked of music and Jake's South Carolina home. Their conversation led to a debate of rice versus cornbread as the optimal side dish. When they finished eating, Mrs. Guthrie asked their visitor, "Would you join us in the parlor while your meal settles?"

"Yes, ma'am." He followed Nell as she pushed her mother's chair.

"Nell tells me that you play the piano at your home."

"Yes, ma'am. We're a string band."

"Perhaps you could play us something." Sitting on the piano bench, Jake ran his hands over the keys for a moment. They made him feel like he had just walked in his front door. Closing his eyes, Jake slowly began to play the tribute to his little brother that he had played on his penny whistle the week before. As his longing for Wade rose, the piano whispered the measured, melancholy song. The room and keys fell away as music filled him and moved his fingers. Wade's crooked smile, his easy laugh when they fished, his concentration when he built a boat all floated through his mind. When the piece ended, Jake felt Wade was resting his hand on his shoulder. Pretending to mop his brow with his handkerchief, he wiped away the tears pooling in his eyes.

"That was very moving," said Alice. "I don't believe I know it."

"No, ma'am. It's mine. It's not done yet." He turned around to face them and noticed Nell's anguished face.

"What do you call it?" asked Mrs. Guthrie.

"I don't have a title for it yet."

"It's a beautiful piece," Mrs. Guthrie said. "You play so well. And you must care for your hands around all those sharp tools, Jake."

"Yes, ma'am. It's a challenge. But I need to be getting back to work," he replied.

"Mama, I think you need a rest," said Nell, getting up from her chair.

"Jake, I'll need to rest for an hour or so. Could you restrain from hammering?"

"Would it bother you if I sawed, ma'am?"

"No, of course not, but it is the hottest time of the day. So, you can rest your digestion. I don't think Thomas will begrudge you a lunch hour in this heat, particularly after your injuries." Turning to Nell, she said with a smile, "But you're a woman, so your work never ends. Some of those green beans would be good for supper."

Nell squeezed her mother's shoulder. "I'm so glad you feel like eatin', Mama. You've gotten so thin."

Alice Guthrie laughed. "I'm just trying to be fashionable. Coco Chanel says I need to fit into a little black dress."

Jake returned to the back yard and was raking wood chips when Nell stepped out of the house carrying her garden basket. Once he noticed her on the porch, she asked, "Would you care to pick some green beans with me?"

"As long as your fiancé doesn't run over me with a truck."

"I don't think we need to worry about that. I broke off my engagement to Asa last night."

Jake raised his eyebrows in surprise. "I hope it was something I said."

Nell smiled as she stepped down to the yard and walked toward the garden. Without saying a word, Jake fell in behind her, followed by Pilot and several chickens. When she reached Harrison's seat under the pecan tree, she sat down and set the basket on the ground.

Nell watched the cluster of hens slowly pecking and scratching around the bench. After sitting in comfortable silence for a few moments, Jake casually leaned toward her and let his hand rest on hers. Without looking down, Nell said, "Well, you don't waste any time. I'll give you that, Jake Parson."

His hand locked in spasm around her fingers when he heard his real name. It hung in the air between them. He felt exposed; his breathing became shallow, while his eyes darted around the garden, searching for an escape. The false identity had acted as a shield between him and the town. Now, the garden fell away, and he closed his eyes. In darkness, he couldn't move and counted his breaths until his thudding heart slowed.

"Jake, are you okay?" Nell asked gently.

Her voice sounded distant, but he felt her stroke his hand and slowly opened his eyes. Gradually, he started to hear Nell's hens clucking a few feet in front of them. Turning his face toward her, he asked, "How did you know?"

"It was so many little things. Your voice sounded familiar, and I remembered the *Jamison* and the *Amelia* had the same homeport of Johns Island. Then in church yesterday, I saw more of your face when you weren't wearing your hat, and I saw how much you favor your brother, Wade. You're looking for the *Amelia*, aren't you? Is that why you're in town?"

How much can I trust her? A mash of emotions warred through Jake's body. He wanted to pull her close to him and hold her, but this racing anxiety wouldn't leave him. A dull ache began to throb in his head. His brother was good at recognizing Jake's panic when different emotions overwhelmed him. For the first time since his disappearance, he could hear Wade speak to him. *It hain't nothing but a windstorm, brother. And she hain't pulled her hand away.* Jake glanced at their intertwined hands that tethered him to the earth. "When I arrived in port, I learned he was missing. I was fixin' to call my parents, but then I figured I would stay in Beaufort to find out what happened."

"But why all the secrecy? Why not just talk to the Coast Guard?"

Jake turned his face away from her, wrestling with himself before he answered. "Well, I was all set to do that, and then Wade's dog showed up."

"The hound?" Nell asked in astonishment.

"He showed up on the town dock, the day after I came into port. That's when I knew something wasn't right. Wade would never sail without him." Saying all this out loud seemed to open the thick wall that encased him, and he gently squeezed her hand.

"Where is he now?"

"In my cabin on the *Jamison*. He'd been living rough and needs some time to heal. And I don't want town folk connecting Wade to me." He smiled ruefully. "Lotta good that did me. You figured it out."

"So, you think Wade might still be here? Why would he be hiding?"

A series of images paraded through Jake's mind. Wade injured. Wade's

120

crumpled body. Or an addled Wade going off to be by himself in the woods or on the water. He gripped Nell's hand before he answered her. "I don't rightly know. But I've been retracing his steps, and I think it might have something to do with the last drop from the *Three Sisters*."

Nell turned to him. "The offshore schooner? How do you know about that ship?"

A wave of anxiety rippled through Jake. *Because I read about it in your log.* "I heard people talking about it around town. Mostly down at Lowell's."

Nell nodded, appearing to accept this explanation. "I remember her load. Emma Grace and I tend to watch and write down the comings and goings in town. Emma Grace's mind is always finding patterns, and I'm always watching the harbor and listening to people's stories. It's been right helpful to the town."

Does she know her log is missing yet? A new wave of distress swept over Jake, causing his body to shudder. He glanced at her face, but she was calmly watching her chickens. *Settle down, my brother,* Wade's voice said.

"I met your brother," Nell continued. "He came into our store, and Emma Grace talked to him when she was painting his boat. He seemed like a kid growing into his shoes."

Jake smiled at the apt description of his quirky brother. Nell understood music, the war, and now his search for Wade. A new thought occurred to him. *Will she feel betrayed when she finds out I stole from her?* He waited a few minutes for his heart to settle into a steadier beat. "It may have been a mistake to let him captain his own boat, but he was so anxious to make a run on his own."

"He's a bit of an odd duck."

"I know what you're saying, but he's brilliant at the same time. He just doesn't have any common sense." Letting go of her hand, he continued. "You mind if we walk around? My legs get sore if I sit too long." He stretched and rubbed his leg to make his point. The truth was that he hoped that movement would help dissipate his panic. His chest still felt tight. She picked up her basket, and they began to stroll around new plants emerging from the soil.

"Wade built the *Amelia*."

Nell caught her breath. "Did he? Mercy, that was a pretty boat."

"What that boy can do to wood," Jake spoke with effort. "Daddy and I can build, but Wade is gifted. His mind doesn't think like yours and mine. It never went from one point to the next point. It was like he was watching a moving picture show in his head. It's hard for him to navigate his life, but he's gifted in design. He could draw better than he could write."

"Where do you think he might be?"

While they walked past rows of early spring lettuce, hot anger began to bubble inside Jake. "I think somebody talked him into refitting his boat to make it faster or to build secret compartments to carry booze. Wade would have felt challenged with a problem like that. He would see it like a jigsaw puzzle." Jake stared off past the backyard fence. "But I don't think he could see the magnitude of what he was getting himself into. There's a lot of piracy and lawlessness on the water now. Asa may have talked him into it. I think he's the brains behind Lowell's bootlegging operations."

Their garden wandering brought them to Nell's plot of green beans. "I know he is," Nell replied in a matter-of-fact tone. Jake glanced at her resolute expression. "When I figured it out, it was the last straw."

Nell crouched, set her basket down, and began to pick beans off their vines. Jake sat on the ground near her and pulled out a cigarette. Sensing Jake's distress, Pilot lay down next to his master and Jake absently stroked his dog's head.

"I think Asa saw Wade as a real goober," said Nell. "But I don't see him using Wade for his runs. He's got a lot of local boys who know the water."

Jake wasn't convinced. There were all sorts of ways that Wade could help a rum-running ring. He could build anything into a boat.

"Lots of boys with half of Wade's sense make good money," continued Nell.

"Maybe. But those boys might have some understanding of how people work and think. Wade doesn't have the head for something like that." Although his brother instinctively picked up on his family's moods and feelings, going into town was agony for him.

Jake inhaled deeply. "I've heard of pharmacists hiring people to transport their scrip for medicinal booze and then pirate them once they're making deliveries."

Nell looked at him in confusion. "Why in the world would they do that?"

"When I was in South Carolina, we heard about a lawyer in Louisville, Kentucky. When Prohibition started, he became a pharmacist, as well. Then he bought several distilleries and had them make medical scrip.. When they ship out the hooch, their own men 'steal' it on the road. That way, they can say they never got their scrip quota and make more booze back at the factory."

"That sounds like it would be fairly easy to trace. Didn't local police figure out the operation pretty soon?"

Jake scoffed. "Not hardly. Couple of bottles of whiskey put them right."

Nell nodded. "Not sure how that would work here. I mean, they're not making liquor, so there's no quotas. They're meeting boats offshore and bringing it in." Her hands were full of beans, which she moved to her basket.

"Maybe there's something we're not seeing. There's a lot of hijackers running up and down the coast these days. Right now, it seems like a big sport, but in the cities, more criminals are getting into the business. Wade could be real stupid about money and not understand how dangerous this could be for him."

"What did Wade want money for?"

"Wade was traveling to Bristol, Connecticut, to work as an apprentice at Herreshoff Boat Yards."

Nell whistled. "Lordy, he must have been able to build himself a boat if he had gotten work there."

"Down the road, he planned to return to Johns Island and expand my daddy's boatyard to build new designs of yachts and workboats with teak and mahogany brightwork. That boy always has four different designs jumping around in his head." Jake paused to remember his peculiar brother. Then he frowned. "What I want to know is where did Wade go after he left Lowell's? My parents and I know he was still in town on April 4 because we received a letter from Beaufort with that date and people saw him around town, but I believe he left the boatyard earlier than that."

Nell stopped picking and fixed her gaze at him, "What makes you say that?"

He was in the soup now; he'd matched the date of the letter with entries written in her log. Before he could answer, Nell turned away from him. Tulla Jaspers was walking into the yard, heading toward the steps on the back porch.

"Oh, I better go greet her," said Nell, gathering up her basket of beans. "I don't want her to wake up Mama."

Jake exhaled a sigh of relief.

Nell raised her voice and started to walk toward the house. "Woo-hoo, Miss Tulla!"

The older woman stopped and looked around when she heard her name. Nell waved and picked up her pace. "Mama's resting right now. Why don't you come into the kitchen, and I'll get you some sweet tea?"

"I could use some of that right now."

Nell glanced back at Jake and he rose from the earth to follow her. She turned and swiftly walked toward the house to open the door for Miss Tulla. While the two women fell into a discussion about tinctures and physical therapy, Jake turned back to work on the ramp.

That afternoon, Jake agonized over Nell's ledger while he worked. By the end of the day, he had made a decision. He was putting his tools away when Nell reappeared in the doorway with Tulla.

"Thank you so much for all your help," Nell was saying to the elderly lady. "I haven't seen the blood flow to my mama's feet like that in I don't know how long."

"Miss Jaspers, I would be more than happy to walk you down to meet Isaac," said Jake.

"I'd appreciate that."

"Could I have a word alone with Nell before we go?"

"Well, surely."

Nell walked down the steps to join Jake, who led her to the henhouse. Jake opened his tool bag, reached deep inside and pulled out Nell's harbor log, which he held out to her.

Nell let out a cry of alarm as she grabbed it from him. Her face clouded with anger. "How did you get that?"

"I took it because I am looking for my brother." When she didn't answer, he added, "I hope you, of all people, can understand that."

Her nostrils flared, but a softness flickered in her eyes. She was still too dumbfounded to answer.

"Would you not give anything to see Harrison one more time?" he asked gently.

Without saying a word, she stormed back to the house, clutching the ledger close to her chest.

124

Jake watched her leave as he walked over to the elderly lady. "So, Miss Jaspers, you all set?"

Watching Nell stomping across the porch, Mrs. Jaspers answered, "Well, now, I reckon I am."

The two started to make their way out of the yard, with Pilot following close behind.

"How's Isaac been treatin' you?" asked Jake.

"Can't complain."

Jake looked over his shoulder and took one last look toward the house. Nell was entering her home without a backward glance. Feeling something precious slip away, he wondered if she would ever speak to him again.

CHAPTER 13

A mixture of guilt and regret roiled inside Jake as he walked with Miss Tulla down Front Street. Nell's final look of betrayal and anger haunted him. Although his heart was breaking, he knew he must focus on his search for Wade. Isaac Jaspers could be the key to understanding Lowell's bootlegging operation, and now Jake was walking home with his grandmother. On the night Jake broke into Guthrie's Hardware, he saw Isaac unloading the skiff behind Lowell's. He glanced sideways at the elderly lady laden with her heavy medicinal satchel. "Can I carry your bag for you a ways?"

"That you can," answered Miss Tulla, handing her bag to him and standing a little straighter.

"After my brother was born, the midwife stayed with us for a right long time," said Jake.

"We always give more time than a doctor."

"Yes, ma'am. Mama was weak, and Miss Libby nursed her through it. She also helped with the baby until Mama was on her feet. She's right special to our family."

"Sometimes, I feel God's love flows through my body when I am healing."

"I can believe that. Some folks have a gift." The sun was setting in front of them, and they squinted against the lowering light. "Miss Tulla, what do you suggest for a chewed-up dog's leg?"

"What bit it?" the elderly lady asked.

"I don't rightly know. Might have been a trap." Looking down Front

Street, Jake saw young Marbles and Tobias jumping off the town dock into the harbor.

"I make an ointment of burdock with willow bark, but it's hard to keep it on a dog, so I mix it with quinine to keep him from licking it." As Tulla spoke, Tobias spied his great-grandmother walking toward them and hollered to Marbles, who was swimming. Within a few minutes, the two small wet boys were racing each other down the street.

"Would you like me to mix an ointment for you?" asked Tulla Jaspers.

"Yes, ma'am. I'd 'preciate that," replied Jake.

Tulla looked down at Pilot. "He look okay to me."

"It's for another dog I found around town," Jake replied.

The two boys reached them, out of breath.

"Hey, Granny," said Tobias.

"Hey, Jake. Hey, Pilot," Marbles panted.

The black Lab greeted them like long-lost friends by dancing on the sidewalk.

"Well, you're growing out your britches just like Tobias," Tulla said to Marbles. "Lordy, you got big!"

Marbles grinned and pulled himself up to look taller.

"We thought we could talk business with you, Mr. Jake," said Marbles in a somber tone.

"Let's not talk about money in front of a lady. Why don't you carry Miss Tulla's big ol' bag for her?"

"Sure," said Marbles. "Will you give us a nickel?"

Jake looked sternly at the boy. "Remember your manners, Marbles."

Marbles hung his head as he lifted the medicine bag and heaved it onto his shoulder.

"Thank you, sir," Miss Tulla said with kindness.

The party made their way down Front Street and turned onto Turner, as the boys chatted non-stop about their crabbing and fishing enterprises.

As they approached Ann Street, Isaac walked toward them from the west. When they reached the corner, Tobias said, "Hey, Daddy."

"Hey there, son." Noticing Marbles straining under his load, Isaac said, "Looks like it's your turn to carry Granny's bag."

"Yessir," replied Tobias as Marbles shifted the load to his friend.

"Isaac," greeted Jake, touching the brim of his hat.

"Mr. Waterson," answered Isaac.

"I've just been telling Miss Tulla what a special healer she is."

"Yessir. We know all about that," Isaac answered, looking affectionately at his grandmother.

"I might need some help on my boat later," Jake said to Isaac. "You reckon you might could help me?"

"Yessir, always glad to help."

Isaac and his family moved to cross the street, and Jake turned to walk with Marbles back to the docks. "Good night, y'all," he threw over his shoulder.

"Thank you for walking with my granny," said Isaac.

Turning his attention to Marbles, Jake asked, "Now, what's this about a business proposition?"

"We thought you might need some help setting up your sails on the *Miss Mary*."

"Well, I might at that. What did you have in mind?"

"We were thinkin'—"

But Jake wasn't to learn what they thought. At that moment, a Dodge truck careened around the corner on Front Street. The engine ran rough and loud, and the flatbed was filled with a group of white teenage boys yelling and laughing loudly. Jake watched them drive up the street, headed right toward Isaac, Miss Tulla, and Tobias as they stepped off the curb.

"Get 'em!" hollered one of the boys, and the driver sped up. Everyone in the truck laughed and whooped uproariously.

Jake's blood ran cold as he watched Isaac look around to see the vehicle increase in speed and head toward them. Isaac yanked his son and grandmother out of the street. The quick action unbalanced them, causing all three of them to fall back on the sidewalk. The truck screeched to a stop, and the drunken boys quickly tumbled out of the flatbed.

"You oughta be more careful where you're walking, nigger," said a large, red-faced teen.

While on the ground, Isaac spoke to Tobias, who got up swiftly and began to run down Ann Street. One of the teens reached for him, but Tobias dodged him and sped down the street.

As Isaac helped his grandmother to her feet, the five boys surrounded them and kicked Isaac, who teetered but didn't fall. Another boy shoved Isaac to the other side of the group and he fell against another one of the teens.

"Why you slamming into me, coon? Don't you know that's disrespectful?"

Miss Tulla trembled as she clung to her grandson. Staring stoically at the ground, Isaac remained silent.

Pilot growled deep in his chest. While Jake's heart pounded, a heightened sense of focus encompassed him. The sensation was frightening and empowering at the same time. He considered approaching the boys and reasoning with them. But their beefy red faces and glassy eyes indicated they were too deep into moonshine to listen. The jeers got louder as Isaac politely shook his head, his eyes not leaving the ground.

Jake scanned the street, considering the scene from all angles. His only option was to create a distraction. He glanced down at Marbles, who never took his eyes off Tobias flying down the street. Kneeling to his height, Jake said, "Marbles, take Pilot and run up to Emma Grace's house and ask her cousin to meet me in a car at the cemetery. Tell them that Miss Tulla needs their help. After they leave, go over to Miss Nell's house. See if she can help you catch Tobias." Jake commanded Pilot to follow Marbles, who took off in high gear after his friend.

Jake looked up to see one of the boys punching Isaac in the face. His head jerked back from the blow. Walking up to Ann Street, Jake quietly turned away from the altercation and headed toward Beaufort's Burying Ground. Keeping his eye on the group at the street corner, he slipped into the cemetery. When he was parallel with Isaac and Miss Tulla, he opened his tool bag and took out a small pouch and several rags.

Setting the pieces of cloth on the ground, he produced a bottle of lubricating oil from the pouch. He poured oil on the rag, then removed his pistol. He opened the chamber, dumped out several bullets, and placed them on the oily rags.

Jake could see Isaac's eye was bleeding. Several of the boys were trying to pull Tulla's medical bag from her, but she curled her body around it. Jake quietly lit the pile of rags and bullets, and then sneaked back in the dim evening light to the other side of the cemetery. The fire smoked with oily fumes, then flared into a flame. The bullets began to explode with loud bangs. They sounded like firecracker explosions to Jake. But to the party on the street, it must have sounded like gunfire. The boys jerked around to find the source of the shots before they ran for their truck and squealed away. Isaac picked up his grandmother and sprinted north on Turner Street toward their home. Jake ran ahead of them and met them at the corner of Broad Street. When Isaac saw him, he veered away from Jake with a vacant look in his eyes.

"Isaac!" shouted Jake, "I got a car coming to pick you up. Those boys'll be coming back. Hide in the cemetery with me."

Rigid with fear, Isaac looked uncertainly at his grandmother. Then they all heard the truck peel off in the distance with a new chorus of shouting, and Tulla shuddered against her grandson. Isaac turned toward Jake and ran with Tulla into the burial ground. All three flattened themselves on the ground behind a row of bushes.

"Wait here," said Jake. He returned to the small fire and stomped out the flames. Gingerly, he picked up the hot casings and returned them to his bag. Before he left the site, he covered up the ashes as best he could. Minutes later, he returned to Tulla and Isaac. The three of them sat low on the ground in the shadows. They heard the truck driving around the block and the drunken boys whooping a Rebel Yell.

Finally, Jake saw Emma Grace's cousin slowly drive by in Thomas Guthrie's truck. Although they had never met, he remembered him as the trumpet player at the Inlet Inn.

"I'll go out and stop him, and when the coast is clear, you can come out." Tulla looked at him with a terrified face. Bracing himself, Jake sauntered casually out of the cemetery and caught up with Winston's vehicle, and he leaned into the open window.

"You, Jake?" asked the driver. "Marbles told me that Tulla and Isaac were in trouble."

"They're hiding in the cemetery," answered Jake. He lazily spat on the ground just as the truck with the drunks rounded a corner and pulled up next to them.

"Hey, Winston," one of the boys shouted, "did you see any darkies walking by here? They shot at us." His head wobbled as he spoke.

"I think a few headed up to the Colored side of town. But y'all might be outnumbered up there." Winston laughed.

"I'd like to see them try," slurred another occupant.

The truck rushed off while Jake remained rooted, watching them leave. Once they were out of sight, Winston drove off Turner Street and parked next to the cemetery. Jake ran into the graveyard and helped Isaac and Tulla get to the vehicle. After Isaac and his grandmother lay down in the flatbed, Jake covered them with a tarp. Then he climbed in the cab and Winston drove toward Nell's house.

Nell was waiting with Marbles, Tobias, and Pilot on her back porch when Winston drove up. She walked up to the truck once Winston switched off the engine. There was a concerned look in her eyes as they swept over Jake's face. Although he knew she was beside herself with worry, he couldn't help but think, *Well, at least she looked at me.*

"I think it's best you get them into the kitchen as fast as you can," she whispered to Winston as she scanned her neighbor's back yard.

When they entered the house, Jake was distracted by the homey scents of cooking fish, cornbread, and fried salt pork.

"Land's sakes!" exclaimed Mrs. Guthrie when she saw Isaac's bloodied face. "We need to call the law. The sheriff can take care of this."

"With all respect, Miss Alice," answered Isaac, as he helped his trembling grandmother into one of the kitchen chairs. "The law's probably talking to those boys right now. They gonna say we were shooting at them. Police listen to their own. I imagine they're looking for us, not the other way around."

The two boys moved over to Miss Tulla. Tobias put his head on his great granny's lap while Marbles leaned into her. Looking tormented, he scrunched up his face in an effort not to cry.

"Do you think they know who we are?" asked Miss Tulla.

"They might. Maybe they'll try to find Annie." Isaac's stoic mask cracked, and genuine terror crossed his face as he thought of his wife. Jake remembered the light-skinned maid who often visited Isaac at Lowell's Boatyard.

The clock ticked off the seconds as everybody huddled against one another in the crowded kitchen. After a few moments, Winston said, "I could pick up Annie in Mr. Guthrie's truck."

Isaac turned his butchered face toward the white man. "Let me go with you."

"You know you can't do that, Isaac," said Jake. "I saw those boys. You can't be on the street tonight. This is no night for Negro folk to be wandering around."

Isaac's agitation increased as his eyes swept the room in panic.

"Maybe we could call over to Doc Davis's house where Annie works," said Mrs. Guthrie.

"Miss Sylvia have a hissy fit anytime Annie use the telephone," answered Tulla.

Isaac stood up and paced around the room, looking trapped and anguished.

"We can get word to Annie," said Winston. "I could pretend to deliver something to the back door."

"Annie might not believe you, Winston," said Isaac. "She don't know you."

Jake's heart raced as he exchanged a worried look with Nell. He was filled with relief that she didn't seem angry with him.

Silence ensued as they all thought. Tobias wrapped his arms around Tulla's neck and shook with sobs. She pulled him onto her lap and silently rubbed his back.

"What about Emma Grace?" said Nell. "Annie knows her from the clinic and Doc Davis."

Everyone considered this option.

"That might be the best thing to do," said Winston.

"Isaac, can you write her a note?" asked Nell.

Isaac removed the small pouch he wore around his neck and said, "Give this to her."

Mrs. Guthrie had been listening to the discussion, but now she pushed her chair up to the table. She spoke directly to Isaac and his grandmother. "Y'all can't go home tonight. You need to stay here."

"We can leave, Miss Alice," answered Isaac as he sat back down. "I got folks that can hide us."

"No. She right," Miss Tulla answered. "If'n we go home, we bring the wolf to their door."

Mrs. Guthrie's head shook as she cleared her throat. The situation was taking a toll on the frail woman. "I hate to think of you out on a night like this. It would haunt me to my dying day if y'all got hurt."

Winston waited for someone else to speak, but everyone seemed frozen at the table. After several long moments, he turned and left the house. The remaining people didn't move as they listened to Winston crank the truck and back out of the long driveway. Nell's fish stew bubbled on the stove.

Isaac's eye was swollen shut, and he moved gingerly.

"I need to take care of my grandson's face," Tulla finally said, placing her medical bag on the table.

"Of course," said Alice Guthrie. "He's going to need some stitches. Why don't y'all clean up in the washroom."

"How about you, Granny?" said Isaac. "You got knocked down pretty hard."

"I ache some, but I think I can heal it."

Nell noticed how difficult it was for Miss Tulla to get out of her seat and softly asked, "Can I offer you some spirits?"

"Perhaps some of Miss Emma Grace's wine," replied the lady.

After Nell returned to the kitchen with a bottle of homemade wine, she was handing a glass to Miss Tulla when they all heard a vehicle speed down Front Street. Startled by the yelling and hollering from the street, Nell sloshed the wine on the table.

"I don't know what got into those boys." Nell shook her head as she mopped up the spilled wine.

"Too much moonshine, most likely," said Mrs. Guthrie.

"The Knights in White are back. They hate everybody now—even Catholics," Jake said with disdain.

Miss Tulla was rummaging around in her medicine bag, muttering, "Mercy, I think I delivered that Hinton boy. He was driving that truck."

Jake opened the icebox and chipped off several pieces of ice from the large block inside. Wrapping the chunks in a dishtowel, he handed it to Isaac, who placed it on his eye. Although there was still a slight tremor in her hands, Tulla took out a needle and thread from the medical kit.

"Mama, we need to call Daddy," said Nell.

Her mother nodded while exhaling a sigh. "Jake, could you help Nell with my chair?"

133

Nell's face still held some reservations from their last conversation by the henhouse, but she allowed him to take the handles of Mrs. Guthrie's chair. Once they were in the sitting room, Nell dropped her voice and said to Jake. "My daddy will have a fit with all these Negro people in the house."

"Mine probably would, too," answered Jake.

Nell sat down in a straight-backed chair next to the parlor table with the candlestick telephone. Noting her mother's gray, ashen complexion she said, "Mama, you look all done in. Why don't you let me talk to him?"

Her mother closed her eyes and nodded.

Nell's hand trembled as she dialed the four digits of her father's store, then positioned the earpiece. When her father answered, Nell spoke into the receiver, explaining the situation. She ended with, "Mama says these folks need to stay at our house tonight."

Mr. Guthrie roared back over the telephone line and Nell pulled the earpiece away from her head.

"We know it will be hard on Mama," Nell answered. "But this is what she wants."

Jake couldn't make out what Mr. Guthrie said, but he could hear the volume of his anger.

"I know it's dangerous Daddy, but—"

Mrs. Guthrie shook her head and held out her thin, gnarled hand. "Let me talk to him." Nell moved the earpiece to the side of her mother's head and wrapped her fingers around the device. "Thomas," she spoke firmly into the phone receiver, "This is no time to sit on the fence. I'm not sending these folks out into the street to be slaughtered or lynched."

Nell and Jake stared at the withered ninety-pound woman. Her frail body seemed to be wrapped with steel. Her husband interrupted again with an angry blast, but Alice Guthrie held her ground. "I will not. Winston is on his way, and Jake is here, so we'll be fine until you get home. I'll not hear another word of this." She handed the earpiece to Nell and spun her wheelchair around to the kitchen. Nell gently placed the earpiece back on its hook and looked up at Jake, her jaw slack. "I hain't nary a time heard my mama talk to my daddy like that."

Jake put his hand to his mouth to hide a smile.

134

Miss Tulla was finishing the last stitches around Isaac's eye when Jake and Nell returned to the kitchen. "This will be a feast of loaves and fishes," declared Mrs. Guthrie in a breezy tone that fooled no one. "Nell, could you take some of the taters in the pantry out to the outdoor pump, and knock some of the dirt off? Marbles, you go on and help her. We'll need to stretch this meal to feed everyone."

"Yes, ma'am," replied her daughter.

CHAPTER 14

Jake and Nell were peeling and chopping potatoes in the kitchen when Winston returned with Annie. Isaac crossed the room in two steps when his wife burst through the door. Tobias clung to her skirt while Isaac took her in his arms. Although the atmosphere was still tense, everyone seemed to exhale.

"I'm gonna head over to Mama's for supper," said Winston. "Give y'all more room around the table. But I'll plan to stay over here tonight."

"Hold up, Winston," said Jake.

Once they had stepped out on the back porch, Winston looked at him intently. "Before all this happened, I reckon half the town saw me walking down Front Street with Miss Tulla. If I leave to check on my boat, somebody might follow me back here."

"I can see that," agreed Winston.

"And then somebody might go after my boat."

Winston nodded slowly. "I can see that, too. Want me to move it?"

Jake hadn't considered that. "That's an idea, but there's also a wounded dog onboard, and he needs food and caring."

"I'll be glad to help out. Is he friendly?"

"Normally, yes. But Yawg's been through the wringer lately, and he might be protective of my boat."

Winston nodded.

Jake thought for a minute. "He knows Marbles pretty well, and I think Yawg would go with him."

"Reckon I should bring him to shore?"

"I'd 'preciate that."

They laid out a plan for Winston to take Marbles in the *Miss Mary* to retrieve Yawg. Jake opened the back door to see the boy lying across two kitchen chairs with his head in Nell's lap. His eyes were half-closed and Nell was crooning gently to him. "You smell like a rose garden, Miss Nell," he said to her. Jake couldn't help but smile.

"Marbles," Jake said. The little boy opened his eyes and lazily looked at Jake. "I got a business proposition for you."

~

Sometime later, Thomas Guthrie appeared at the back door of his home. His face darkened as he surveyed the crowded kitchen. Opening the door, he stomped through the room to the parlor without uttering a word. Nell followed him, pushing her mother's chair while Annie and Tulla watched the fish stew and cornbread. The scent of bubbling stew filled the kitchen, but Jake could also detect the stench of sweat and fear that reminded him of a battle. Sitting at the table, he could hear snippets of Mr. Guthrie's harsh conversation with his wife and daughter.

"Danger to my family . . ." said Nell's father, his deep voice rumbling through the house. Followed by, "Just a bunch of rebby boys . . . could hurt business at the store . . ."

Although Mrs. Guthrie's tone was softer and weaker, her conviction resonated in her voice. ". . . ox is in a ditch . . . Christian thing to do . . ." Her voice grew louder, ". . . Tulla is part of this family . . . it's not safe . . . he's only a little boy . . ."

A few minutes later, Nell pushed her mother's wheelchair back into the kitchen, and everyone looked up in anticipation. With a forced smile, the lady stated, "We're gonna all have a nice supper, and then y'all can spend the night in the shed for your own privacy."

Tulla and Annie exchanged glances, "If it's all the same to you, Miss Alice," said Annie. "We can eat our supper out in the shed."

"Don't be silly, Annie," Nell's mother answered.

"We can see y'all don't have much table space, Miss Guthrie," said Annie. This wasn't true; Jake could see there was plenty of room around the parlor table. But he sensed that breaking bread with the white family was as awkward for the Jasper family as it was for Mr. Guthrie to find a Negro family in his home. The steamy, cramped quarters began to close in on Jake.

Mrs. Guthrie hesitated. "If that's what you would prefer, but I ask that we say grace together before you go back to the shed."

"Yes, ma'am."

"Jake, could you go fetch Mr. Guthrie for supper? I believe he is out on the front veranda."

Walking around the house, Jake approached the front porch but stopped when he saw Nell's father. Thomas Guthrie was cleaning and oiling a shotgun with a grim, determined look on his face. When he lifted his head to look at Jake, there was a hard, dull stare in his eye. Jake cleared his throat. "Supper's almost ready, sir."

Thomas Guthrie nodded and turned his attention back to his gun.

Everyone gathered in the kitchen and stood around the table, now groaning with cornbread, fish stew, green beans, black-eyed peas, peach preserves, and homemade bread.

Mrs. Guthrie smiled at Tobias and said, "Would you like to say the blessing tonight?"

Terrified, Tobias sought his mother's face. Annie gave him a quiet, reassuring nod. Everyone bowed their heads as Tobias inhaled and began the prayer with a quavering voice. "Dear Lord, thank you tonight for these many blessings and this good food . . ."

After the Jasper family had filled their plates, they paraded out to the shed in the shared garden. The sun had set, and the cover of darkness hid them.

Back inside the house, Jake ate with the Guthrie family in uncomfortable silence. Twice during the meal, the carful of drunken boys drove by the house, whooping and hollering. When Nell began to clear the dishes, Jake spoke to Nell's father. "It wouldn't surprise me, sir, if these boys try to come over here tonight. It's my understanding that they do their best work when it's dark. If it meets with your approval, I'd like to assist you and Winston. If you take the front flank on the porch, sir, me and my dogs will cover the watch from the back." When Mr. Guthrie didn't answer him, he added, "I served in Europe, sir."

Thomas Guthrie chewed the inside of his mouth and glanced over at his daughter. "I don't want you near the house. You stay in the shed."

Jake looked over her father's shoulder and caught Nell's eye. The corners of her mouth curled up at him, but Jake kept his face impassive. "Yessir."

When it was apparent that Mr. Guthrie had no more to say, his wife gently coughed. "Do you reckon you and Nell could take some cobbler out to the Jaspers?"

"Yes, ma'am," answered Nell. "We may as well carry some bedding out, as well."

Loaded with cobbler and blankets, Nell and Jake closed the door to the house behind them and stepped out on the back porch. Jake filled his lungs with the crisp musk of the cool evening. While trapped in the cramped kitchen, he'd begun to smell the acrid stench of the trenches. He glanced at Nell, and they exchanged a bemused look.

"Your daddy protects his own."

"That he does," she replied as they walked toward the garden.

It was the first moment they had been alone since Jake had returned her harbor log. "Nell, I—" Jake started, but Pilot interrupted him by barking. Then the dog turned and ran back toward the house. Nell and Jake followed him and met up with Winston driving up the driveway. Once Marbles set down Yawg, the hound hobbled over to Pilot, and greeted him like a long-lost castaway.

"The *Jamison's* anchored off a creek in the Town Marsh," Winston said to Jake. "You can't see it from town. I'll take you out to it when you're ready to go."

Jake exhaled with relief. "Thanks for all your help, Winston," he said as he grabbed the younger man's shoulder. He stooped down to Marbles. "Your mama's gonna be worried sick about you. It's time to go home."

"But I wanna stay for the fightin'," cried Marbles.

"How 'bout a nickel instead?" Jake held up the shiny silver coin.

Marbles snatched the coin from his hand and took off at a run through the garden toward his house. "See ya, tomorrow, Jake," he shouted over his shoulder.

After the three young people watched the little boy run back to his house, Nell handed Winston a pile of blankets. Together, with the two dogs in tow, they walked toward the shed in the garden. Yawg's bowlegged gait made Jake chuckle. "That dog's been on the boat for days, and now he needs to get his land legs back." He looked over at Nell. "Do you reckon your daddy will ever like me again?"

Nell scoffed. "What makes you think he liked you to begin with?"

"Well, he hired me."

"He thought you'd be cheap."

"Got that wrong. I'm costing him a fortune in worry and aggravation and turning his family upside down."

"And stole our log," Nell said under her breath. Jake glanced at her in the dusky light, but he could see no malice in her face. He felt a great weight lift from his shoulders. As they passed by the chicken coop, the two men waited while Nell scooped feed from the bin and fed her hens.

"You know," said Winston, his words coming slowly. "When you think about it, Mr. Guthrie changed a lot after Harrison died."

All the light went out of Nell's eyes. "It was a double blow for all of us. He lost Harrison, and then it was all we could do to keep my mama alive."

"She seemed to be holding her own tonight," chuckled Jake. "She brought your daddy to Jesus on the phone."

"That's a fact," she smiled along with him.

"Sorry, I missed that," said Winston lightly. "Ya know, it's sad, though. Thomas was right fun when we were growing up. My daddy's away fishing so much, and Thomas would take us out fishing and such."

"I remember that," said Nell. The path under their feet felt soft and spongy from rain. "He's more afraid now. And the drink doesn't help."

Jake remembered the unconscious Thomas in the hardware store the night he broke in.

Nell continued. "He pretends he doesn't drink, but he's not fooling anyone. Sometimes, I see a glimpse of the old Daddy. Like when he lets me leave work to take the *Harmony* out to sail or when I play music he likes."

"Did he ever find out that you played with the band at the inn that night?" asked Winston.

"Oh, Lordy, no. And when I did that, I thought that I'd be married by the time he found out, so I wouldn't have to answer to him."

"The best-laid plans . . ." tsked Winston.

The familiar smells of dust and motor oil greeted Jake when they entered the shed. The small structure was full of the miscellaneous junk that no woman would ever allow in her home: outboard motors in various stages of disassembly, carpentry and gardening tools, and a wide assortment of jars and cans. Amongst the disorganized jumble, he was startled to see a myriad of musical instruments, including a Jew's harp, two pennywhistles, and several harmonicas hanging on one wall amongst the hammers, drills, and screwdrivers. Then he remembered that Nell often played with Winston and Harrison. He figured they must have practiced in this shed.

As Nell, Miss Tulla, and Annie began to lay blankets and bedding over crates and benches, Winston advanced to the far side of the room. Lifting the curtain draped from the workbench, he pulled out a wooden crate containing corked wine bottles. When Jake knelt down to help Winston pick up the box, he was greeted with the scent of fruity fermentation drifting from an array of large earthenware crocks under the bench.

"Is this where you make your wine?"

"Emma Grace makes it. She's a genius at it." Jake could hear the pride in Winston's voice when he spoke of his cousin. "She uses strawberries, dandelion, blackberries, apples, and whatever else grows in a year. Sometimes grapes."

Placing the crate on the workbench surface, Jake noticed several smaller bottles on the far side of the bench. "What's in these?"

"She moved on to bitters," explained Winston. "She collects bark, roots, herbs, seeds, and plants that have strong smells. She uses spices like nutmeg, oranges, and cinnamon when she can get them. Lots of people just throw everything together, but Emma Grace steeps them out separately and then mixes them at the right moment. They put a zing in a Bacardi. I'll grant you that."

"I use a lot of her tinctures in my healing," added Miss Tulla, as she fluffed out her bedding. "She know her herbs."

Jake's eyes drifted over to a set of beakers and burners stacked on the end of the bench. "I'm afraid to ask what she uses those for."

Nell drifted over to the two men. "Scent distillates," she answered simply, as though every household owned them. "She reads everything she can on Coco Chanel's perfumes. She started distilling her own flower scents like lavender, jessamine, and wildflowers when she was in school. But her first good scent was the rose extract that I always wear." Jake looked at her in surprise, and she laughed at his reaction. "You thought I smelled liked roses all on my own?"

"Well," said Jake, "that's what Marbles told me."

Winston pulled several full wine bottles from the crate and set them on the workbench. "My cousin loves science. Can't remember a time she wasn't experimenting, and before that, she was always studying bugs."

Nell nodded. "One more reason for girls at school to hate her."

Winston handed Jake two bottles. "Why don't you open these tonight? They'll help you get some sleep."

Annie pulled up a crate for the cobbler, and everyone sat around it to eat up the sweet dessert.

Jake noticed Isaac studying the wall of instruments. "You play?"

"A little."

When they were ready to settle for the night, Nell packed up the dishes in her basket. Jake selected a Jew's harp from the wall while Isaac picked out a harmonica. Then they went outside with Winston and Nell.

"I told Mr. Guthrie that Isaac and I would sit sentinel with the dogs outside," said Jake. While Jake and Isaac were setting up two chairs outside the shed, Winston walked up to Nell's house, where he would share shifts with Nell's daddy.

"I reckon I'll see y'all in the morning," she said, surveying Isaac and Jake. She gave a quick look at her house before she said softly. "I'll plan to come down here before Daddy wakes up tomorrow. That way, you can leave without seeing him."

Isaac chuckled. "'preciate that."

"Nell, let me help you carry those," said Jake as he took the basket of dirty dishes from her. They turned away from Isaac and the shed. Her rose scent enveloped Jake, but this time he thought of Emma Grace's distillate apparatus. Although the cobbler and wine eased his tension, the guilt of stealing her harbor log rose in him.

"Nell, look, I'm sorry, I—"

She cut him off. "Let's never talk about it again. Bigger things to worry about."

And just like that, it was over. As they walked, he stole a glance at her face and noticed faded freckles dotted over her nose.

Nell glanced at him. "Don't you even think about kissing me, Jake Parson. My daddy hain't but about ten feet away with a loaded shotgun."

"Yes, ma'am." Jake peered around in the dark.

142

They stopped when they reached her porch, and handed the basket to her. He watched her walk back toward the house. She looked back and smiled at him, making him feel settled for the night. Despite the harrowing evening, he felt at peace.

When he returned to the shed, Miss Tulla was examining Yawg's paw. The dog watched her with reverence. "Well, hain't he been mommicked," she muttered.

"Yes, ma'am," replied Jake. "I never saw anything like it."

Miss Tulla turned Yawg's paw over. "I'll get an ointment to you when all this mess is over."

She bid them goodnight and entered the shed while Jake settled into his chair across from Isaac. "Thomas Guthrie put me out in the shed to keep me away from his daughter. "

Isaac looked up at the Guthrie home. "Reckon I can't blame him for that."

Jake chuckled. "No, I reckon not." While he scratched Yawg's head, he reached down for one of the wine bottles next to him and began to work out the cork. He thought back to all the barracks and trenches that he'd shared while in the war. "I've never had a Colored man for a bunkmate," he said absently, working the cork with his penknife.

Isaac looked up. "I never had any man for a bunkmate."

They both laughed. Jake leaned back in his chair and looked up at the stars. For a moment, he felt transported to these beacons of light that had guided him so often on the water. As the wine settled them, the strain of the day slipped away from him. His mind wandered back to the day he'd taken the ride out to the lumber yard when Isaac hadn't said more than a few words to him.

Now, he sat with a blanket on his knees, looking relaxed and unguarded. He longed to ask Isaac about Wade, but he knew this wasn't the right time.

After their first glass of wine, Isaac pulled out the harmonica and began a smoky rendition of "When the Saints Are Marching In," which quickly became comical when Jake added percussion on the Jew's harp.

∽

It was still dark the following morning when Nell carried biscuits and a pot of coffee down to the shed. Isaac and Jake were slumped asleep in their chairs, and Nell gently kicked Jake's chair to wake him up.

"Can you get the door?" She asked softly, indicating the tray in her hands.

Once inside, she gently set the tray on the crate. Scratching his head, Isaac followed them as his family slowly started to wake up.

"I'll be back for the dishes later. I think Winston will drive you home."

As she turned to leave, Isaac cleared his throat and addressed her in a formal voice. "Your family showed mercy to us last night, Miss Guthrie." He paused. "Annie and I would like to repay the kindness by extending an offer of supper to you later this week."

Nell straightened up. "I would be glad to accept your invitation. Please let me know when it will be convenient." Jake noted that she made no mention of her parents.

"Yes, ma'am." The large man inclined his head before sitting down to join his family.

CHAPTER 15

Over the next week, everyone took precautions, and to their great relief, the truck of angry drunks didn't re-surface. As the trauma of that night began to fade, Nell learned there was more heartache in store for her. Venturing downtown to shop for staples, she approached a cluster of girls gathered on the sidewalk. Just as she was ready to greet them, they all turned in unison and walked away. News of her broken engagement had spread through town, and Nell was feeling the sting of Mrs. Davis's invisible hand.

Feeling brittle and raw, Nell retreated from town as hot tears spilled down her cheeks. When she entered her home, her mother patted her hand. "I loved Asa for so long," Nell sniffled recalling her dreams of being Asa's wife, studying music in Richmond, and helping his business grow. But those hopes unraveled with his bootlegging lies and liaisons with Luanne. Now, she saw that he never worried himself about her music. Maybe the idea of being his wife had always been a fairy tale for her.

While Nell cried, her mother gently stroked her hair. "Our best bet is to have this blow over soon enough. Then Sylvia can move on to be unhappy about something else."

When business started to fall off at her father's store, Nell stayed home, took care of her mother, and practiced her music. Dreading her Wednesday night Bible study, Nell begged her mother to stay home.

"You back down, they win," her mother replied. "This is when you hold your head high. You can't let Sylvia run your life." In a show of support, Emma Grace decided to join her.

"You realize this is a testament to our friendship that I'm going to this hen party," Emma Grace groused as they walked to the church.

"Yes, you mentioned that a few times," Nell replied, watching her friend's ire rise. "Please don't mess with them."

But it was worse than either of the girls could imagine. After they returned home, Nell teared up while recounting the evening. "Oh, Mama. It was just common. They acted like I wasn't there. And then when they did talk to me, they were so nicey-nice." She shuddered at the patronizing way the leader had addressed her.

"Steady girl," said Emma Grace, wrapping her arm around her friend. "Once they know they've scratched your skin, they'll smell blood and go in for the kill." She turned to Mrs. Guthrie. "It was the worst. Nell would offer an answer to the scripture reading, and that hag Karen Russell would say 'isn't that nice' as if butter wouldn't melt in her mouth."

"What was the lesson on?" Nell's mother inquired.

Emma Grace let out a bark of a laugh. "Forgiveness."

Alice laughed while she shook her head in disgust. "I think you'll feel better after the Oyster Shuckers' visit tomorrow—that was the earliest I could get them together."

$$\backsim$$

The following afternoon, Alice Guthrie convened the faithful group of friends who dated back to their work at the mollusk cannery before husbands and family complicated their lives.

Emma Grace arrived first with her Mama Beatrice, a plump woman tending infant Edward, the newest addition to the Willis family. She was a no-nonsense woman who didn't take guff from any of her seven children. Since her husband, Donnie, was away fishing most of the time, she ran her household with love and punctuality.

Tisdale sailed from Harkers Island and left a bag of clams by the back door before entering the home. Tisdale's married name was Delight Jones, but she earned her nickname in high school when she was never without one of her romantic Tisdale novels. The odd woman often walked around town with her pet goat, Eloise, wore mismatched clothes, and was always in a dither. Today, she arrived in a checkered skirt with several layers of sweaters. Although she had lived in Beaufort during high school, her family was from Harkers Island. After she married a man from the island, she moved back. Speaking in the Harkers Island brogue, derived from the Scottish dialect, she declared, "Honey, there was some wind out there tonight, son."

Once everyone had settled, Nell served iced tea and applesauce muffins, and Emma Grace's sweet rice pudding. Mrs. Willis and Emma Grace took turns tending to Edward, while Tisdale unpacked her knitting. Everyone shook their heads and clucked in disgust as Nell and Emma Grace unrolled the week for them.

"You would think these Christians could find a better use of their time," said Mrs. Willis.

"The trouble with Sylvia Davis is that she doesn't know how to fry her chicken!" spat Tisdale.

"Honey, don't I know it," replied Alice.

Mrs. Willis noticed Nell's confusion and explained. "Tisdale means there hain't nary a time she wouldn't put herself in front of everybody else."

"Sylvia always thought she was too good for this town," added Alice.

"She's got those damn—darn cotillion lessons and people just eat it up," said Tisdale.

Speaking in a snobby, falsetto voice, Mrs. Willis added, "I'm from Richmond, where everything is perfect."

Nell giggled, thinking of the woman she'd admired for so long.

"This reminds me of when we were in school, and she got everybody to be so mean to Mathilda Lewis after her mama ran off with that railroad man," said Alice.

The other two ladies nodded in agreement.

"Anybody would have left her daddy. He were as mean as a skunk," said Tisdale.

The women tried to think of ways to make this passage easier for Nell. Initially, they considered avenues of retaliation.

"I could get the boys to deliver salt instead of sugar to her house," suggested Mrs. Willis.

"It would only bring us down to her level," answered Alice.

Emma Grace studied her aunt for a moment. "Well, we could get Winston to go around—"

"You keep Winston out of this!" Mama Beatrice said in a loud voice. "Lord have mercy, that boy is too ornery for his own good. Just keep him out of this."

As the afternoon came to a close, the women leaned into Nell before getting up to leave.

"Now, listen, Nell," Mrs. Willis said. "The only thing we can offer you is our support. If you're feeling lonely out there, get word to one of us, and we'll come down and help you."

"That's right, honey," added Tisdale. "You hain't alone in this. Asa got what he deserved, and you're better off without him. That old witch of a mother is doing his dirty work."

Mama Beatrice nodded. "Nell, what you need to remember is that men get justice in the courtroom, and women get justice in the bedroom and the parlor."

"That's a fact," agreed Tisdale.

Nell almost knew what they meant.

After the women had gone home, Alice Guthrie stayed in the kitchen as Nell prepared supper. "These friendships are more precious than rubies."

Nell nodded as she scrubbed the mud off the clams that Tisdale had left them. "Emma Grace and I are going to Horse Island with Winston later this week."

"Now, you know that'll be fun."

On Friday, Thomas Guthrie traveled to New Bern to pick up motor parts, so it became imperative that Nell work at his hardware store. The day dawned gray with a heavy overcast that stretched from horizon to horizon. As she walked down the driveway with Emma Grace, her friend commented on the seamless sky. "I think most of this cloud cover will burn off. Don't ya reckon?"

Nell sighed, dreading the day ahead at the store. She followed Emma Grace's gaze toward the sunrise but didn't answer. Fragile rays of pink and orange were fighting the gloomy mantle. Emma Grace squeezed her friend's hand, and they turned to walk toward town.

Once they arrived at the hardware business, Emma Grace hugged her friend goodbye. Waiting for Nell at the door was a shipment of galvanized tin buckets. She decided to arrange them in a pyramidal display in front of the store.

By mid-morning, Nell was sorting through a tray of bolts, nuts, and screws when Buddy Taylor bobbed into the store with his bouncy gait.

"Well, hey there, Buddy," said Nell with some surprise.

"Hain't you a sight for sore eyes," the man said, taking in her appearance from stem to stern.

"Thanks, Buddy. I could use some sweet talk right about now."

"I heard about you and Asa. I wish I could say I'm sorry."

Nell laughed softly. "You never give up, do ya?"

"Not a chance, sugar." He looked around the store as if he were searching for something. "Have you got your bodyguard with you today?"

"Bodyguard?"

"The big hunky guy. Likes to *load your lumber.*"

"Oh, you mean Jake Waterson? No, he doesn't follow me around town. Why? Do I need a bodyguard?"

"Dressed like that, you do."

She looked down at her simple dress and then back into his face to catch his mischievous grin. She broke into a heartfelt laugh. "You're terrible, Buddy. Just shameful." She was still laughing as she turned around to shelve some nails behind the counter. "No, Daddy just hired him to build the ramp for my mama's wheelchair." She glanced at him and saw a skeptical look on his face.

"I thought your daddy only hired *local* people."

"He'd seen Jake make a skiff in about a half-hour. I reckon he figured since he worked so quick, it would be cheap to have him build a ramp," said Nell.

"So, he's good with wood?"

"I think he said his daddy has a boatyard in South Carolina." Nell noticed a cloud pass over Buddy's face. "Does that worry you?"

"Oh," said Buddy casually. "No, I just don't want local people to miss out on any work."

Something in Buddy's tone didn't ring true, but just as Nell started to question him further, the phone rang. "Guthrie Hardware," she answered. The line went dead.

"Cowards," Buddy sneered.

Nell looked down at the jumble of mixed hardware on the counter so Buddy couldn't see her hurt expression. "I 'preciate you stopping by," she said without looking up. "I know you do a lot of business with Mrs. Davis's friends."

"I have other customers," Buddy answered curtly. "I don't appreciate people who bully my friends. I tend to push back at that type of thing."

Hearing an edge in Buddy's voice, Nell looked up in surprise. She studied this light-hearted man who was the master of the double entendre and practical jokes, but she could also recall his bursts of anger on the playground when they were growing up. "Well, who knew you carried around a bottle of vinegar in your pocket, Buddy Taylor."

"Oh, darlin'," he replied with a weary exhale, "you don't know the half of it."

Nell imagined that being the odd man out in his family weighed heavily on him. She smiled. "I did want to tell you that I enjoyed seeing your Sugar Shack collection the other day."

The gloom lifted as quickly as it had settled, and Buddy's face broke out into a wide grin. "Who knew I had such good taste."

"What does your mama think of it?"

"Oh, good Lord! I've never shown it to her. She would take one look around that shed and call it the devil's nursery. For all she knows, it's just an old shed on the lumber yard property."

"Have you ever thought about opening up your own furniture store?"

"Whew, that would mean working regular hours and rubbing elbows with townsfolk. I'm not the most diplomatic of people."

"Maybe you need a partner to help you with all that." She walked across the store to the wall bins and began to return the sorted hardware to the appropriate containers.

Buddy meandered behind her, lingering along the way to examine vices, chains and spools of rope. "I can't think of a soul I could work with."

Nell thought for a moment, then turned back to face him. "What about that friend of yours from Richmond that I ran into at Asa's house? He looks like he comes from money, and he would 'preciate decorating."

"Who was that?"

"Mr. Ramsey. Edgar Ramsey. He's a distant cousin to Mrs. Davis."

"Oh, him," Buddy groaned as he ran his finger along the side of a barrel standing in the aisle. "We've traded from time to time. Kinda persnickety. I can't say I know him all that well."

"Huh," Nell furrowed her brow for a minute. "I got the feeling he knew you better than that."

"Not really," replied Buddy.

They both returned to the counter, where Nell pulled out the harbor log to write entries. Buddy dumped a new container of hardware bits onto the tray and began to quickly sort the remaining hooks, nuts, and bolts. Buddy always worked quickly, and soon the small pieces were dancing around the counter. "Although, I wouldn't put it past Ramsey to give that impression; he's always working some angle."

Nell laughed as she watched Buddy's manic fingers speed through the sort. "I can certainly imagine that about him. My Lord, but he brought some excellent wine with him the last time I had supper at Asa's house."

"Did he?" Buddy stopped the sort with his hand in mid-air and looked up at her, his eyes round. "You don't remember what it was called?"

"I think he called it The Black Horse, or however you say that in French."

Buddy studied her for a moment. "I don't believe I've heard of that."

"The label had a running horse and all. Goodness, that was good wine."

"I don't recall it, but I'll certainly ask him the next time I see him."

"It's a sad day indeed," Nell sighed, "when the most you can say about your ex-fiancé is that you'll miss his wine." She paused to write several entries in the log. "Listen, Buddy, a bunch of us are going to gig for flounder and are having a clam bake on Horse Island tomorrow night. Think you might want to come?"

"Woo, I hain't been floundering since forever. Who's coming?"

"Midgett and Winston, not sure about Emma Grace because—" As she spoke, Nell saw Asa walk past the store, look at Nell, and scowl. When Buddy noticed the smile slip from her face, he pivoted to follow her gaze out the front display windows. "Daddy said he walked by about every hour this week." She shivered as if a cold wind had passed over her.

"Well, at least he's not coming into the store."

Nell made a skeptical face. "Not yet, anyway. Now that he's seen that I'm working today, I'm sure he'll be back."

151

Buddy looked toward the front window. "Nell, I just remembered that I needed one of those new buckets out on the sidewalk."

She looked over at the spring arrangement. "Do you like my display?"

"I do," he replied enthusiastically. "You have a real eye."

With some apprehension, she followed Buddy to the sidewalk, worried that Asa was still in close proximity. When she reached for one of the tin pails in the stacked pyramid, Asa turned around and started walking back toward her. His pace quickened as his face contorted with rage. Nell froze, suspended, still holding the bucket in her hand as she locked eyes with Asa. Vaguely aware of Buddy's shoulder pressing against hers, she let out a cry of surprise when Buddy slipped his arm around her waist.

Asa closed the distance between them. "Well, you didn't waste any time," Asa spat at Nell. Her eyes darted from the silly expression on Buddy's face to Asa's bitter rage.

Buddy's bemusement seemed to anger Asa more deeply. "I'd watch my step if I were you," he said to the short man, jabbing Buddy in the chest with his finger. "You never know what's going to float in on the tide."

"I just came in for some line and nails, Asa," Buddy replied as his mouth twisted, trying to suppress his mirth. "We haven't had time to hop in the sack."

Nell screamed as Asa uncoiled and knocked Buddy to the ground. They rolled on the sidewalk before Asa straddled Buddy's torso and began to punch him unmercifully. Nell's cries brought people running toward the brawl, and several men pulled Asa off Buddy. Searching Asa's face, Nell tried to find the man she'd loved for so long, but he squinted back at her in disgust. The last good memories of Asa evaporated, and she felt like she was looking at a stranger. While a crowd gathered around them, Nell knelt to help Buddy into the hardware store. Although he cupped both hands around his nose, blood gushed between his fingers. "Dang, when y'all break up, y'all really break up. I have never seen Asa that mad before!" He snuffled through the blood.

"Did you have to provoke him like that?"

"Nobody ever said I was smart," Buddy said, wincing against his pain.

CHAPTER 16

The following evening, Emma Grace, Nell, and Winston loaded Nell's *Harmony* with gear and food for their clam bake at Horse Island. Scanning the horizon, Nell noted all the boats in the harbor, knowing that Asa or his friends might be watching them and could follow them across the sound.

"Buddy and Midgett went on ahead of us, so they should already be there," she said to Emma Grace.

"I invited a few friends, too," replied her friend.

Nell nodded in a distracted way as her eyes continued to sweep the water.

Winston cast them off, and the boat glided away from shore.

Sailing with sunlight during the day clarified and delineated the seascape, but sailing by points of light at night was fun and mysterious for Nell. As the *Harmony* skimmed through the harbor, she felt the thickening darkness obscuring other parts of her life. With only the stars, moonlight, and a few points of light onshore for guidance, the boat moved away from the busy details of the town. Propelled by a gentle sea breeze, the *Harmony* made small ripples behind her. The notes of a waltz floated out to them as they passed the Inlet Inn, but once they glided past the town and entered the channel, Nell heard only the music of the lapping water, spring peepers, and occasional cry of the night heron. She looked back at the receding town one last time as they rounded the end of Carrot Island. When she couldn't see any boats following them, her heavy mantle of anxiety slipped away, and they sailed into the night.

They soon spied Midgett's cookfire looming on the horizon as the brightest point in the sound. As the skiff drew closer to the beach, Emma Grace jerked up the centerboard, while Winston adjusted the sail to slow the boat.

When the boat stalled, Coast Guard Commander Elijah Midgett waded out to pull them onto the shore. "Nell, darlin'!" he exclaimed when he caught sight of her at the helm, "I wasn't sure you were coming."

Nell hopped out of the boat and allowed the massive comfort of Midgett's arms and body to swallow her in a hug. The chilly water and soft sand felt divinely familiar to her feet.

"You feel as good as a sack of oysters," said Midgett.

She chuckled. "No one's told me that in a long time."

"So, where's your other half?" Midgett asked, glancing around the boat.

Winston and Emma Grace halted their unloading to stare at Midgett.

"You must be the only person in Carteret County who doesn't know Asa and I broke up on Sunday," Nell answered.

Midgett studied her for a minute, before he roared, "I'll arrest that boy for stupidity one day."

She smiled at him.

"Well, spit me out and call me tobacco juice," said Buddy. "Here I go defending your honor, and take a punch from your ex, but this brute of a man gets all your hugging and loving."

"'Defending my honor'?" Nell repeated with incredulity as she pulled away from Midgett. "More like poking a rabid bear."

"Po-tah-to, po-ta-to," replied Buddy.

"How's your nose doing?" she asked, as she gingerly bussed him on his cheek. She held up her lantern to examine the bandage and bruising on his face.

"It's seen worse."

Nell reached into the boat and pulled out a canvas bag full of liquor and wine bottles.

"So, hero of the surf," Winston said to Midgett, "think you could help me unload this here boat?"

"My work is never done," sighed Midgett as he waded to the skiff and pulled out a sack of clams and a flounder gig.

154

"Fame brings out the surliness in a man, don't you think, Emma Grace?" Nell said.

"That's a fact."

"Oh, by the way, Midgett," Winston said, "we ran out of Bacardi. We only got 'shine left."

Midgett dropped the sack of clams into the water, creating a loud splash. "I came all this way for moonshine?"

"Don't listen to him," said Nell. "He's messin' with you. He got a whole sack of rum for you boys off the *Polaris* a few weeks ago."

"You reckon you'll have to arrest us for drinking?" Emma Grace asked Midgett.

Midgett laughed as he reached into the water to retrieve the clams. "I doubt it, considering I'm planning on drinking all of Winston's rum just for aggravating me."

"Midgett only enforces the good laws," Winston explained. "Not the stupid ones written by people who would feel better if they had a drink in their hand."

"Can't you get in trouble for that?" asked Buddy.

"Can't we all?" replied Midgett.

"'Lips that touch wine will never touch mine,'" Nell quoted the temperance slogan as she batted her eyes at the Coast Guardsman. "But in truth, Emma Grace and I stick with wine. Keeps the Methodist in us." She rummaged in the canvas bag and pulled out several bottles filled with their homemade wine. "Besides, you boys might take advantage of us."

"This way, we can get you drunk on Bacardi, and we'll have our way with you," Emma Grace said to Midgett.

The burly man set the heavy sack of clams next to the campfire. "Oh, mercy," said Midgett as he clutched his heart. "Let me die and go to heaven."

Emma Grace and Nell giggled.

"Is that the real reason why ya don't drink the hard stuff?" asked Buddy.

"Nah," answered Nell. "Emma Grace works at the clinic, and she sees what homemade liquor does to people."

"You never know where that bottle of rum has been," Emma Grace said, pointing to Winston's booze bag. "Sometimes it's mixed with moonshine that's been run through car radiators, or people mix it with wood alcohol. Either way, it can poison you."

Buddy looked suspiciously at the bottle that Winston had just handed him. "I'm beginning to see the light."

"I get patients who have liver failure, or go blind," continued Emma Grace.

Buddy stared at the bottle before popping the cork. "Here's to sobriety," he said, taking a long pull. "We're all gonna die of something."

Emma Grace exchanged a glance with Nell. "Boys will be boys."

The young women began to set up their clams near the embers to bake. "Don't y'all have some floundering or something to do before we can eat?" asked Nell.

"Come on, Buddy," said Winston. "We can see when we are not needed. Or wanted." The two of them turned toward the sandy dunes covered with low brush, carrying flounder gigs and swinging two lanterns.

Emma Grace took a drink from the wine bottle and passed it to Nell, while Midgett dragged a massive log to the fire for their seating. Emma Grace scanned the water now dappled with reflected moonlight. She let out a gasp of surprise. "Looks like he came after all," she said with satisfaction.

Nell followed her gaze, squinting into the dark to make out a faint silhouette of a sailboat gliding toward them.

"Who else did you invite?" asked Nell.

Emma Grace reached into her bag, pulled out a set of binoculars and handed them to her friend. "I thought it might be a nice surprise."

As the vessel neared, the firelight revealed the sails on the silent boat. On the bow, Nell could see a hound and a black Lab wagging their tails. She turned to her friend. "You little vixen."

Emma Grace smiled.

Nell re-trained her binoculars to study Jake on the helm and thought of the night he showed compassion for the Jaspers and stayed in her shed. Feeling lightheaded, she sucked in her breath while a warm sensation pulsed through her body. She squeezed Emma Grace's hand.

A few minutes later, Jake beached the *Miss Mary*.

"He'll need some help off-loading his skiff," Emma Grace said, nudging Nell.

She glanced at Emma Grace and then she waded over to the boat.

"Fancy meeting you so far from shore," she said to Jake when she reached the stern.

156

Jake looked up from the boat's well and met her eyes. He hopped overboard to stand in the water with her.

"Yeah," he said, grinning down at her, "Imagine that." His hand reached out to caress her face. Then he cupped his hands on either side of her head before leaning into a tender kiss. The island fell away for Nell when Jake pressed against her, triggering a surge of desire. His hands moved down to the small of her back, and she trembled. After the kiss ended and she pulled away, she saw that Pilot and Yawg were watching them with great interest while vigorously wagging their tails. Their enthusiasm made Nell giggle into Jake's shoulder. "Looks like we have a peanut gallery." Jake turned to the dogs, and he laughed along with her.

"Everything okay out there?" Emma Grace asked from shore.

"Everything's . . . just right," Nell answered.

Jake smiled at her. Reluctantly, he turned to the boat and commanded, "Pilot, off ship." The big dog sailed over the gunnel and landed with a glorious splash. Jake scooped up the hound and placed him in Nell's arms. The dog gave her a kiss, and when she released him on the sandy beach, he began to wag his way toward Emma Grace and Midgett sitting by the fire. Nell picked up the bowline of the *Miss Mary* and pulled the boat onto the beach.

Then without warning, Yawg dropped his nose to the ground, and the fur on his back bristled. Despite his paw injury, he frantically tracked a scent by circling the campfire in a frenzy. Everyone stared at him as he became increasingly agitated. Finally, he threw back his head to release an ear-splitting, anguished bay.

"Yawg!" reprimanded Jake. "Hush, now."

But the dog ignored him as his distress increased, and he followed the scent toward the brush. Midgett was closest to Yawg and grabbed him just before he disappeared into the thicket. But the hound wouldn't quiet and struggled to free himself from the man's grip.

"That dog loves his rabbit," sighed Jake. But his brow furrowed. "He's usually so easygoing." He walked up to take hold of the hound, who continued to strain against Midgett's grip. Pilot ran up to comfort Yawg by sniffing his face, but Yawg's attention never wavered from the shrubbery behind them.

"Do you think there might be something out there?" asked Emma Grace.

"Nah," said Jake with conviction. "If there was something in there, then Pilot would be having a fit. I've seen Yawg do this before, and it doesn't help that he's been cooped up on the boat for days. He wants to run. But I can't have him going off with his leg still boogered up." Stooping down, he wrenched the dog from Midgett. "Nell, could you grab some line from my boat, and I'll tie him up 'til he settles down." Yawg whined as Jake dragged him back toward the campfire. After Jake tied the hound to the large log they were using as a bench, Yawg quieted but maintained his focus on the interior of the island.

Jake waited until Nell sat down on the log before placing himself next to her and pressing his leg against her thigh. She smiled as a secret intimacy passed between them. "I think you met Midgett at the inn." She looked around behind her. "And you met Buddy at the lumber yard the other day, but it looks like he ran off with Winston." She searched the island for their bobbing lanterns.

"They said something about flounder and firewood," said Midgett. "I reckon we won't see them for a while. They were carrying two rum bottles, so we'll be lucky if we see them before morning."

As they sat around the warmth of the fire, Nell stroked Yawg and spoke softly to him. But the dog ignored her and kept his back to the group while he watched the brush with earnest intensity. Emma Grace noticed the clams were opened and ready to eat. She used tongs to scoop them out of the fire before setting them on a board. When they had cooled, she passed them around to her friends.

"It's the hound in him," commented Jake drily, popping a mollusk into his mouth. "They're stubborn, and they can't let go of a scent."

"Sounds like most men, I know," said Emma Grace, digging an elbow into Midgett.

The big man smiled down at her.

"Lots of hard-working boats on the water tonight," said Nell, scanning the horizon.

"I noticed that," said Midgett, turning his gaze to the sound.

"Reckon you'll have to go chase them down?"

"Hardly. But Lord, they got me running ragged," replied Midgett. "I wish they would repeal all this mess. It's gonna get worse before it gets better, and it's taking money away from buying new rescue equipment."

158

"Are you involved in a lot of rescues?" asked Jake.

"I reckon."

"I bet you got a whole mess of stories to tell," Nell said as she leaned in toward Midgett with interest. Yawg lay down in the sand with his nose toward the shrubbery. "I heard that the *Amelia* was lost, but there was no wreckage." She felt Jake's body stiffen next to her. Knowing how vital his secret was to him, she made a point of looking away from him when she spoke.

"Yeah, that came through about three weeks ago. That call went out from here to Rhode Island, where he was headed, and I think it went on to Boston— just in case he got caught in a storm and was blown off course. Since Beaufort was the last known port, we went up and down the coast and searched from the water, but that boy's been gone a long time.

"When did he sail from the harbor?"

"The family wasn't sure of the date—they were going by letters he'd sent them. So, we asked around the docks, but nobody seemed to know much about the boat. Or they thought Parson had left a few weeks before the family thinks he sailed."

"I remember that boat," said Emma Grace. "I made a watercolor of her when she docked. My, she had nice lines."

"She was hard to miss on the water because she is so unique," said Nell.

Midgett continued. "I went back and checked our log when the call came through, and I sent them everything I had. Then when I went around town, a couple of folks remembered that the captain took her out for a day sail a few days before she left port."

Nell felt Jake's body tense, and he leaned in toward Midgett. "What day was that?" asked Nell.

Midgett thought for a minute. "That was around the beginning of April. I remember it was about four or five days before she sailed out of port for good."

"Did they say who was on the boat during the day sail?" Nell could hear that Jake's breathing was becoming rougher and more ragged. His forehead was shiny with sweat.

"The witnesses could see the captain and somebody else, but they couldn't make out the other person."

"Does anyone remember them coming back to the harbor?"

Midgett shook his head. "Not really. When I got all these details, I mentioned them to Commander Brainerd. But he gave orders to stop pursuing it any further."

"Why?" Jake demanded. Nell placed her hand on top of his and squeezed. He looked down and then gripped it as if it were a lifeline.

"I don't rightly know." Midgett sighed and took a pull from the Bacardi bottle. "I think partly because it was a rumor; no one was real sure about it. But with all this whiskey traffic, things aren't as straightforward as they used to be. Booze is beginning to bring in some real crooks—it's not local boys in skiffs anymore. It's already started in New York and Chicago. Landlubbers want more control of ports, and there were so many things that didn't add up in that case. Like, no one saw him return from the day sail the week before the family says he left port for good. There were rumors that he might be smuggling. I think Brainerd wanted it to be someone else's problem. He may have been worried about his statistics and success. If a lot of boats get lost outta Beaufort, then they might replace him. Or they may not entrust him with better equipment or faster boats. Everything's about politics these days."

The group stared transfixed at Midgett as the firelight danced across his face. Nell glanced at the hound next to her and remembered it was Wade's dog. For weeks, the missing *Amelia* felt distant and remote, but now it felt close and urgent. "Do you think it's possible she wasn't lost at sea?"

Midgett shrugged. "Anything's possible." He looked up at Nell. "I was thinking about that after I talked to Commander Brainerd. We're seeing more boats re-surfacing under other names. So many vessels are getting re-registered with ownership in other countries. If we catch a smuggler using a foreign boat, then we can't impound it like we can an American boat. Maybe the captain of the *Amelia* staged its disappearance so he could re-register it."

Nell exchanged glances with Jake. Judging by his stunned expression, she saw that he had never considered this. Still, it seemed unlikely that Wade would not have written his parents.

"That boat was so distinctive, you couldn't really disguise it," said Nell. She could feel a tremor run through Jake's body. Feeling both excited and dismayed, she thought of more possibilities for the *Amelia's* disappearance.

"They would probably have to alter it some," replied Midgett, as he scratched his chin.

"It's also possible that it was hijacked and someone else registered it under a foreign flag," Jake said. "I mean, it wouldn't have to be the captain."

"That too," Midgett conceded. "But I always thought—"

Midgett never finished his thought because, at that moment, Yawg jumped to his feet and began to bark frantically. This time, Pilot joined him with raised hackles and a low growl. A moment later, shouting erupted from the island's interior. Everyone rose to look in the direction of the noise. Nell could see two lanterns bouncing through the darkness just as a volley of angry retorts drifted to her on the wind. Standing on tiptoe, Nell was peeking over a dune when a single shot cracked through the air. Before she could think, Jake pulled her down into the sand. Terror gripped her as she remembered Asa's intense rage the day before. Could he have followed her to kill her?

Despite the panic of the moment, Jake spoke with deliberate calmness. "Get down, take cover." Turning to his dogs, he commanded, "Hush boys." They immediately silenced. Nell untied Yawg and scrambled with Emma Grace and Midgett to the dune. Jake brought up the rear, crouched over in a run.

Once everyone was together, Nell glanced at Jake and saw a focused but distant look on his face. She remembered seeing this stare in other veterans. Her eyes widened when he reached into his bag and pulled out a pistol. "I started carrying this with me after I got knocked out behind the inn."

Running footsteps advanced through the undergrowth before them. Light from the dancing campfire silhouetted several figures running past at full speed through the brush. Nell's heart began to pound as Yawg whined but didn't bark. Nell recognized the cries of Winston and Buddy. In all likelihood, they surprised someone recovering hidden liquor.

"Stay back," Midgett directed to the two young women. When Emma Grace opened her mouth to protest, he added, "Please. You're not armed." He looked at Jake. "Will you stay with the women?"

Jake nodded.

Midgett ran after the figures.

Jake hunkered down into the dune grass in front of Emma Grace and Nell. While sweat poured off his body, he maintained a distant, icy concentration.

Several long moments passed before Nell heard a boat engine start from Midgett's direction. Then a second engine roared to life. She followed the sound of the motors as they traveled away and grew distant.

After a few moments, Winston shouted his presence as he walked up. After he caught up with them, he bent over to catch his breath. "Midgett and Buddy took off in Buddy's boat," he panted. "Buddy's got a lot of horsepower."

"What happened?" asked Emma Grace.

"We were floundering, and we heard some noises behind us. Buddy thought we should separate so we could flush them out. Buddy wasn't gone more than a few minutes when the bastards fired. I heard the bullet fly right over my head. Then they ran past me and I recognized Chadwick and a couple of his friends. Buddy was right behind them, so I took off after all of them."

"We'd best leave," said Emma Grace. "We may have made someone mad out here."

"If Chadwick was here, then it's most likely Asa's crew," said Nell.

"Why don't we put out this fire and come back for the rest of your gear in the morning? Could probably find 'em more easily in the daylight," said Jake.

"Sounds good to me," said Winston, kicking sand on the fire.

Within minutes, they extinguished the fire and loaded the two sailboats. Nell trembled as she waded back to her boat. Her earlier self-confidence at the helm had slipped away, and she felt trepidation about returning to town.

"I could use some crew," said Jake, looking at Nell.

Nell hesitated. Earlier that evening, it had been magical to feel his strength as she sat next to him by the fire. Now, since they were returning to the mainland, she could feel the weighty judgment of the town. And Asa could be nearby on the water. "I think I need to stay with my friends tonight."

"No, you don't," said Emma Grace. "We got Winston to chaperone me and Midgett." She looked over at Jake. "That man needs crew." Emma Grace walked over to her friend and dropped her voice. "Nell, don't let Sylvia Davis take over your life. Think of all the music you can make with that South Carolina boy." Nell studied her friend's face, recalling how a provincial group of girls had shamed her throughout high school. But here she was, strong and solid and still standing up to all of them.

"Okay," she said, turning to wade over to Jake's boat. "First mate coming aboard." The two dogs greeted her like crew.

"Actually, that title goes to Pilot," Jake said. "So, you and Yawg need to work out rank."

Climbing into the boat, she shot him a sardonic look. He pulled her toward him and kissed her. "How about a special title for you," he whispered. "What about 'Best Mate'."

Although dreading what might await them on the water and onshore, Nell didn't feel alone. Nestling into Jake's arms as he steered the boat, she felt alive and contented. Thinking back to his response to the shot fired on the island, she could see something distant, something unknown about him.

They set sail and pulled away from the island, and the night engulfed them. The *Miss Mary* moved silently through the water. They spoke little and felt like the only two people in the world. And Nell remembered why she loved to sail at night.

CHAPTER 17

The following morning, Nell walked with Emma Grace and her family to their church. They made a small procession down Ann Street with Winston and Marbles in the lead, followed by Nell and Emma Grace pushing infant Edward's stroller. Mama Beatrice brought up the rear with the three remaining siblings.

As they approached the white clapboard church, Emma Grace dropped her voice and said, "Isaac Jaspers got word to Winston that they would like us to stop by tomorrow for supper."

"I remember they invited us when they stayed at our house that awful night. I'm not sure Daddy would want me to go. He got pretty spooked when he heard Chadwick and his gang showed up at Horse Island."

"Does Thomas need to know?" asked Emma Grace.

They snickered.

"Maybe not."

When they arrived, Emma Grace and her family entered the chapel, but Nell remained outside to meet her parents. Her mother woke up feeling little pain that morning and decided to attend service. The new ramp enabled Nell's father to help his wife into their Ford.

Nell didn't relish standing alone while friends she'd known all her life snubbed her as they walked into the sanctuary. Searching stoically for her family's truck, Nell was terrified that Asa would arrive with his family and make another scene. When the organ music began to spill out of the building, Nell thought of Mrs. Davis's influence within the church and wondered if she would ever be asked to play again. Despite anguish washing over her, she began to hum along with the music, and her shaking hands steadied.

While she searched the stream of parishioners, she also kept an eye out for Jake. The street and church melted away from her. *Why is it so much easier to talk to Jake than to Asa?* She hummed and laughed at herself. *The music, of course.* On the sail home that night from Horse Island, they'd hummed songs and talked about jazz. Absently, she ran her tongue over her lips as she remembered his kiss. Asa had never wanted to talk about the war, but Nell knew it was always in Jake's thoughts. She wondered when they could be together. *What would happen when Jake found his brother? Would he leave?* Maybe that was part of her attraction to him, and she frowned. With Asa, it had all been mapped out—their move to Richmond and their rise to prosperity. Jake was unknown and exciting.

Lost in her thoughts, she didn't realize that Mr. Edgar Ramsey was standing in front of her. She recalled Mrs. Davis's cousin from the last supper she'd attended at Asa's house. That night now seemed so distant. Her heart raced, and her eyes darted for an escape. *Is he going to shame me right here in front of the church?*

"Why, Nell Guthrie, how charming you look," the Virginian's words harmoniously floated out of him.

Still cautious, Nell exhaled. His voice sounded sincere, and she recalled the little jokes they had shared before supper at Asa's house. Having been dismissed by so many of Mrs. Davis's friends, she was reticent to let down her guard. "Thank you, Mr. Ramsey."

He dropped his voice and leaned in towards her. "I wanted to tell you how much I enjoyed your music at the inn last week."

Nell smiled at him, feeling a warmth return to her limbs.

He continued, "I also wanted to say I was so dismayed to hear about you and Asa."

In a polite tone, she answered, "That's very thoughtful of you."

"Listen, Sylvia's my kin, but I recognize how difficult she can be."

"You seem to have a way with her."

He studied her face for a moment as the congregation streamed around them. His casual demeanor slipped, and his eyes softened with concern. Placing his hand on his heart, he said, "Please let me know if I may be of any assistance to you. I know how special creative spirits can be. Your music touched my soul." While his words left her speechless, Nell was distracted by the large silver and garnet ring that adorned his hand.

"Thank you, Mr. Ramsey," she stammered as gratitude overwhelmed her.

"I also heard about your incident the other evening on Horse Island. I hope it wasn't too unsettling."

"I'm concerned that Chadwick is still missing," said Nell. "Midgett put out an alert for him and suspected accomplices, but he hasn't surfaced."

At that moment, Nell looked behind Mr. Ramsey to see Buddy Taylor with one of his brothers helping their ancient mother slowly shuffle around the corner of the church.

Mr. Ramsey turned as Buddy said to his brother. "You reckon you could help Mama? I need to talk a little business with Nell and her friend."

His mother glowered at him. "Sunday is not a day of work; it is a day of rest."

"Yes, Mama," replied Buddy. But when his brother turned his mother toward the church steps, Buddy glided away from them to Nell and Ramsey. "Hey, y'all."

Nell thought he looked like he'd been freed from a possum trap. "Well, hey to you, too. Ready to receive your weekly spiritual blessings?"

"Today, I think I will atone for my sin and get my weekly quota of damnation," replied Buddy. His eyes danced as they swept over Mr. Ramsey.

The Virginian smiled at Buddy, rocking back and forth on his heels. "That sounds like a very tall order."

"We were just talking about how Chadwick disappeared after we saw him on Horse Island," said Nell.

"Is that right?" Buddy replied. "I wouldn't worry too hard over him. He can be right squirrelly."

Ramsey chuckled. "I happened to see his mother the other day. I think it's rather indicative that she didn't seem to be worried."

Relief swelled inside Nell, and they shared a grin. People on Harkers Island had a different set of rules and protected their own. "Guess she knows something we don't."

Buddy turned away from his friends to look back at the church. At the top of the steps, his mother was throwing him a ferocious look. "Time to be forgiven," he stated flatly. Still, he lingered, and Nell noticed a sadness sweep over his face as he looked at Mr. Ramsey. She could sympathize with her friend, who would have to sit next to his Draconian mother during the sermon.

Mr. Ramsey reached out and plucked a hair off Buddy's shoulder, then briefly brushed the dark fabric with his hand. "Well, at least you'll look your best."

Reluctantly, Buddy pivoted and dragged himself up the stairs. It was unusual to see him moving so slowly.

"Buddy tells me that y'all have done some work together."

Ramsey was watching Buddy enter the church. "Now and again. I often get a better price for his collectibles in Virginia."

Nell lowered her voice, "His Sugar Shack is so much fun."

Mr. Ramsey raised an eyebrow. "You must be a close friend indeed to have seen Buddy's inner sanctum."

"Well, I reckon." She scanned the street and saw her father pulling up in his truck. "You'll have to excuse me. I need to help my mama get into church."

"Is there any way I could assist?" asked Mr. Ramsey.

"Well, you might could take her wheelchair up the steps."

"I'd be delighted."

Mr. Ramsey waited as Nell gingerly helped her mother out of the truck. "Daddy, I got someone to help me. You can go park the Ford." Her father's mouth hardened when he glanced at Mr. Ramsey in his impeccable suit with a crimson pocket square peeking out his breast pocket.

"Mama, this is Edgar Ramsey."

"How do you do," said Alice Guthrie.

"Madame, I must say it is delightful to see you in church this morning."

As they chatted, Nell reached into the truck bed, removed her mother's wheelchair, and rolled it toward the church. While Mr. Ramsey helped her mother up the stairs, Nell followed them, dragging the empty chair up each step.

At the top of the stairs, they settled Mrs. Guthrie into her chair. Nell moved out of the cool, spring air into the church's dusty warmth. As her eyes adjusted to the diminished light, she made out Jake sitting near the front of the church. When he winked at her, she felt the hateful week fall away, and they were the only two people in the sanctuary. She turned away from him and began to walk down the aisle to the pew filled with Emma Grace's family. Mr. Ramsey followed Nell wheeling her mama's chair.

Once everyone was seated, Nell pushed the wheelchair up the aisle where it would be stored during service. When she reached the back of the church, Nell froze when Asa and his parents entered. Her former fiancé clenched his fists, and his hooded eyes glared hot rage.

Unable to move, Nell watched Mrs. Davis's eyes narrow, darting back and forth between Nell and the Virginian who was slipping the chair out of her hands. "Let me take that from you," said Mr. Ramsey at Nell's shoulder. "You go sit with your mama while I put this away." Brushing against Mrs. Davis, he said, "Well, hey there, Sylvia."

A shudder rippled through Nell as she slid into the pew next to her mother, leaving room for her father. As Asa and his family walked past, Nell busied herself with opening her mother's hymnal to the first song.

"Nell," said her mother, "I know you want to help Emma Grace with the baby; why don't you step over me." Although clumsy in the narrow pew, Nell squeezed by the other parishioners just as her daddy slipped in from the aisle.

The music stopped, and service began with prayer and announcements. When it was time for the children to leave for Sunday school, the adults tucked their feet under the pew to allow Marbles and his siblings to clamber over them into the aisle.

After the congregation settled, Rev. Saunders began his sermon. "Last week, I spoke of the evils of alcohol floating in on a tide of immorality. This week I ask you this: what lures men to crash their boat of righteousness upon the rocks of vice? What beckons them? What do they hear? What force drives our young folk away from God's safe harbor? What makes some people turn to sin and others toward rectitude? The Bible is black and white, but new sciences cast us into ambiguous seas of gray."

Nell sighed deeply. *Another sermon with sea imagery.* She exchanged bemused glances with Emma Grace.

"Let us look into the soul of a young captain of the boat that has been cast astray," Rev. Saunders droned on. "When the sailor leaves the shore, he may have a good grounding in God's word, but ill winds can still steer him off course."

The sermon stirred up Nell's memories from the evening on Horse Island. Chadwick and his friends came out of nowhere that night. *How had I missed their boat when I was watching the water so closely? Where was he now?*

168

Why is he hiding? She stared at the back of Asa's head, sitting just a few rows ahead of her.

Nell's gaze drifted over to Mr. Edgar Ramsey. Although he was odd, she felt a genuine kinship with the man, who always found the humor in a situation. She imagined him stepping back from oil painting to get the full view; he would never be fussed with small brush strokes.

She turned her attention back to the pulpit. "The new century has brought a flood of modern sciences. These ill winds challenge and attempt to demolish religious thinking. Our young navigator may seek false prophets. Of course, I am referring to the greatest demon of this century, the Austrian, Sigmund Freud. Many young people turn to 'The Love Doctor' to justify their own heinous acts."

The reverend paused as his audience tittered. Emma Grace leaned over and whispered to Nell, "You know, I never had anyone quote Freud to me in the back seat of a Model T."

Nell stifled a giggle as she put her finger to her lips to hush her friend. The smile slipped from her face when she saw her father's disapproval.

Rustling in the church abated, and the preacher continued. "These new deceptive beliefs confound and befuddle the modern man. And perhaps I should add the modern woman. The path of purity is narrower for the woman. She is the vessel and the guide of children. Freud would have us believe that we are not responsible for our actions. For the true answers, says Freud, we must troll the unconscious. The Love Doctor would have us look to our dreams for guidance. This is a heresy." The minister paused. "Again, I ask the question, what lures a boat captain to crash his boat upon the rocks of the vices of smoking, dancing, and lust?" Rev. Saunders drew the last words with emphasized disdain. "What calls them to shore? What do they hear? What calls to them from the speakeasy? The answer is the siren song of jazz."

A second ripple spread through the fellowship. A few people stole glances at Nell, who stared at the wall behind the preacher, feeling trapped and constricted sitting on the narrow pew. Emma Grace stifled a deep chuckle, but she stopped when she saw Nell's panic-stricken face.

"In the words of the great evangelist, Billy Sunday, 'our youth is turning its moral compass from Jesus to jazz.' With its jungle rhythms, this so-called music has a hypnotic effect on innocents today. The irregular beat unbalances and disorientates a person. It is the antithesis of the civilized, stabilizing tempo of a waltz or hymn."

Emma Grace reached for Nell's hand and gave it a reassuring squeeze, but Nell was too paralyzed with shame to respond. She sought Jake's face in the audience. He looked back at her, concerned and helpless. Other parishioners were giving her swift, disdainful glances. Nell's father's face flushed to a molten shade of purple. As the preacher droned on, her daddy stared resolutely at the church rafters. Mrs. Guthrie looked down at her hands folded in her lap.

"Jazz comes to us from cities." The minister's voice rose. "From the dirty, disreputable, decaying corners of the metropolis. It comes from dangerous parts of town where life is cheap. It is not the music of pastoral goodness, where nurturing food is grown. The dance floor is our new battleground against depravity! We have scientific proof that the dance floor's devious beat can lead a person to hedonistic debauchery in the bedroom." The reverend paused to mop pools of sweat from his brow.

Nell could no longer breathe. The heat of the crowd was suffocating her.

"The strength of this lewd music influences the most vulnerable of our community: the innocent and the unscathed. When a young girl is subjected to this primitive rhythm, she is more susceptible to be driven out of her righteous mind."

The preacher looked up from his podium and looked directly at Nell. A wave of bile rose in her throat.

"The woman who has fallen the farthest is the female jazz musician. Not only have her scruples been tarnished and destroyed; she is the enchantress who lures other girls to their moral decay."

A hush fell over the congregation while panic tore through Nell. The room pulsed with condemnation. Her mother's gnarled hand clasped hers, but Nell was too ashamed to look at her.

"Let us pray."

⌒

"You defied me," Mr. Guthrie boomed. He had waited to explode until they were home. "I didn't want you playing jazz. You went against my word. I hate that music in my own home, and I never want you to play it in public."

Nell sobbed as her mother gripped her shoulder with her arthritic hand. The sermon had wracked Mrs. Guthrie, who was gray with exhaustion.

"I was just helping out Winston," Nell choked out between her tears. "They were in a bad way. Their piano player didn't show up."

"I forbade you, Nell," her daddy roared back. "And now the preacher has come down on you. And for some godforsaken reason, you broke up with Asa."

"What do you mean?" asked Nell. Her daddy had been close to Asa, but she now heard something else in his voice.

"He could have saved you from all this sinful music. You're on the wrong path, but he would have supported you." Her father's tough exterior was cracking, and he started to pace the room.

It was Nell's first glimpse into her father's fears and concerns since her brother died.

Although still angry, Nell's father lowered his voice. "I felt bad that you couldn't go to school after Harrison died. It was shameful to me that I had to put my daughter in my store."

In an instant, Nell remembered how cold her father had been to her while working in town.

"I won't be able to support you if you become an old maid." His face contorted with pain and anger. "Now, I'm worried that there won't be enough money for you and your mama if something happens to me."

Nell stared at her father. She chose her words carefully. "Daddy, Asa lied to me. He was seeing other girls, and I'm right sure he was having relations with someone while he was engaged to me." Thomas Guthrie stopped his pacing and stared at Nell. "And he was breaking the law. He's smuggling liquor."

Nell didn't look away and held his gaze. Turning to his wife, Thomas Guthrie asked, "Did you know this?"

Alice Guthrie paused. "I suspected."

"When I was little," continued Nell tentatively, "You and Mama were so much in love, and you treated each other so respectfully. I didn't feel that with Asa. I loved him, Daddy, I really did, but I can't imagine what would have happened if I was alone with him in Richmond with none of my family."

"Why didn't you tell me all this?"

Nell looked to her mother for help. The truth was, she hadn't been able to tell her father anything for years.

171

Voices and footsteps floated from the back porch. Emma Grace and her family were arriving for Sunday dinner.

"Thomas," said Alice, "why don't you and I continue this in our bedroom? Nell, go wash your face before you greet Beatrice and her family."

"Yes, ma'am."

Nell hurried to the bathroom to freshen up while Emma Grace entered and began to warm up their dinner in the kitchen. Once Nell joined them, Emma Grace shared her heated remarks. "It was the most pitiful thing I ever heard." She held fussy Baby Edward on one hip while she stirred beans on the stove. "I swear, he directed it right at you, Nell. I bet my bottom dollar Sylvia Davis put him up to this. You should have seen the smug look she gave us when we left." Although Emma Grace's voice held steady so as not to further upset the infant, Nell could see she was agitated.

Nell could hear Emma Grace's cousins playing in their back yard. Mama Beatrice entered the kitchen carrying Edward's bassinet. She set it on the side table, and took the baby from Emma Grace before settling in the rocking chair.

"Sylvia Davis certainly looked full of herself," hissed Emma Grace as she stirred the bubbling pot.

"I'd like to know how she got to the preacher," muttered Nell, while pulling bread and preserved peaches from the cupboard.

"Like everything else in this town. Sylvia Davis has so much money that people listen to her," replied Emma Grace.

Mama Beatrice thought for a moment. "It's more likely she knew how to talk to the preacher, bend his ear. You know Billy Sunday's been saying that mess for years." She rocked the baby soothingly. "I wouldn't be surprised if that scrimmage with Asa and Buddy in front of the hardware store shook up Sylvia Davis, and she wanted revenge."

"Maybe Beaufort's not ready for rag and jazz yet," said Nell, slicing the bread.

"Well, you wouldn't know it by that crowd at the Inlet Inn," said Emma Grace. "Winston and that band brought the best music to the inn since I don't know when," said Emma Grace. "Lordy, everyone was on their feet."

As they gathered to eat around the table, Mama Beatrice glanced with irritation at Winston's empty seat. "Did you see what happened to your brother?" she asked her children. "He was supposed to walk home with us."

"He took off right after the minister finished," said Emma Grace.

"He'll have to answer to his father one of these days."

When Mr. Guthrie pushed his wife's wheelchair into the room, a heavy pall settled over the table. Although calmer than he'd been before the Willis family arrived, Mr. Guthrie's mouth was still set in a grim line. Nell stared at her plate when he said grace. No one spoke as they served themselves. As silence enveloped the table, the clattering of silverware became more noticeable. When Nell tried to eat anything, it tasted like cardboard and rested in a lump in her stomach. Eventually, she simply pushed the food around on her plate.

Finally, Mama Beatrice spoke up. "That preacher was horrible to Nell. But I was glad to hear someone stand up to that Love Doctor. Laugh all you want, but that man puts the stamp of approval on sex outside of marriage."

Nell glanced at her father's reddening face. He shoved a forkful of chicken pot pie into his mouth.

"Well," said Alice, waving her hand dismissively. "I dare say, he'll fade by the wayside before you know it—just one more fad like flagpole sitting or dance marathons."

"Well, Billy Sunday will live on in the hearts of Americans forever," proclaimed Mama Beatrice.

"Freud is saying that we all have these impulses," said Emma Grace, spearing a green bean with her fork. Nell looked up at her daddy's face and watched it deepen into a beet-red color. She reached under the table and squeezed her friend's hand, but Emma Grace ignored her. "Being aware of impulses makes them easier to recognize. Rather than feeling shame about them, we can understand them better."

"That's enough of that kind of talk at Sunday dinner!" bellowed Mr. Guthrie, angry and upset. His volume startled the baby, and the smaller children stopped eating in fright. Baby Edward started to howl, so Emma Grace unstrapped him from the highchair and carried him into the kitchen.

Alice Guthrie shot a poisoned look at her husband. Everyone stopped eating. An awkward silence thickened over the table. After a few moments passed, Mama Beatrice looked up from her plate and exclaimed, "My! Whoever made these lovely sweet potatoes?"

When the long meal ended, Nell ducked into the kitchen with a stack of dirty dishes. Emma Grace was pacing and singing softly to lull little Edward to sleep. "You have nothing to be ashamed of," Emma Grace told her friend.

"It doesn't feel that way," said Nell, who felt drained. "I feel like this town is roasting me in the flames of hell." After she set the stack of dishes in the sink, she wiped hot tears from her swollen eyes.

Crossing the kitchen to the pantry to retrieve two rhubarb pies, Nell heard a gentle knock on the back door. Both girls looked up to see Jake standing on the porch. "Hey, Nell. Hey, Emma Grace," he said politely.

Holding a pie in each hand, Nell felt a wave of contentment flood over her. His face looked concerned but reassuring. Pushing her misery aside, she remembered their wonderous night sail from Horse Island. Now, he was braving her father on one of the worst days of her life. She steadied herself and willed herself not to break into tears. Looking behind him, she saw the happy, panting faces of Yawg and Pilot. When she didn't invite him in, he opened the door and stepped into the kitchen. Emma Grace smiled at him as she slipped outside with her infant cousin.

"I was worried about you after that big brouhaha at church." He gently took the pies from her and set them on the table. Placing his hands on her shoulders, he smiled with soft reassurance. She closed her eyes as he kissed her tender eyelids before his lips traveled down to her mouth. When their kiss ended, she leaned into his chest, and a gentle peace settled over her. "Don't let those bastards take your music away." The rumble of words bounced around inside his chest.

When she answered him, her voice sounded distant. "Jake, don't swear on Sunday."

He laughed softly. "That preacher's a coward," he said with scorn. "He doesn't speak music." And she knew this was true. For the first time since the sermon, she felt herself strengthen as her shame slipped away.

They held their embrace for a moment before they heard Marbles shout from the parlor, "Where's the pie?"

"They're wondering where I am," said Nell. "Why don't you come in and sit down with us?"

She picked up the two desserts and entered the parlor with Jake following. Since he'd changed out of his Sunday best into work pants and shirt, he looked vulnerable among all the church-clad family. "Look what the tide carried in," said Nell with a strained cheerfulness. She turned to Jake. "I'm not sure if you've met Mrs. Willis and her passel of young'uns."

"Ma'am," said Jake, inclining his head toward her.

"Jake!" shouted Marbles and started to lunge across the table.

"Michael James," said his mother firmly, and the boy sat down in his seat, squirming with impatience.

While slicing the pie, Nell glanced at her father, who seemed to be chewing his tongue. She smiled when she placed the dessert in front of him, but his face remained impassive. Once Nell sat down, Jake pressed his leg against hers under the table, making her feel warm and shivery at the same time.

When Marbles and his sister began to argue over which pie tasted better, Mrs. Guthrie turned to Nell and said, "Why don't you and Emma Grace give Mama Beatrice a breather and take these young'uns down to the shore. Jake can help you, too."

Emma Grace looked to her aunt for direction. "Just leave the dishes. We can all wash them when you get back."

The younger children scraped their chairs as they pushed back from the table and stampeded toward the door.

The briny essence of a low tide greeted the young adults as they approached the shore. While Emma Grace bounced the baby, her younger cousins stalked sand fiddler crabs in the marsh grass lining the shore. Pilot and Yawg joined the children, and soon everyone was covered in wet sand. Emma Grace glanced over her shoulder at Nell's house and said, "I reckon your daddy wants me to chaperone you two." They all laughed.

Nell longed to take Jake's hand but knew it would only fuel ugly rumors. Although the street looked deserted, she knew no one was ever alone in Beaufort. She stood close to Jake as they studied the harbor. "What's so odd is that I feel the spirit when I play. It's as though God or an angel is moving my fingers. Sometimes, I feel as though I am dreaming or in a trance when I'm on the piano. I don't have to read the music; it's a part of me. Even when I was a child, before I could read music, I could play."

"Of course, you did," Jake said simply, as if everyone in the world understood this.

Marbles stopped chasing his sister for a minute and looked up at Nell with some alarm. "Are you going to marry Jake, Nell?"

Nell felt a hot blush rise in her cheeks.

Jake kept his gaze on Marbles and said, "Not today."

"But I meant—"

"Look out, Marbles!" said Nell. "I think I see a blue crab near your toe." The little boy hopped around in the water and mercifully forgot his next question.

The children were in the middle of a game of tag when Nell looked up to see her father walking toward them, sober as a judge. Winston followed behind him, looking equally downcast. "What happened?" she asked with alarm.

Jake and Emma Grace looked up when they heard the concern in her voice. Mr. Guthrie said to Marbles and his sisters, "I want you young'uns to go to the garden, now."

"We just got here," wailed Marbles. But a second look at Thomas Guthrie's face made Marbles and the others walk toward the house without a word.

"The manager at the inn canceled the band's booking," said Winston.

"What? Why?" cried Nell.

"He caught up with me as I was leaving church and said he didn't want the band to play. He'd heard the preacher's sermon, and he remembered that you helped us out on Friday night."

"Oh, for the love of—" started Jake, but Nell silenced him with a look.

Winston laughed mirthlessly, "I told that son of—" He paused, struggling with himself. "I told him that the preacher said jazz was immoral, not you."

"Then he got right confused. I reckon he's not the sharpest tool in the shed. He sort of mumbled that he'd heard things about you.'"

"So, I got up in his face and said, 'Well, what did you hear?' He beat around the bush. Finally, he said you'd been going off to some of the rooms and . . .'"

"Oh, goodness. How can he say that!" cried Nell, covering her ears in an attempt to stop the words. "Daddy, it's not true!" She felt as though a knife had been run through her heart.

"That's what I told him," said Winston. "He said he thought we were good musicians, and we could get people to dance, and the hotel makes good money when we play, la de da, la de da. But there is an unsavory perception of you in town right now, and he can't hitch the hotel's name to it."

"He actually said 'unsavory'?"

"Like a half-baked roast."

Jake began to move toward Nell, but she caught her father's eye and pivoted away. "Who did he get to replace you?" he asked Winston.

"The Razzle Dazzles."

"Oh, good Lord, they can barely play a waltz," said Emma Grace.

Nell's father stepped in front of Winston. His dark Sunday best suit and starched white shirt, coupled with his stricken face, reminded Nell of an undertaker. She fought the urge to take a step back away from him. "I know you didn't intend any of this, Nell." She noted the change in his tone. While his anger and disappointment still rolled in waves off of him, his words had lost their fire. "But there's a lot at stake for all of us now. Most of all, your safety and your reputation."

"Yessir," she answered.

"I want you to stay close to the house."

"For how long?" She searched his face for an answer, feeling powerless and beaten.

"I don't know. We need to talk this over with your mama."

Her head hurt from the injustice of Rev. Saunders' words, but now she could see the concern in her father's eyes. Mr. Guthrie turned to Jake. "I think it's best if you not visit Nell."

Looking down at the ground, Nell felt her strength drain from her.

Mr. Guthrie glanced at his daughter. "I can see where this is headed. I'm sorry, Jake, I think you're an upright boy, but people will take it the wrong way if you start courting Nell so soon after her engagement to Asa."

With a great effort, Jake straightened to his full height. "I understand, sir." He turned to Nell but didn't speak. He wore the same vacant expression she'd seen when they were under siege on Horse Island. Slowly and mechanically, he turned from her and whistled for his dogs. Yawg and Pilot fell in line behind him, and the three of them started walking away from her down Front Street.

SUE ANGER

Nell wanted to go after him. A part of her was leaving with him. She saw herself climbing into Jake's boat and sailing out of the town that disowned her. Mr. Guthrie turned back to the house. Emma Grace moved over and stood next to her friend, leaning in with a reassuring presence. Nell knew her father would not want her to break down and cry on Front Street. So, she fought her tears and watched Jake and his dogs walk away until they were nothing but three distant specks.

CHAPTER 18

Dear Mama and Daddy,

I got your letter that talked about Wade's crew that returned to Stono Creek. Doesn't sound like they can help much.

I'm thinking Wade might have refitted the Amelia *into a rum boat. Things are getting mean on the water.*

Coast Guard Commander Midgett says that they saw the Amelia *go on a day sail around April 9, several days before Wade sailed out of port. He also said sometimes boats resurface under different names and different flags, so keep your eye out in Charleston for the* Amelia. *She was one of a kind, but they may have converted her.*

I'm gonna go over to talk to a man who worked with Wade at a boatyard up here. Wade mentioned him in his letters, and I'm betting I can trust him.

Each night I look out over the water and up at the sky, and I feel Wade's presence. He is so close, I can feel him here.

Your loving son, Jake

From the cockpit of the *Jamison*, Jake finished the letter and placed it in an envelope. His fingers slowly traced his home address, lingering on his family name. Although he hadn't had much appetite since he left Nell and her family the day before, he suddenly had a hankering for his mother's Frogmore Stew.

His eyes drifted to the boats setting out from the harbor for nighttime work. Some would set nets with the tide, while others would check crab pots. As they left port, he imagined pulling up anchor, catching the building sea breeze, and sailing out to open water. When could he get away from this petty town that could rip the soul from Nell?

Jake didn't blame Thomas Guthrie for running him off. The man was only a father protecting his daughter. Still, when Jake closed his eyes, he could feel Nell's warm body pressing against his during the damp night on their sail back from Horse Island.

Eventually, Yawg and Pilot reminded him it was suppertime and he fed them from his limited provisions. When it was time to go ashore, he spruced up and put on a clean shirt. Both of his dogs hopped into his dinghy and supervised his row across the harbor. Once onshore, Jake searched Front Street and spotted Emma Grace and Winston several blocks away. Without thinking, he looked for Nell before remembering she couldn't join them. As the cousins came closer, he saw that Emma Grace carried a large flat basket covered with a cloth. Although her dress was simple, it was a rich blue hue. A dress like this stood out in Beaufort, where girls wore summer white cotton. Walking down the dock to join them, Jake raised his voice to say, "Emma Grace, I must say, you know how to wear a dress."

"Thanks, Jake," she replied, looking pleased with herself.

They crossed the street, and Jake posted the letter to his parents.

"How's Nell doing?" Jake asked.

"Not well," replied Winston. "Thomas won't even let her work at their hardware store. I reckon he thinks she'll sail away with you."

"Can you blame her?" asked Jake. "This town has kicked her to the curb."

"She didn't even want to play the piano," added Emma Grace.

The weight of these sad words fell heavily on Jake. Turning away, he recalled the gripping despair that prevented him from playing after he returned from Europe.

As they walked down Front Street, Jake noticed that Yawg kept up with them while still favoring his injured paw. Turning north, the three young people fell into step together as they made their way to the home of Isaac and Annie Jasper.

During the Civil War, Confederate forces stationed at Beaufort and Fort Macon were overtaken by Union troops in 1862. As the Yankees advanced into the state, enslaved people ran away from their owners and sought shelter in occupied Beaufort. Most of them settled north of Cedar Street in a neighborhood that became known as Union Town. Jake and his friends now crossed over the invisible border into this part of town. Now, the houses were small and weathered. Some looked no bigger than shacks. Although the front yards were hard-packed dirt, Jake could see the homes were in good repair, and many had well-tended vegetable gardens. Several residents were sitting on their porches, but stopped chatting and turned to stare at the three white people as they passed. "Do you feel safe on this side of town?" Jake asked Emma Grace.

Emma Grace snorted. "Safer than I feel at the Inlet Inn."

Her confidence settled Jake's concern, and he nodded slightly to a group of silent people staring at the trio and their dogs. One of the elderly men returned his nod. They turned on Pine Street, lined with several stores serving the Union Town community. These included a pool hall, grocery store, and a barber shop.

As they approached the Jasper home, several dogs in the front yard barked while simultaneously wagging their tails in greeting to Yawg and Pilot. After Emma Grace knocked on the door, they heard footsteps, and young Tobias greeted them. "Come on in, y'all."

Jake barely recognized the beaming little boy who was always so scruffy on the dock. Tonight, he wore his Sunday best with a scrubbed face and parted hair.

"Well, Tobias, don't you look handsome," exclaimed Emma Grace.

"Thank you, Miss Emma Grace," replied Tobias formally. "May I take your basket for you?"

"Yessir," she answered. "You best be careful, though; my rhubarb pie is in it."

Tobias's eyes widened as he turned to lead the way to the family table.

Jake felt his usual shortness of breath when entering a house for the first time. Following Emma Grace and Winston, he took a few moments to steady his breathing. The cramped living room was spotless and connected to a kitchen at the back of the home. Emma Grace was eyeing strings of drying herbs stretched across the back of the room with interest. These would be used in tinctures and poultices.

Miss Tulla was standing at the stove tending to her fry oil in a skillet, while Annie was setting serving dishes of black-eyed peas and cornbread on a large table laid out for eight people.

Isaac's wife was an unpretentious woman with dark, luminous eyes. Tonight, Annie was dressed in a floral dress that set off her nutmeg skin tone. Now that she was in her own home, her face and movements reflected a gentle easiness.

"Oh my," said Emma Grace, admiring the groaning table. "Doesn't all this look good." She looked at Tobias and asked, "Did you help the womenfolk make all this food?"

Breaking into his wide smile, he answered, "I helped Mama with her sweet potato pie." His small body almost shook with excitement as he unwrapped Emma Grace's pie from her basket and gingerly set it on the sideboard.

Jake looked over at the older woman, whom he had all but thrown into Winston's truck a few days ago. Today, she looked robust and relaxed as she worked at the cookstove. The room smelled heavenly after his weeks of canned and dried food on the *Jamison*. Although the oil of the fish fry hung thick and warm in the air, he could also detect the black-eyed peas simmered with ham and the hint of cinnamon from Tobias's sweet potato pie.

As the three guests stood around the table, Isaac entered from the back door with an armful of wood that he stacked next to the stove. When Annie looked up to greet her visitors, a shadow of concern passed over her face. "Where's Miss Nell? Is she feeling poorly?"

Emma Grace shifted uncomfortably. "Her daddy didn't want her out in the evening right now."

Cooking fork in hand, Miss Tulla turned around from the popping grease to study them.

"There was a mishap at the church," Emma Grace looked to Winston and Jake for help.

"Nell was shamed and re-named by the preacher in church yesterday," Winston said with some heat.

The eyes of the three Jaspers adults widened in surprise.

"According to Preacher Saunders, Nell is the anti-Christ with her ragtime music and her wanton ways," said Jake.

Winston offered more details about the sermon as a hush fell over the room.

"In any case, her daddy didn't want her running around right now," finished up Emma Grace.

"Hain't that something," said Isaac, shaking his head. "There's no nicer girl in the county."

"You know Miss Sylvia is behind all that," sniffed Annie, clucking her tongue in disgust.

"She looked pretty satisfied with herself when she left church," admitted Emma Grace.

Annie reluctantly took up the place setting for Nell.

Miss Tulla removed the sizzling fish from the frying pan and set the platter on the table.

Jake, Winston, and Emma Grace waited until the family had found their seats before they sat down.

Isaac led them in grace that ended with, ". . . and let us now repay our gracious guests for the kindness they have shown us."

The laden dishes were passed around, and Jake piled food on his plate. He recognized the fried spot fish, named for the single dark mark on its flank. Folks never bothered to filet the small fish, and the flavorful, flakey meat was one of Jake's favorites. He tucked into the dish. "Mmmm, mmmm, mmmm. You know that's good eatin'."

Miss Tulla looked pleased. Once their initial hunger abated, Emma Grace spoke to the healer, "Your dried herb collection is impressive. Are you growing all of these in your garden?"

"Mostly, but some I find out in fields, along the road, and such."

Jake remembered Emma Grace's tinctures and distillates concocted in the wine shed.

"Did those rebby boys ever come back and bother you this week?" asked Winston.

"Mercy, no," replied Miss Tulla, exhaling with great relief.

"I've been talking to other maids in town," Annie said as she filled her fork. "The story I heard is some boys came in from the farms down near Russell Creek. Mitchell Lewis drank a snootful with them. Somebody saw it was Mitchell's truck and told his mama, and she fussed him out good. She know Miss Tulla as a healer and told Mitchell he was shameful."

"I pray it's over," said Miss Tulla, shaking her head.

"Y'all have certainly had a time," said Emma Grace.

When Isaac eased back in his chair, Tobias impatiently squirmed and eyed the sideboard. When his mother began to clear the table, the boy jumped up to assist her. Annie set out clean forks, while Tobias and Emma Grace collected the two pies from the sideboard. After everyone was served a slice from each pie, a silence settled over the table. Tobias tasted both, laid down his fork, and closed his eyes. "These pies taste like springtime."

"You know that," chuckled Isaac.

Winston finished both pieces and pulled the rhubarb pie towards him for a second slice. His cousin jerked the pan away from him and gave him a look that indicated he had the manners of a barn animal.

Isaac glanced down at Tobias's empty plate. "Son, why don't you go on to bed now."

"But Daddy," Tobias whined before he glimpsed his father's stern face. "Yessir." He walked over to his mama and hugged her.

"Good night, Tobias." Annie stroked the top of his head. "I'll be by in a minute."

After the boy entered the bedroom off the kitchen, Emma Grace reached under the warming cloth in her basket and pulled out two bottles of her homemade wine. Annie walked over to her cupboard and retrieved six glasses, and set them on the table. Then she walked to the sideboard and picked up a sewing basket while Emma Grace splashed purple-black liquid into the glasses.

"Here's to happier tomorrows!" Emma Grace said as they all toasted.

"Amen to that!" replied Miss Tulla.

Jake let the sweet berry wine sit on his tongue before he swallowed it.

"How's Dr. Davis this week, Annie?" Emma Grace asked.

"Oh, he always nice to me," answered the soft-spoken woman. "Lord knows how he keep his mind between Asa and Miss Sylvia. They're having a time of it."

"She's so lucky to have you," replied Emma Grace.

Tulla harrumphed. "She just don't know it."

"Miss Sylvia about run Nell to death when she was at her house."

"What do you mean?" Jake asked Annie, but it was Emma Grace who answered. "As far as Sylvia Davis was concerned, Nell was still in her cotillion class. 'Sit up straight, cross your ankles,'" Emma Grace imitated a rolling Richmond drawl.

"Why did Nell put up with that?" asked Winston.

Emma Grace sighed deeply. "After Harrison died, Nell thought she was a burden on her family."

Jake's eyebrows raised in surprise. "Why would she think that? She runs the hardware store and takes care of her mama."

"Nell and her daddy were close when she was a young girl. But after Harrison died, Mr. Guthrie withdrew from everyone and fell into the bottle. I think Nell's been trying to win his love back ever since. And it didn't help that they were slammed with her mama's doctor bills right after they'd lost Harrison. I think Nell truly loved Asa, and she forgave him when he lied and ran around on her because she knew how much her daddy liked him."

Annie looked down at her plate and shook her head. "What Nell didn't know was that she was the only thing keeping that boy together. He don't know what to do with hisself now that Nell gone—and her doing the goin'—he can't figure out what he is."

Jake tensed as a slow burn built in his chest. He pictured Nell stuck between her daddy's distant coldness and Asa's hot erratic anger.

Annie threaded a needle and took out a small, well-patched shirt from a household basket. The wine flooded Jake with courage as his eyes swept the table, but his familiar panic rose in his throat. Coughing gently, he forced his voice to sound casual. "I know you work over at Lowell's, Isaac. I was wondering if you remember a boat that was here a few weeks ago. It was a schooner called the *Amelia*."

"Yessir," replied Isaac. "We fixed her mast."

"Do you remember her captain?" asked Jake, picking at the remaining pie crumbs on his plate.

"Sure I do. I never seen a man work like Cap't Wade," Isaac said, shaking his head. "He knew wood. It like he could talk to wood, and it do what he wanted. Mr. Lowell had some juniper, and he charged Cap't Wade top dollar for it."

Jake turned to Isaac. "I'm his brother. My name is Jake Parson."

Winston and Miss Tulla caught their breath and stared at him. Annie's hand, which was in the middle of pulling her needle through the fabric, now hung suspended in midair. But Isaac nodded his head while he placidly replied, "Yessir."

"You don't seem surprised," Jake said.

"When I first seen you, I seen that you favored him. I figured it was something like that when you picked over the wood and then rode out to Taylor's with me. Your brother's the only other person ever been that particular. Then you build your skiff—practically had Cap't Wade's name on it." Isaac pulled out the pocket watch that Jake had seen when they were riding in the dray.

"And I notice that you knew this watch. Cap't Wade paid me with it for the lumber for his mast and the work I did on his boat. I was gonna sell it, but I got right attached to it." After he fingered it for a moment, he pushed it across the table to Jake, who picked it up and felt its warm smoothness. As he held the timepiece in his palm of one hand, his fingers traced his grandfather's engraving while he remembered the Sunday morning when he and Wade had received their watches. "Now you are men of the world," the old man had said. "This will show people you are men to be reckoned with."

A part of him longed to make Isaac an offer to buy it back from him, but he knew this wasn't the right time. The information that Isaac could possess took precedent. Reluctantly, Jake handed the watch back to Isaac. "Does anyone else know who I am?"

"Not by me," Isaac answered as he returned the watch to his pocket. "I figure this got somethin' to do with him being missin'. I knows when to keep my mouth shut. That keep me alive in this town."

"Well, aren't you full of surprises," Winston said to Jake. "Does Nell know?"

"Yes," replied Emma Grace. "She figured it out and told me."

Jake turned his attention back to Isaac. "Did the Coast Guard talk to you?"

"The officer come around Mr. Lowell's shop and asked questions, but they never talk to me."

"But you did work with him on his mast?" asked Jake, leaning across the table.

"Yessir."

"They think the *Amelia* left Beaufort on April 10," said Jake. "But I don't think Wade was on the *Amelia* when it left port. Wade wrote my mama once a week, and he always let us know when he was due to sail. The last letter we got from him was dated April 2, more than a week before the *Amelia* set sail. He never mentioned a sail date."

"Maybe one of his letters got lost," said Annie.

"Maybe. But then, when I got to Beaufort, Wade's dog, Yawg, found me after I got to port. Wade would not go to sea without him."

Everyone at the table stared at him. "His dog is here?" Annie finally asked.

"Sitting right out there on your porch," pointing through the front doorway. Pilot and Yawg were pressing their noses against the screen door. "That hound right there."

Chairs scraped as everyone at the table turned to look at Yawg and Pilot. "I knew I remembered him, but I couldn't think where I'd seen him," said Emma Grace.

Isaac got up from the table and walked to the screen door, looking down at the hound. He studied him for a while and then returned to the table, shaking his head.

Jake looked at Miss Tulla. "His foot looked awful when I found him, but I used your tincture on him, and it fixed him right up."

"Your mama must be out of her mind with worry," Miss Tulla said in reply, her brow crimped in consternation.

Everyone was silent while Annie pulled her needle through Tobias's shirt.

"Did y'all refit the *Amelia*? Does she look different now?" asked Jake.

Isaac shook his head. "I don't rightly know."

"Do you think Chadwick or Asa may have approached him about making a booze run?" asked Jake.

"I reckon not," replied Isaac. "He like to use local boys. They knows the water better."

"We wondered if he got outfitted for speed. Maybe added an engine for a whiskey run," said Jake.

"If he were, it weren't at Mr. Lowell's," replied Isaac. "From what I seen, he got his mast fixed, and then I thought he'd be going up North. But then I seen him around town. He'd need to be dry-docked for a refitting like that. There's a whole mess of people do that around town. If you got a rail line, you can do it in somebody's back yard," said Isaac.

Jake nodded. He had figured this out from Nell's harbor log. After Wade left Lowell's, there had been no further entries regarding the *Amelia*, although references to Wade had popped up in speakeasies and on the waterfront.

When Jake didn't reply to Isaac, Emma Grace spoke up. "Do you remember what liquor Asa was picking up that week? What boats were passing by offshore during that time? There were probably a lot sailing north after wintering in the Caribbean."

Isaac leaned back and closed his eyes. "In early April, we were getting a whole mess of water traffic."

While Isaac spoke, Jake pictured the pages of Nell's log. "*The Three Sisters* came up from Nassau that week, but didn't make port."

Isaac took a sip of wine and closed his eyes in concentration. "Mr. Asa come around to talk to Mr. Lowell about the *Three Sisters.*" He nodded while deep in thought. "They needed boats to meet her offshore. Now that I be thinking about it, there was something right peculiar that week at Mr. Lowell's," said Isaac. "Miss Sylvia come down to the docks all that time. Usually, you don't see her so much."

Emma Grace's mouth fell open in astonishment. "Sylvia Davis?" Jake and Winston also starred at him in disbelief.

Annie chuckled softly. "Yes, ma'am, she help out Asa a lot."

"She does?" asked Winston.

"She the one who handle the law mo' time. She and Jimmy go way back. She always keeping her eye on Asa."

"Well, shut my mouth," said Emma Grace.

Annie looked up from her mending in her lap to study the stunned faces of her three guests. "Oh, Lord, yes. Miss Sylvia be out there driving the truck if she ever learn to drive."

Emma Grace shook her head as if she wanted to erase the image of Asa's mother driving a truck.

Annie set down with her mending and poured herself another glass of wine. "There's a whole lot Miss Sylvia don't want people to know. Miss Sylvia got Nell all turned around. She good at that. Oh, that woman about worked her to death."

Emma Grace stared at her, listening intently.

"Somebody need to keep an eye on Asa. Lord knows I looked after him for a many a year," said Annie, shaking her head.

"Well, he can be stupid when he drinks," said Emma Grace.

"If only it were just that," said Miss Tulla.

Emma Grace furrowed her brow. "What do you mean?"

Annie exhaled. "Asa got into all kinds of trouble in Richmond. Mighta had something to do with the hospital he working at. Miss Sylvia still think he can go back up there. She got no sense where that boy's concerned."

"I thought he was gonna open a chain of drug stores," said Winston.

"He want to do that, but it take money. I hain't sure the banks will give it to him," said Isaac.

"Asa would hate Richmond over time," said Annie, setting her glass back on the table. "Whenever those Richmond people come down, they be so bossy. It's easy for Asa down here. He just don't know it. Here, he his own boss. He gonna have to work for somebody up there."

Jake thought of Asa's anger the day he accused Marbles and Tobias of stealing candy. He'd recognized that restless, demanding rage in Charleston's elite. Rules didn't seem to apply to them.

"He weren't good with books like his daddy and granddaddy," said Miss Tulla.

Isaac laughed. "But, oh, dear Lord, can that boy run booze. He cussin' his boys out of one side of his mouth, and sweet talkin' them fancy people out of the other."

Annie nodded. "Keep him happy, too. That boy always moving and dodging. Lord knows he like that when he was a young'un."

"They pay top dollar for booze in Richmond," Isaac said with a nod. "Good booze off the ship, not 'shine, and Asa never deal in no shine. Never water it down."

"When he run that good liquor up to Richmond from here, it keep Miss Sylvia in good with all her friends," said Annie.

"How does he get it up there? Does he take his car?" asked Jake. "The roads are terrible from here to Richmond—mostly marsh and swamp."

"I hain't sure." Annie paused to think. "Asa go up to Richmond, but he go by train, but he don't carry that much with him when he go."

"Where does Asa store his supply down here?" asked Jake.

Annie and Isaac exchanged glances. "I hain't sure," Annie replied. "It hain't at the house."

"It hain't at Lowell's, neither," said Isaac.

"We get a lot of visitors at Doc Davis' house, and most come by train," said Annie as she picked up her sewing. "Maybe them summer folk come down here and pick it up. I hain't sure."

Miss Tulla added, "Sometime they come down 'cause they want somethin' special—liquor or champagne or a wine that's hard to fine. Asa try to find what they want."

Emma Grace suddenly sat up straight. "Annie, do you remember who might have been visiting Mrs. Davis when the *Three Sisters* sailed by?"

"Oh, goodness, that was a busy time. There were all kind of folk down from Richmond that week, and they about wore me out. Most of them come down with Mr. Ramsey." Annie scrunched up her face in concentration. "I think some big wedding or somethin' was gonna happen in Richmond. They talked about rye and bourbon, but they also wanted champagne and wine for they's party."

"What does Ramsey look like?" asked Jake.

"He dresses better than I do," replied Emma Grace.

Jake nodded, thinking of the man who interacted with Chadwick at the Inlet Inn. "Black hair and wears it a little long?"

"He's hard to miss." Emma Grace turned back to Annie. "I don't remember making any entries in our harbor log regarding lighter fare in April. Usually whatever is passing by shows up in town."

Jake sat back in his chair. "Maybe it didn't come through Beaufort. Maybe they shipped it in by different route."

The table was quiet while everyone thought about this.

"Mighta gone through Morehead," said Winston.

"But that would double their sail time in passing by Fort Macon. Double their chances of getting caught," said Emma Grace.

"Maybe they brought it in Down East," said Winston, referring to the string of communities located east of Beaufort.

While everyone thought about this, Annie clipped the end of her thread and knotted it.

Isaac rubbed his chin. "Sometimes, I hear about those boys from Harkers Island working a haul over to Shackleford."

Jake pictured the nautical chart in his mind. This island was part of the Outer Banks located just below Cape Lookout.

Winston took a sip from his glass. He picked up the bottle of wine and swirled it around, but only dregs remained.

"Mama, you gonna say good night to me?" Tobias's voice rang out from the bedroom.

"Be right there, boy," said Annie as she rolled up her mending and tucked it back into her basket.

"We best be getting on so y'all can get to work tomorrow," said Emma Grace.

Everyone said their goodbyes, and Jake and his friends stepped out into the darkened street to begin their walk home. The sun had recently set, and there were no streetlights in this part of town. Twilight and the light from the homes helped them walk through the Jaspers' neighborhood.

"You're mighty quiet," Emma Grace said to Jake.

"I'm just trying to imagine how you could run booze into Harkers Island. When you look at a chart, you can't see a channel between Shackleford and Core Banks. And then the sound is so shallow around Cape Lookout."

"Well, they got the Drain at Lookout," said Winston.

"The what?" asked Jake.

"The Drain," repeated Emma Grace. "It's just a trickle of a channel—more creek than inlet, but you can get a skiff through it. It might not be on the chart."

"Shoot, those boys don't need an inlet. Some of the boats they build only draw about three inches."

Jake thought of the shallow, flat-bottomed boats made by the local fishermen.

They crossed the train tracks that ran down the middle of Broad Street and continued to walk toward the waterfront.

"So, they could land the crates of liquor on the beach near the bight," said Jake. "Then go up the Drain to the sound side. But if the Drain was too shallow, or it was low tide, they would carry it over by foot." He knew the barrier island was narrow at that point, less than half a mile. "Another team could pick it up on the sound side and take it pretty much wherever they wanted."

"Sounds about right," answered Winston. "Those Coast Guard cutters draw too much water to get up in there."

Jake thought about this. "But you would need someone who knows the water. Nobody from Richmond, that's for sure."

"Or Johns Island." Emma Grace exchanged a glance with Jake, and he smiled.

They walked a few moments in silence. "I reckon I'll take the *Miss Mary* over to Harkers Island tomorrow and ask around. Find out who's running booze from there," said Jake.

Emma Grace and Winston burst into laughter. "I reckon you've never been to Harkers Island," Emma Grace said once her laughter was under control.

"It's not like you can just go and talk to that crowd out there," said Winston.

"They make Charlie Lowell seem like a trusting man."

Winston wiped the tears of mirth from his eyes. "That's a fact—we'll need to find someone we know from Harkers Island and start there."

"I'll tell you what," said Emma Grace. "I have a patient I need to check on who lives on the island, and I'll make the sail with you. I think I know just the person to help us."

CHAPTER 19

The following morning, Nell awoke to silence. She usually heard music playing in her head when she transitioned out of sleep, but now a deadened emptiness greeted her. For a moment, she felt disoriented and scanned the room in confusion until she recognized the photo of Harrison by her bedside. Staring at the picture grounded her, but it did little to lift the combined weight of Rev. Saunders' humiliation coupled with the loss of Jake. When Harrison died, she'd been shattered, but determined to fill her emptiness. Her fingers and heart always led her to music, but now they were still.

She lay in bed, straining to pull a tune into her head, but none came. Eventually, she dressed and rose to prepare breakfast. Putting water on for coffee and grits, she heard her father begin to stir for the day. Eager to stay out of her daddy's way before he left for the hardware store, she quickly picked up her basket and went outside to collect eggs from her henhouse.

Stepping out on the back porch, Nell lifted her eyes to see a single gargantuan cloud filling the eastern sky. It rose from the horizon to the heavens, now aglow with the soft pink of the rising sun. Although stationary, its billowy nature provided a sense of movement. She felt herself rise with its airy ascent. She forgot her sorrow and imagined herself floating and swirling in the soft crevices of the cloud, going higher and higher.

The clucking hens returned her to earth. She lowered her gaze and studied the ramp that Jake had built. It reminded her of the wretched vision of Jake and his dogs walking away from her, growing smaller and smaller into the distance on Front Street. Swallowing hard, she stepped down from the porch while her head pounded from a lack of tune. Mechanically, she moved to collect her eggs before plodding back to the house. Any other day, she would have noted the growth in her garden, but the emptiness of the day spread out before her. Barren days lined up in front of her without end. She would make breakfast. She would bake, or wash laundry, or clean house. Her daddy wouldn't let her leave their home, or work at the store. Abruptly, she stopped walking. *He's ashamed of me.*

Like a sleepwalker, she entered her home. While serving her parents a breakfast of grits and gravy with eggs, Nell heard a soft knock on the back door.

"Woo-hoo," said Beatrice. The jovial greeting jarred the family's heavy stupor. "Sorry to walk in on your breakfast. Whew!" the big woman exhaled as she lumbered inside.

"Hey, Miss Beatrice," Nell answered, making an effort to smile.

"Hey there, Nell," Mrs. Willis replied as she sat down in a chair to catch her breath. "Emma Grace needs to sail over to Harkers Island to look in on Anna Lee Rose. Remember, she was the young'un who landed on the flounder gig when the engine jumped? Emma Grace needs to look in on her leg, make sure it's not infected."

Nell pictured the sail to the island under the luminous eastern cloud. Now she was in the cloud, floating over the sea, her lungs filled with air and hope.

Beatrice continued. "She needs to catch the tide, and she could use some crew. Thomas, you reckon you could spare Nell to sail with her?"

Holding her breath, Nell stared at the fried eggs in the pan that she gripped tightly. One word from her daddy and she could walk out the front door, leave the house, sail away from shore. Beatrice's labored breathing filled the kitchen as everyone waited for her father to bellow out a command to keep her in the house. Nell tentatively raised her eyes to peek at her parents, who were staring at each other. Alice Guthrie's mouth was set in a grim line. Watching their strained silence, Nell realized she'd heard her parents talking long into the night. While enshrouded in her haze of misery, she'd listened to her mother's steady voice dominating the conversation. Now, the seconds ticked off the wall clock in the sun-drenched kitchen. Without looking away from his wife, Nell's father quietly cleared his voice and replied, "I reckon that would be alright."

Nell nearly dropped the skillet in astonishment. When he turned his head to look at her, she noticed a new softness around his eyes. "Thank you, Daddy."

"That's wonderful," Beatrice exclaimed. "I'll run and tell Emma Grace right now." She opened the door to leave.

"Beatrice, wait," added Mr. Guthrie. Nell sucked in her breath, fearing he would change his mind. Emma Grace's aunt stopped at the door and turned back to him. "I want Nell to finish the dishes before she goes, so she'll meet Emma Grace at the dock."

"Yes, sir," said Beatrice over her shoulder as she moved out to the porch.

Nell scooped the eggs out of the pan and onto their plates before sitting to say grace with her family.

"Nell," said her mother. "I want you to stop by Tisdale's house on Harkers Island and give her a note from me. She needs to know about the quilt squares we're making."

"Of course, Mama."

∽

The tide was rising as the two girls set sail in Nell's *Harmony*. Nell's contentment increased proportionately the farther the boat pulled away from the shore.

"Your daddy probably didn't want to see you moping around your mama all day."

"Maybe," replied Nell, remembering the clarity she glimpsed in his eyes that morning.

Emma Grace continued. "That, and he figures that Harkers Island is the end of the earth, and they haven't heard of your downfall out there."

Nell smirked before setting her course toward the mouth of the harbor. Since the tide was running against the little boat, she hugged the island side of the channel. Once the small vessel entered the sound, Nell let out the sail into a broad reach while Emma Grace scanned the horizon with binoculars. "I see three working boats, but there's a sharpie coming out of the channel, poking along in the weeds. It might be headed our way."

"What does it look like?"

"Eighteen feet. Two masts with gaff rigs."

"Sounds like Jerry Adams. He's one of Asa's men." Nell scoffed. "You'd think he'd have something better to do."

"It's all about him being the boss," said Emma Grace in a distracted tone.

As they sailed, Emma Grace shared what they had learned at Isaac's the night before. When she told her friend about Sylvia Davis' involvement, Nell laughed. "I wish I could've been there."

"It sounds like they might could walk a shipment over Shackleford Island."

"If anyone would know anything, it would be Tisdale."

Once they were in the sound, the swells gently quartered on Nell's stern, lifting and lowering the boat in a lazy rhythm. A chill ran down Nell's spine when she glimpsed the steeple of the Methodist church while Rev. Saunders' words echoed in her head. Fighting the desire to look away, she continued to study the church tower. Something was nagging at her. She remembered how she had been waiting outside as the stream of people entered the church. "Emma Grace, did you say Mr. Ramsey was staying at the Davis' house when the *Three Sisters* came through?"

"That's what Annie said."

"When I saw Mr. Ramsey at church on Sunday, he hinted that Chadwick might be hidin' out on Harkers Island."

Emma Grace stared at her. "Hain't that sumthin."

"Yes, ma'am."

"So, Chadwick gets chased by Buddy and Winston on Horse Island and then goes and hides with his mama on Harkers Island."

"Doesn't sound like an innocent man."

A strong, steady wind blew them quickly across the sound, and within an hour, they were approaching a small dock at Harkers Island. A tall, lanky man wearing a wide-brimmed straw hat walked down to greet them. Emma Grace threw the bowline to him to tie off the *Harmony*. Once she stepped off the boat onto the dock, Nell looked up into the man's face under the hat. Jake Parson grinned back at her.

Flustered, she stammered. "Oh, Jake . . . how did—" she looked over at Emma Grace, who smiled, as well. "You set this up!" Nell said in alarm.

She turned to Jake, "My daddy would have a fit if he knew you were here."

"Well, he hain't here," answered Emma Grace.

Nell's panicked eyes darted back and forth between the two of them. She hated to lie to her daddy.

"Nell," said Emma Grace gently, "more than hemlines are changing right now. Even Methodist girls can vote. You don't have to treat your daddy like he's the hand of God."

Nell looked back into Jake's face, full of tenderness. She realized why she hadn't recognized him right away. "You shaved off your mustache."

"I figured if I wasn't fooling you or Isaac, then I couldn't keep hiding behind the damn thing."

She studied this new face, exposed and vulnerable, etched by lines of worry and sadness.

"Rev. Saunders hain't gonna walk around the corner here on Harkers Island," said Emma Grace.

"I don't know what you're worried about," Jake added. "We got Emma Grace here as a chaperone."

They all burst into laughter. Jake stretched his hand out to his girl. Tentatively, Nell smiled, took his hand, and he pulled her close to him. Emma Grace busied herself with tying down the sail and unloading the boat, while Nell leaned against Jake's chest, listening to the endless drone of the crickets and the lapping water. The natural sounds blended into a simple melody, and she nearly cried when her music returned. Jake sensed her relief and held her tighter.

After they pulled away from each other, Jake whistled to his two dogs, who were waiting patiently on the *Miss Mary*. They bounded off the skiff and greeted Nell like a sister. The three friends followed the dogs down a narrow road made of crushed shells bordered by acres of live oak trees. At the top of a high dune, they paused to admire the crowns of the trees, woven together into a single leafy canopy. Rooted in the hilly dunes, the grove rose and fell like sculpted waves of a green ocean.

"Now, there's a sight," said Emma Grace. "It looks like you could sail on it."

The other two nodded in agreement, watching the leaves quiver and tremble.

As they walked down the other side of the dune, Jake asked, "Did anyone follow you?"

"We mighta seen Jerry Adams when we left the harbor. How 'bout you?"

"I'm not sure, but I made note of a few boats." They walked along, talking about each vessel Jake had seen and trying to guess who they might be.

When they approached a small spur off the main road, Emma Grace said, "This is where I leave you. I promised Doc I would look in on Anna Lee."

"Jake and I will walk on to Tisdale's house," said Nell. "Maybe we can catch her at home."

"If she's not, she can't be far. She's gotta be on the island, somewhere," said Emma Grace.

Once their friend was out of sight, Jake pulled Nell to him for a lingering kiss. Although they'd only been apart for a day, Nell felt every part of her body aching for him. The steady breeze rustled while spring peepers sang a ceaseless refrain. His kisses traveled down her neck and eventually tickled her. Nell giggled, "My daddy would have a fit right now."

Jake pulled back to look at her. "Don't talk about your daddy right now."

Nell laughed out loud. She took his hand, and they continued down the road.

"I assume you remember our Tisdale," Nell said.

"You mean the lady who saved my bacon when Asa was pounding on me over five cents worth of candy?"

Thinking back to the day Marbles and Tobias had walked into Asa's drug store, she replied, "That's the one."

Several rabbit chases later, Yawg and Pilot arrived with Jake and Nell on the porch of Tisdale's home. "Miss Tisdale!" Nell hollered through the screen door. She watched as the tiny lady, accompanied by her pet goat, made her way from the back of the house and opened the door.

"Well, now. Hey there, honey. What brings you all the way out here?" The thick brogue rolled off of her tongue.

"Oh, Miss Tisdale," Nell said as she embraced the woman. "You're a sight for sore eyes." Tisdale's authentic ease brought a restorative swell of faith and goodness to Nell. "Well, hey there, Eloise," she said to the goat, who answered with a tail twirl. Unsure of this hooved creature, Pilot and Yawg remained behind Jake.

"I'm not sure if you remember Jake Waterson."

"Oh, my Lord, honey! You took on Asa and Jimmy after Tobias and Marbles got mommicked at Asa's pharmacy."

"Yes, ma'am," said Jake, extending his hand. Eloise made her way around Jake and began to nibble on Yawg's ear. Looking politely aggravated, the hound gave Jake a questioning look.

A look of concern passed over the woman's cheery face. "Is your mama poorly?" she asked Nell.

"No, ma'am," Nell answered, quick to reassure her. "She asked me to give you this note." Nell reached into her pocket and handed the woman a sealed envelope. "We were hoping you could help us with a problem we're having."

"Oh, my, that sounds like we might need some sweet tea. "Why don't y'all come through to the kitchen?" Company could be a welcome treat on the island.

Leaving the dogs and goat on the porch, Nell and Jake stepped over the threshold and followed Tisdale to the back of the house. Nell caught glimpses of Tisdale's treasures from the sea: driftwood carved and polished into sea creatures, wooden loons and duck decoys, and oysters adorning bleached horse skulls.

Tisdale bustled around as Jake and Nell settled onto their chairs.

"Mama wanted me to tell you they were starting another sentimental quilt."

"Who are they making it for?"

"I'm not sure. I think all that is in the note I gave you."

Tisdale nodded sagely and turned to her icebox for her pitcher of tea.

"I'll make her a whole passel of quilt squares. Can't wait to see how it will come out."

Nell watched Tisdale dart around the kitchen as she retrieved cookies and biscuits to go with their tea. Throughout her life, Tisdale had worked alongside her sons and husband while they shrimped and fished. Despite her age, she moved deftly around the kitchen. Once the tea was served, Nell and Jake began to lay out their story. "Well, Jake here was working down at Lowell's—"

"Oh my, bless your heart," interrupted Tisdale, shaking her head.

Jake simply replied, "Yes, ma'am."

"And he's been hearing lots of funny things," continued Nell. Three glasses of tea and several biscuits later, Nell finished her story by saying, "So, right now, we're looking for Chadwick. And since he has kin on the island, we thought you might be the best place to start."

"That's a fact." Tisdale bit into her biscuit as a generous blob of fig jam oozed out and plopped onto her plate. "I hain't nary a time seen him to the island, but for this past week. And I hain't at all sure where he's been a'lighting nowadays. But I have nary a doubt he's working over to Island Boatworks with hiz'n uncle, Elmer Lewis. I reckoned something happened there to town when he come home so quick. But Chadwick likes to keep to himself, so I let him be. And he's his own man. He gets that from his daddy."

Jake nodded, remembering how the young man often walked away from Charlie Lowell in midsentence during one of his rants at the boatyard.

"We figured it was something like that," said Nell.

"Do you know of someone making booze runs to Cape Lookout?" asked Jake.

"Half the island, just about," Tisdale replied matter-of-factly.

The animals had moved to the back of the house, and Tisdale's gaze wandered out the back door. She seemed lost in thought as she watched Eloise chase the two dogs around the back yard. Then the canines turned the tables and playfully chased the goat.

"You can't just go down yonder and talk to him, son," Tisdale said thoughtfully. "Folks out here won't nary a time talk to someone off island." The lady tapped her tea glass absently with her fingernail. "And he would look like evil to his friends if you showed up and were a'talking to him. It's best for me to go by myself to fetch him from the boatyard. I'll have to make up a story to get him here."

Long shadows were streaking across Tisdale's kitchen when Jake and Nell heard footsteps on the back porch. Nell looked up to see Chadwick open and step through the back door. He was breathing hard when he entered the kitchen. His eyes quickly searched the room. "Where's Mama?"

Nell and Jake didn't reply, waiting for Tisdale, who came panting up to the back door. "Whew! Young'un, I thought I lost you." She bent over and clasped her knees to catch her breath. Straightening up, she said, "I'm sorry, child, I told you a white lie. Your mama didn't fall and hurt herself."

Chadwick looked confused as she gently closed the heavy winter door behind her and stood in front of it. The young man became increasingly wary when Tisdale rested her hand on his arm. His eyes jumped between Nell and Jake while he furrowed his brow in anger.

"They're not with the law, Chadwick. Can you just talk to them, young'un?"

Determined, the islander clamped down his jaw. "I reckon I will," he retorted sarcastically.

"Chadwick," said Nell softly, "we don't care what you were doing on Horse Island that night. We don't care that you shot at us."

"I didn't shoot nary a time." The young man's voice rose in irritation. "I don't have no gun. It might have been Len—the boy I was with—he always said he's got a Luger, but I hain't seen it. I broke away from him after we heard that shot."

"Okay," Nell replied in a soothing voice. "I believe you. That shot could have come from anywhere." She smiled at him.

Chadwick turned his unblinking eyes to Jake but spoke to Tisdale. "He's the law. He's a revenue man."

"Asa started that rumor so no one would trust him," Nell said. "He's not a revenue man." Nell noticed a wave of fear ripple across Chadwick's face when she mentioned her ex-fiancé's name.

With a clear and deliberate voice, Jake spoke to him, "I know you don't know me, but I believe you can help me." When the youth didn't respond, Jake continued. "My brother is lost at sea, and you may have been one of the last people to see him before he left shore."

"I know nary a thing about that."

Tisdale glared at Chadwick and spoke firmly. "Let the man speak. You don't even know who he's talking about."

"We don't care if you were running booze," Nell said with a laugh. "Remember, I was engaged to Asa and dated him half my life. I reckon he's run some liquor."

"Son, you've had a time living like this," said Tisdale. "You've been holed up like a rat this past week. Can you not listen to what they have to say?"

Without taking his eyes off Jake, Chadwick looked resolute and stubborn.

"I want to talk to you about the *Amelia*," Jake said.

"I don't know nothing about that," Chadwick replied. His voice was angry, but there was fear in his eyes.

Holding Chadwick's gaze, Jake took a step closer. "Wade Parson is the captain of the *Amelia*. He's my brother. I'm Jake Parson. The *Amelia* is missing."

"I told you I know nary a thing about it." But his look of anguish said otherwise.

"He hain't foolin', son," Tisdale said to Chadwick. "This is serious business."

"We think Asa's friends from Richmond might have planned something," said Nell.

"All them people from up North are the same to me."

"We think Edgar Ramsey was involved," said Nell.

"I don't know him."

"You let him into the speakeasy at the Inlet Inn last Friday night," said Jake.

"That means nary a thing. I let a lot of people in. That's my job. Or it was anyway."

"What do you mean 'was'?" asked Nell. "Aren't you working with Asa anymore?" It didn't surprise her. When Chadwick disappeared, she figured he was either running from Asa or the law.

When he didn't answer, Jake asked, "Are you working with Ramsey?"

Tisdale stepped up to Chadwick. Despite being a head shorter and standing on her tippy toes to look him in the eyes, she cut an impressive figure, and Chadwick stepped back. "Now, you listen to me, Franklin Chadwick," she said, shaking a finger into his face. "You can't keep living like this—hiding out on an island, sleeping in your mama's attic, looking over your shoulder all the time. You're gonna have to go to the mainland eventually. You're living like an outlaw, and it hain't natural."

Chadwick looked like a possum who had been treed by hounds. "They could—" He didn't finish the sentence. Everyone waited as he looked down at the ground and squeezed his eyes tight. "They might hurt my mama."

"Sheriff Styron's not gonna go after your mama," said Tisdale, more gently.

"It hain't Jimmy I'm worried about," he shouted. They waited for him to continue, but he just looked miserable.

"What are you scared of, son?" pressed Tisdale.

Chadwick started to shake all over.

"You weren't working for Asa when you were out on Horse Island," Nell spoke slowly. "Now, you're afraid he found out. That's why you're hiding out here—you're not afraid of the sheriff; you're scared Asa will come after you."

Chadwick looked paralyzed with fear, but his eyes locked on Nell. "Chadwick," Nell continued, drawing out her words carefully, "We believe the *Amelia* met with foul play. Did you help unload her back in April?"

The young man looked away from her without speaking.

"Whoever harmed the crew on the *Amelia* might come after you."

"Why?" he nearly wailed.

"Well, we're not sure. But you were one of the last people to see Wade, and now he's missing. Do you want to go over to Fort Macon with us?"

"Oh, no, ma'am," Chadwick stepped back from her. "They might arrest me."

"We trust Elijah Midgett over at the Coast Guard station. He'll do right by you."

"Your mama can't protect you from Asa's people," said Tisdale.

Chadwick looked uncertainly at her. "You really think Midgett will help me?"

"I know he will," replied Nell.

Tisdale reached over and picked up one of Chadwick's hands. "You need to tell them what happened; you can't keep living like this."

"Tell us about the night you met the *Amelia*," Jake said.

Chadwick collapsed into a chair as his anger drained from him. They waited a few minutes in silence as Chadwick wrestled with himself. Finally, he looked into Tisdale's eyes and drew a breath. "Me and Johnny Davis met the *Amelia* in my skiff just down from the hook on the Cape. After we got the booze, my crew met us on shore, and it took us most of the night to move the cargo across the island. It's not but about a quarter of a mile right there. Some of it, we carried up the Drain, but it was so close to the lighthouse, and we were afraid someone would see us, so we moved down the beach.' Bout half that crowd were drunk or passed out by the time we were done. But I stayed sober. Well, mostly."

"Where did the *Amelia* go after you unloaded it?" asked Jake.

Chadwick thought for a minute. "I don't know. I didn't watch it. I was too busy onshore."

Jake nodded and Chadwick continued. "Since it was starting to get light, we buried the haul in the dunes on the sound side 'cause the cutter patrol over yonder could see us during the daytime. I stayed with the drop the whole next day, mostly 'cause I thought the boys who unloaded would come back and steal it. The next night, the crew met me on the sound side, and we carried it over to Lenoxville Point."

Nell pictured this deserted peninsula at the eastern end of Beaufort. "Who met you there?"

"Mr. Ramsey."

Nell and Jake exchanged looks.

"Chadwick," Nell said. "Who was on the boat when you met the *Amelia*?"

The young man hesitated. "I didn't see their faces all that good. We all covered our faces with bandanas. Most of us had hats pulled down low. We all did that. I knew my crew, but if we get caught, we figured we would say we couldn't recognize anybody." He paused for a moment. "Now that I'm thinking on it, they didn't say much. Just pointed and such."

"Can you tell us what you remember about the boys on the *Amelia*?"

"There were two of them." Chadwick thought for a moment. "One of them had brown hair."

"How tall was he?" Jake asked.

"The one on the helm never stood up, so I don't know how big he was."

Jake took a small, framed tintype photograph of Wade from his breast pocket and showed it to Chadwick. "Was he there? He worked on his mast with Isaac at Lowell's."

Chadwick squinted at the photograph. "I remember him from the boatyard. I can't tell. It was dark. And we were right busy. There was some surf that night."

"Was there anything you remember about them?"

The young man closed his eyes. "The one on the helm was wearing a ring. When we were rafted up against the *Amelia*, the helmsman threw me a line since it was right choppy. When he cleated it off, I saw he was wearing a big ol' ring. There hain't nary a man around here that wears a ring like that. Particularly on a boat where they can get all messed up. It had a big ol' stone."

"What did the ring look like?"

"It were a big, dark red, square stone with silver metal."

Nell exchanged glances with Jake. She knew she'd seen a ring like that, but she couldn't remember where. Jake looked equally confused.

"What were they bringing in, Chadwick. Rye?" Nell asked.

"There was some rye, but most of it was wine."

"Wine?" Nell and Jake said together in surprise. Locally, people only bothered to move hard liquor since they could make their own wine.

"Is that what the boys were drinking?"

Despite his trepidation, Chadwick broke into a wide grin. "Shoot, most of those boys didn't want money for all that hauling. They wanted the hooch. All they'd ever had was 'shine."

Tisdale was watching his face closely. "You kept some of it for yourself."

"Mr. Ramsey said I could have it," cried Chadwick.

"Do you have any left?

"Nah, we drank 'em all."

Nell studied his face. "But you kept the bottles." It was a statement, not a question. She knew wine bottles were used and reused for homemade vintage. If the bottle had a good label, it might pass for the real deal.

Chadwick looked away from her, clenching his jaw in a mulish fashion.

Tisdale was adamant. "Chadwick, it's important that you show us the bottles." When he didn't answer, she added, "The bigger sin is lying to these people, son."

"Chadwick, I want to take one of the bottles over to Midgett at the Coast Guard Station."

"Why?" said the young man, nearly whining. "They're mine."

"Evidence," stated Jake. "When we tell them what happened, we need to prove that there was contraband from the *Three Sisters*."

Chadwick looked crestfallen.

Jake crossed the room to him. "Let me buy them from you."

The young man considered this but still looked resistant.

"Name your price," pressed Jake.

The waterman hesitated. "It's just that, those bottles had a swell label."

"What did it look like?"

"It was a black horse with his mane blowing in the wind."

Inhaling sharply, Nell looked wide-eyed at Jake. "That's the wine they served at Asa's house the last time I had supper there."

CHAPTER 20

Dusk was falling on the island when Nell, Jake, and his two dogs made their way back to the harbor. Two empty wine bottles wrapped inside a sweater were nestled inside Nell's canvas satchel. Chadwick had led them to a large stump in a small crop of trees. After scraping off moss and sandy soil, he pulled out several wine bottles.

Despite Tisdale's pleas, Chadwick refused to leave with Nell and Jake and sail to Fort Macon since he was afraid of retaliation if anyone saw them together. On the promise he would follow them later that night, Nell and Jake reluctantly parted from him in the woods.

As they walked down to the island harbor, Nell said to Jake, "When I had supper at Asa's house, Mr. Ramsey said he'd brought the French wine down with him from Richmond. Now that I think about it, Asa got right riled up about that."

"He must've realized Ramsey had picked up the load on his own."

"I think Mr. Ramsey stays at the inn when he's in town. So, where would he store his cargo?"

When they arrived at the shore, Jake fed and watered his dogs before sitting down next to Nell. Dangling their feet over the edge of the dock, they listened to the spring peepers singing their frenzied song of courtship while they waited for Emma Grace. Nell rummaged around in her bag, and pulled out the wine bottles. "You'll need these when you get to Fort Macon."

"You know you're welcome to come with me," said Jake, circling the top of her hand with his finger.

Mesmerized by his touch, she felt weak and hazy. "My daddy would have a fit," she replied, but there was no heart in her answer.

"I would never have figured out this much without your help," Jake whispered as he leaned in and nibbled her ear.

She pulled back, searched his bare face, and then let her eyes rest on his lips. "You don't know that for sure," she said. Her voice sounded distant.

"Sure, I do," he answered, but she wasn't listening. He gently covered her hand, sending an electric pulse racing through her body. When he kissed her, everything fell away from Nell. She couldn't hear the mating frogs anymore, and she felt like they were the only two people on the island. She didn't care what Rev. Saunders or Sylvia Davis or any of those Beaufort cows thought of her.

"Can't leave the two of you alone for a minute," Emma Grace said as she stepped on the dock. Jake and Nell reluctantly pulled away from each other.

"How did it go? Did you find Chadwick?"

"You might say that," Nell said, slowly standing up. The couple recounted their day with Tisdale and Chadwick. When they finished, Nell held up the two wine bottles as if they were trophies.

Emma Grace whistled as she studied the label. "Y'all had quite a day. No wonder you were kissin'."

"How is Anna Lee?"

"Driving her mama crazy. But her leg has healed right nice." She kneeled to grab the bowline of the *Harmony*.

In a resigned, bitter tone, Nell said, "I've got to get back to the house. Jake, here, is gonna head over to Fort Macon and talk to Midgett about the *Amelia*."

Emma Grace stopped pulling the line to look at her friend. "Nell, you have to go with him."

"That would just about kill my daddy."

Emma Grace stood up to face Nell. Tilting her head at her friend, she stated, "Nell, this is your life you're living—you have to see it all the way through."

Nell exhaled and closed her eyes. In an instant, everything that had happened in the last few days paraded in front of her: the fall from grace at church last Sunday, life-long friends turning their backs on her, the silent, soulless morning despair and her father's anger.

Emma Grace cleated off the bowline. "Nell, if I hadn't stood up to those girls in high school, and if Harrison hadn't believed in me, my spirit would have died. Those girls will never like me, but I found people who do love me. If you don't push back and fight, they'll take everything from you."

Nell nodded slowly. "Okay," she said, turning to Jake. He moved over to her and wrapped his arms around her. Swallowing an enormous lump in her throat, Nell pulled back to look at him. "I do know the channel better than you."

Emma Grace watched them for a moment. "Should I alert Rev. Saunders when I hit the town dock?" She smirked. "He could speed up the ostracism."

Nell smiled. "No, but I would appreciate it if you stopped by and let my daddy know I'm sorry I disappointed him."

Emma Grace considered this. "I'll tell your mama. She can tell your daddy."

"Emma Grace," said Jake in a somber tone, "I think it's time we told Mr. Guthrie about my connection to the *Amelia*." He exchanged glances with Nell. "Y'all have put yourselves out for my family and me, and we need to let Nell's family know what she's doing for us."

Emma Grace saluted him. "Aye, aye, Captain."

"Are you okay going back to Beaufort by yourself?" asked Nell.

Emma Grace scoffed. "I could do it in my sleep."

"Watch your back. The night has eyes."

Nell and Jake eased back down to the dock and watched Emma Grace climb into Nell's boat, set sail, and pull away from shore. The *Harmony* grew smaller and smaller until they could no longer discern it from other lights on the water. The couple remained on the dock, listening to the maniacal insect chorus that grew louder with the night. As they waited for the cover of darkness, Nell shifted and pressed her back into Jake, watching the lights from Beaufort and the Coast Guard Station twinkle on the horizon. When it was sufficiently dark, they set sail without running lights in case anyone was following them.

With Jake at the helm, Nell scanned the water with binoculars, looking for any boats that might be following them. Then she pointed to the distant point of light off their port side. "That should be Fort Macon."

"That's what I figured."

Jake set a course close to the headwind and turned the bow into the gentle oncoming waves. Soon, the *Miss Mary* was lifting and falling in an easy, steady rhythm. After twenty minutes, an enormous yawn overtook Nell, and she curled up next to Jake as he steered the boat. The two dogs wedged themselves on either side of the couple, and the four of them shared body heat in the moist evening air. Nestling closer into Jake, she felt both protected and free. The mesmerizing beat of the waves, combined with the caressing wind, soothed her like a gentle lullaby and she fell into a light sleep . . . Chadwick digging holes in dunes . . . the black stallion prancing by while tossing his flying mane . . . swaying trees on Lenoxville Point . . . a figure in the woods with his back to her, he's turning around. . . .

The skiff jolted, and she awoke to see Jake tacking to stay in the channel. She automatically reached for the sheet and adjusted the sail before securing the line for their new tack.

"Thank goodness I had you to guide me through the channel."

"Sorry about that," she said sheepishly. "I was dreaming, and I saw the ring that Chadwick was talking about. It was on Mr. Ramsey's finger when we had supper at Asa's house."

"That would put him on the helm of the *Amelia*."

"What I don't understand is how the crew working with Chadwick came to trust Mr. Ramsey."

"I thought of that, too," said Jake.

"I mean, people from Harkers Island don't just open to highfalutin, hoity-toity people from Richmond."

"Ramsey must be working with someone local."

"And they're doing it right under Asa's nose."

"I reckon he wouldn't appreciate that very much." Shivering, she remembered the thugs who guarded Asa's speakeasy at the Inlet Inn, enormous men who pulled nets on ships when not onshore. "In my dream, I saw that black horse on the wine label. Why do you think Mr. Ramsey brought that French red wine to supper at Asa's that night? It wasn't very bright. I mean, he gets that wine all the way up to Richmond, and then he brings it back down, and waves it around right in front of Sylvia Davis."

Jake was silent for a few moments. "Maybe it never left Beaufort—or part of it didn't. Chadwick had a few bottles, so there may have been more around town."

"That would make sense." The wind shifted, and Nell trimmed the sails. She nestled back into Jake's chest. "The other thing that occurred to me is that I believe Chadwick when he says he didn't do the shooting on Horse Island."

"Yeah," agreed Jake. "He looked right scared, but it didn't look like he was lying."

"So, there was somebody else out there with a gun."

While they sailed in silence, Nell searched the horizon for boats. The waves beat out a rhythm against *Miss Mary's* hull and created a gentle rise and fall of the boat. The hypnotic movement made her want to sail out to the open sea with this man she was learning to trust. Nell had been so wrong about Asa. The hope of having a future with him sustained her after Harrison died. They were always looking forward to moving to Richmond, building a business, raising a family. Nell never saw what was right in front of her: his mother's interfering, his overbearing demeanor, and his dishonesty.

Now, curled up next to Jake under the starry Southern sky, she felt at home. There was something familiar and comforting about Jake, like playing a tune for the first time, but feeling she had been humming it all her life. As she tenderly traced the buttons on his shirt, a new consideration danced through her head. Emma Grace's father had sailed into port, fallen for her mother, and then sailed away. No one heard from him after he left. Her Mama Beatrice said he was an Italian sailor. Did he know he had a daughter? Had he died at sea? Would Jake sail away and never see her again?

"Penny for your thoughts," Jake asked.

Nell sat up and studied him in the light from the moon. She knew people left Beaufort. They visited during the sunny months of summer, splashed in the ocean, and then left when the shad boats returned in the fall.

"Jake." She cleared her throat.

When she didn't continue, he took his eyes off his course momentarily to glance at her.

"You reckon you're gonna stay in Beaufort? I mean, after you find Wade and all."

Jake stared at the water in front of him before he spoke. "The honest answer is, I don't know. I have commitments to my family in South Carolina."

The skiff plowed on against the charging waves. It was some minutes before Jake spoke again. "But whatever I decide, I want you to be a part of it." Then he added, "I know that's not a simple thing to say. But when your daddy sent me away on Sunday, it felt like coming back from the war with a missing limb."

Nell turned her face up to him and they kissed. Since he was holding the tiller, the boat shifted when they embraced. He quickly released her to right the skiff.

"Of course," continued Jake. "After tonight, your daddy might shoot me. Decision made."

"That's a fact," she answered. It would have to do for now. There had been promises and plans with Asa. Jake could offer music and a sail on his skiff. She knew neither of them would rest until they knew what became of Wade. And that was enough for now.

They sailed for an hour, both feeling at peace with the bright moon, the sea, and the starry ceiling above them. All too soon, the lights of Fort Macon Coast Guard Station appeared on the horizon. "Going to shore," she said with a sigh.

"Going to shore," Jake repeated with similar reluctance.

∽

When Jake had first arrived in Beaufort, he sailed past the brick, pentagon-shaped Fort Macon located on the eastern end of Bogue Island. Since Beaufort Inlet was a valuable port on the North Carolina coast, it was susceptible to naval attacks from pirates and national enemies. Although the impressive garrison had defended the port since 1826 and played a significant role in the Civil War, it was now unoccupied.

Adjacent to Fort Macon, several modest white clapboard buildings housed the burgeoning United States Coast Guard. Before Prohibition, this site was home to the local Life Saving Station that rescued crews from stranded ships off North Carolina's shallow, treacherous coastal waters. Now, with the onslaught of illegal smuggling of alcohol, the Coast Guard focused on rum-running operations and rescues using power boats and seaplanes.

When Nell and Jake sailed up to the station's dock, several uniformed men greeted them and tied off the *Miss Mary*. After the couple stated their business, they accompanied the servicemen to the larger, wooden building.

Radio static greeted Nell and Jake when they entered the dining quarters. Framed nautical charts interspersed with photos of naval commanders lined the walls. When she sat down at the mess table, Nell noted that it was almost two in the morning by the wall clock. She knew her parents would be worried sick about her. Midgett entered from the station's kitchen and set steaming cups of coffee in front of them.

"So, what brings y'all out here in the middle of the night with no running lights?"

Jake glanced at Nell before he spoke to Midgett. "My real name is Jake Parson. My brother, Wade, built the *Amelia* and sailed it to Beaufort in March."

Midgett hesitated before he replied, "I'll be damned."

"Nell and her friends have helped me uncover some important information regarding my brother and his boat."

Midgett nodded, sat back, and fixed his attention on his two visitors. Over the next quarter of an hour, Jake unraveled everything they'd learned, starting with the information shared by Annie and Isaac Jaspers. He noted that the disappearance of Wade coincided with the *Three Sisters* passing by offshore. Midgett merely raised his eyebrows when Jake mentioned Sylvia Davis's involvement in Asa's smuggling operation. He recounted their meeting with Chadwick, who had confirmed the drop from the *Amelia* near Cape Lookout after the date of Wade's last letter home. Several days later, Wade's boat had made a final sail out of the harbor. Now, they wondered if he had been on the helm. He ended the story with the surfacing of Yawg in Beaufort long after Wade supposedly left port. When Jake finished his recollection, Nell pulled the empty bottles of *Le Chevel Noir* out of her bag and set them on the table.

"We also came out here 'cause we're worried about Chadwick's safety," added Nell. "We think Asa suspects him of picking up this wine behind his back so he would be really mad at Chadwick."

Midgett picked up one of the bottles and examined the label. "I haven't seen this around town at all. I would have remembered it."

"I don't think my brother left port on the *Amelia* because he would never have left Yawg behind. I don't think he was lost at sea." The words sounded raspy as they tumbled out of Jake. Nell could see that he'd wanted to say this for a long while. "And we think Wade got involved in this bootlegging crowd, so there's a high likelihood he mighta been hijacked. Knowing my brother, he would have fought to the death if he thought his boat was being pirated." He turned his face away from them.

Midgett absently nodded and began to speak slowly, bringing all his thoughts together. "The Coast Guard posted an All Bulletins for the *Amelia* when your family first reported it missing," said Midgett. "But we're finding that smugglers change a ship's registration to a different country and that can deter us from hunting them down." He rubbed his chin in thought. "But when we made the post, we didn't know about this connection to the *Three Sisters*. If we knew her crew or her load, we might could track it back to *Amelia* and follow her route. Since the Whiskey Road runs from Nassau to New York, it's more than likely the *Three Sisters* is headed north. I can radio the naval station in Norfolk and see if they have an update on it. But there probably won't be anyone there who knows anything until daybreak."

He paused and focused on the wall behind them. "If someone wanted to disguise a boat, you could change the sails and fool people from a distance. But some folks might recognize the hull. You couldn't just dock anywhere; you'd have to hide it. Tell me more about the *Amelia*. I mean, I know she was a schooner, but what else can you tell me?"

"She had a short draft with a rounded, overhanging stern, and a short, stabilizing, weighted keel. It made for a smooth sail." Jake paused, staring at the wall behind them. "She sailed more like a yacht than a workboat. Wade went down to the dock in Charleston and bartered with the crew on the ships. He ended up getting mahogany for the brightwork." His gaze returned to Midgett and Nell. "I reckon there's not another boat like it."

Midgett got up from the table and went into the office, returning with pencil and paper. "Reckon you could draw it out for us?"

Jake sketched out the *Amelia* and handed it to Midgett, who studied the drawing. "So, it could be used in very shallow water. What did she draw?"

"I reckon about three feet with no load. But if she had a load—maybe four feet."

"It's more than likely she's in the Caribbean—Nassau is so big right now. And it's lawless."

After further questioning, Midgett made a radio call to Norfolk for information regarding the *Three Sisters* and provided additional information regarding the *Amelia*.

"Midgett," Jake started, "Do you have authority in Beaufort? Wouldn't the local law be involved if someone disappears?"

"Maybe, but right now, everyone thinks the *Amelia* was lost at sea with your brother abroad."

The three of them sat in concentration for a few minutes, tapping their coffee cups.

"It all comes back to Asa and Ramsey," Midgett said after several minutes.

Jake nodded. "Asa was running liquor, but we think Chadwick identified Ramsey on the *Amelia* when they made the drop at Cape Lookout."

"We need to find out what Ramsey knows, and we can't do that by coming in the front door," replied Midgett. "We need to get to Ramsey first, so Asa and his crew, and that would include Sylvia Davis and Sheriff Jimmy Styron, don't destroy evidence or leave town."

"I know Mr. Ramsey's in Beaufort because I saw him at church," said Nell. "But I'm not sure if he's at the inn or with Asa's family."

"So, if we need to find Ramsey, I could start with Sylvia. She's the weakest link," said Midgett.

"Hold up," said Nell, raising her hand. "It's still dark out, and Dr. Davis isn't at their house."

"He's not in town?" asked Jake.

She gave the two men an exasperated look. "No," said Nell, "he's not at his house. Everyone in town knows that. He's sleeping at the clinic now. I guess he finally had enough of his wife. But if she's all alone in that house, she'll never come down and answer the front door. She'll just call Jimmy or Doc Davis. We need to start with Asa."

The two men nodded.

"We have to be careful about how we come into town. If we ride in on one of the Coast Guard vessels—it's going to wake everyone up," said Midgett. "They may already be alerted because one of Asa's men could've followed you. If Asa's involved, Jimmy Styron won't make this easy."

"If we sail into port with the *Miss Mary*, we could catch Jimmy and Asa unawares and learn more," said Jake. "The tide and wind are with us, so we'd make good time."

"Could you find a way to distract Jimmy?" asked Midgett. "That would buy some time to get to Ramsey."

Nell nodded. "That shouldn't be too hard. I'll think of something on the way into town."

Midgett looked thoughtful, slowly nodding, and turned to the man operating the radio. "Ensign Marshall."

The man turned to look at his commander. "Yes, sir."

"You're in charge of the station until my return."

"Yes, sir."

"I'm going ashore in Beaufort. I'm expecting a radio call from Norfolk that will provide information regarding the *Three Sisters*, the *Amelia*, or Wade Parson. I want an immediate report if they contact us."

"How do I reach you, sir? I have no radio contact to Beaufort."

Midgett looked at Nell. "You reckon your daddy would help us out?"

Nell exchanged looks with Jake. *How did Emma Grace's conversation go with her mama and daddy? Would her father be willing to help?* "I don't rightly know."

Midgett turned back to his ensign, "Forward the message to Camp Glenn in Morehead. When I arrive in Beaufort, I'll find a way to contact them."

"Affirmative, sir."

Midgett glanced at the station's wall clock. "If you haven't heard from me by 0900 hours, send the cutter over to Beaufort Town Dock."

"Affirmative, sir."

Now, Midgett sighed and turned to the couple. "I'm gonna keep you out of the investigation. I can't risk harming two civilians."

Jake and Nell looked at each other. "I think you need us, Midgett. We can question Asa, who can lead us to Ramsey," said Jake.

"Asa's a liar," said Nell. Both men waited for her to continue. "I learned to read him pretty well, so I can tell when he lies. If he stalls you, we could lose time."

Midgett looked like he was struggling with himself. "Alright," he replied with reluctance, "But I'm gonna need to deputize you."

Within minutes, Jake and his dogs, Nell, and Midgett boarded the *Miss Mary*. With Jake on the helm, Nell set up the running lights on the bow of the boat. Speed, not stealth, was their main concern right now, and she had no desire to come upon a shoal or collide with another boat in the harbor.

Midgett scanned the water as he let out Jake's mainsail. "Damn. I'm gonna have to call in the feds. I hate those people."

"Aren't you a fed?"

Looking aggravated, Midgett replied, "I'm not a revenue fed. They're nothing but goons with guns."

"So, where should we dock after we get to Beaufort?" asked Jake.

"If we go to the town dock, everyone in town will know we're there."

"Let's go to our dock at my house," sighed Nell. She weighed her father's uncertain mood. "We might as well deal with my daddy first. Depending on how that goes, you might have to hunt the bad guys by yourself."

A look of concern passed over Jake's face. "You didn't by any chance hide his shotgun before you sailed?"

Nell grimaced. "Maybe I should go ashore first after we dock."

CHAPTER 21

The Beaufort Harbor was slumbering when the *Miss Mary* glided past several dozen fishing boats docked behind the stores or moored throughout the harbor. Nell tensed when they approached her house. "Oh, my goodness. The light in the parlor is on. I'm in a scrape now."

Jake eased the boat toward the dock in front of Nell's house. She held her breath as she watched her daddy open the door and pass under the streetlight. His measured footsteps didn't reveal his mood, and she couldn't read his expression in the dim light. She glanced at Midgett and Jake, who looked as apprehensive as she felt.

Nell moved to the front of the boat with the bowline, ready to jump on the dock, while Midgett dropped the sail. Jake guided the craft into the slip.

After Nell tied off the boat, she turned to her father waiting on the dock. Unable to move, she looked at him. "Daddy, I'm so sorry. Jake needed help, and we found the wine bottles, and we wanted to protect Chadwick after we talked to him. . . ." Her voice trailed off as she looked up at her father's face, expecting to see it colored in a purple rage. But his expression softened when he looked down at her with understanding in his eyes. There was none of the cloudy, unfocused mess she'd seen for the past five years.

"Emma Grace told me the whole story. And I talked to your mama." His voice sounded even. "Let's get inside where we can talk."

Nell looked back at Midgett and Jake, still sitting in the boat, looking equally confused.

"I'll clean up the skiff if y'all want to go inside," Midgett offered.

Jake looked like he preferred to stay with Midgett, but he stepped onto the dock and offered his hand to Nell. Reluctantly, they walked beside Nell's father into the house, with Yawg and Pilot trailing behind them.

"So sorry to hear that your brother disappeared," the older man said to Jake.

Looking uncomfortable, Jake replied, "Thank you, sir."

Walking beside him, Nell realized that her father didn't smell of booze, and his gait was steady and sure-footed. The determined look on his face reminded her of Jake when they were under fire on Horse Island.

Keeping his eyes on the ground, Mr. Guthrie began, "Your mama and I talked, and then Emma Grace showed up and told me what you were up to." Without looking at her, he cleared his throat. "I think you've been very brave."

This was her old daddy. This was the man who would wake her up in the middle of the night when shrimp were running. Nell wanted to throw her arms around him and hug him. Instead, she politely replied, "Thank you, sir."

Jake squeezed her hand, and she held his tight.

"I just got your mama to lie down," Mr. Guthrie explained while he quietly opened the back door to the kitchen. "She made you sandwiches and coffee. Nell, you reckon you could serve us?"

"Yes, sir." The plate of sandwiches was on the side table, covered by a bowl. After she set the plate in the middle of the kitchen table, she turned to retrieve the coffee pot, plates, and mugs.

"So, what's your plan of action?" asked Mr. Guthrie. And then Nell saw it. This was her daddy's war; the one he'd wanted to fight instead of sending off his only son. He was avenging Harrison's death by protecting his little girl. Feeling overwhelmed with relief, she turned away from the table.

Jake picked up a sandwich and then recounted what the three of them had worked out on the sail from Fort Macon. "We need to find Ramsey. Before he disappeared, Wade unloaded the *Amelia* with a load of booze off Lookout. We think Ramsey was working with him. We're not sure where Ramsey is, and we don't want to wake up the whole town, so we thought we'd start with Asa. Nell says she knows when Asa is lying, so she's coming with us. Midgett is waiting to hear from his men regarding the *Three Sisters*, the offshore boat that Wade

218

and Ramsey were meeting. After we talk to Asa, he's gonna wake up half the town, so we'll need to distract Jimmy."

Mr. Guthrie snorted. "He's in it up to his neck with Asa."

Nell sipped her coffee and asked, "Daddy, you reckon you could help us take care of Jimmy?"

"I'm not sure what you mean."

"Midgett wants to send Jake down to the store with you and somehow get the sheriff's attention away from us when we go and talk to Mr. Ramsey."

Jake shifted uneasily.

"How do you feel about that?" Mr. Guthrie asked Jake.

"I'd rather stay with Nell," he replied, chewing the inside of his cheek.

Nell placed her hand on his white-knuckled fist resting on the table. "But Midgett figured it would be like waving a red flag in front of a bull if you go to Asa's house. He's already beat up Buddy."

They both looked at Mr. Guthrie, who thought for a moment before answering. "I reckon we could make it look like someone broke into the store and then call Jimmy to check out the robbery."

"I like that idea," answered Nell, nodding slowly. "There's something else, Daddy. Could Midgett and I use your truck?"

"The keys are in the ignition," her father replied without hesitation.

"Thanks, Daddy. Why don't you come down to the dock with us and check in with Midgett before we take off?"

Nell started to stand up and then looked at Jake. "When y'all leave for the store, you reckon you could go over to Emma Grace's and see if someone could come here and sit with Mama? I know she'll not want to be alone when she wakes up."

Jake smiled at her and nodded.

"I reckon you need to come down to the dock and check with Midgett to see if we forgot anything," Nell said to both men.

Once the three of them were outside on the back porch, Nell leaned forward to rub the heads of Jake's two dogs before everyone walked down to the dock. When they rounded the house, Nell bent her head against the rising wind. Despite her apprehension about confronting Asa, her daddy's change of heart bolstered her resolve to find Wade.

"Hey there, Midgett," Nell cried out as they approached the landing. She could hear an engine-powered boat making its way through the harbor. The town was beginning to stir.

In the dim light, Midgett turned away from the water. When he saw the three adults and two dogs headed for him, he looked apprehensively at Mr. Guthrie.

"My mama talked some sense into my daddy," Nell said triumphantly as they walked toward the Coast Guardsman. She hugged her father, who awkwardly put his arm around her shoulders. "He's ready to loan us his truck, and he and Jake will keep Jimmy out of our hair while we talk to Asa."

Smiling broadly, Midgett exclaimed, "Well, that's good news!" After shaking hands with Thomas Guthrie, he asked, "Did Nell ask you if we could use your phone at the hardware store? I need to call Camp Glenn to get in touch with my men before nine o'clock."

"Sure thing," replied Mr. Guthrie. "I'll put a call through when we get down there."

"I reckon we'll meet up with you at the store when Midgett and I get finished with Asa," said Nell.

As Nell listened to the men's conversation, the boat engine on the water became louder as it moved closer to their dock at a high speed. As the boat approached, Nell saw a small woman at the helm. Tisdale's voice rang out in distress across the water, and the party ran to the end of the dock to greet her. "They come up to the house and surrounded it!" she cried.

"What's all this?" Nell asked.

Tisdale cut the motor and coasted to the dock while throwing the bowline to Midgett.

"There's a whole crowd over to Chadwick's house. They come over after y'all left. They dumped a whole load of rotten fish on the porch. It was common."

Midgett turned to address Nell. "Somebody must've seen you talking to Chadwick. Asa's got everyone thinking Jake's a revenue man."

"There hain't nary a secret to the island," Tisdale added. "Chadwick's sitting inside with his mama and his shotgun. They're scared out of their wits."

"I know you promised Chadwick that we wouldn't bring any government boats over to the island. But I reckon we'll need to notify Jimmy," said Midgett.

220

"Hang on, Midgett," replied Nell thoughtfully. "There might be another way around this."

～

A short while later, Nell was standing beside the Coast Guard commander as he pounded on Asa's front door. "Open up! Official Government Business!"

Several minutes passed before Nell said, "He's here, Midgett. He wouldn't go anywhere without his car."

"Asa!" Midgett shouted, "I know you're in there, and I'll wake up the whole town if you don't open up."

Nell heard shuffling from inside the house; someone was swearing and bumping into furniture. Several minutes passed before the door opened.

"I hain't deaf, Midgett, damn. Break my door down why don't you?" said Asa. His eyes were bleary, and he reeked of bourbon, vomit, and sweat. Despite their differences, it hurt Nell to see Asa suffering.

The young man's eyes randomly drifted from Midgett to Nell before he smirked. "Well, if it hain't The Lonely Virgin."

Nell's head snapped back as if she'd been slapped.

Asa paused to inhale from his cigarette. "Or maybe not, now that you're making the rounds through the whole damn town. First, Buddy, now Midgett. You've certainly become real popular in town, but I wouldn't know."

Nell winced, but managed to stare back into Asa's sneering face. This was the man she'd planned to marry, the man for whom she was going to leave her family and her town. A shudder gripped her body, but instead of hurting her, Asa's cruelty strengthened her resolve.

Midgett stepped menacingly toward Asa. "You always did have a potty mouth when you're drunk, Asa. Or any other time for that matter. Too bad you're too stupid to realize that Nell was the best thing that ever happened to you."

Nell impassively studied the face she'd cherished for so long. She saw the corners of Asa's mouth momentarily droop before they stretched back into a hardened grimace. "Did you get me out of bed in the middle of the night to insult me?"

"We need to find your cousin, Ramsey," Midgett said.

"He hain't here."

"You want me to go wake up your mama?"

Asa sneered as his head jerked up. "I'd like to see you try."

"We got a situation brewing on Harkers Island."

"Who are they stringing up? Frankie Chadwick?"

Midgett and Nell stared at Asa. The silence lengthened. "That's a very interesting statement, Asa Davis," the serviceman said slowly. "Did you know Nell talked to him yesterday?"

Asa swayed slightly and looked behind them into the street, "Shit," he said. "It's all over town, is all."

"What's all over town?" said Midgett.

Nell could see rage building in Asa. "Whatever happens to that dimwit serves him right." He spat between Midgett's legs. "Talking to a revenue man."

"Where were you last night?"

"None of your business." Asa pulled his chin down and away from them.

Nell remembered how he had made this movement when she'd asked about Luanne. She knew this indicated that he was lying. "Chadwick could be dead right now."

"That would be tragic," he said indifferently. "But I can't imagine how it concerns me."

"Were you over at your mama's last night?"

"I told you, it's none of your damn business."

Midgett grabbed Asa by the shirt, yanked him out of the doorway, and slammed him against the side of the house. "I am investigating the hijacking of a ship. A man who probably worked for you could be in great danger. I credited you with a bit more respect for human life and your own friends."

Asa made several drunken attempts to break Midgett's hold, but had no chance against Midgett's enormous strength. The more Midgett locked him in, the more it fueled Asa's rage. "You piece of trash, Midgett! I will protect my family with my dying breath—and that goes for their friends, too. Just because you're in the service—"

Distanced from his temper, Nell objectively scrutinized Asa's face closely as he spat out his words. "He just mentioned family and friends, Midgett. His mother is involved. And Mr. Ramsey might have been at his mother's house."

Asa stopped flailing at Midgett to look at Nell with disdain. "Did the *Love Doctor* teach you how to read people's minds? On his couch?"

His venomous reference to Freud smacked Nell back to the shaming sermon directed at her by Rev. Saunders. She took a step back from Asa without breaking her concentration on his face. Somehow, she knew that if he had said this a week ago, his words would have devastated her, but tonight she could feel a strength rising in her.

Midgett leaned his full weight into Asa to regain his attention. "Tell us where we can find Ramsey, and I won't turn you in."

"Like I'm gonna help you."

"Is he at your daddy's house?"

Asa laughed and held Midgett's gaze.

"Is he at the inn?"

He tucked his chin down, "Got nothing to say."

Nell caught the movement of his chin which she correlated to earlier falsehoods. "He's at the inn." She turned to walk off the porch, but looked back at Asa before she said, "We're wasting our time here."

Midgett held Asa until Nell was opening the door to her daddy's Ford. Then he slammed the drunk against the house with a force that stunned him. Asa slid down the wall and sat. Midgett turned and walked off the porch. When he reached the bottom step, Asa revived and launched himself over the railing.

"Behind you," Nell cried to Midgett. The officer dodged to one side, causing Asa to land facedown in the sandy dirt.

"You're worthless, Midgett!" he cried in pain, holding his face and rolling in agony.

Midgett climbed into the passenger seat and drove away with Nell. Once they were some distance away, Midgett glanced at Nell's contorted face. "You okay?"

"Yeah," she replied. "I'm glad I was able to help you." Then she added, "Don't you want to put a man on his house, so he won't wake up the whole town?"

"We're in the thick of it now. At this point, I reckon he'll flush all the rats out of their hidey-holes, so I don't have to go look for them."

"But he might get to Mr. Ramsey before we do."

"He might, but from all the time I've been doing this, it's usually a good thing to get everyone out in the open because they start pointing their fingers at each other."

They drove down Front Street just as the fiery fuchsia and orange light of dawn began to streak across the eastern sky.

$\backsim$

Jake and his two dogs were waiting with Mr. Guthrie in his hardware store when Nell and Midgett drove up. Pilot and Yawg greeted Nell by wagging their entire bodies.

"We figure Ramsey's at the Inlet Inn," said Midgett.

"Asa told you that?" asked Mr. Guthrie.

Nell knelt to stroke the two dogs. "In a manner of speaking." Feeling bruised and shattered by her encounter with Asa, she longed to be embraced by Jake or her daddy. For now, she settled for this hearty canine welcome.

"Asa's moving a bit slow. If we act now, we might get to Ramsey before he does," said Midgett.

Mr. Guthrie looked at Nell, "I reckon it's time to start tearing up the store and then call over to Jimmy to keep him busy for a while."

She turned to Jake and Midgett. "Why don't the two of you get over to the hotel, and I'll catch up with you shortly?"

"Nell, I really don't know if you should be going over—" Midgett started.

"I'd like to see you stop me," she retorted in a flat, but challenging voice.

Midgett stepped back and exchanged strained looks with Jake.

Mr. Guthrie broke the tension by saying, "Oh, Midgett, I called over to Camp Glenn. Your men had left a message about a boat in Norfolk." He handed the note to Midgett, who read it and passed the message to his two friends.

"Hain't that interesting," Jake commented.

"Y'all need to get going. I'll keep the boys here with me," said Nell, indicating the two dogs. "They might slow you down once you get to the inn."

Yawg and Pilot sat at attention when Jake sternly commanded them to protect his girl. They listened to their master like two soldiers with their chests puffed out, ready to be pinned with war medals.

Before turning to leave with Midgett, Jake caught Nell's eye and held it for a moment. A longing passed between them. After Asa's blasphemous condemnation, Jake's face was a welcome sight to Nell. From the store's front window, she watched the two men walk up the street to the Inlet Inn. Then she turned to her father and said, "Alright now, let's tear it up."

~

As Jake walked away from the store, he fought the urge to run back and shield Nell from danger. When he and Midgett entered the Inlet Inn, they approached the night clerk working the front desk, who was struggling to keep his eyes open. Midgett slammed his hand on the counter to stir some life into the young man. He held up his Coast Guard identification and stated, "Official Business. We are investigating a crime. We need to find your guest, Edgar Ramsey."

Still working his way out of his doze, the young man answered, "Yes, sir." He swayed over to the counter and pulled the desk registry toward him. He ran a finger down the list of guests before he looked up and said, "Room 201. My manager will have to escort you for entry." The clerk disappeared into the office behind the desk and the rotund manager appeared moments later. Flanked by Midgett and Jake, he ascended the hotel staircase to the second floor. When no one answered his knock at Room 201, the hotel manager opened the room with a passkey.

When Jake stepped into the room, his foot rolled on an empty wine bottle left on the floor. Gaining his balance and adjusting to the dim light, he could detect an overturned nightstand, several overflowing ashtrays, and strewn clothes around the room. Ramsey lay sprawled on the bed, snoring and naked, tangled in the sheets.

"Sweet Jesus," the manager muttered as his foot slipped on a half-eaten sandwich discarded on the floor.

Midgett turned over the prostrate figure and shouted, "Ramsey!" He gently slapped the sleeping man's face while he repeated, "Edgar Ramsey!" The man's eyes fluttered, but he couldn't open them. Jake picked up one of the discarded wine bottles and examined the label with the familiar prancing stallion. "It's that Black Horse mess." He sniffed the open bottle. "But I can't

225

imagine he could be this far gone on wine." He turned to the hotel manager and said, "You want to go find some coffee and ice?"

"Sure thing," the man replied as he left the room.

Midgett pulled Ramsey to a sitting position on the bed's edge.

Working together, Midgett and Jake dragged the man to the bathroom and lifted him into the tub, where they turned on the cold-water faucet.

Ramsey sputtered and fought them as he tried to climb out of the tub. His head lolled with heaviness. Jake grabbed the ceramic pitcher from the bedroom and filled it with cold water. Ramsey groaned when Jake poured the water over his head. "There's definitely some laudanum involved here. He reeks of it," Midgett said.

When the manager returned with a small block of ice, a pot of coffee and several cups, Ramsey was sitting in the bed. The bedsheets covered his hips, and his head tilted to one side, but his eyes were open. "Oh, dear God in heaven, allow me to die this instant," he muttered, straining to focus on Jake's face.

Midgett chipped off a piece of the ice, wrapped it in a washcloth, and pressed it against the back of Ramsey's neck, then moved it around to his forehead.

"Oh, that hurts so much it's heavenly," the semi-conscious man slurred.

After several minutes, Ramsey leaned against the headboard and said, "How can I help you, gentlemen?"

"We need to talk to you about the *Amelia*."

"The what?"

"Ramsey," Midgett nearly shouted, "I am an officer of the law. Do you want to do this with Jimmy down at the jail?"

"Good heavens no." A visible shudder wracked the man's body. "Could you pour me some coffee—I can smell it, but I need to swallow some." The words sputtered out of him.

Jake poured a cup. "We know you had something to do with the disappearance of the *Amelia*. It was the boat loaded with this." He held up one of the empty bottles of *Chevel Noir* close to Ramsey's face.

The artifacts dealer took a long sip of coffee and stared at the wine bottle. His hand stretched out to stroke it. "Is it a crime to love a good Bordeaux?"

"Ah, well, according to the Eighteenth Amendment, yes."'

Ramsey replied, "Oops, how true."

"The *Amelia* is a boat that has been missing for about three weeks," Jake repeated. "Frankie Chadwick helped you move your cargo from the *Three Sisters* onto Shackleford back in April."

"Running lights . . . signals in the dark. . . ." the Virginian murmured as he closed his eyes and slumped sideways on the bed. Midgett caught the coffee cup before Ramsey's grip on the saucer slackened.

Midgett looked down at the unconscious man on the bed and sighed. "This may take a while."

CHAPTER 22

While Jake and Midgett were sobering up Mr. Ramsey, Nell and her father were creating a distraction designed to lure Sheriff Jimmy's attention away from the inn. Their plan was to set the stage for a phony robbery at the hardware store. Nell smashed a back window of her father's store to make it appear as the point of entry, while Mr. Guthrie pried the cash register open with a screwdriver and overturned several barrels of hardware. When they determined that it looked as though someone had rifled through the store, they called Jimmy.

While they waited for the lawman to arrive, Nell watched Front Street through her binoculars by the front window.

After a few moments, her father sat next to her.

"It was hard when Harrison died," said Mr. Guthrie.

Nell set down her binoculars and looked at her daddy. "Don't I know it."

"Grief hits us all in different ways. You still had your mama and your music. But it felt like everything I had, died with Harrison. Last night, your mama pointed out that you kept the family together."

Nell thought back to their collective grief when they learned of Harrison's death. She'd gone through the motions of life, cocooned in her solitary misery, removed from everyone, including her parents. In that moment, her parents had needed her. "I can't think of anything else I would have done."

Her daddy shifted. "I wish you had talked to me more about Asa."

"I didn't want to burden you, Daddy. I thought it would be easier if you didn't have to worry about me. You just seemed so sad about everything."

"Little girl," he turned to look at her, "you are the most precious thing, other than your mama, to me." She leaned into him, and he wrapped his arms around her.

When she pulled away, Nell saw several store owners were opening up their businesses for the day, and shoppers were arriving on foot, on bicycles, and in wagons. Her daddy got up to unlock and open his front door. Across the street, several of Asa's men walked up when his clerk arrived to open the drugstore.

Nell swiveled and turned her binoculars toward the inn and spotted Asa shuffling from his house with an unsteady, weaving gait. When Nell turned to tell her father, she noticed Jimmy walking up from the other direction. As he got out of his police vehicle, the sheriff noticed Asa turning into the Inlet Inn. Now, the lawman stood indecisively on the sidewalk. Nell didn't want Jimmy to run down the street and talk to Asa at that moment. She jumped up and ran out to the sidewalk, crying, "Oh, Jimmy, you just have to help us. I think some of those men from the boats broke in from the waterside. Let me show you the back door." She locked onto Jimmy's arm and pulled him into the store.

"Thomas," Jimmy greeted Nell's father.

Nell nattered on at high speed. "We got so much riff-raff coming in off the boats. You have no idea who might be moving in and out of the harbor. I counted twenty-seven boats rafted against the dock." As she led Jimmy to the broken glass at the back of the store, her father took up the watch at the front window. A few minutes later, Mr. Guthrie walked back to Nell and handed her a stack of letters. "Let me finish up with Jimmy here. You need to take these to the post office for me."

Nell looked at the letters and nodded. Now that everything was in place, it was time to join Midgett and Jake at the Inlet Inn. "Sure, Daddy," she answered, taking the letters. She remembered Jake's parting words and knew he wanted her to keep his dogs with her for protection. "Come on, boys," she said to Pilot and Yawg, who were snoozing on the floor. They jumped up like it was Christmas and practically danced out the street-side entrance. They soon fell in step behind Nell as she walked down the sidewalk. When she was a few paces away from the store, she tucked the letters in her dress pocket and broke into a trot to the Inlet Inn.

A few minutes later, Nell stood at the hotel's front desk talking to the clerk, whom she recognized from school. "You know I can't tell you that, Nell," the young clerk said when she asked him for Ramsey's room number. His tone was both firm and apologetic.

"Jerry, I'm working with the law on this now."

"It's one thing for Midgett to come in and demand personal information, but I just can't give out room numbers to a citizen."

She narrowed her eyes at him. "If you don't tell me in the next fourteen seconds, I am going to stand on this desk and tell everyone in this lobby what you do with raw oysters. And it won't be pretty."

"I don't do anything with—"

"Oh, it won't have to be true," she retorted fiercely.

The color drained from Jerry's face as his eyes darted around the lobby. He swiveled the guest registry around so Nell could read the list of registrants. Turning away from the desk and raising his voice, he declared, "I believe I am needed in the office."

Nell read the registry and found the entry for Mr. Ramsey in Room 201. Returning the registry to its place, she walked away from the desk with Yawg and Pilot on her heels.

As the three of them walked by the office door, Jerry jumped out of the doorway. "Nell," he said, mustering every ounce of authority, "I cannot allow you to bring your dogs up to a guest's room." He walked over to her and lowered his voice, "I would most definitely lose my job."

Nell considered this for a moment. "Can they wait behind the kitchen?"

"Of course."

She pivoted toward the side entrance of the hotel, glancing into the dining room as she went. Asa was rising from a table and would soon be walking toward her. Nell checked the lobby and saw that Jerry had returned to the front desk. She ducked across the office doorway and diverted down the empty servants' entrance with the two dogs on her heels. "Okay, boys," she said, once they were some distance from the office. Their ears perked forward. "No, speak." They wagged their tails. "High alert." Their movement stopped, and their bodies became taut with anticipation.

The three of them stole down the corridor to the dumbwaiter. Nell opened the small elevator used for food trays and commanded the dogs, "Up."

Without hesitation, both dogs jumped into the dumbwaiter and settled themselves. She tucked in their tails, closed the door, and pulled the adjacent rope to carry the lift to the second floor of the hotel. When it stopped, she ran up the flight of stairs, checked the hallway, and released the dogs from the dumbwaiter.

Nell noticed Yawg put his nose to the floor and began to circle a scent that caused him to whine. She was watching this erratic behavior when she heard loud voices erupt from the direction of Mr. Ramsey's room. Peeking around the corner, she saw Asa walking away from her toward the room. Throwing the door open, he cried, "What the hell are you doing to my cousin?"

"Come!" she commanded the dogs as she ran to Room 201 and entered in time to see Asa charging Midgett. Jake tackled Asa from the side, and they collapsed onto the floor, where they began to scuffle. When Jake pinned down one of Asa's arms, Nell kneeled on it as Jake shifted his weight to straddle and restrain Asa.

"Stay!" commanded Jake when he saw the hackles rise on his dogs. They froze at their master's command, but their eyes remained fixed on the pharmacist.

"Asa!" said Midgett bending over to look into his face. "We are trying to wake up Ramsey. He was passed out when we came in."

Asa looked up at Midgett with disgust. "I don't appreciate you coming to my house, making insinuations about my mama, roughing up my friends with your revenue man—"

"I'm not a revenue man," said Jake.

"Do you take me for an idiot? Running around town, asking questions, and spying on decent folk."

"I'm Jake Parson. I'm Wade Parson's brother."

"Who?"

"Wade Parson. The captain of the *Amelia*, you heartless bastard. He worked for you."

Nell held her breath when Jake clenched his fists in rage and she wondered if he would start pounding Asa.

Asa stopped resisting and stared at him. "Well, don't that beat all."

"Now we're going to let you up, but you have to remember your manners," said Midgett. Using caution, Jake shifted his weight off Asa while Nell stood up but remained near the entrance of the crowded room.

Slowly, the pharmacist rose from the floor, rubbing the arm that Nell had pinned down. "This doesn't end here, Midgett—"

"Be nice, or Jake's dogs will rip you to shreds," answered the officer.

Asa glanced at Yawg and Pilot, who bared their teeth at him.

"Hush up now, Asa. You're acting like a baby," Nell said. "We don't have time for this. We need to help Chadwick, and we need to find Wade and his boat."

Asa's face contorted with anger and he lunged for Nell, but Midgett stepped in front of him and punched him in the face. The blow opened up the gash from their early morning encounter and covered his face in blood. "Jesus Christ, Almighty," Asa screamed as he clutched his nose and fell back into a chair. As he continued to scream obscenities, the two dogs advanced on him for a second time. Jake commanded them to remain near Nell. Although they obeyed, they growled and walked away from Asa, stiff-legged with their hackles raised.

Nell turned to look at Mr. Ramsey, who had hardly stirred during the brawl. His head lolled from side to side and his eyelids labored, but he was aware that everyone was watching him. "My, that was entertaining. You big strong men." He sighed deeply.

Midgett poured a new cup of coffee for Mr. Ramsey and handed it to him. "We were talking about the *Amelia*."

"Oh, yes," replied Mr. Ramsey, accepting the cup with shaking hands. "Back to business."

"Funny thing about the *Amelia*," Midgett continued. "Actually, there are lots of funny things about that boat. We don't know where the *Amelia* is, but we can put our hands on her cargo." He stooped to pick up one of the bottles on the nightstand table, "In fact, there appears to be a bunch of it in this room. This wine came in on the *Three Sisters*."

"It could have come ashore anywhere along the coast," said Asa, spitting blood on the floor.

"But it didn't," said Midgett. From his pocket, he pulled out the message from the U.S. Naval Station in Norfolk that Mr. Guthrie had scribbled for him at the hardware store. "My men got this message this morning: *We apprehended the* Three Sisters *off Willoughby's Spit. No Le Chevel Noir aboard. The captain stated they picked up the* Noir *in Nassau and sold the last of it to the*

232

Amelia." Midgett tucked the note back into his pocket. "It's a very specialized wine, so people tend to remember it."

"You stupid idiot," Asa glared at his cousin. "What are you up to?"

Pale and sweaty, the man in the bed turned his face in the direction of Asa.

"You brought a bottle of that wine into my mama's house last week. You said you brought it down from Richmond. Where the hell did you get it, Ramsey? Did you meet the *Three Sisters*?"

"Cousin," Mr. Ramsey replied in exasperation, "think about it. What on earth could I do on a boat? You know I can't sail ten feet without tossing my cookies. And how could I possibly pull all those ropes and work all those grinders on deck." He shivered.

"We know you were working with Chadwick," Jake said. "He told us that yesterday. You unloaded the *Amelia* near Lookout, carried it over Shackleford, and on to Lenoxville Point.

"What was left of it." Mr. Ramsey shook his head. "Those boys drank about half of it before it got to town."

"You son of a bitch!" Asa cried as he advanced toward the bed, causing Pilot to growl. This time, Jake did not command him to stand down. The Labrador lowered his head and bared his teeth. Keeping his eyes on the dog, Asa stopped and stepped back from the bed. Contempt spread across his face. "You double-crossed me and my mama."

Stunned, Nell stared at him. Despite Annie's testimony, there was a part of her that couldn't believe the proper, genteel Sylvia Davis was smuggling liquor into Beaufort Harbor. Now, her son confirmed it.

"We paid you for getting hooch up to Richmond," Asa bellowed at Ramsey.

"I got tired of being your delivery boy. I wanted a daring adventure." He paused to sip his coffee.

Midgett was watching the exchange. "Our concern right now is for Chadwick. Last night, a mob surrounded his house."

Mr. Ramsey turned to the officer. "But I have an alibi and a witness for last night and most of this morning. I am reluctant to share my personal life with you here. However, if it comes to the question of the gallows, I promise you I will not be so gallant."

Nell could see that despite his casual demeanor, Mr. Ramsey seemed to be hanging by a thread. His hand shook as he gripped his cup and his eyes still had a glazed, fuzzy look to them. Gently, she asked, "What did you do with *Le Cheval Noir* once you picked it up from Lenoxville Point? None of us saw it circulate around Beaufort."

Mr. Ramsey seemed to recognize Nell's compassionate attempts to talk to him, and he took a sip of coffee. While she focused on the man's face, Nell became aware of voices emanating from the corridor outside the room. Yawg also noticed and began to sniff under the door and emitted a soft whine. This was different from his earlier protective posture spurred by Asa's outburst; now, he looked distressed and agitated. Nell looked up at Jake, who looked equally confused by his dog's anguish. *When have I seen Yawg act like this before?*

After looking around at all the faces in the room, Mr. Ramsey's gaze lingered on Asa's hostile demeanor. "Perhaps it might be safer for me to answer that question down at your jail until this all gets untangled. May I, as they say, go peacefully." Mr. Ramsey held out his wrists to Midgett with a surrendering look.

"I think you were on the *Amelia*," said Jake.

"I already told you, I would be worthless on a boat."

"Chadwick remembers your ring."

"Ring?"

"Ring," repeated Jake, crossing the room and holding up Ramsey's hand. Moving the bloodstone and silver ring inches from Ramsey's face, he said, "Folks usually don't wear them on boats—they get caught in winches and lines and such. Chadwick remembers seeing this ring when the *Amelia* was near the bight at Cape Lookout."

For the first time that morning, Nell saw genuine concern cross Mr. Ramsey's face, something akin to both regret and comprehension. At the same moment, Yawg began to growl and scratch at the door. "Hush now," she knelt and spoke quietly to the dog, not wishing to interrupt Mr. Ramsey's narrative.

Ramsey struggled to collect himself. "Let me clarify. You are correct; I often wear this ring." Then he laughed. "But I wasn't wearing it on the *Amelia* the night it came to shore because I wasn't there."

Yawg's pacing became frantic, but Nell kept her focus on the man in the bed.

"Several months ago, I made a gift of an identical ring for a friend. Someone who had admired it for some time as he greatly appreciated its originality. Someone who would bargain his mother away for the right price; someone who collects the unusual, the unique, and the beautiful."

Nell looked down at Yawg and remembered his agitation the night they were at Horse Island. The hound had gone crazy when he disembarked from the *Miss Mary*.

Ramsey's face hardened as he turned his head toward Nell. "Anyone come to mind?"

Nell looked up from Yawg and caught her breath, "Buddy?"

The words had no sooner left her lips when she felt someone grab her hair and wrench back her head. "Asa, stop!" she screamed in surprise before she realized that Asa was standing in front of her, looking just as perplexed. Her assailant had opened the door to the corridor and grabbed Nell. "You're hurting me!" Nell cried as she flailed and twisted to look at her captor.

Asa, Midgett, and Jake involuntarily rushed to help her. But they froze when Nell heard a familiar voice say, "Get back y'all."

Recognizing Buddy Taylor's voice, Nell felt a gun's cold muzzle against the side of her head. At that moment, everything became distant for Nell, and no muscle in her body could move.

"I'll shoot her if you come any closer."

"Buddy!" Nell cried in disbelief.

There was a pleading, wrenched look on Ramsey's face as he stared at Buddy. "Don't do this."

Despite the bluster and bravado, Nell felt Buddy's grip jerk when Ramsey spoke. The gun shook in his hand, but he dragged Nell by force toward the door. "She's going with me, and y'all are gonna let me go, or I will shoot her dead," said Buddy.

"Buddy, what in the world is wrong with you?" cried Nell. "You've known me all my life, how can you—"

"Y'all think I'm so stupid. 'Look at fancy Buddy with all his knick-knacks,'" his voice parroted a sing-song. Nell could feel Buddy's body quiver with indignation as they faced the room with Asa inches away. "You think you're so smart with your rum-running, and your money, and your fancy ways. I just wanted my cut. I wanted my own shop. Y'all need to respect me now!"

Nell cried in pain as he twisted her hair. Ramsey's face turned ashen.

"We respect you, Buddy," said Midgett. He held out his hands with his palms down in a calming motion, but his eyes never wavered from Buddy's face. "Look how well you've built your own business in this town. Just tell us what happened that night."

The room was silent but for Buddy's labored breathing.

Sensing the heightened danger in the room, the dogs never took their eyes off Buddy. Pilot advanced toward him, issuing an unearthly, demonic growl, causing the short man to pivot. In the split second that Buddy glanced down at the dog, Jake lunged for the hand holding the gun. In the same movement, Pilot sunk his teeth into Buddy's ankle. The gunman cried in pain while Nell twisted away from him and out of his grasp. Yawg joined Pilot by latching onto Buddy's leg, while Jake struggled to wrestle the gun out of Buddy's hand.

"Get these dogs off me!" Buddy bellowed. Then all at once, Asa slammed his full weight against him. Nell screamed when Buddy hit the floor. His gun discharged into Asa's shoulder, who swore and cried in agony. Buddy's eyes darted back and forth in disbelief between Asa and the gun in his hand. Jake lunged and pinned Buddy's left arm and shoulder beneath him. Yawg turned and locked onto his other arm, which held the gun. Nell backed into the corner of the room and crouched down when it looked like Buddy might squeeze off another shot. Growling, Yawg began to worry the arm as Buddy cried in pain. After an eternity, Buddy's grip loosened, and the gun clattered to the floor. Jake kicked it away and commanded the dogs to release their prey.

Nell struggled into a sitting position with her back to the wall. While he held Buddy down, Jake looked at her, and she nodded to assure him that she wasn't hurt. When she heard Asa groan, Nell crawled over to him. She applied pressure to his shoulder wound to stanch the bleeding like Emma Grace had taught her.

Midgett, who hadn't been able to advance from the far side of the room during the melee, now used the hotel phone to call the clinic. When Buddy struggled to free himself from Jake's grip, the veteran leaned into his face and ground his words out through clenched teeth, "Move, and I will break . . . your . . . arm."

With intense loathing, Buddy spat, "Go to hell."

236

CHAPTER 23

Profane cries fueled by pain echoed through the hotel as Asa thrashed on the floor. Midgett knelt to subdue him, allowing Nell to increase the pressure against the bleeding from his shoulder. Dr. Giles Davis arrived before the local police and leaned over his son. "Be still, Asa," he said in a calming voice. "The more you move, the more blood you'll lose." Nell moved aside as the doctor's shaking hands injected a syringe of morphine into his son. Asa emitted one loud moan, before his body slackened, and the doctor cradled his son with tenderness.

Feeling detached, Nell leaned against the wall while Asa was loaded onto a stretcher and carried out of the room. Buddy slumped in a chair in the hallway; his left arm dangled from his shoulder while his other wrist was handcuffed to one of Midgett's men. Ramsey pulled on trousers and a white shirt but remained shoeless. He slowly fumbled into the corridor, using the wall for support. When he leaned over to speak quietly to his friend, Buddy turned his head away.

Nell looked down at her hands and saw that they were covered in Asa's blood. Her gaze drifted to her dress, stained with large, red splotches. She willed her feet to carry her to the bathroom, where she vomited into the commode. When she felt strong enough, she began to wash her hands in the basin. The warm water brought feeling back to her icy skin. She sank to the floor as every nerve in her body re-awakened. She could hear the water running in the sink, sounding distant and remote.

"You okay, Nell?" Midgett asked from the doorway.

She turned her head toward him, unable to speak. Jake appeared behind him and knelt to her while Midgett turned off the water. A soft, agonized sob escaped from Nell when Jake took her in his arms and rocked her. Sitting in the washroom, they held each other as she fought her way back.

When they returned to the bedroom, it was empty except for Midgett, Ramsey, and the two dogs. Leaning into Jake, Nell answered Midgett's concerned look by saying, "I'm better now." Pilot and Yawg approached Nell and pressed their bodies against her legs, but she was too weak to pet them.

At that moment, Emma Grace entered the hotel, scanned the room, and ran to Nell to hug her. "When the call came in, Doc asked me to get more nurses from Morehead, so he has extra help at the clinic. He wants me to stay here."

"Buddy and Asa are at the clinic," said Midgett. "Buddy's shoulder is dislocated, and no one knows about Asa. He got shot pretty bad."

Nell tilted her head in a nod. "When will the revenue men be getting here?"

"My understanding is that they're still in Harlowe busting up several stills." Midgett glanced at his two men standing guard in the hall. Leaning toward Nell, he smiled and lowered his voice. "I may have forgotten to call them."

Nell smiled back at him. "You need to get right on that, Commander."

"I have to get over to the clinic and keep Jimmy away from Buddy," replied Midgett. "That sheriff's probably involved in this mess up to his eyeballs and would hinder an investigation."

"You got that right," answered Jake.

"But we still don't know what happened to Wade," said Nell.

"And we've only got a few hours before the revenue men take over," added Midgett.

Nell looked over at Ramsey, who was attempting to put on his shoes but kept falling over. Although she still felt queasy and out of sorts, a new idea jolted her out of her stupor. "Midgett, why don't I stay with Ramsey?"

Both Jake and Midgett stared at her in alarm. "Nell, are you sure you're up for that?" Jake asked.

"You got your hands full with Buddy and Jimmy." Her eyes darted between the two men. "Ramsey likes me. And I like him. And he knows a lot about what happened. He seemed overwhelmed when everyone questioned him earlier. I think he'll talk to me." When they didn't answer, she added, "You weren't getting anywhere with him before Buddy came in."

"You don't know what he could pull on you when you're alone with him."

"I can stay with her," added Emma Grace. "Doc Davis was worried y'all might be suffering from shock." She looked over at Ramsey struggling to put on his shoes and added "Or alcohol poisoning. I think it would be easier on Nell and Ramsey if we didn't move them to the clinic right away. Sylvia Davis will be pitching a fit right about now."

Nell glanced at Ramsey. "I can smell laudanum on him, and he's half out of his mind, so his guard will be down." Nell studied Jake's face, creased with worry. Feeling humbled that both men cared so much for her, she said, "I got Emma Grace and my two bodyguards." She indicated Yawg and Pilot, who wagged at her in delight. "They already saved me once today." Raising her hand, she gently stroked Jake's face. Somehow, she knew the answers were close, and they had been working toward this moment.

Midgett looked thoughtful. "It's not a bad idea. Nell was right helpful when we were questioning Asa at his house this morning."

Nell turned to Jake. "You're worried about my reputation." Although he couldn't answer her, Nell could see Jake was concerned. "Half the town thinks I'm a demon-driven slut already, so I don't care anymore what people think." Without taking her eyes from his face, she added, "We just need to find Wade." Jake's body tensed at the mention of his brother's name.

Midgett inhaled deeply. "Okay, bring him down to Doc Davis's clinic as soon as you can."

When he turned away, Nell leaned in and hugged Jake. "I know you're scared," she whispered, "but this is our best shot."

The stout manager of the inn entered the room. When his eyes fell on the blood and debris, his face turned a pale green. When Midgett walked up to him, he took a step back. He remembered the enormous waterman from the altercation with Emma Grace the previous Friday night. Midgett peered down at the hotel employee. "Could we move Mr. Ramsey to another room? The federal agents will need to see this one. He's a material witness, but we'll need to sober him up."

"Of course," the hotel manager answered, nodding profusely. He attempted to smile, but his mouth merely twisted into a contorted grimace. "I'll open up 203 for you." Jingling room keys, he hurried out of the room and down the hallway.

Once he was gone, Midgett sat down next to Ramsey on his bed. "Nell and Emma Grace are gonna stay and keep you company. But I'll need to take your razor."

Still shaky and clammy, Ramsey slowly rummaged through his carrying bag, pulled out a shaving kit, extracted his razor, and handed it to Midgett.

"Why don't you boys help Mr. Ramsey carry his luggage down the hall?" he said to his two men.

Nell and Emma Grace positioned themselves on either side of Ramsey and slipped their arms around his waist to steady him. The weakened man leaned unsteadily on them as they walked out of the room and down the hall, followed by Yawg and Pilot. Once they were all inside Room 203, the two Coast Guardsmen took their places outside the door. Jake's dogs flopped down, but continued to watch Nell as she moved around the room.

Once Ramsey reached the bed, he sunk into the soft quilted coverlet. Soon his entire body began to shake. Seeing his sorrow made Nell relive how close she'd come to death. Emma Grace pulled Nell into an embrace and stroked her hair. Together, they moved to the other side of the room to give Ramsey privacy. After a few moments, it dawned on Nell that Mr. Ramsey was crying for more than a friend. When he had composed himself, Nell said, "You know, I have known Buddy all my life. I can't imagine him doing anything like this."

Ramsey wiped his eyes with his handkerchief. "Well, the odd thing is, I can." He exhaled slowly. "He never felt like he was part of this town, and so much rage built up inside him. I begged him to leave, but something still tied him to his family."

"How long have y'all known each other?" Emma Grace asked gently.

Ramsey waved his hand dismissively. "Sylvia introduced us years ago." His eyes became distant. "There's a vulnerability about him. I always wanted to take care of him."

The tenderness she heard in Ramsey's voice caused conflicting feelings in Nell. Her eyebrows knit together in confusion to learn of such intimacy between two men, while a wave of queasiness overtook her. Emma Grace remained unphased as she stroked Nell's hand.

They sat for a moment before Nell walked into the bathroom, wet a small washcloth, and rubbed one corner of it against the bar of soap on the sink. From the bathroom, Nell could hear Emma Grace ask, "Mr. Ramsey, I know you want to protect yourself and Buddy. But something went amiss with your operation, and Jake's family is suffering. And Chadwick and his mama are under siege."

Ramsey exhaled and wiped his eyes. "Well, I really don't know how much I can tell you."

When Nell walked out of the bathroom, Ramsey rose from the bed and put one hand on the wall to steady himself while he crossed the room. His eyes were red and weary from weeping. Nell sat down in a chair and dabbed at her dress with the small towel making the spots of blood fade to pink.

Once he reached the washroom, he turned on the faucet to wash his hands and face.

"I should like to add," said Nell, "that Midgett has called the federal revenue agents. At the moment, they are otherwise engaged, and I understand they'll be here in a few hours. When they arrive, everything will be out of Midgett's hands, and he's the only lawman we trust in the county."

Ramsey groaned, "My head feels like the inside of a brick oven."

When he didn't continue, Nell looked up and saw him staring down at the sink. "The way I see it, you were running booze for Mrs. Davis before you started to work with Buddy."

Turning off the water, he replied, "That's right; you'd be surprised how many doors open to you when you introduce a good merlot in the Fan. In my business, that's invaluable."

"How did you get it from here to there?" Emma Grace asked. "The roads aren't paved, and half the time they're washed out."

After he dried his hands and face with the towel, he looked back into the room at the two women. "Why, on the train, of course."

Nell nodded. "Oh. That would make sense. All those big wooden crates filled with Buddy's treasures and antiques. Didn't anyone ever wonder?"

Ramsey dug out his comb from his bag. "Well, people on trains get thirsty, too."

Nell could see the critical role Ramsey played in Asa's operation.

"Do you know why Buddy showed up when he did? I mean, why was he here in the hotel?"

"He was setting up the speakeasy in the room next to mine. It was rumored Asa was leaving the business, and now that Chadwick had disappeared, well, Buddy saw an opening."

So, Asa had tried to quit, thought Nell. *Or at least that's what he'd told people.*

Ramsey continued. "Buddy and I met up late last night. I'm not sure why he wasn't around when y'all arrived. Knowing Buddy, he went down to get something to eat."

Nell recalled how she'd scanned the dining room earlier that morning. She'd spotted Asa but hadn't seen Buddy.

"So, what do you remember about last night?" Emma Grace asked

"Ah, seems so long ago, now. I was having supper at Sylvia's, in part, because Buddy wanted me to keep an eye on Asa. We weren't sure how he would respond to Beaufort's newest speakeasy." Ramsey looked in the mirror as he ran a comb through his hair. "I was sitting in her parlor when Asa's boys came to the back door. When we went back to the kitchen, they were talking about how they had followed you to Harkers Island and seen you talking to Chadwick." He paused to look at Nell. "But I believe what really fried their oysters was when you turned off your running lights after you left the island."

Nell continued to dab her dress while Ramsey walked out of the washroom to sort through his bag. "Giles returned from the clinic not long after Asa left with the boys. Sylvia was rather undone by all the late-night activity, particularly as it related to Chadwick. Once she calmed down from the interruption, she was . . . well . . . rather drowsy, so I took my leave."

Nell recollected how fond Mrs. Davis was of her wine and aperitifs.

"Buddy was waiting for me here at the inn when I returned." Nell followed the bloodstone ring on Ramsey's hand as he laid out his vest and necktie on the bed. "We had a nightcap together in my room. A lot of people from Raleigh stopped by Buddy's speakeasy, so he was over the moon." He paused for a moment. "When I think back on it, he did ask me about supper, and I mentioned that Asa's men had come by. It was so mysterious . . . boats shuttling around with no running lights . . . shadowy figures . . . a moonlit evening. So, hush, hush."

242

Nell inhaled a deep breath to steady herself while she concentrated on rubbing the bloodstains out of her dress. She thought of Chadwick and his mother barricaded in their home while their neighbors terrorized them. And here Ramsey was making this sound like a chapter from a dime-store crime novel. City folk could easily romanticize the hardscrabble lives of seafaring people.

"Weren't you staying with Dr. and Mrs. Davis for the week the *Three Sisters* passed through?" Emma Grace asked.

"Yes, I was, but I hardly remember anything from that week. Sylvia keeps a . . . fluid household."

"But you would see Buddy from time to time," added Nell.

"Oh, yes. I heard about *Le Chevel Noir* on the *Three Sisters* at Sylvia's. They talked about it in regards to a big ball at the governor's mansion in Virginia, but I didn't think that much about it. But when I mentioned it to Buddy, it just set him on fire." Ramsey paused and his shoulders sagged as he thought of this memory.

"Why did you want to do it?" Nell asked abruptly.

He gave her a startled look. "Because it was fun. It was like being in a motion picture: having a rendezvous with a boat on the water, dodging police officers, watching train engineers enjoy their first remarkable Cabernet. And when I delivered all that wine to Gov. Trinkle, I was a hero. In the end, it helped my business enormously. But when we were planning it, I was doing it for Buddy. He wanted status and recognition and to get away from cutting lumber. And his mother." A shiver rippled through his body.

Nell looked up from her dress. "What about the night we had supper at the Davis home about a week ago? You came in with a bottle of *Le Cheval Noir*. Didn't you think that would be a problem? You and Buddy took Asa's delivery right out from under his nose, and then you bring the booty into their house?"

"Well," replied Ramsey reluctantly, "when you put it like that, I do sound like a dolt. I didn't even think about that wine until Asa got all agitated. After the ball at the governor's mansion, I didn't give it another thought from that day to this."

"But you didn't carry that bottle down from Richmond, did you? It was already here."

Ramsey laid his necktie under his collar and began to knot it with his clumsy fingers. "You're right. I stopped by Buddy's. When he wasn't there, I wandered out to his Sugar Shack, and I saw one of the bottles, and I just took one—I knew we would settle up later."

Nell couldn't recall any wine in the Sugar Shack the day she and Jake picked up lumber for the ramp. "So those cases of smuggled wine were just sitting around the Sugar Shack?"

"Something like that," replied Ramsey. He turned away from the two young women and began to hum a tuneless song. His movements shifted from clumsy to mechanical and deliberate. In her mind, Nell made an inventory of everything she had seen in the Sugar Shack, but she couldn't remember any crates of wine. *There has to be a hiding place.*

"There were several bottles in your room last night. Who brought all of those?"

"Buddy must've," Ramsey replied. "Now that I think about it, it was rather bold of Buddy to bring all those bottles over."

Pilot rose, walked across the room to sit next to Nell's chair, and rested his head in her lap. Without taking her focus off Ramsey, she absently began to scratch the dog's head. "So, how did the evening end?"

Ramsey paused. "I remember enjoying the wine. I must have had too much and fallen asleep."

Feeling a hot flush rising from her collar, Nell leaned forward in her chair and rested her elbows. She couldn't bring herself to ask the indelicate questions she needed to ask Ramsey.

Emma Grace noticed Nell hesitating and picked up the conversation. "What I think Nell wants to ask is," she paused to clear her throat. "How and when did you fall asleep? Do you have any idea what time you returned to the hotel?"

"When we found you, you'd been left for dead, so we're trying to figure out how that happened," added Nell.

When Ramsey didn't answer, she looked up from Pilot's head to see the man staring into space. "I have no earthly idea. I left Sylvia's after midnight, but things just got so fuzzy after Buddy arrived. I can't even recall . . . it was rather sudden."

"Tell me what you were drinking."

244

"We had some *Le Cheval Noir* . . . when I first came in. Then we might have had some later . . . the next thing I remember, the Coast Guardsman was slapping me awake."

"It sounds like you passed out," Emma Grace said. "Have you ever done that before?"

"No," said Ramsey thoughtfully. He rubbed his head in apparent frustration.

"I think you had some help."

Ramsey turned to them in confusion.

"Does Buddy ever take laudanum or morphine?" asked Emma Grace.

"Doesn't everyone?"

"Mr. Ramsey," Emma Grace chose her words carefully. "Did it occur to you that Buddy drugged you?"

A wave of anger swept through Ramsey. "Buddy wouldn't do that." His face contorted and his eyes were blazing when he turned to look at them. "I don't believe it."

"When we came into your room this morning, we could smell laudanum. And Buddy was desperate when he showed up." Nell flinched at the memory. "Last night, when you told him how we were talking to Chadwick, I think he got real scared. I think he wanted to look into things, but he didn't want you involved."

Ramsey was shaking with anger. There was a cornered look in his eyes.

"Maybe he was just trying to protect you," said Emma Grace gently.

Comprehension appeared to dawn on Ramsey's face, and the anger drained from his body. "But why would he leave all those bottles of *Le Chevel Noir*? I mean, it made everything point to me."

Nell shrugged. "Buddy doesn't always think things through."

She waited for Ramsey to reply, but he remained quiet, motionless, lost in thought. "Oh, my goodness." He sank into the bed and looked out the window to the harbor and the inlet beyond. "You might be right."

The hotel clock clicked off several minutes. Finally, Ramsey sighed deeply and looked down at the vest on the bed, staring at the piece of clothing as if he'd never seen it before. When he fumbled to put the vest on, Emma Grace crossed the room and helped him slip into the garment. Then she held his jacket for him. Once dressed, the Virginian gently shook his shoulders to settle the clothing on his body. His stride was steadier when he crossed the room to check himself in the full-length mirror. Although weariness was still etched into his mournful eyes, he snapped his cuffs out of his sleeves with confidence. He wore the immaculate clothing like a mantle of armor. Turning back to his traveling bag, he reached in and pulled out a small Bible, which he tucked into the inner pocket of his jacket. "Come now; I know they're waiting for us."

With the Coast Guardsmen and two dogs in their wake, the three of them left the room and walked out of the hotel. As they strolled down to the clinic, it was hard to ignore the clusters of people now gathering to watch them. By now, the news of the early morning escapades would have traveled throughout the town. Nell and Emma flanked both sides of Ramsey as they walked down Front Street.

"I must say, Nell, you seem to be revealing a whole new side of yourself," said Ramsey. They exchanged a friendly, sideways glance. "Until this morning, I imagined you as the sweet little thing playing *Claire de Lune* on her harpsichord."

"I've done a lot of growing up in the past week now that I'm considered a jazz siren."

Ramsey sighed, "The provincial charms of a small town. I know them well. Do you think there will be a place for you here after all this?"

Nell had wondered about this ever since the damning sermon. She'd thought of her music, her love of her daddy and mama, Emma Grace, and Jake. She also knew the Oyster Shuckers stood behind her.

"There'll always be a place for Nell here," replied Emma Grace.

"Yes, there will be a place for me here," Nell added. "But it will be very different." She saw her church slip away from her, but she could see herself at the helm of the *Harmony* flying out in front of a southeast breeze. Smiling to herself, she lifted her chin defiantly while the crowd grew deeper as they walked down the street.

CHAPTER 24

The Davis Emergency Clinic had been built on the second floor of a commercial building in the middle of Beaufort's mercantile center. As Nell approached the clinic, she recognized Sylvia Davis's remote screaming and wailing from the back of the infirmary. When they entered and climbed the stairs, Nell commanded the two dogs to remain outside. Once in the waiting room, with her eyes adjusted to the indoor light, she saw Jake and Midgett huddled in one corner.

"Why don't I take you to Buddy's room?" Emma Grace said to Ramsey.

Nell turned to look at Jake and saw his concern and longed to hold him, but knew it would fuel hateful gossip in town. Instead, she looked away to ask Midgett, "How's Asa doing?"

Midgett looked thoughtful. "Doc Davis is operating on Asa now, and his mama is pitchin' a fit."

"She is not one to suffer in silence," replied Nell. The wails continued to fill the small building. Dropping her voice and leaning into Midgett and Jake, she said, "We were right. Mr. Ramsey moved his booze to Richmond by train." She quickly told them that Buddy had opened a speakeasy at the Inlet Inn. She added that Buddy and Ramsey created the plan to meet the *Three Sisters* to supply *Le Chevel Noir* to the wedding in Richmond. "It sounded like some of *Le Chevel Noir* is still hidden in the Sugar Shack. I imagine Buddy got spooked last night when he learned that we were poking around on Harkers Island. He probably thought we were coming to get him. So, have you been able to learn anything from him?"

"We were waiting to hear what you had to say," replied Midgett. "I think they need to pop his shoulder back in place, but I asked the attending nurse to let me question him before she gives him any morphine," said Midgett. "If he's all doped up, it might not be admissible in court. But if I can't get him to talk, I may ask them to give him a dose. I figure if it makes him loopy, maybe it will help us find Jake's brother."

"Any word on Chadwick?" Nell asked.

"Not yet," replied Midgett. "But I imagine your flotilla is probably arriving on Harkers Island right about now."

Nell smiled. When Tisdale had told them that Chadwick's house was surrounded by their angry neighbors, it had been Nell's idea to send over Winston and several of his friends. After they loaded their skiffs with Emma Grace's homemade wine, they sailed to the island to negotiate with the posse harassing Chadwick. "I just figured that if Winston could convince that crowd that Jake isn't a revenue man, and we were just trying to find the *Amelia*, they might back down."

"Well," replied Midgett, scratching his head, "If anyone could do that, it would be Winston re-enforced with Emma Grace's brew."

Midgett glanced over at the room where Emma Grace had taken Ramsey and inhaled deeply. "Okay, deputies, follow me."

Entering Buddy's room, the faint smell of disinfectant pine oil mixed with rubbing alcohol and ether caused Nell's eyes to water. The icy, disassociated feeling that Nell felt at the Inlet Inn returned to her. Her hand went to the place on her head where she'd felt the cold steel of the gun muzzle. When a small moan escaped from her, Jake glanced at her and clasped her hand, holding it tight. She leaned into him and felt his warmth restore her.

Buddy was sitting in a rattan wheelchair with his face slightly turned to Ramsey, who spoke to him in a low voice. When Buddy had held her at gunpoint in the hotel, she hadn't been able to see his face. She only heard his menacing voice and felt his tensed body when he grabbed her. Now, shrunken and withdrawn in the oversized chair, Buddy reminded Nell of a pouting yet defenseless toddler strapped into a stroller. Transfixed by the dwarfed figure in the chair, she recalled the years she had spent with her erratic friend: softball games played during high school, Buddy's delight with his treasures in the

Sugar Shack, and running off with Winston to gig flounder in the middle of the night.

Ramsey stood up and reached into his breast pocket to pull out the small holy book that Nell had seen at the hotel. "I brought my Bible for you, Buddy," said Ramsey, placing it on the nightstand next to the bed. When Buddy glanced down at the small book, the hardened defiance around his eyes softened. But when he turned his head and saw Jake enter the room, he snarled, "Get this maniac away from me. He told his dogs to kill me at the inn."

Nell felt Jake start to lunge toward the man in the chair, but she leaned into him until he pulled back.

"Nobody's trying to kill anyone, Buddy," replied Midgett in a calm voice as he sat down and stretched his legs.

"Why isn't Jimmy handling this case?" asked Buddy.

Midgett reached into his pocket and pulled out his cigarettes. "Sheriff James Styron is preoccupied with other crimes at the moment." He paused to tap his cigarette against the case. "Smuggling liquor from the *Three Sisters* in international waters and transporting over state lines. Those are federal charges." He cupped his hand and lit the cigarette. "The feds are on the way, but they're still tied up in Harlowe. I'm covering 'til they get here, and I deputized Jake and Nell. They brought the situation to my attention, and we're short on manpower. This investigation will soon be out of my hands." He could have been talking about picking beans from his garden.

Emma Grace walked over to Buddy and untied the sling holding his arm in place. "I understand you injured your shoulder."

"That's right," answered Buddy. "And those dogs mauled my arm."

Emma Grace opened the bottle on her tray and poured the liquid onto gauze while examining the wounds on his arm. When she dabbed the gashes, Buddy cried, "Lord have mercy, don't that burn!"

When she finished cleaning and bandaging his wounds, Emma Grace poked Buddy's arm, which dangled loosely at his side. "Looks like a dislocated shoulder. I can take care of that."

Buddy winced as she moved the arm around. "Can you give me something for the pain?"

"We need to keep you alert so we can talk," said Midgett. He glanced out the window and flicked his ash on the floor.

Buddy gritted his teeth and cried out as Emma Grace worked the arm backward and forward. Ramsey winced and stepped toward them, but Midgett barred him with one of his legs.

"What about Asa and Sylvia?' Buddy shouted.

"What about them?" answered Midgett.

"Why aren't they being charged?" The color in Buddy's face deepened as his voice grew petulant and whiney.

"As far as I know, they didn't transport *Le Cheval Noir* over state lines." Midgett drew out the French name with a southern drawl.

"I want a deal. I can testify against them."

Midgett sighed. "What would the deal look like?"

"I get immunity if I tell you about bootlegging operations in Beaufort."

"Yes, that would be helpful," said Midgett. "But our bigger concern is what happened to the *Amelia* and her captain."

Buddy grimaced as Emma Grace manipulated his arm, making grinding and popping sounds. Ramsey turned away with clenched fists.

"You were the last one to see the *Amelia*."

"Says who?" said Buddy, gritting his teeth.

"Says Captain Wade's dog."

Buddy's eyes flashed as if an electrical pulse had blasted through his body. "That don't mean nothing. All dogs hate me." But his eyes betrayed him; he looked cornered.

"That dog knows you. He picked up your scent at Horse Island, and he knew you this morning at the inn, and he doesn't like you," said Midgett.

Jake's breathing was becoming labored and ragged.

"Ahh," cried Buddy in agony as Emma Grace lifted his arm over his head. Sweat broke out in a sheen on his forehead. "I'm not saying no more." The words were directed at Midgett, but he didn't take his eyes off Jake, who was ready to uncoil on him.

Emma Grace pressed down with force on her patient's shoulder. Buddy struggled to move out of her grip.

Midgett thought for a minute. "This is gonna be out of my hands shortly. Where is Wade and the *Amelia*?"

"I don't know what happened!" Buddy shouted.

"You'll have to do better than that," said Midgett.

Nell heard a loud snapping sound as Buddy roared with pain. "It's in," Emma said, as she walked away from her patient.

Ramsey moved forward and cradled the elbow on Buddy's arm. "Let's get you into that bed." He helped Buddy rise from the chair and shuffled toward the bed.

Once he was lying down, Buddy remained tense, but now he was swallowed up by bedsheets and blankets. His expression remained dark, and his mouth was clamped tight.

Ramsey looked over at Emma Grace. "I think you can give him something for the pain, now."

Emma Grace exchanged looks with Midgett, who gave her a slight shrug. She turned to her tray as she spoke to Buddy, "I'm going to give you a shot of morphine." She uncovered a syringe on the tray, tested it for air bubbles by thumping it, and pushed the plunger.

After Emma Grace had injected her patient, Buddy's body began to unclench. He gave Ramsey a dreamy look. "I understand the cook hasn't come into work yet. Do you reckon you could get me a blue plate special from Dora Dean's? Lord knows when I'll eat anything halfway decent after they take me away."

"Of course," said Ramsey, as his hand swept Buddy's cheek. "Now, don't forget your good book," he said, gently rubbing the Bible on the stand. "Spirit is often our best defense." Buddy glanced at the Bible and then looked up into Ramsey's face. Time seemed suspended as the pair lingered for a moment. Ramsey picked up Buddy's hand and held it as his face became wistful, and tears pooled in his eyes. Eventually, Ramsey turned away and began to walk toward the door.

Nell and Jake began to file out after Ramsey.

"Nell, wait." Buddy's voice sounded defeated.

She hesitated without turning around.

"This might be the only chance we can talk," the weak voice said from the bed.

Nell turned around. "Jake needs to stay with me."

A shadow passed over Buddy's face as he peered at Jake. "Keep that lunatic on the other side of the room."

Jake slowly nodded and settled himself into a chair.

251

Nell slid into the chair next to the bed. For several minutes they were silent. Nell took several deep breaths. When she was ready to look into Buddy's face, she saw a distant look in his eyes. The morphine was making him hazy. After a few minutes, he said, "I always liked you, Nell. You always had style. And moxie. Don't let this town take that away from you. Small minds will always be closed to what's important."

As he spoke, she knew it was true. In Sunday school, they giggled together every time the teacher said, "begat." Many of their classmates thought they were odd.

Nell's hand involuntarily flew up to her hair. *And a few hours ago, you put a gun to my head.*

"I'm sorry I scared you so bad." Buddy's face became etched with sadness.

Nell exhaled. She reached into her heart to find the friend that she knew. "I know you are, Buddy. You were scared. You wanted respect. You've built so much with the Sugar Shack, and you wanted to leave town."

Buddy nodded, "I got Nadine in Norfolk. I rescued her."

"I remember you telling me that," Nell replied, recalling the bare-breasted mermaid figurehead designed to plow through the surf. "The hooch was bankrolling your business, and you wanted more of the action. When Ramsey told you about the *Three Sisters* and the governor's wedding, it all fell into place. That could have been your ticket out of Beaufort."

Buddy laughed lazily. "Ramsey made it sound like a lark, but I knew he needed the money." He scoffed. "And he couldn't do it alone. We both knew he'd puke his brains out on a boat. But the problem was, we needed a boat that Asa wouldn't tie back to me."

"And then one came to you."

He turned his head toward her. "Parson had spent a few days at Lowell's and heard about all the money everyone was making. He sailed the *Amelia* up to our yard at Russell Creek to pick up lumber."

His voice drifted away, and when Nell looked at his face, Buddy's eyes were closed. She could feel Jake behind her, silent but aware.

Leaning over the bed, Nell whispered into Buddy's ear. "I think some boats have souls in them."

Buddy's eyes opened slowly, and he nodded. "Like the *Amelia*. She was special, like Nadine."

Nell nodded.

"You could tell there was something wrong with that boy. He didn't like being in town. He didn't like people. He wouldn't look you in the eye, and he barely talked. 'Who the hell let him near a boat?' I kept wondering. He wasn't all there."

Jake shifted behind Nell.

"But the longer the *Amelia* stayed in your yard—the more you wanted it. Desire grew in you."

"When we made a deal with Parson to meet the *Three Sisters* on his boat," replied Buddy, "I told him I had to sail the *Amelia*. I told him it was because I knew the shallow water better than he did."

"But it was more than that."

Buddy turned his face toward her. She felt she was on the deck of the schooner with him.

His speech became melodic as if he were riding the swells. "She came right up to the surf and drew barely three feet. She was fast with beautiful lines, perfectly balanced, and a shallow draft. The detail and mahogany on her were beautiful. Once I sailed her, I wanted to own her."

Nell watched his faraway look and waited. "But everything changed when you came ashore."

Buddy stiffened and his mood soured. "That Lowcountry trash was going to desecrate it." A pained look flitted across his face. "He wanted to rip her open and put in an airplane engine. It was obscene. That boy picked up on emotions and knew what people were feeling. He reminded me of a dog." Buddy's distress increased.

"When we were sailing up the Newport, Parson started saying how he wanted to get his dog and move his boat that night so he could anchor it in the harbor. I started offering him money for the boat, but he acted like he couldn't hear me. He just turned away and wouldn't answer."

"We'd left the dog onshore 'cause I didn't want him on the boat with me. When we docked, he didn't even want to get off the *Amelia*; he just wanted to sail away." That dog came out when he heard Parson's voice, and when he got on the boat, he could tell that Parson was upset. He started to snap and snarl at me." Buddy looked at her. "I hate dogs, Nell, you know that."

"I do know that," Nell agreed. "I remember how they used to chase you."

"I pulled out the gun that I always carry with me when I'm on the water. I was just gonna shoot it near the dog—not hurt it, but that Parson boy threw himself on top of the dog, and I got him in the head."

The words came out in a rush and bounced around the room. Then everything was silent except for Buddy's labored breathing. *So, Wade really was dead.* Nell glanced at Jake's face, which was still as stone, enveloped in a fog of grief. She'd seen that look when they were on Horse Island, distant and absent.

"Please believe me when I tell you it was an accident," the muted voice said from the bed.

A deep, unearthly groan escaped from Jake. His voice sounded rusty. "Did you ever talk to Wade about the *Amelia*?"

Buddy's eyes drifted over to Jake. "I could barely understand half the things he said."

"If you had ever talked to him," his voice trembled, "Then you mighta learned that Wade designed and built the *Amelia*."

Buddy looked skeptical, and his voice sounded angry. "How would you know that?"

"He was my brother."

Buddy stared, frozen. Nell looked at Jake; her heart felt like it would burst.

Swallowing, Jake continued in a measured voice. "If he had lived, the *Amelia* would have been the first in a fleet of boats."

The magnitude of what he had done crashed over Buddy. She knew that he would clam up now that he knew Jake was Wade's brother. She walked over to the door and spoke to Midgett. "Why don't you take Jake outside and let him get some air?"

When Midgett started to usher Jake out of the room, Nell added, "He might want to sit with his dogs."

The two men left, and Buddy stared at the closed door for several minutes. Eventually, his eyes wandered to the ceiling. "There's evil in me, Nell. I've done terrible things." The resonance in his voice reminded Nell of Rev. Saunders' sermon. "I always struggled with my wickedness. So many things I don't understand about myself. Look who I chose to love." He glanced at the doorway as if Ramsey would walk through it at any moment.

"I loved Asa half my life," Nell replied. "Look how bad he's treated me in the past week."

"You've lived through one week of scorn. Imagine having a lifetime. A secret that kept you apart from everybody. I always felt so outside of everything. Then I met Ramsey." He closed his eyes as if he was savoring a rich piece of chocolate. "It seems like we never really choose who we love."

Nell nodded thoughtfully.

His face darkened. "My mama told me all my life that people like me are sinful."

"Doesn't seem to bother Mr. Ramsey. I reckon it's something you can't help."

"Ramsey puts up a good front, but it's not easy for any of us. We're despised and abused. I found solace in material objects. Surrounded myself with beauty." He closed his eyes as if he was taking an inventory at his Sugar Shack. "But I knew Ramsey could never love me the way I love him. So, I grabbed the crumbs from his table whenever he was in town."

"Mr. Ramsey doesn't take anybody seriously."

Buddy nodded, looking thoughtful. "Imagine living a lie your whole life, Nell. Pretending to be somebody you're not. All the time."

"You had me fooled."

He turned his head toward her and gave her a rueful smile. "When I fell in love with Ramsey, I came to believe laws didn't really apply to me. I was already breaking Christian law. I was already going to hell, and there was nothing I could do about it." Buddy closed his eyes.

Nell nodded. "I don't know about sin so much anymore. It used to be clear. It used to be all black and white. Now that this town has turned its back on me, so many things are gray for me. You can still make it right. I'll help you at the trial."

Buddy turned to look into her face, "You were always good people, Nell."

"Midgett will protect you," Nell said. "He'll make sure the feds move you out of the county." Nell pulled the chair to his bedside. "I know that Jake's family is suffering awful. They want to put Wade to rest. Now that you know what Wade could have achieved, I think he'll haunt you. I think if you talk through that, you're going to feel a lot better."

Buddy was silent for several moments. "I buried him way back in the woods near the lumber yard. His dog knows the spot. He stood guard over it. I'd see him in the woods and wanted to kill him, but I could never pull off the shot. I set traps out for him."

Nell felt bile rise in her throat as she remembered Yawg's butchered paw. "I guess he ended up in town."

"We need to get the *Amelia* back to his family. It's all they have left of him now."

"When I set out to acquire the *Amelia*, I thought I was saving her. Protecting her. If I'd known . . ." his voice cracked as his face twisted with misery. "Now that I look at it, Parson was different. Like me. And Jesus warned us against hoarding material possessions."

Nell waited, watching her old friend.

"The *Amelia* is just north of Norfolk," continued Buddy. "It's docked at Madison's Wharf in Newport News near that big shipyard. I renamed her *Astor*. You'll find the exact address in my desk in the Sugar Shack."

Nell started to stretch her hand out to her friend but pulled it back. "Thank you, Buddy. That will help the family."

Buddy closed his eyes and dipped his head in acknowledgment.

After a while, Buddy asked, "Could you see what's keeping Ramsey? I am ready to eat my arm."

"Sure thing," said Nell. Once outside the room, she leaned against the wall and breathed deeply. One of Midgett's men stationed in the waiting area came to her side. "Could you get Jake?" she whispered to him.

Jake appeared a few minutes later with Midgett on his heels. Her sweetheart wrapped his arms around her.

"He's asking for Ramsey."

"There might be a crowd at Dora Dean's, and that's holding him up."

"Have you gotten any word about Chadwick and his mama?"

"They're safe, but really shaken."

"I can imagine." She leaned forward and put her hands on her knees, fighting her light-headedness. It had taken all her strength to talk to Buddy.

A few moments later, Ramsey walked up to them, holding a plate of food covered in wax paper. "Nell, can I give you a few hush puppies?"

"Oh, thanks, Ramsey, I can't eat. But Buddy was asking for his food."

Ramsey turned the doorknob and stepped into Buddy's room. "Oh, no!" he cried as he dropped food, shattering the plate. "Help! Help!" he shouted.

Midgett bound over to the door.

"Get a doctor! Nurse!" Ramsey was shouting from the threshold. "It's Buddy!"

Jake tore off toward Dr. Davis's office. Nell followed Midgett into the room and saw Buddy lying motionless on the bed with a syringe in his hand. His empty eyes remained fixed on the ceiling. Nell could see that he wasn't breathing. Next to Ramsey's small Bible on the table stood a vial that Nell had not seen when she left the room.

"Oh, Buddy," Nell cried, stepping into the room and studying his conflicted face. Memories of a lifetime with Buddy swirled around her, lingering on the moment they shared in front of the hardware store when Buddy provoked Asa into smacking him in the nose. Now, she saw how Buddy had stepped out of his own darkness to confront a bully. She knew his confession was a gift to her and Jake. Looking at him now lifeless in his bed, she hoped he was at peace. Weakness overtook Nell, and she sank to the floor.

EPILOGUE

Several weeks later, on a balmy Sunday morning, Nell looked up from the piano to see twenty of her closest friends and family crowded into the Guthries' living room. This intimate group was finishing their prayer service, having no desire to return to Rev. Saunders' ministry after his damning sermon targeting Nell.

While the last notes of her original piece entitled "Oyster Harmony" hung in the air, the small congregation clasped their hymnals to their chests and bowed their heads. Thomas Guthrie read the closing scripture, his resonating voice rolled over them. When he was finished, he bellowed, "Amen."

"Amen," answered his congregation. A split second later, the younger children bounded out of their seats and ran out the back door to the garden. Nell and the womenfolk followed them, carrying covered side dishes, rolls, and coleslaw from the kitchen. Mr. Guthrie brought up the rear, pushing his wife's wheelchair across the back porch, down the ramp, and over the bumpy ground to Harrison's bench under the shade of the pecan tree.

During the service, Winston and several of his friends had tended the cook fire that had now burned down to glowing embers. As people queued up with outstretched plates, the young men removed the grilled spot fish from the steady heat. Tisdale trotted up to the food table with her goat, Eloise.

"You still getting fish from folks on the island?" Nell asked.

"Yes, ma'am," replied Tisdale.

When the details of Tisdale's role in helping Chadwick clear his name became known to her neighbors on Harkers Island, they thanked her with a steady supply of fish. "Lord, every time I open up the icebox, I got a new set of eyes staring out at me. Sometimes people just drop it off when I hain't home. People are also giving me taters and green beans and such since we helped Chadwick. Thank the Lord we're hosting these prayer services because me and my family could never eat all that food."

Nell nodded with approval. "Just goes to show you that a tide can turn."

Mrs. Guthrie looked at her old friend. "We have you to thank for that."

Tisdale sniffed. "Hain't got nary an idea what you mean."

Nell and her mama exchanged a smile, knowing the Oyster Shuckers implemented strategical maneuvers after the damning sermon. Beatrice and Tisdale launched their own whisper campaign. They would often attend Bible studies and quilting circles and stage remarks such as: "Why, that Nell Guthrie's been caring for her mama for six years now," and "That's right; she gave up school after her brother died." Then they would drop their voices to a whisper and add, "And did you know that Sylvia Davis has been helping Asa sell all that liquor."

And on it went until Nell began to feel the thaw. Beaufort's good citizens curbed their overt hostility. It was a different story on Harkers Island, where they treated her as a living saint.

Nell and Emma Grace sat on Harrison's bench under his tree and began to eat from the plates balanced on their laps. Nell smiled with gratitude at all the people in the back yard, but one face was missing.

"Nell, honey, do you know when Jake will be coming back from South Carolina?" her mother asked.

"No, ma'am. I haven't heard from him." *And he may not be coming back.* "Soon, I hope." Her throat tightened, and her appetite dimmed. She looked down at her plate and pushed the food around with her fork.

"He'll come back," Emma Grace whispered.

Nell leaned back and gazed up into the leaves of the pecan tree. "Maybe."

Within hours after Buddy Taylor's death, Midgett had accompanied Nell and Jake to Buddy's lumber yard. With his nose to the ground, Yawg quickly led them to Wade's shallow grave. After they recovered his body, Nell watched the light drain from Jake's eyes. As long as Wade had been missing, Jake held hope that he would see his brother alive again. Once he accepted that Wade was dead, he retreated into the vacant, thousand-mile stare worn by so many shell-shocked veterans.

Jake withdrew to the *Jamison* while he coped with his loss. When people learned of Nell's role in the recovery of Wade, they soon arrived at Nell's house laden with food as offerings of condolence.

Nell caught glimpses of Jake and his dogs on his boat or Carrot Island. But this self-imposed exile didn't last, and within days, Jake stopped by her home. In silence, they walked through her garden and sat under the pecan tree on Harrison's bench.

Finally, Jake started to speak with difficulty. "Nell, I'm going to South Carolina to lay Wade to rest. Would you accompany me?"

She glanced at her home. "I already asked my daddy if I could go with you, and we decided I shouldn't," she replied. "But I want to."

Jake nodded.

She exhaled, "I just got my daddy back, and I don't want to lose him again." Thomas Guthrie had remained sober since the day of Buddy's capture, and her family had settled into a restful amity. Nell's parents often sat together on their porch in the evening, and her daddy listened to her piano and allowed Nell greater freedom in town. But the serenity felt tenuous and fragile. "I know it's important for him to have some say in the things that I do now. At least he's letting me play jazz outside the house."

Jake traced her cheek with his finger. "Still daddy's girl."

Nell returned his smile, but then her face darkened. "Leaving town with you could stir up all those ugly rumors . . . like before."

She leaned into him, and he wrapped his arm around her. Looking up into his face, she ran her index finger over his lower lip. "But I'm holding you to your word, Jake Parson. I remember what you said when we sailed from Harkers Island to Fort Macon that night."

"Hmm, can't remember anything about that night." A faint smile turned up at the corners of his mouth. She punched him gently in the arm. "You said 'whatever I decide, I want you to be a part of it.'"

"Oh, yeah, that," he chuckled as his arms tightened into a tender embrace.

The next day, Jake's parents arrived by train, and the three of them left Beaufort with Wade's remains. That had been a month ago, and she had received no word from him.

Now, at the backyard Sunday picnic, Nell's father joined them under Harrison's pecan tree with an overflowing plate. "You sound more and more like a preacher every Sunday, Daddy."

His sobriety and spiritual growth had opened so much between them. They often sat at the back of the store after hours and watched the harbor while drinking ice-cold Pepsis. They'd even gone fishing a few times.

Thomas Guthrie grinned at her before glancing at her bobbed hair and looking away. Beaufort's male population mourned the cropping of Nell's hair. So much so, Winston made a tiny coffin for her plait. Nell squeezed her father's hand and said, "Just remember, Daddy. I did it for the band. I can't play jazz and rag when I'm wearing a granny bun." From a practical view, she was thrilled she didn't have to fuss with her hair in the morning, and she could now easily wear a cloche hat.

Nell and Winston were playing rag and jazz whenever they got the chance. The duo played modest venues, such as speakeasies, pig pickin's, and parlor dances. Although the Inlet Inn had yet to ask them to return, it was no secret attendance had dropped significantly at the hotel's weekend events.

"I hear Rev. Saunders might not be long for Beaufort," said Beatrice, walking up to them with several of Emma Grace's younger siblings trailing behind her.

"Is that right?" said Nell.

"He referred to Asa's injury as a blow from the staff of God, casting out the decay of bootlegging."

"Oh, my."

"They say they had to carry Sylvia out of the church. You reckon you'll go back if he leaves?"

"I don't know," said Nell as she looked around at the children playing in the back yard and the adults holding groaning plates of food. "Kinda like what we started right here. We might even put Daddy in a revival tent."

Each week, different folks would lead the discussion of a Bible passage or another spiritual topic. By playing such an active role in her religion, Nell connected and embraced spirit and her music more deeply.

Midgett was sitting next to Mrs. Guthrie, with a cluster of children gathered around his ankles. "Show me again, Mr. Eli," Marbles demanded. The Coast Guard commander dramatically opened the small wooden box that held his newest medal. After a few moments, the children lost interest and scattered.

"Have you heard anything about Jimmy Styron?" asked Nell.

"Got the best defense team in the state," said Winston. "It might not go to trial."

Nell nodded. "He knows where the bodies are buried." Her hand flew to her mouth, "Oh! No pun intended."

"Sylvia needs to protect her interests."

When the feds had taken the sheriff into custody, he was charged with accessory to illegal blockade running, but oddly, they could find no witnesses. To date, Jimmy hadn't rolled on Sylvia or Asa, and everyone agreed that Buddy was a rogue, solitary smuggler.

"Has the court heard Ramsey's case yet?" asked Mrs. Guthrie.

"Last time I spoke with him, it sounded like they might settle," answered Midgett.

When the facts of Buddy's lifestyle became public, his family was so enraged they refused to bury him. In the end, Ramsey interred Buddy's remains privately. When the will of Richard Taylor, otherwise known as Buddy, was read, his family was incensed to learn that he'd left all his worldly possessions to Edgar Lionel Ramsey. Since his mother partially owned the lumber yard, she padlocked the property while she contested the will.

"The last I heard, Ramsey gave up all claim on the land but requested the contents of the Sugar Shack," said Nell. "But the family still won't give him access. We're going with him tomorrow with a state-appointed official to empty it."

"My Lord, honey, but he's had a time of it," Tisdale replied.

Emma Grace walked up with a plate of second helpings from the cookfire. "Oh, Nell, I forgot to ask you to help me tomorrow morning. Since Asa's out of commission, Doc Davis asked me to collect the medical supplies off the train. I could use some help."

"Of course," replied Nell.

The next morning, Nell drove Emma Grace down to the Beaufort Train Depot. The station had a deep overhanging roof to shelter passengers from inclement weather as they boarded or departed trains.

"How's Asa doing?" Nell asked as they stepped out of the truck and walked over to the bench in front of the train station. She knew the pharmacist had moved back into his parents' house while recovering from his shoulder injury. Nell absently rubbed the back of her head, thinking back to that terrible day at the inn. With mixed emotions, she remembered that Asa had stepped in front of her in order to shield her from Buddy's bullet.

Emma Grace laughed. "Well, the doc says Asa's healing well, but I don't know if Sylvia will survive. Lulu is about to drive her insane."

Nell chuckled about her former rival. "That explains that queer look she gave me in the store the other day. It mighta been wistful."

"I almost feel sorry for her," said Emma Grace.

Nell raised an eyebrow and looked at her friend. "I hear Dr. Davis moved back in."

"Well, not really; he still stays at the clinic. From what I can see, they called a truce of sorts during Asa's recovery."

Nell sighed deeply. "It's such a shame; my mama can remember when they truly loved each other."

Emma Grace got up from the bench to speak to the conductor. A few moments later, Nell was leafing through her friend's latest *Ladies' Home Journal* when the train pulled into the station. She was engrossed in an article when two dogs came up and greeted her. It took her a moment to realize they were Pilot and Yawg. Looking up, she saw Jake walking toward her. At first, she didn't recognize him since he was dressed in a light suit, not his usual dungarees and work shirt.

"Oh, my," Nell managed to say as she stood up to meet him. They moved toward one another, but stopped before they touched, for the sake of appearances. "Jake!" she whispered as their eyes locked. She longed to feel his arms around her but knew inquisitive townsfolk surrounded them. Though his frame was still thin, the color had returned to his face, and his eyes were clear.

"Howdy, stranger," Emma Grace said, joining them. "I used to know someone who looked like you, but I can't be sure."

"It seems like you are always bringing us together," Nell replied, thinking of their evening on Horse Island and again on Harkers Island.

Emma Grace shrugged. "I might be your fairy godmother."

Later that day, Nell was weeding in her garden when she looked up and saw Jake leaning against the pecan tree. Pilot and Yawg sat in front of him, thumping their tails. "Thought I'd stop by."

Instinctively, Nell glanced around to see if anyone was watching them. When she determined they were alone, she joined Jake on Harrison's bench. After many long, warming kisses, he told her of his stay in South Carolina.

"I made a few skiffs with Daddy while I was there, and we felt close to Wade while we worked. It was as if he was guiding our hands."

"I can imagine."

"It was good to hear people remember Wade at the funeral. But when it was over, I talked with my family, and we decided to search for the *Amelia*. It was tearing us up, not knowing where she is."

As Nell watched her hens scratching in the garden, she marveled at how nice it was to hear his voice again.

He leaned in to kiss her neck. "I realized when I was down there; I wanted to come back to Beaufort." I think there are people in town who know more about the *Amelia*. And I want to start the boat-building business that Wade was born to do."

She waited for him to continue. But when he said nothing, she turned away and sighed deeply.

∽

The next morning, Winston, Midgett, Jake, Emma Grace, and Nell piled into the *Miss Beatrice*, the *Harmony*, and the *Miss Mary* and made their way up the Newport River to Russell Creek. The small flotilla was part memorial for Wade and part salvage operation.

Ramsey, haggard and ashen, was waiting for them at the dock of the lumber yard with a dour-looking state official. Once the Sugar Shack was opened, everyone stood in disbelief as they surveyed a scene of demolition and destruction. Every bookcase, knick-knack and teacup was shattered. Nell didn't know who looked more upset: Ramsey, who lost all remnants of his trusted lover and friend, or Jake, hoping to find some clue regarding the *Amelia*.

They spent the day sifting through scraps of paper in hopes of finding information regarding the missing boat. On his last day on earth, Buddy had told Nell that he'd sailed the *Amelia* to the Madison's Wharf outside Norfolk, but Midgett's inquiries had yielded nothing. Ramsey revealed a secret nook where Buddy had hidden the bottles of *Le Chevel Noir,* now reduced to a ruby puddle and broken glass. In the middle of the rubble, Nell found the scarred and butchered wooden head of the beautiful Nadine, the last remains of the sea nymph figurehead Buddy had rescued in Norfolk. Knowing broken women could heal, Nell gently packed the remains of the mermaid away on the *Harmony.*

At the end of the day, the group made a bonfire of the remaining debris. Staring deep into the mesmerizing flames, Nell and Ramsey leaned on their shovels as everything that Buddy held dear curled up in smoke.

"I think a lot about what a jury might have done with Buddy," said Nell. "I mean, Wade's death *might* have been an accident . . . ." Her voice trailed off.

"Hmmm, given Buddy's proclivities, I don't think a jury would have found much mercy for him," answered Ramsey.

"Ya know, Ramsey, once they moved Buddy out of the clinic that day, I don't remember seeing that Bible you brought to him. They found that extra morphine bottle near his bed, and it didn't match the clinic stock. I always wondered how that syringe and morphine found its way into Buddy's room."

Ramsey turned his head to look at Nell; his face etched with grief. "I offered him a choice. I let it be his decision." He sighed deeply. "You have to understand, people like us don't last five minutes in jail. This way, he just got high one last time."

Nell let Ramsey's words tumble inside her mind, recalling them with Buddy's last revelations. She shuddered to imagine how Buddy and Ramsey must have faced disdain and violence every day of their lives.

Later that week, Nell sailed the *Harmony* out of the harbor to rake for clams in the Back Sound. That same day, Jake sailed toward the inlet on the *Miss Mary* accompanied by Pilot and Yawg. The couple met on Shackleford Island and waded along the shore while the dogs chased rabbits through the brush. When the lovers found a protective dune, they nestled into welcoming sand.

"I told my parents all about you," said Jake. "My mother can't wait to meet you."

Nell turned away from him and looked out over the sound. "Have you heard anything about the *Amelia*, or the *Astor*, or whatever they're calling her now?"

"I've written to the Navy and every boatyard around Norfolk, but no one has seen hide nor hair of the boat."

"I reckon you'll need to go up."

"Yes."

"Do you know when?"

"Not sure, but I know I'll need some help when I get up there. I need a cracker-jack mind that sees the patterns and clues no one else can see."

"That sounds like a special person."

"She is," and he pulled her into a kiss. "You and I are gonna go up to Norfolk and search for her."

Nell sat up and looked at him. "Jake, you need a real detective—a Pinkerton man to hunt her down."

Jake shook his head. "You found Wade. You knew the people in this town, and you knew how to talk to them in the right way. Nobody else could talk to Asa or Ramsey or Buddy the way you did."

Nell stared at him. "Well, I guess I did. Never really looked at it that way." She thought for a minute, "Just as well the town doesn't either; I'd be run out on a rail."

She leaned into him, picking up fistfuls of dry sand and letting it run through her fingers.

"When I was in Stono Creek, my mama wanted me to give you this." From his breast pocket, he took out a silver ring with small diamond chips clustered around a blue sapphire. He gently slipped it on her finger.

"Jake, I can't take this," Nell said, staring at the ring. She remembered how everything fell apart after she accepted Asa's engagement ring.

"You helped bring my brother home, Nell. You were the first person outside the family to listen to me." He paused. "Will you be my girl?"

"I don't know how I can wear it," she replied, thinking of their clandestine affection. Tears sprang to her eyes as she fell under the spell of the sparkling facets of the ring.

"I'll understand if you don't wear it in town right now. But I'm hoping it can be our secret."

Her tear dropped on the stone and mingled with the sapphire's hidden star, where it glistened and danced as if it were a piece of the sea.